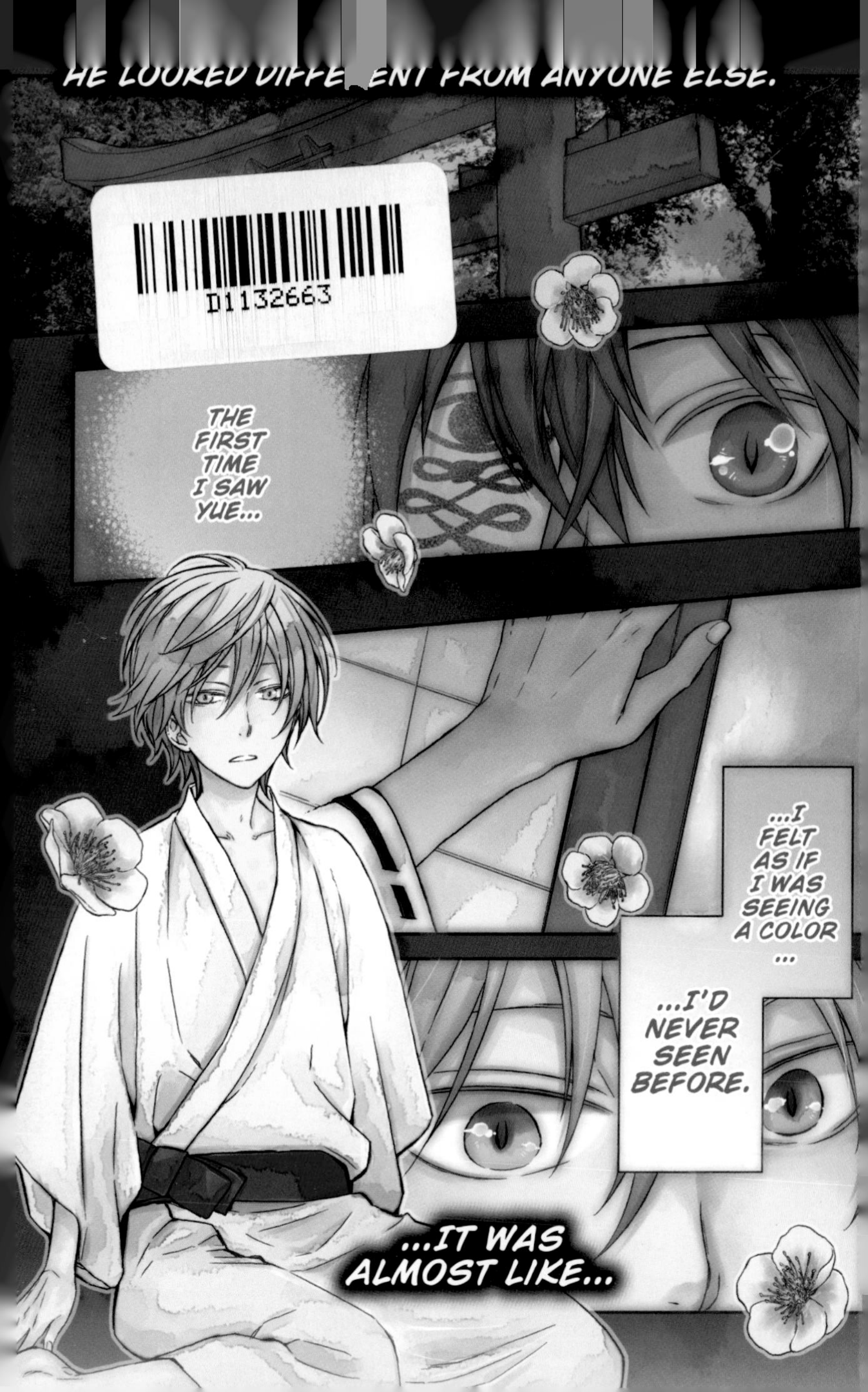
HE LOOKED DIFFERENT FROM ANYONE ELSE.
THE FIRST TIME I SAW YUE...
...I FELT AS IF I WAS SEEING A COLOR ...
...I'D NEVER SEEN BEFORE.
...IT WAS ALMOST LIKE...

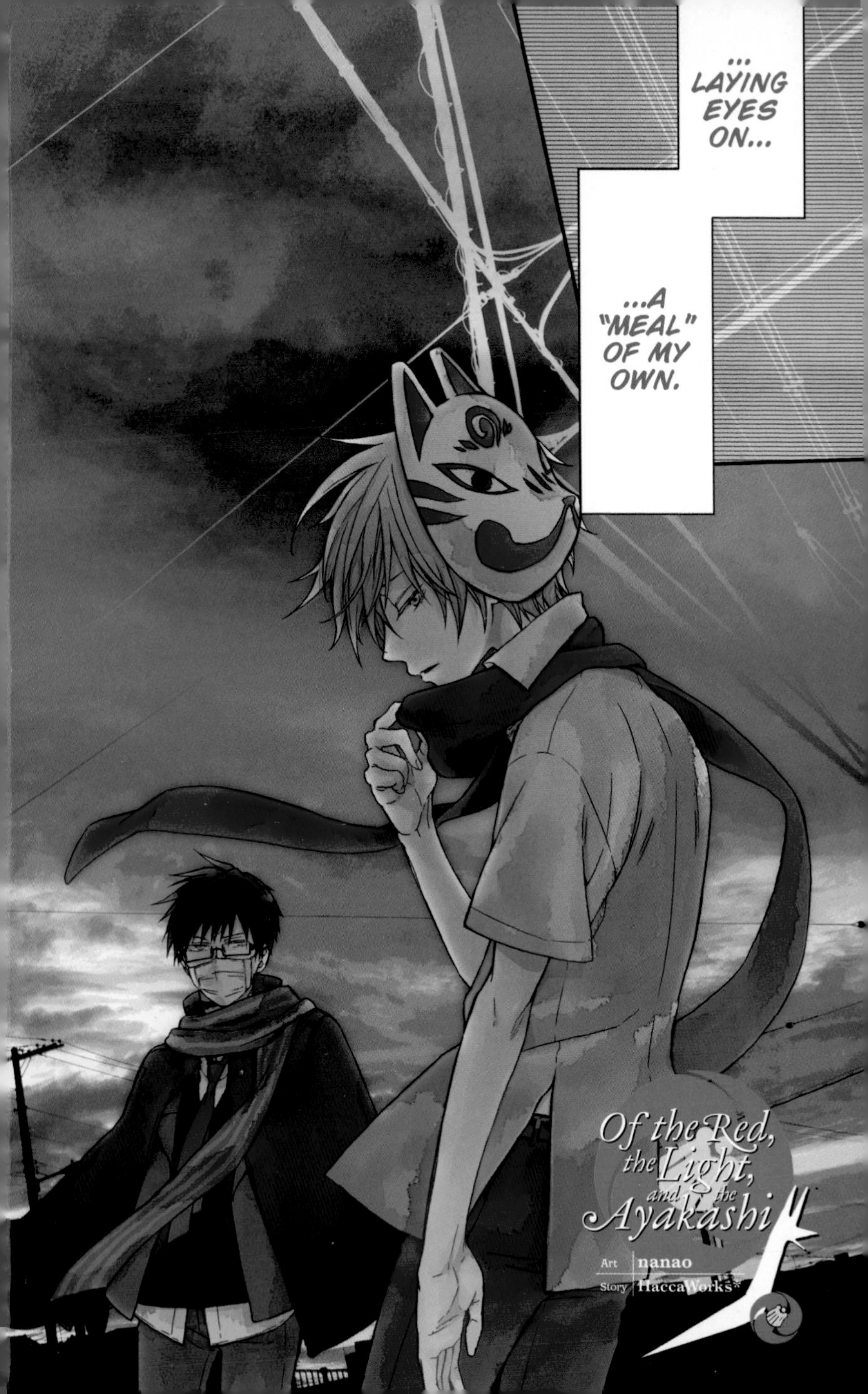
...LAYING EYES ON...
..."A "MEAL" OF MY OWN.
Of the Red, the Light, and the Ayakashi
Art nanao
Story HaccaWorks*

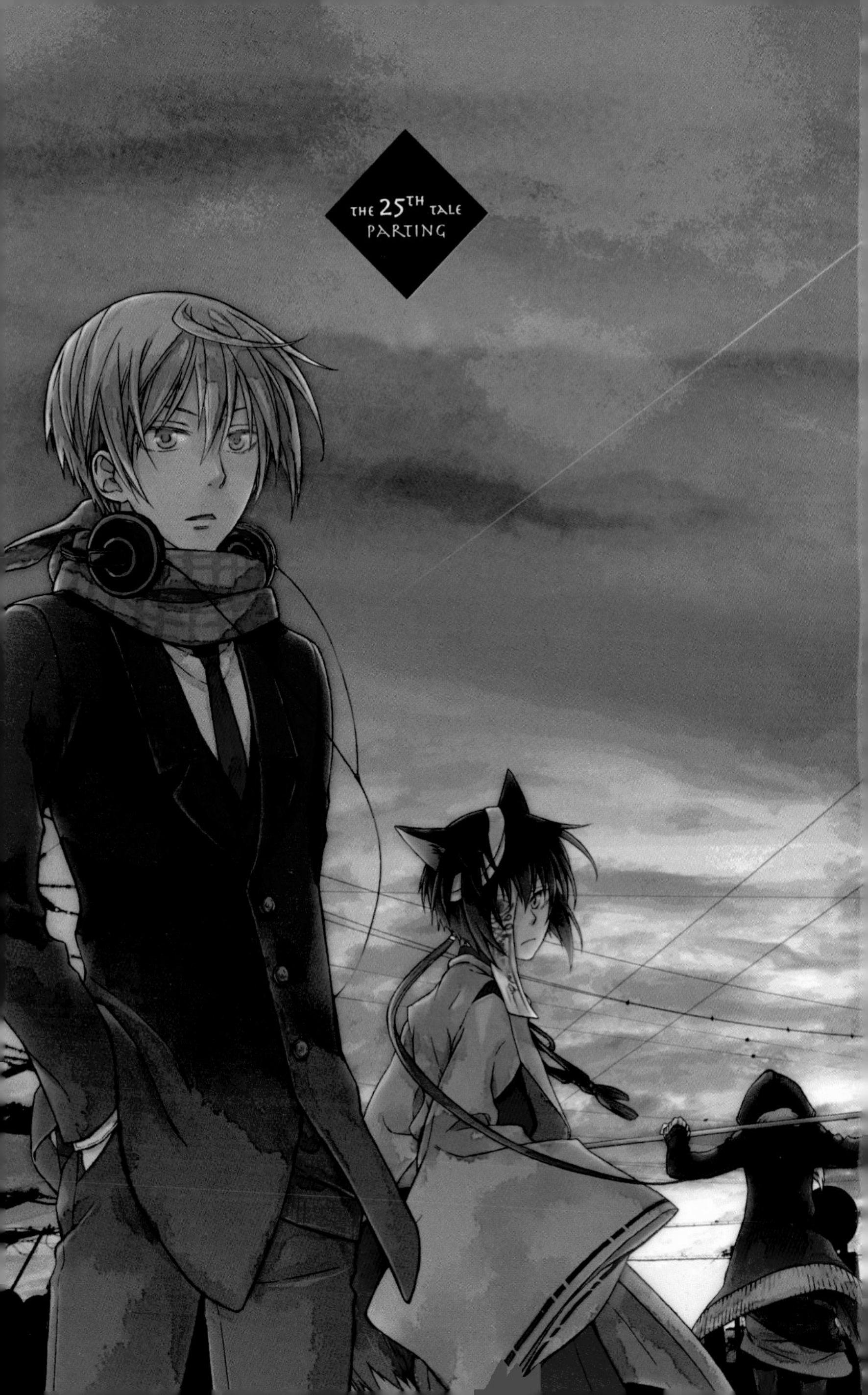
THE 25TH TALE
PARTING

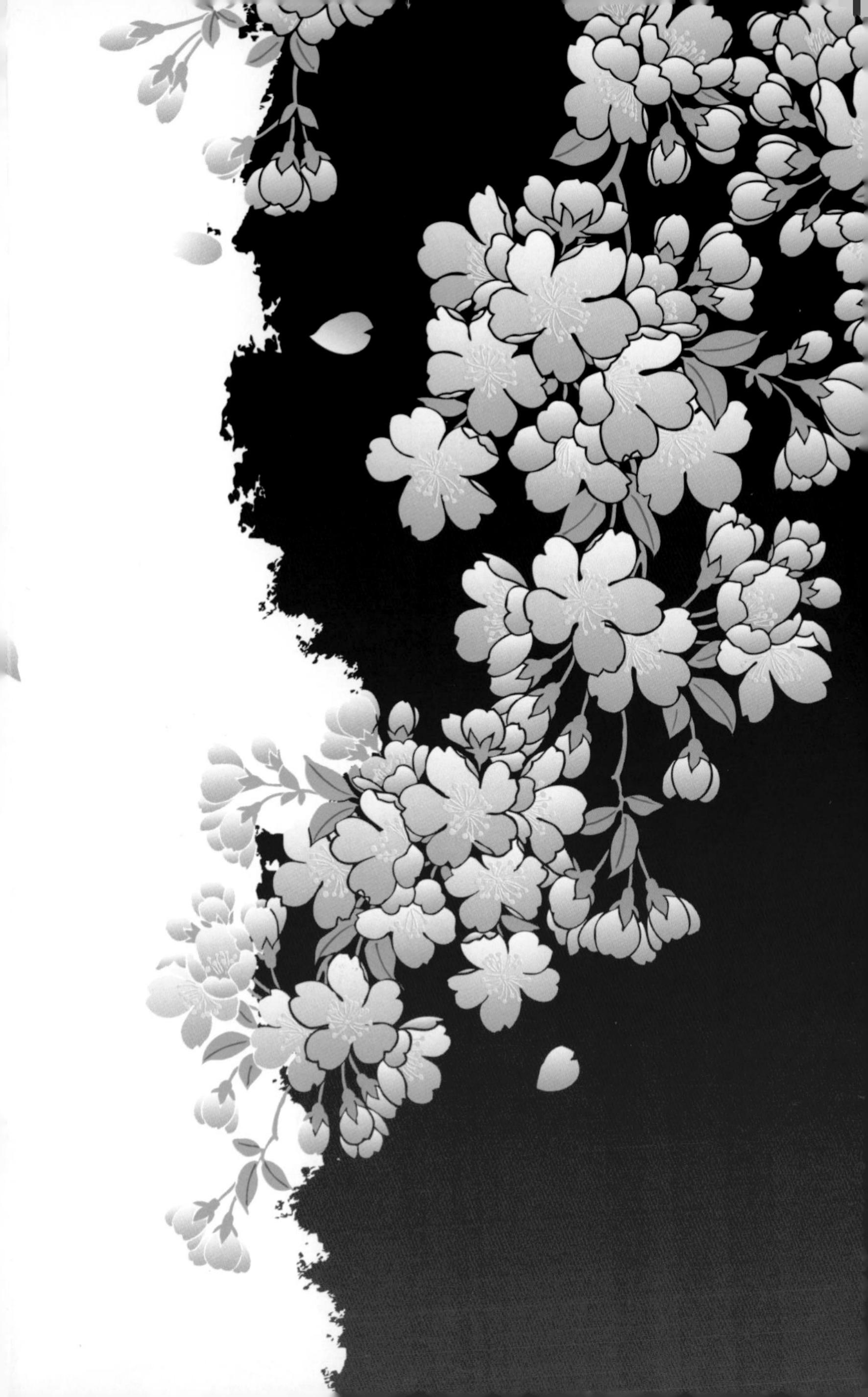

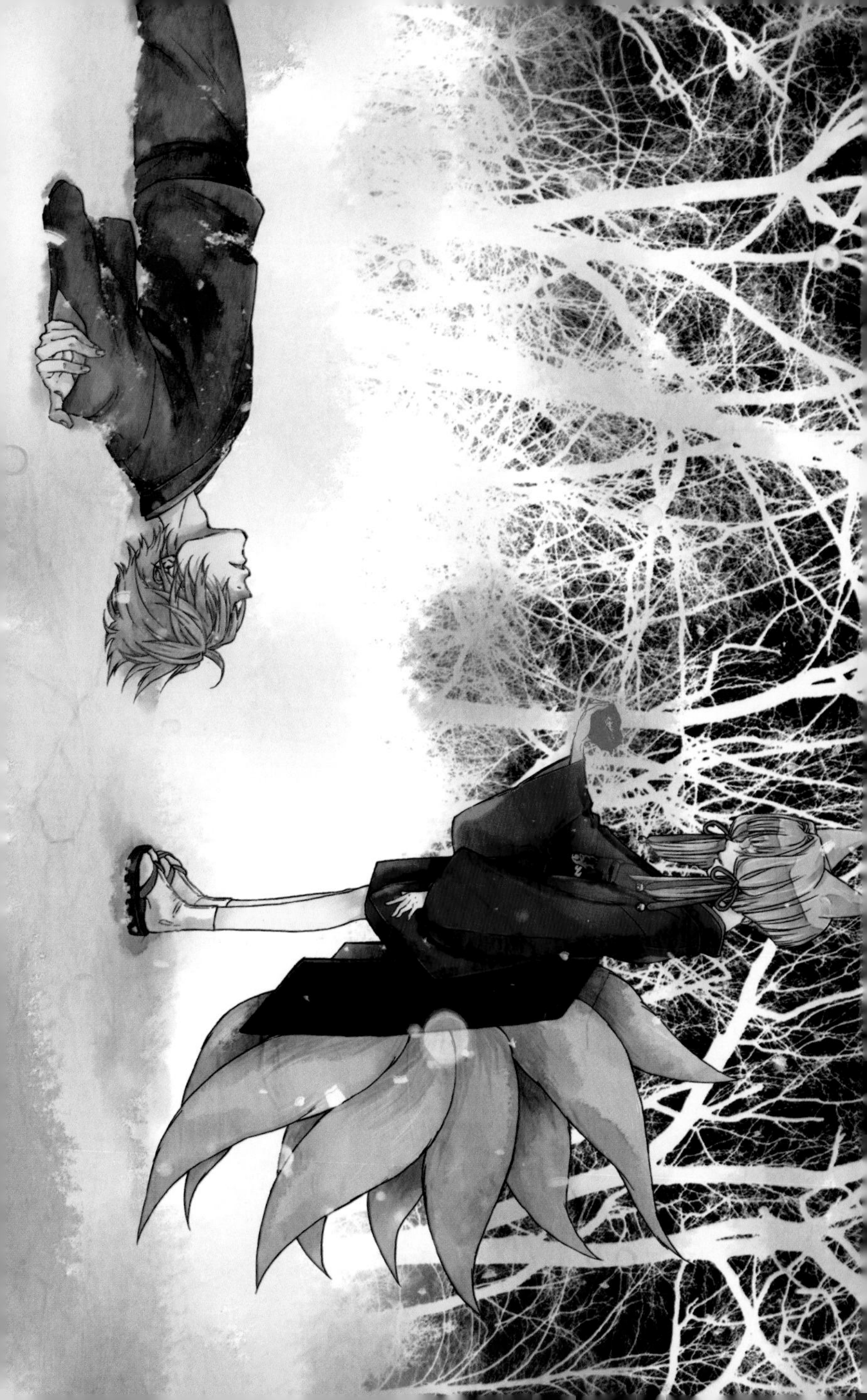

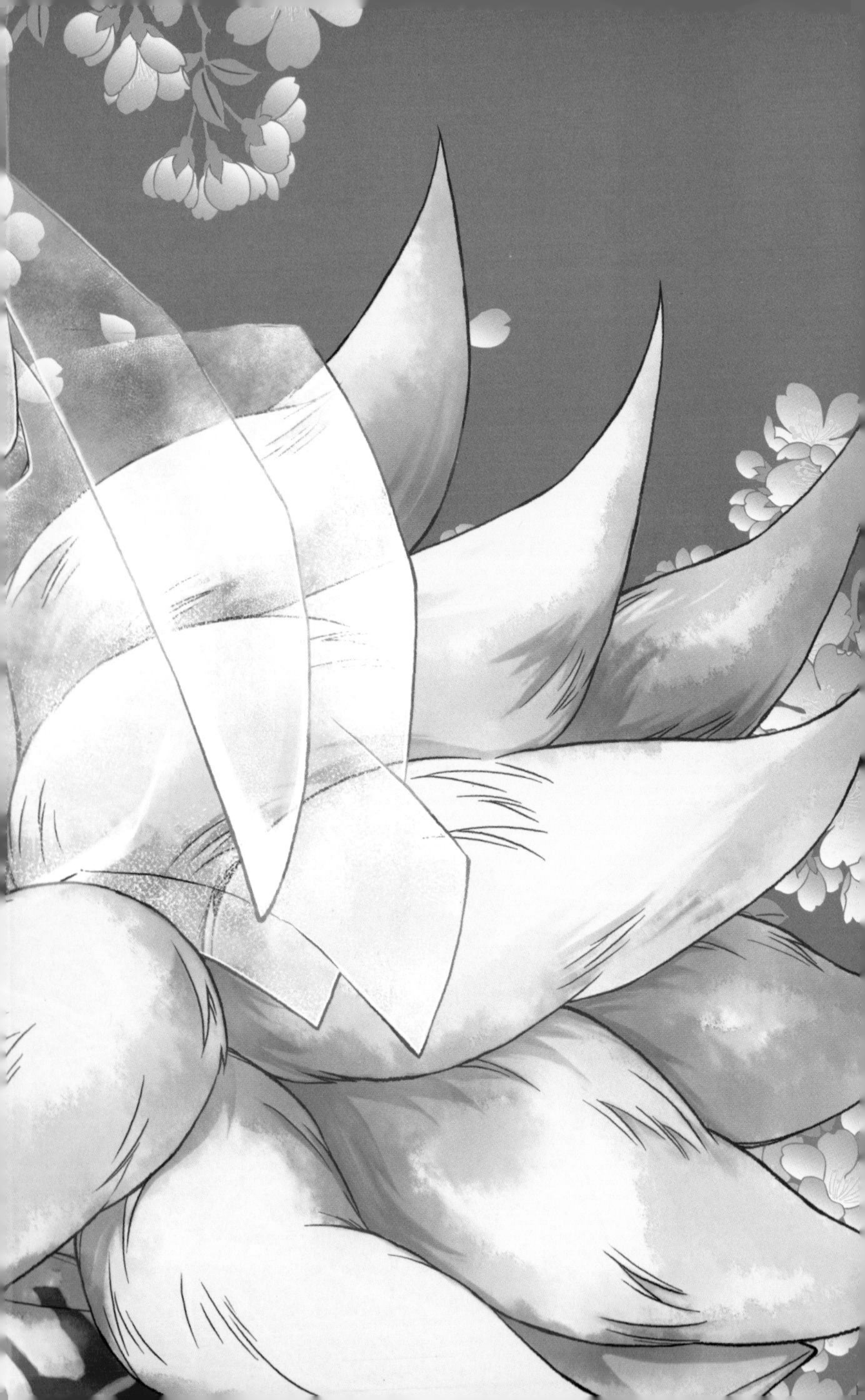

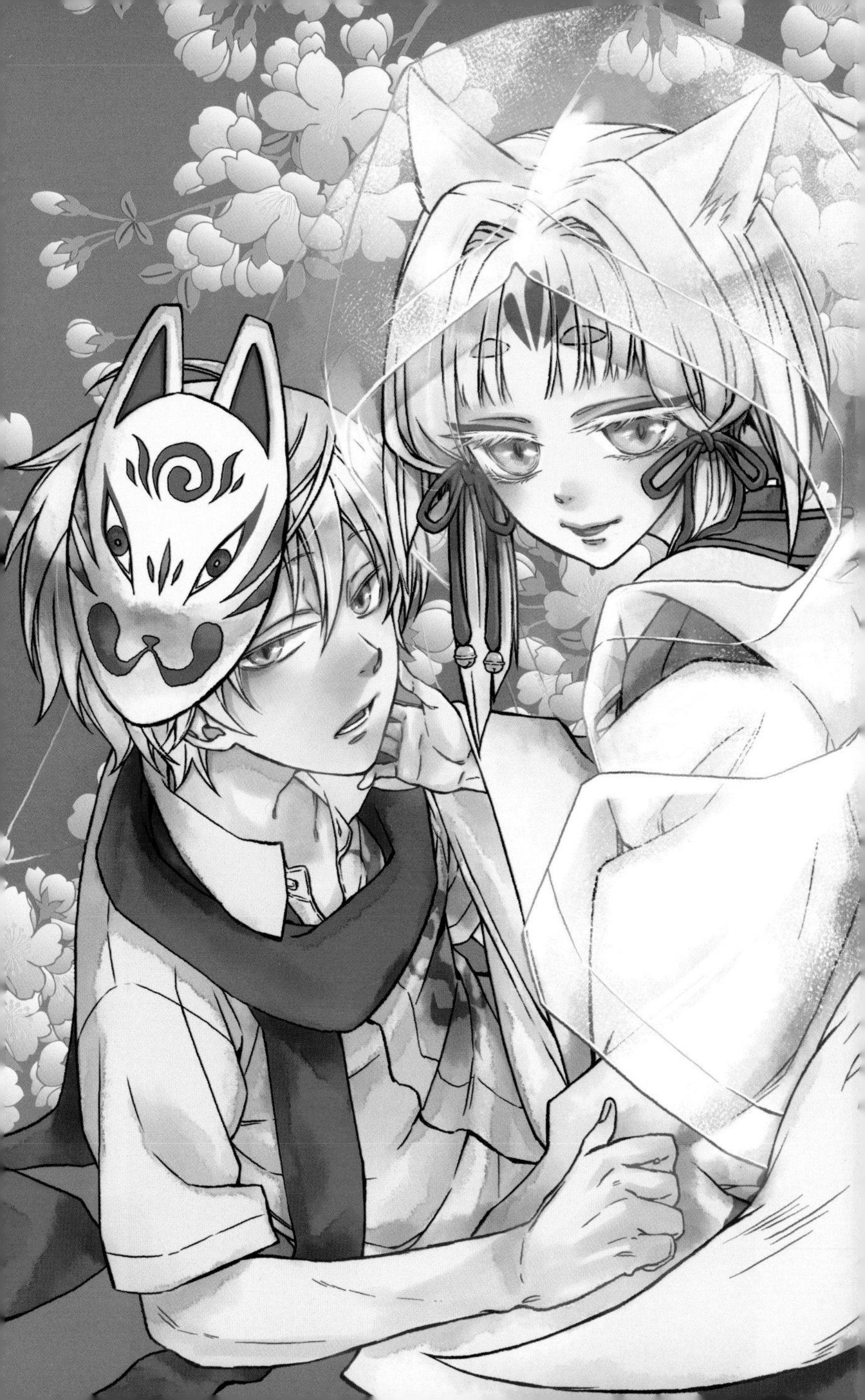

CONTENTS

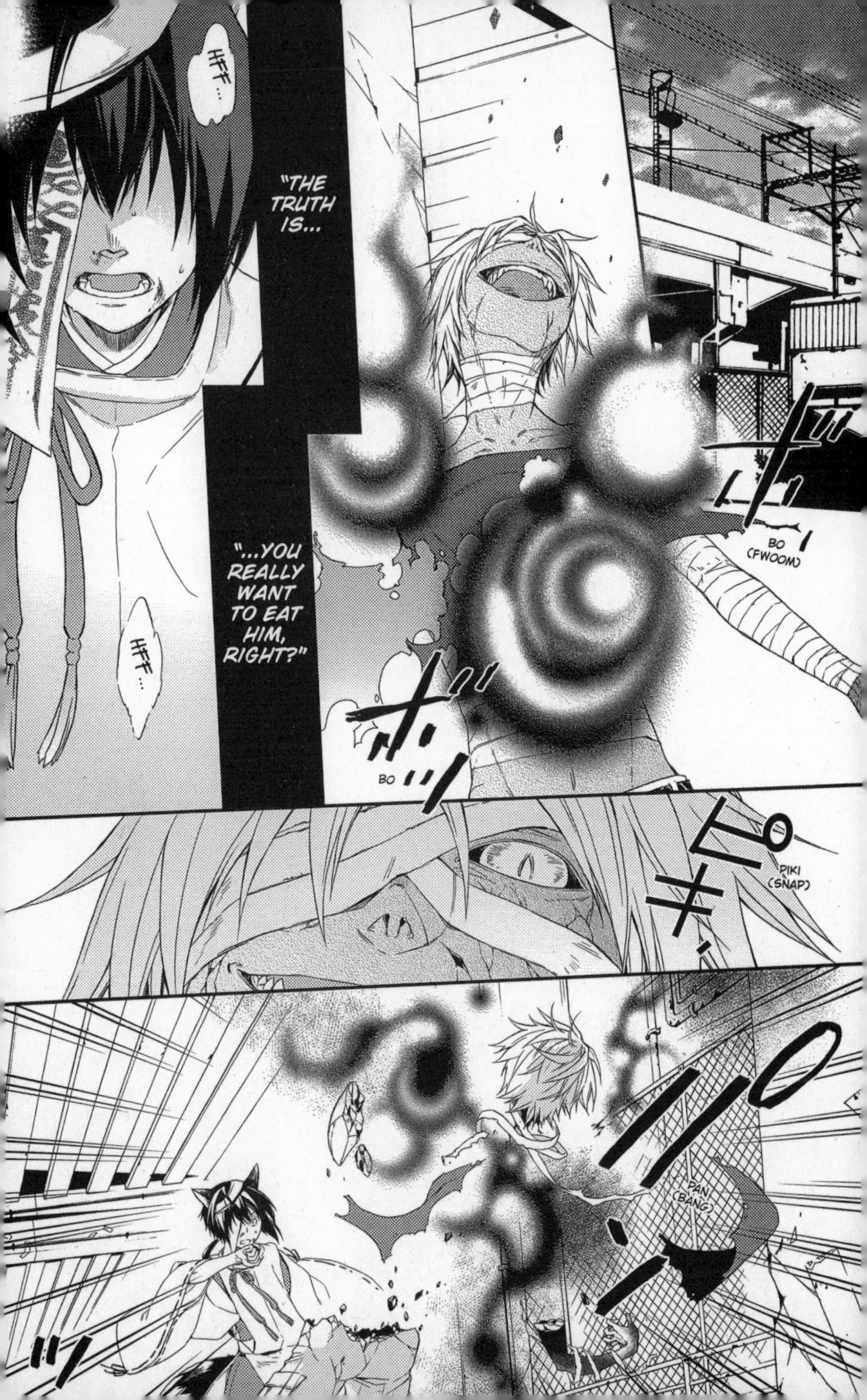
BO (FWOOM)
BO
HFF...
"THE TRUTH IS...
"...YOU REALLY WANT TO EAT HIM, RIGHT?"
HFF...
PIKI (SNAP)
PAN (BANG)

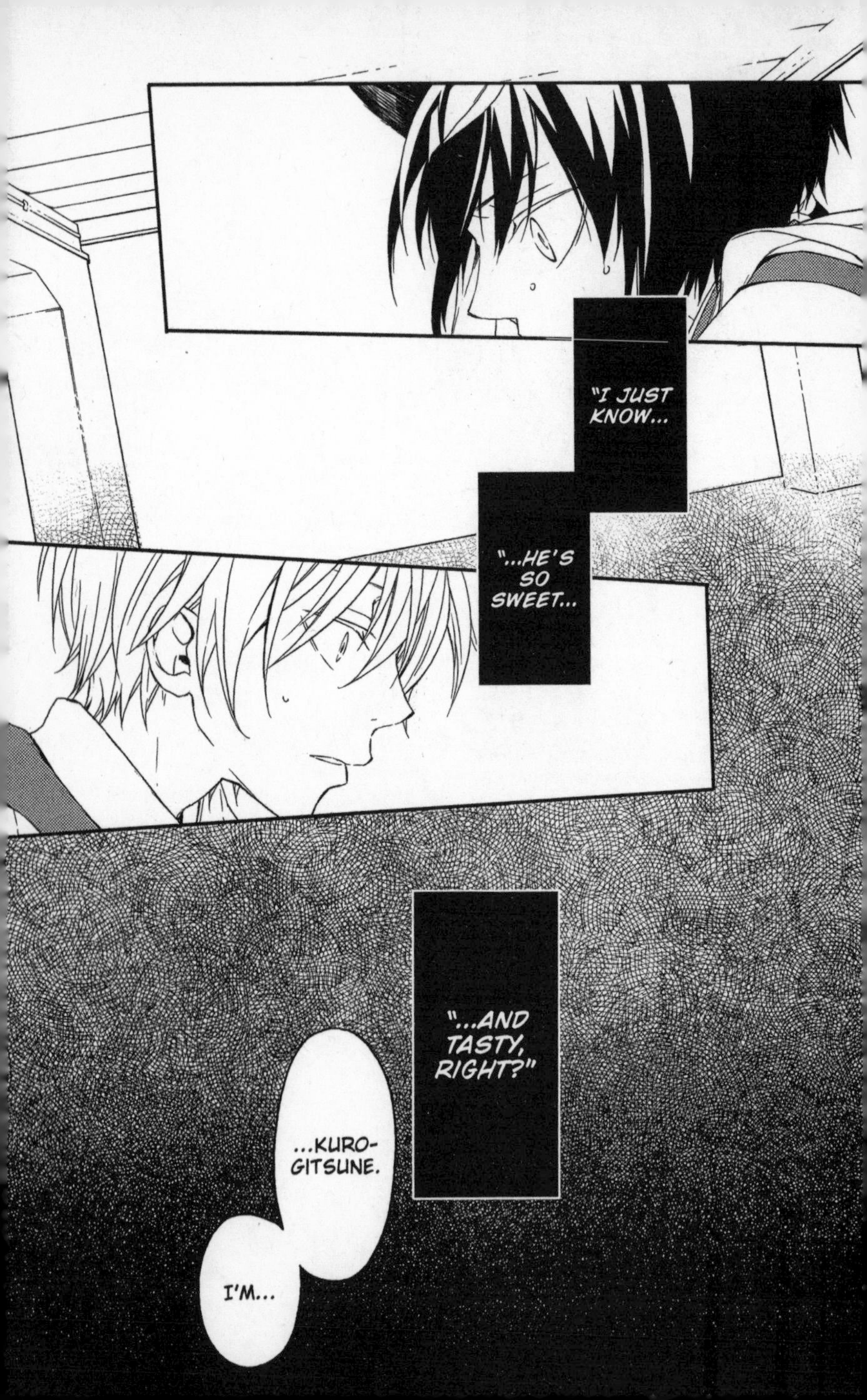
"I JUST KNOW...
"...HE'S SO SWEET...
"...AND TASTY, RIGHT?"
...KURO-GITSUNE.
I'M...

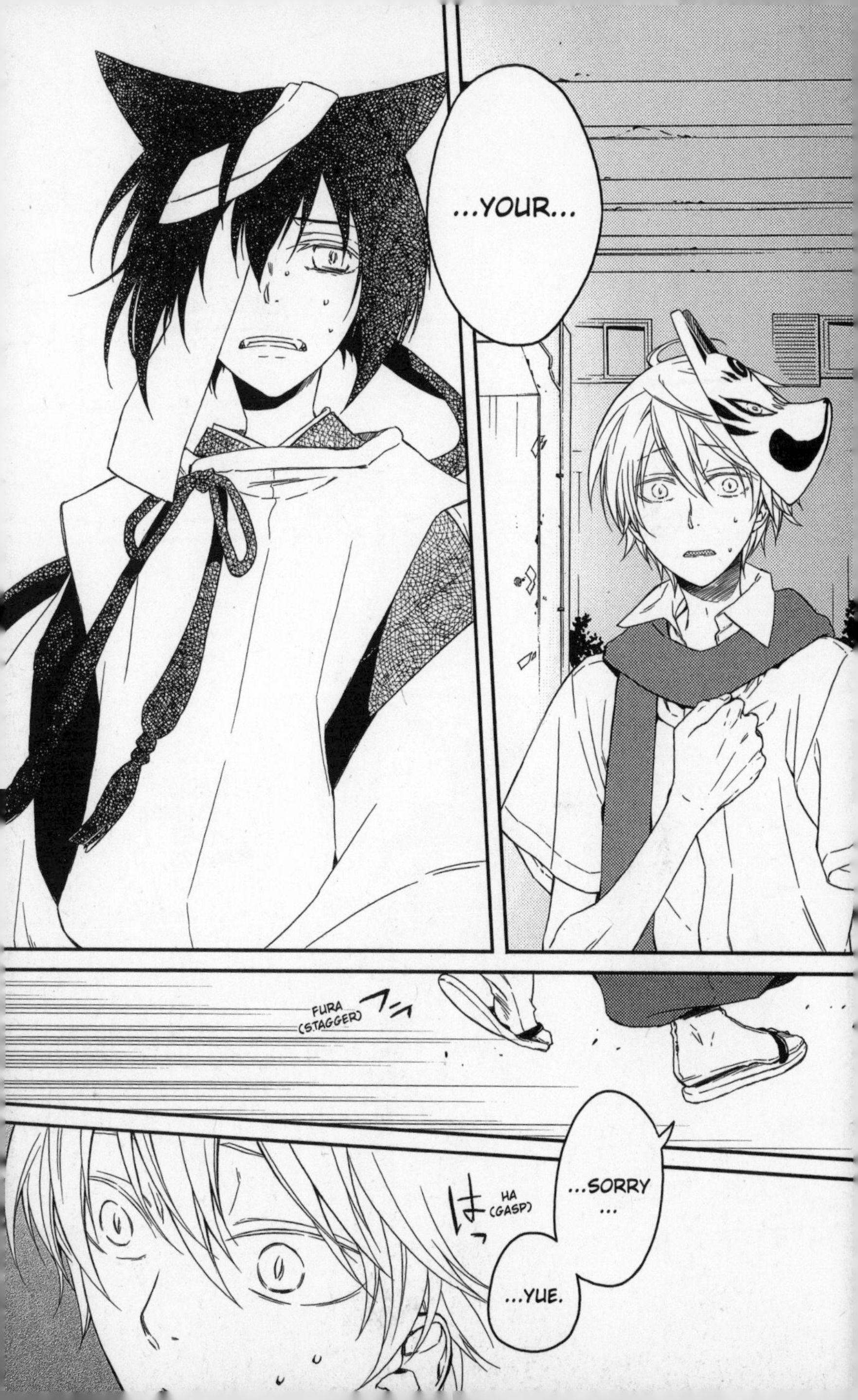

...YOUR...
FURA (STAGGER)
...SORRY ...
...YUE.
HA (GASP)

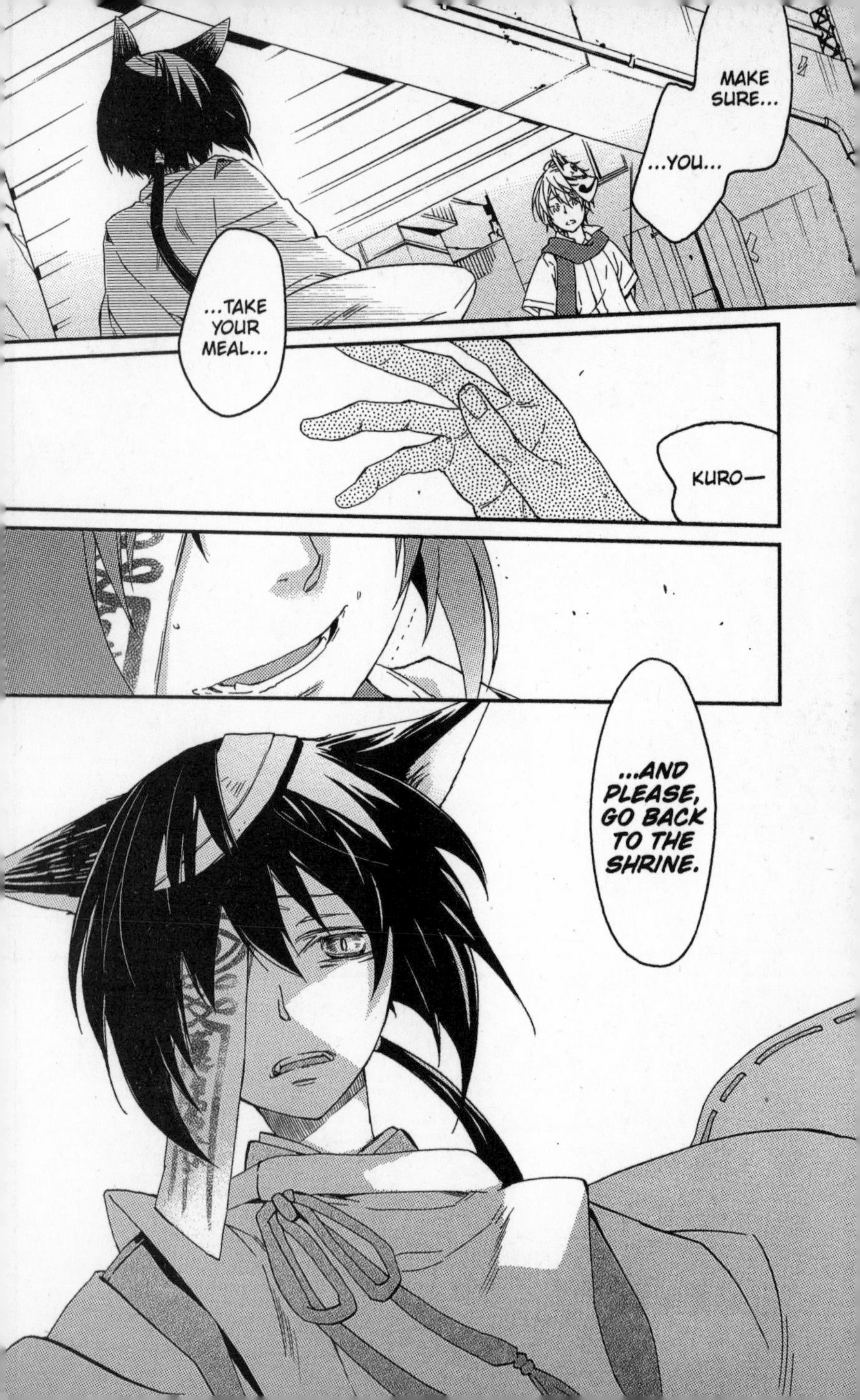
MAKE SURE...
...YOU...
...TAKE YOUR MEAL...
KURO—
...AND PLEASE, GO BACK TO THE SHRINE.

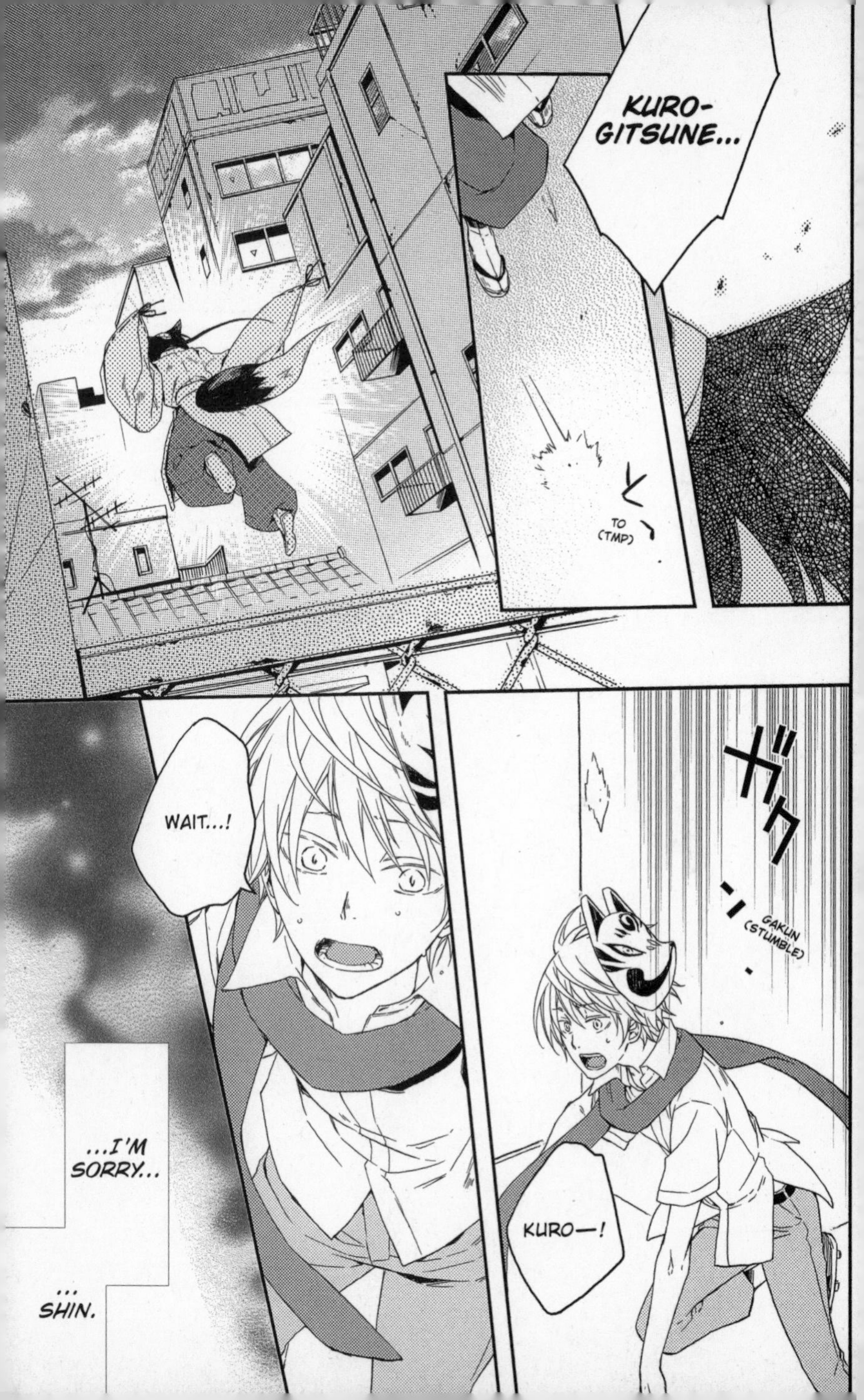
KURO-GITSUNE...
と
TO (TMP)
ガクッ
GAKUN (STUMBLE)
KURO—!
WAIT...!
...I'M SORRY...
... SHIN.

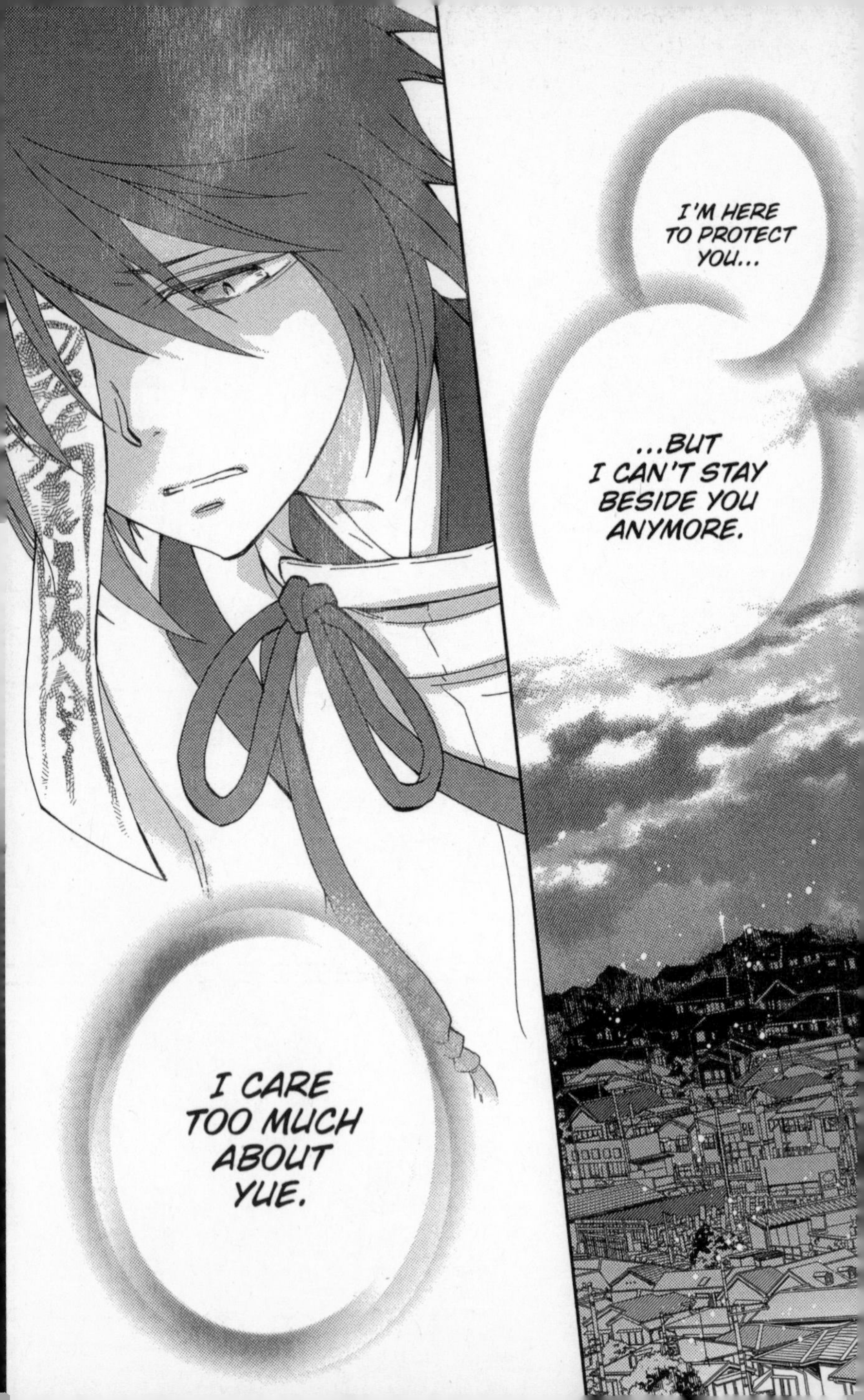

I'M HERE TO PROTECT YOU...
...BUT I CAN'T STAY BESIDE YOU ANYMORE.
I CARE TOO MUCH ABOUT YUE.

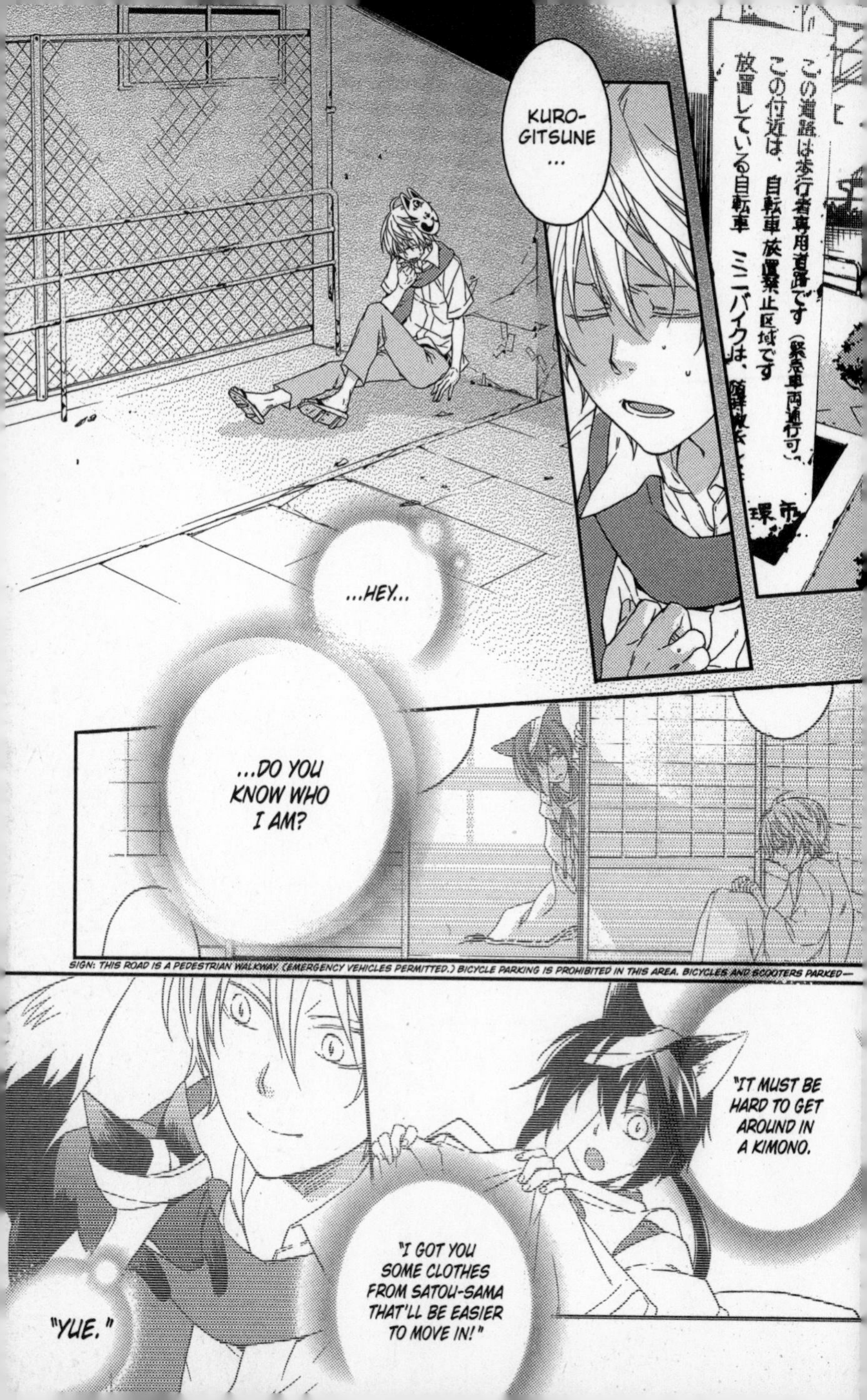
この道路は歩行者専用道路です（緊急車両通行可）
この付近は、自転車放置禁止区域です
放置している自転車 ミニバイクは、
KURO-GITSUNE ...
...HEY...
...DO YOU KNOW WHO I AM?
SIGN: THIS ROAD IS A PEDESTRIAN WALKWAY. (EMERGENCY VEHICLES PERMITTED.) BICYCLE PARKING IS PROHIBITED IN THIS AREA. BICYCLES AND SCOOTERS PARKED—
"IT MUST BE HARD TO GET AROUND IN A KIMONO.
"I GOT YOU SOME CLOTHES FROM SATOU-SAMA THAT'LL BE EASIER TO MOVE IN!"
"YUE."

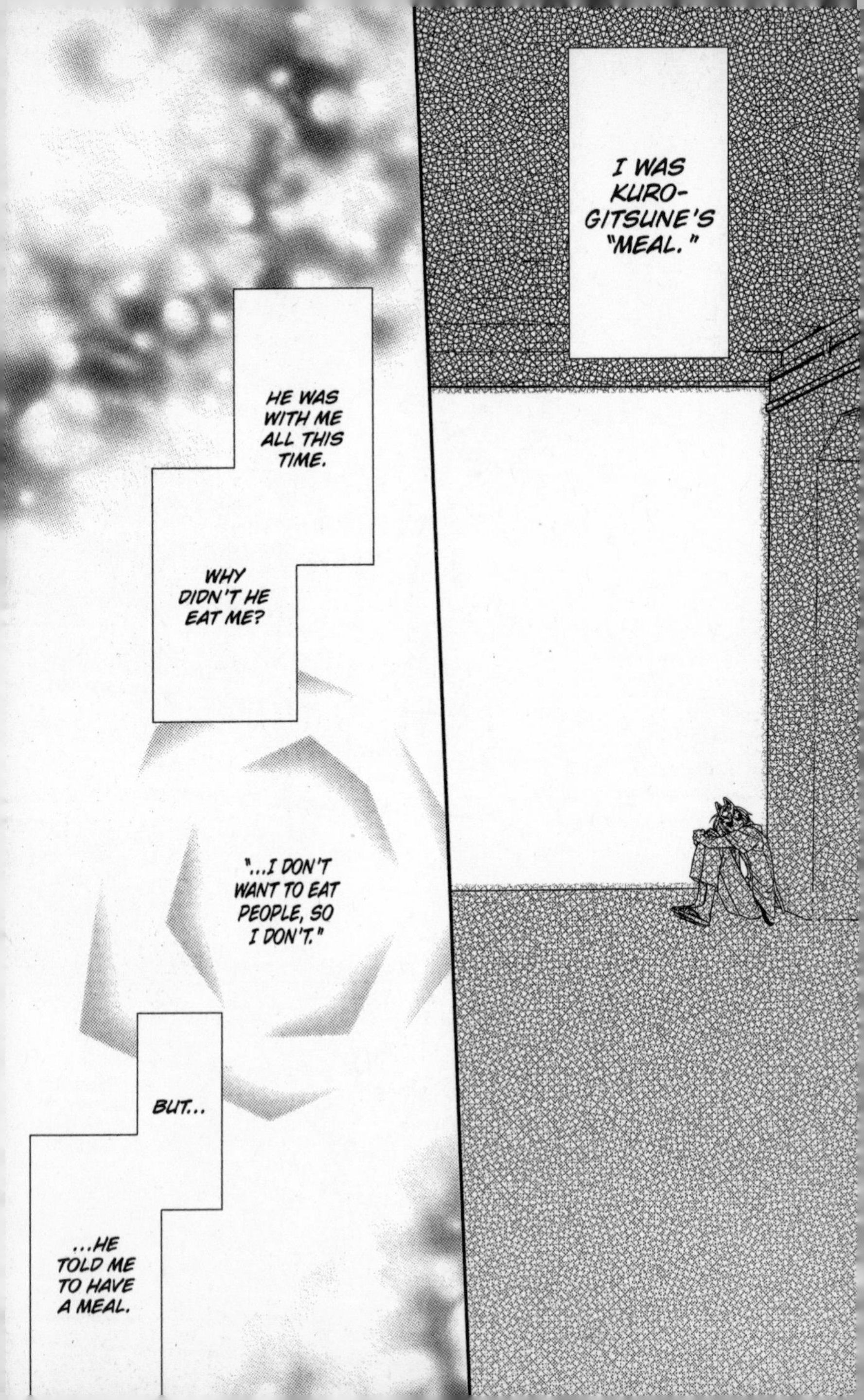
I WAS KURO-GITSUNE'S "MEAL."
HE WAS WITH ME ALL THIS TIME.
WHY DIDN'T HE EAT ME?
"...I DON'T WANT TO EAT PEOPLE, SO I DON'T."
BUT...
...HE TOLD ME TO HAVE A MEAL.

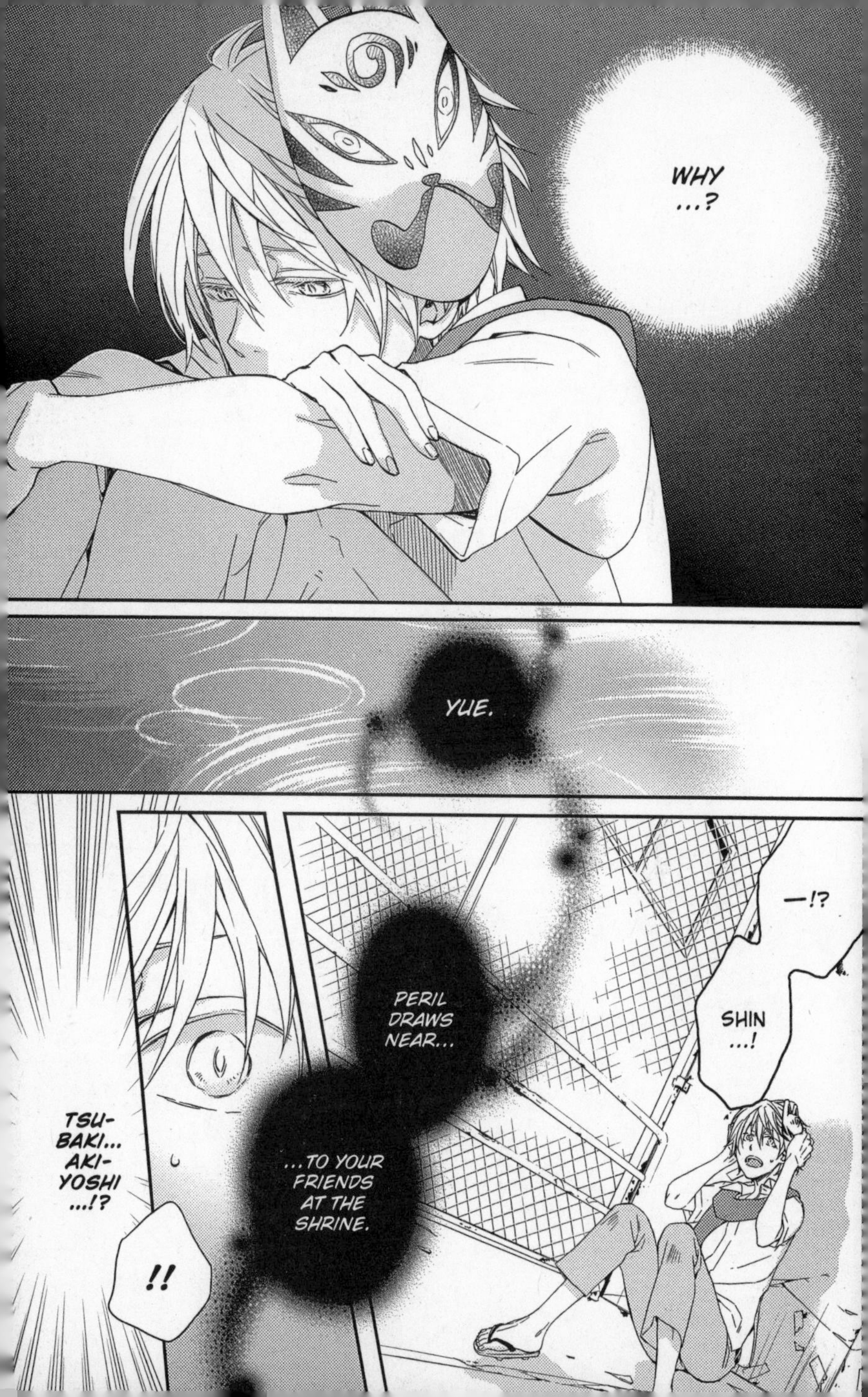
WHY ...?
YUE.
—!?
SHIN ...!
PERIL DRAWS NEAR...
...TO YOUR FRIENDS AT THE SHRINE.
TSU-BAKI... AKI-YOSHI ...!?
!!

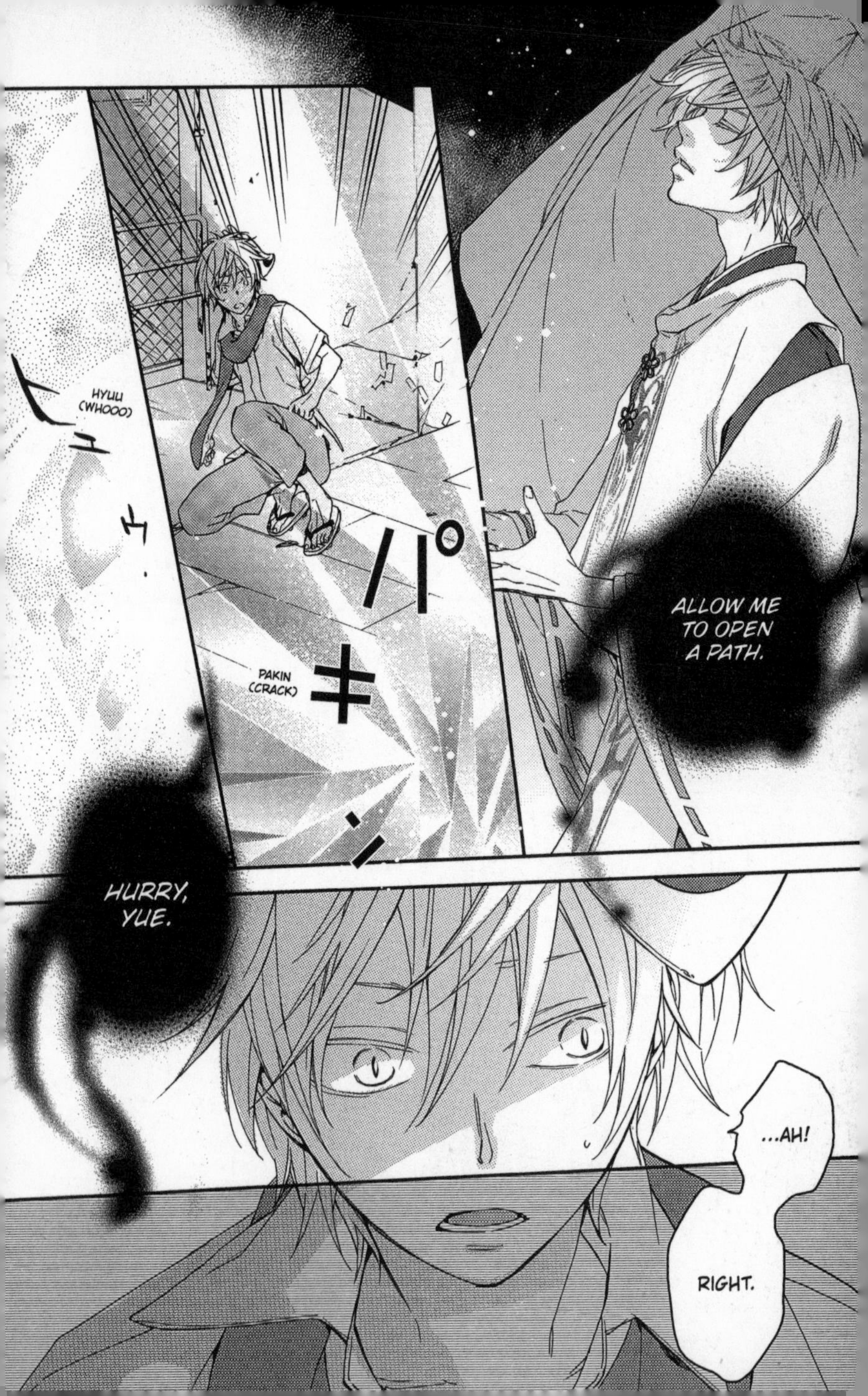
ALLOW ME TO OPEN A PATH.
PAKIN (CRACK)
HYUU (WHOOO)
HURRY, YUE.
...AH!
RIGHT.

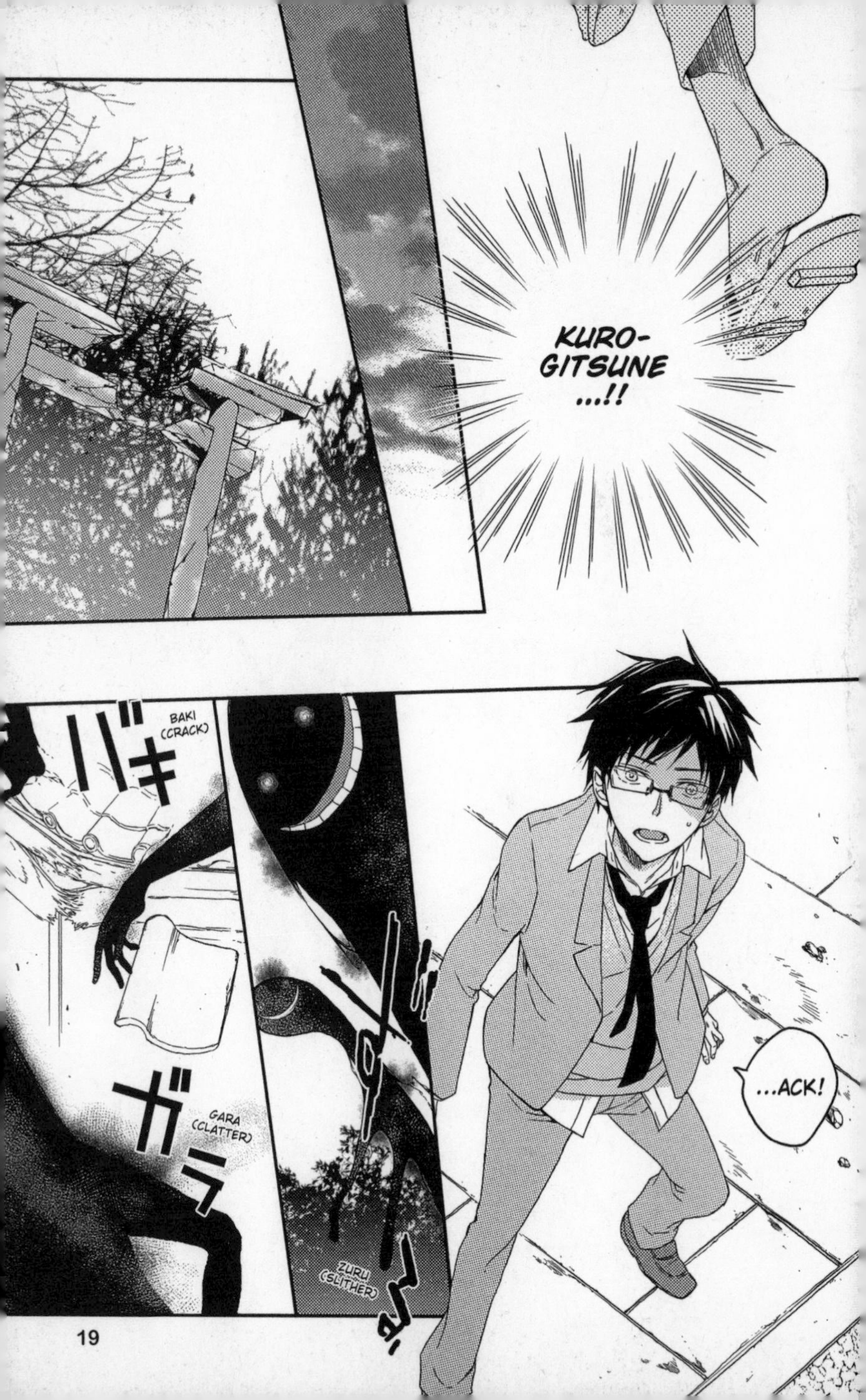
KURO-GITSUNE ...!!
...ACK!
ズル
ZURU (SLITHER)
バキ
BAKI (CRACK)
ガラ
GARA (CLATTER)

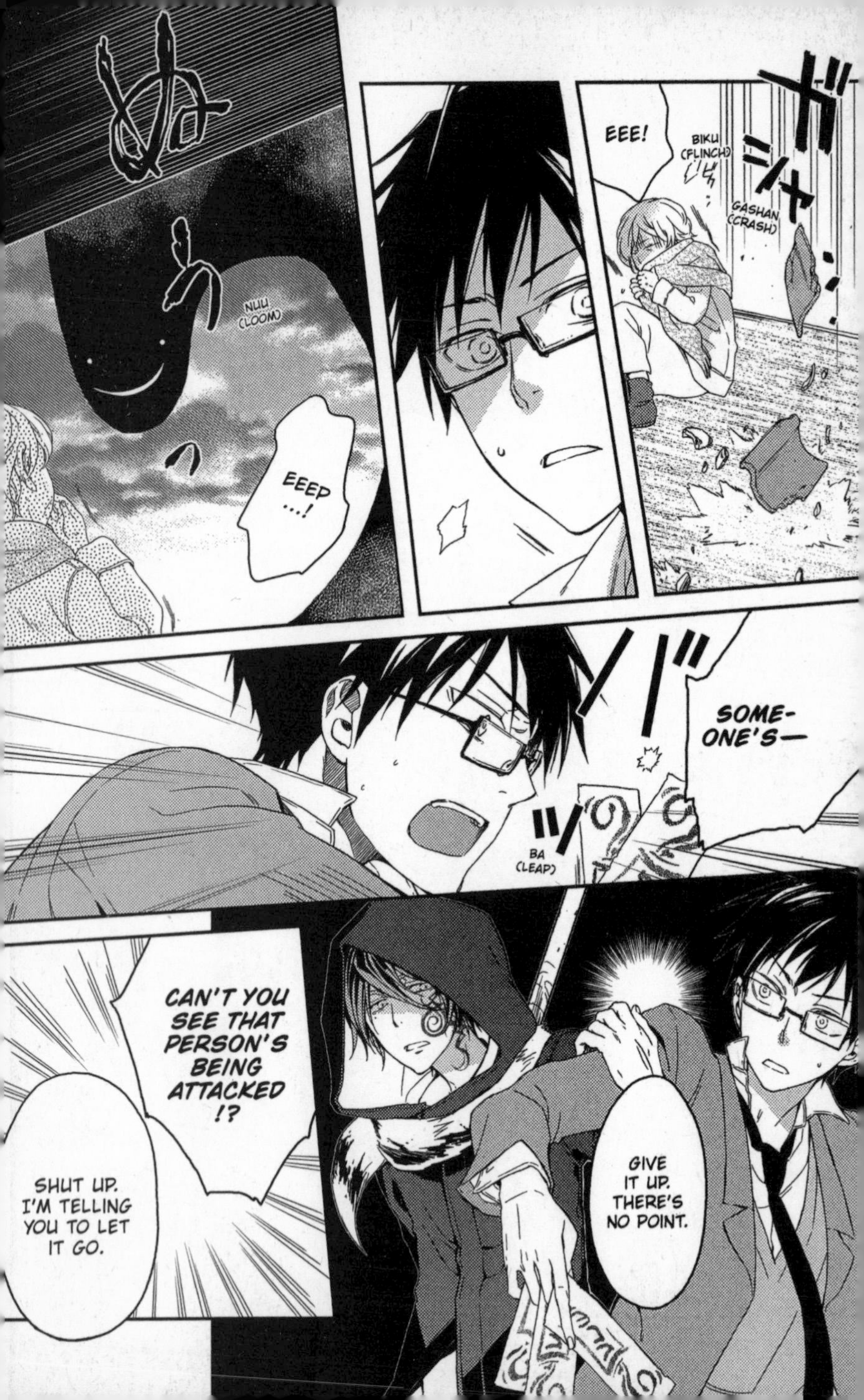
EEE!
BIKU (FLINCH)
GASHAN (CRASH)
NUU (LOOM)
EEEP ...!
SOME-ONE'S—
BA (LEAP)
GIVE IT UP. THERE'S NO POINT.
CAN'T YOU SEE THAT PERSON'S BEING ATTACKED!?
SHUT UP. I'M TELLING YOU TO LET IT GO.

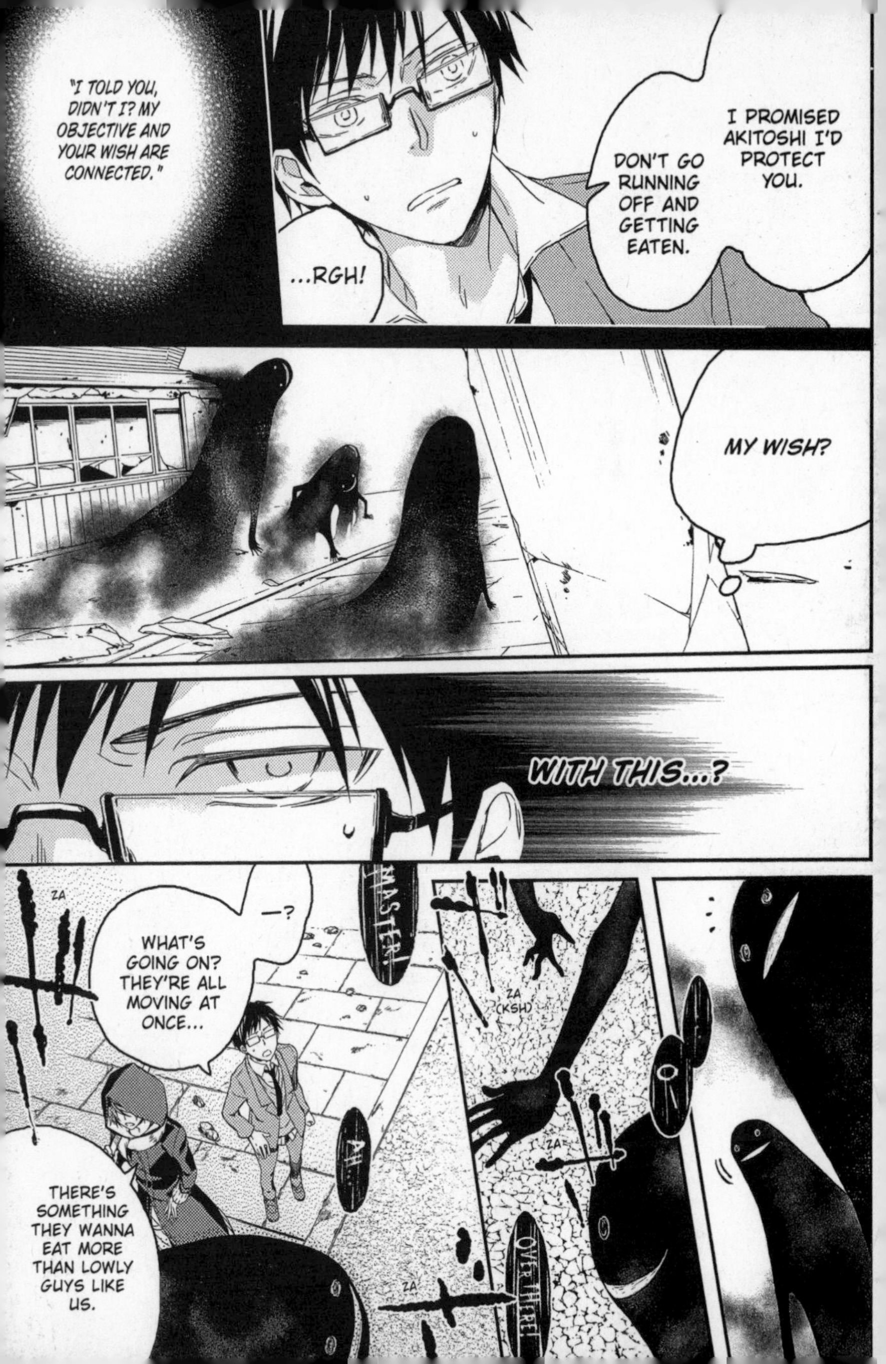
I PROMISED AKITOSHI I'D PROTECT YOU.
DON'T GO RUNNING OFF AND GETTING EATEN.
...RGH!
"I TOLD YOU, DIDN'T I? MY OBJECTIVE AND YOUR WISH ARE CONNECTED."
MY WISH?
WITH THIS...?
...
ZA (KSH)
ZA
OVER THERE!
ZA
MASTER!
—?
ZA
WHAT'S GOING ON? THEY'RE ALL MOVING AT ONCE...
AH
THERE'S SOMETHING THEY WANNA EAT MORE THAN LOWLY GUYS LIKE US.

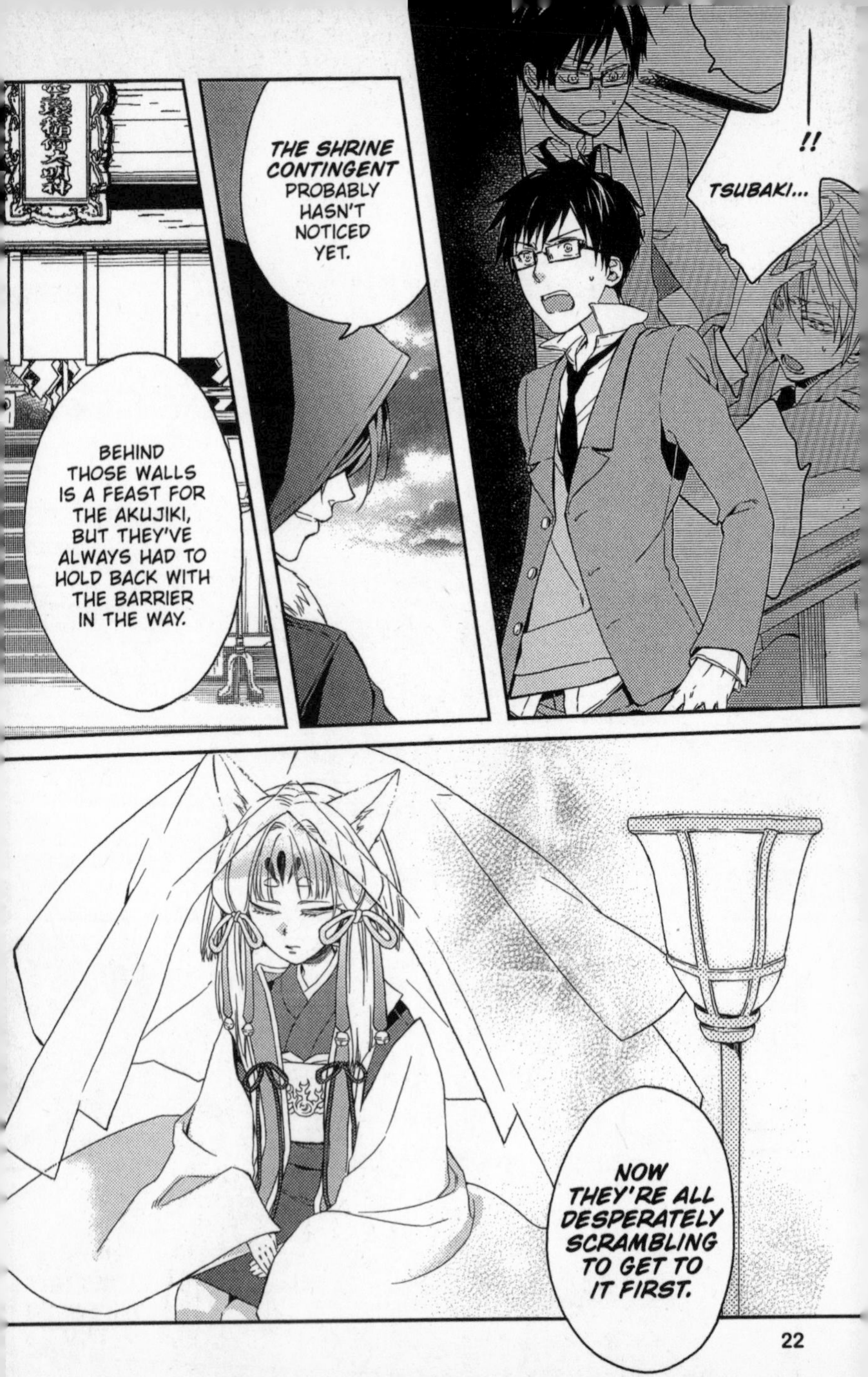
!!
TSUBAKI...
THE SHRINE CONTINGENT PROBABLY HASN'T NOTICED YET.
BEHIND THOSE WALLS IS A FEAST FOR THE AKUJIKI, BUT THEY'VE ALWAYS HAD TO HOLD BACK WITH THE BARRIER IN THE WAY.
NOW THEY'RE ALL DESPERATELY SCRAMBLING TO GET TO IT FIRST.

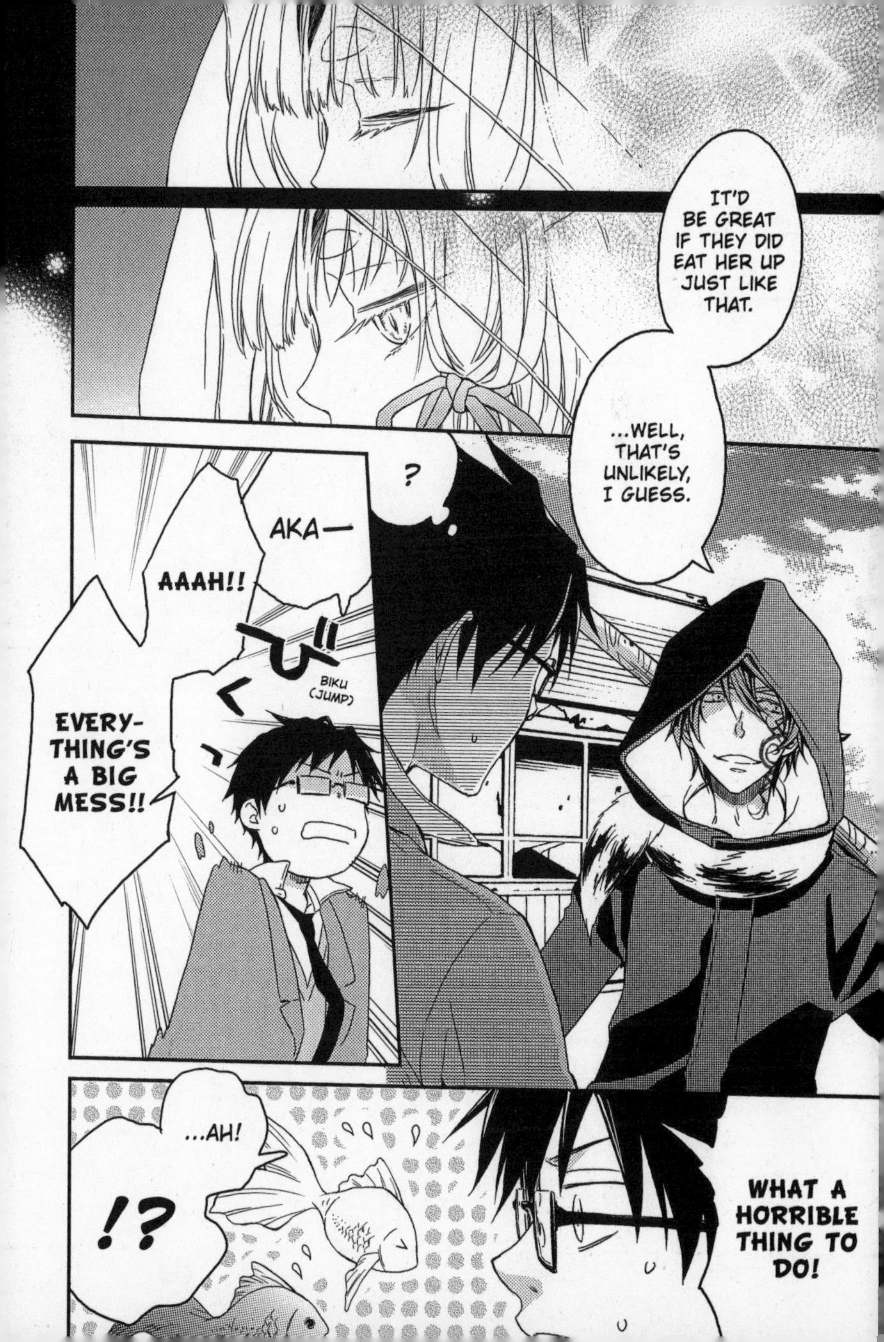
IT'D BE GREAT IF THEY DID EAT HER UP JUST LIKE THAT.
...WELL, THAT'S UNLIKELY, I GUESS.
?
AKA—
AAAH!!
BIKU (JUMP)
EVERY-THING'S A BIG MESS!!
WHAT A HORRIBLE THING TO DO!
...AH!
!?

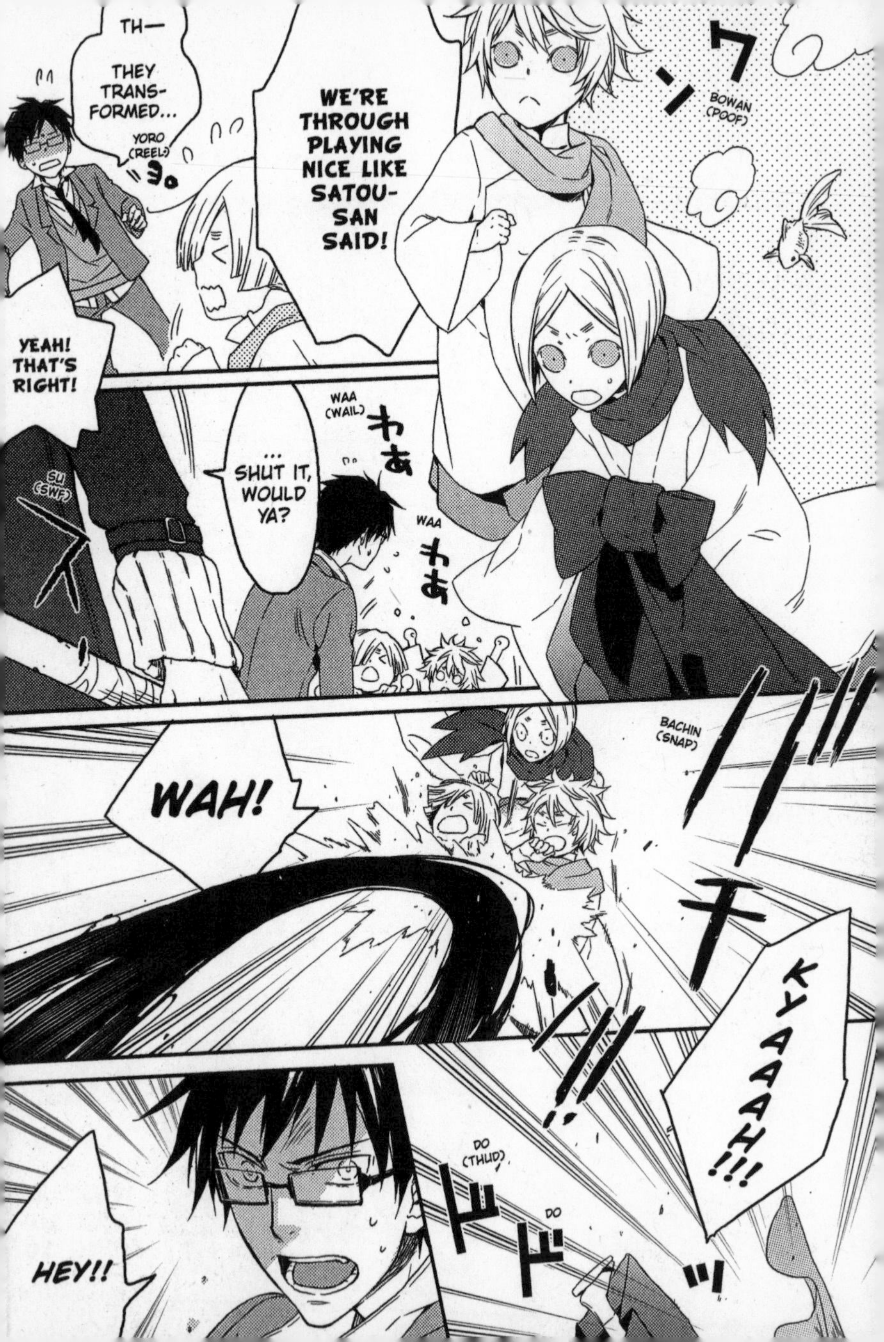
BOWAN (POOF)
WE'RE THROUGH PLAYING NICE LIKE SATOU-SAN SAID!
TH— THEY TRANSFORMED...
YORO (REEL)
YEAH! THAT'S RIGHT!
WAA (WAIL)
WAA
... SHUT IT, WOULD YA?
SU (SWF)
BACHIN (SNAP)
WAH!
KYAAAAAH!!!
DO (THUD)
DO
HEY!!

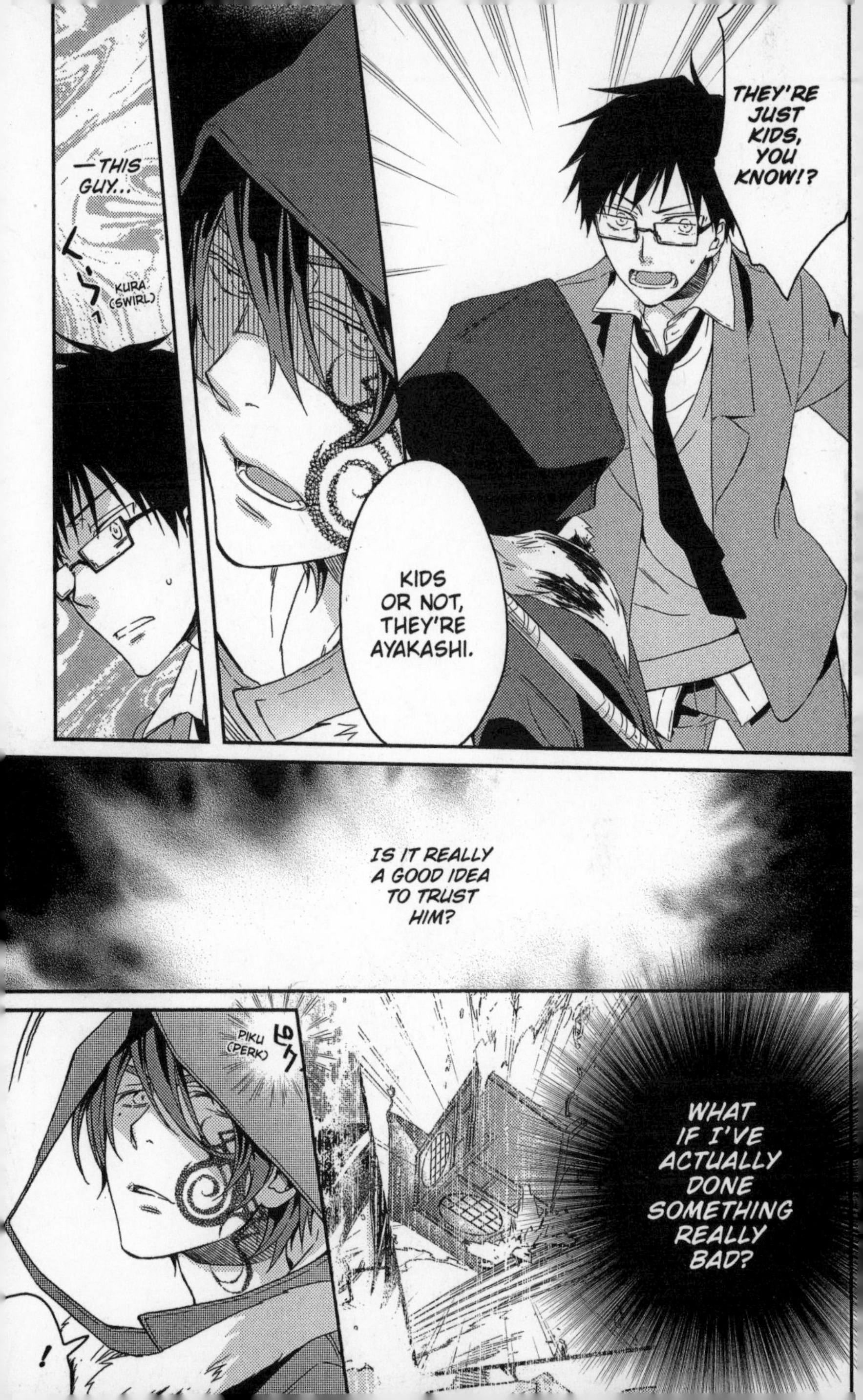
THEY'RE JUST KIDS, YOU KNOW!?
KIDS OR NOT, THEY'RE AYAKASHI.
—THIS GUY...
KURA (SWIRL)
IS IT REALLY A GOOD IDEA TO TRUST HIM?
WHAT IF I'VE ACTUALLY DONE SOMETHING REALLY BAD?
PIKU (PERK)
!

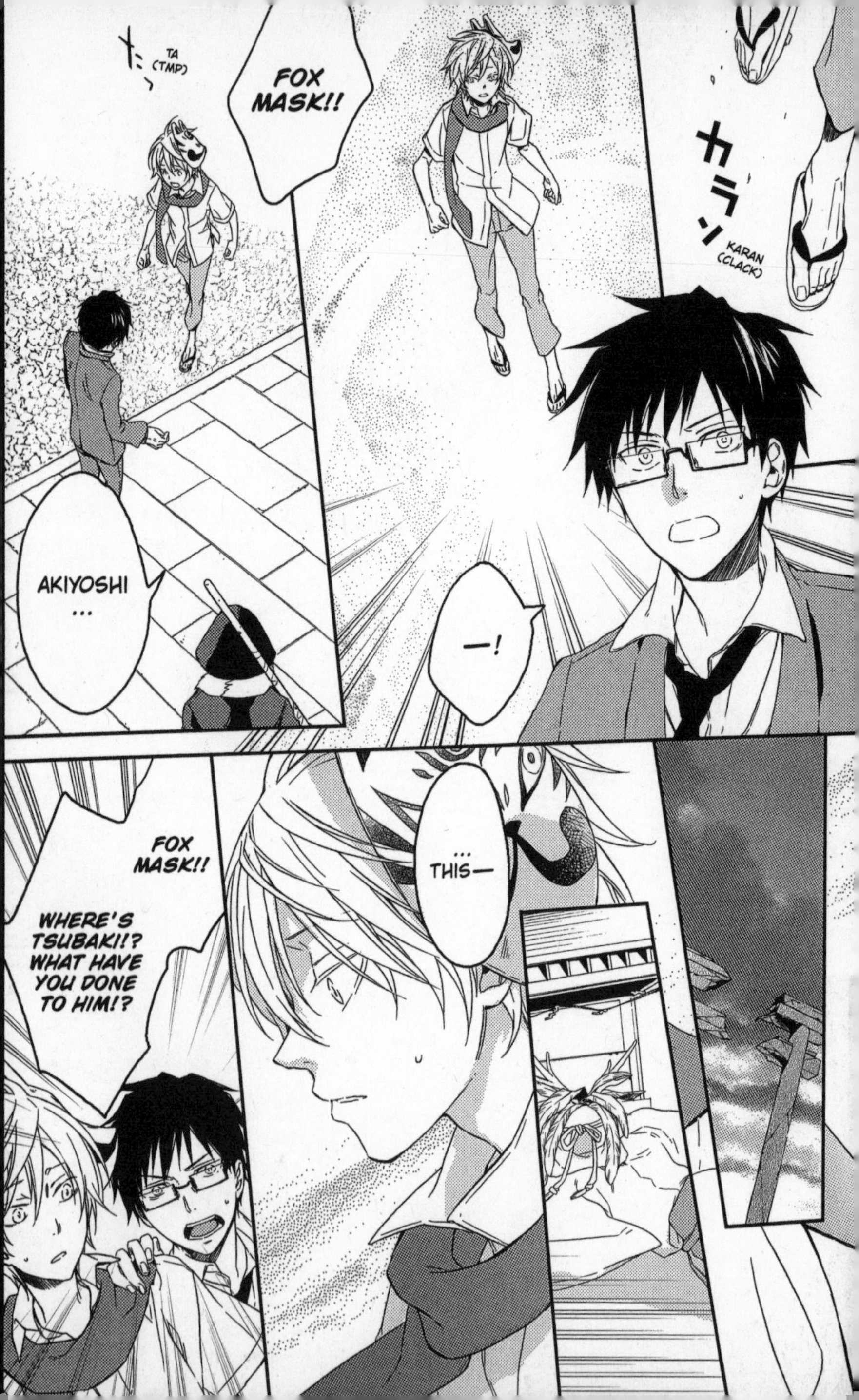
カラン
KARAN (CLACK)
FOX MASK!!
—!
たっ
TA (TMP)
AKIYOSHI ...
... THIS—
FOX MASK!!
WHERE'S TSUBAKI!!? WHAT HAVE YOU DONE TO HIM!?

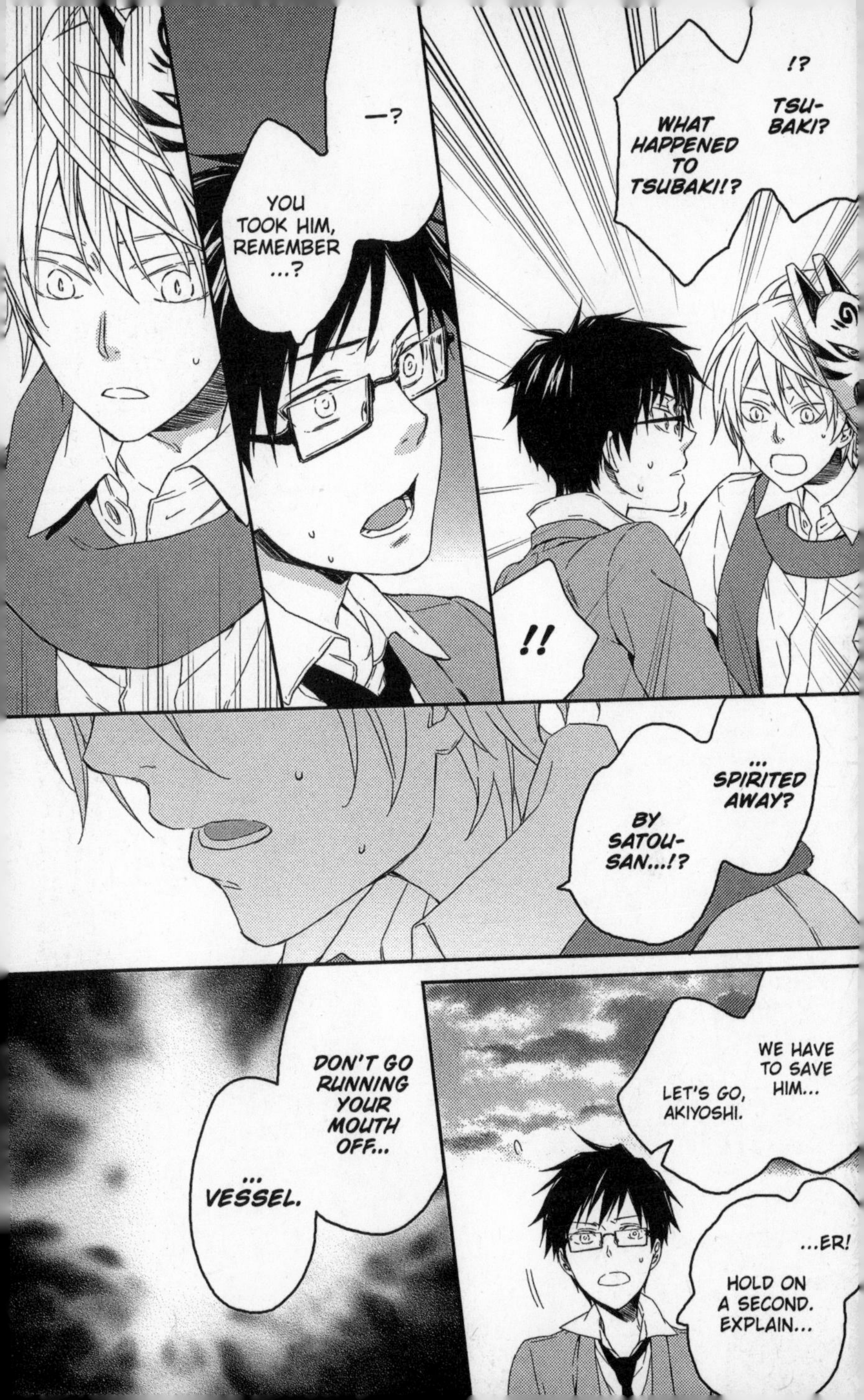
!?
TSU-BAKI?
WHAT HAPPENED TO TSUBAKI!?
!!
—?
YOU TOOK HIM, REMEMBER ...?
... SPIRITED AWAY?
BY SATOU-SAN...!?
WE HAVE TO SAVE HIM...
LET'S GO, AKIYOSHI.
...ER!
HOLD ON A SECOND. EXPLAIN...
DON'T GO RUNNING YOUR MOUTH OFF...
... VESSEL.

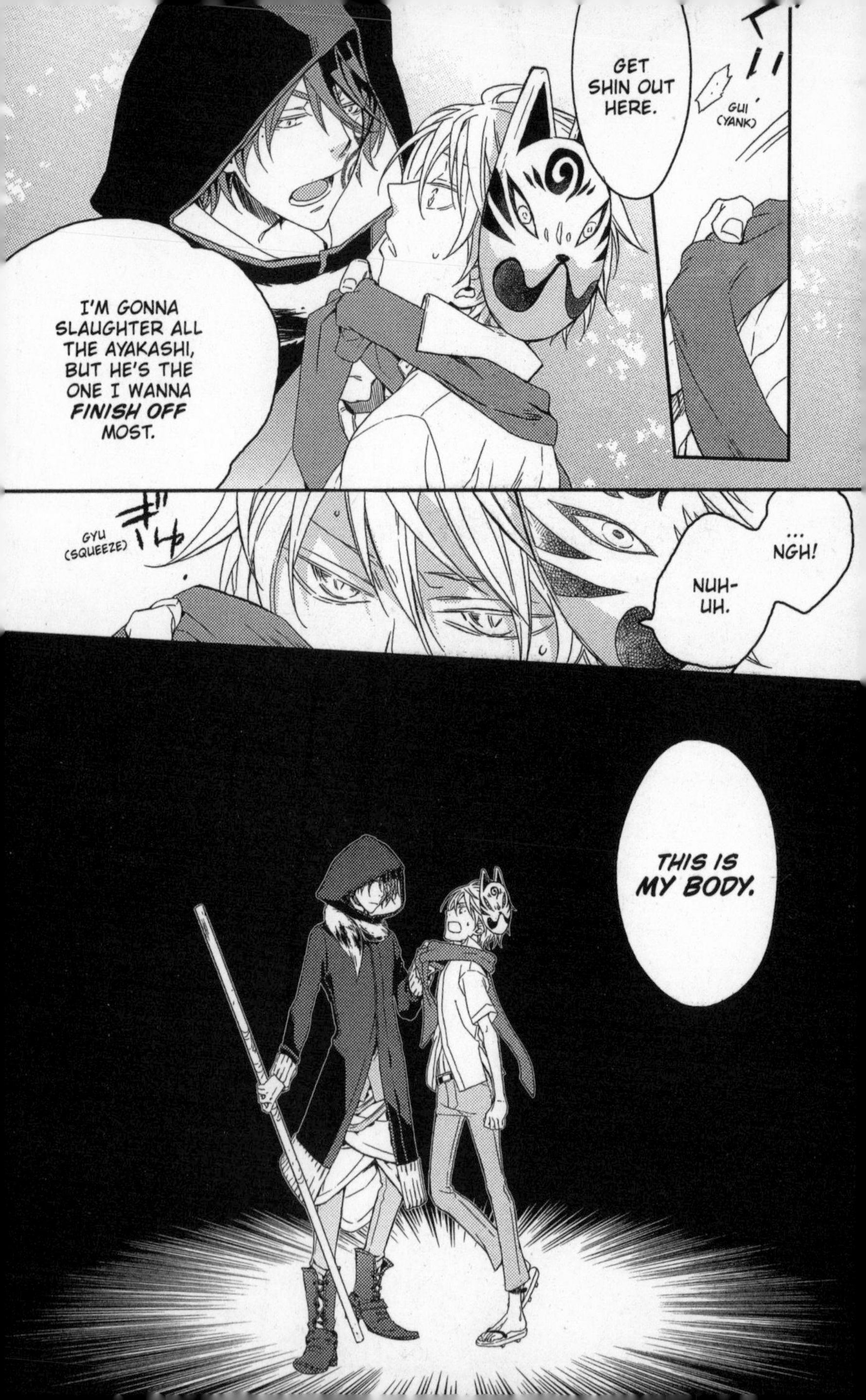
GUI (YANK)
GET SHIN OUT HERE.
I'M GONNA SLAUGHTER ALL THE AYAKASHI, BUT HE'S THE ONE I WANNA *FINISH OFF* MOST.
...NGH!
NUH-UH.
GYU (SQUEEZE)
THIS IS MY BODY.

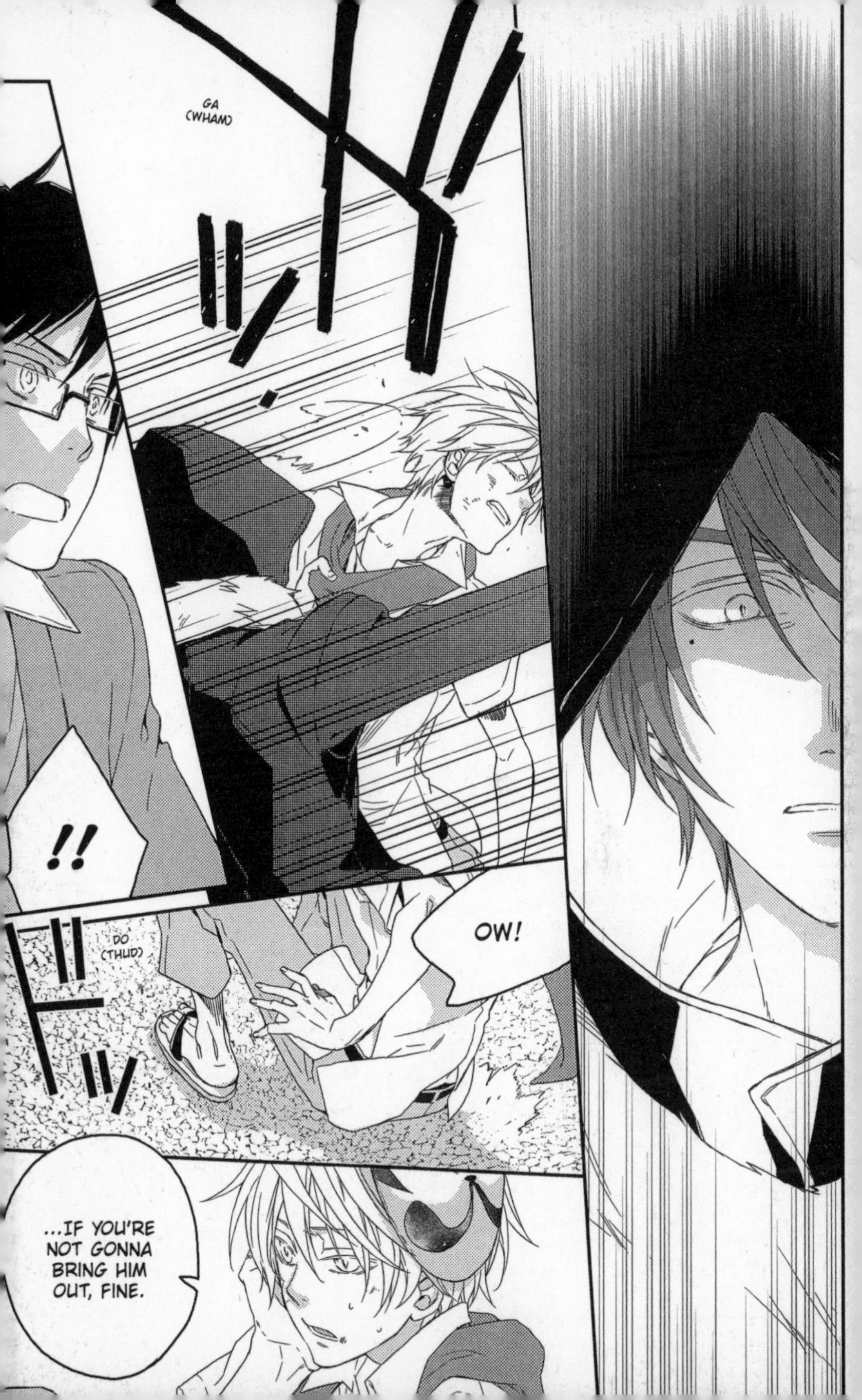
GA
(WHAM)
!!
OW!
DO
(THUD)
...IF YOU'RE NOT GONNA BRING HIM OUT, FINE.

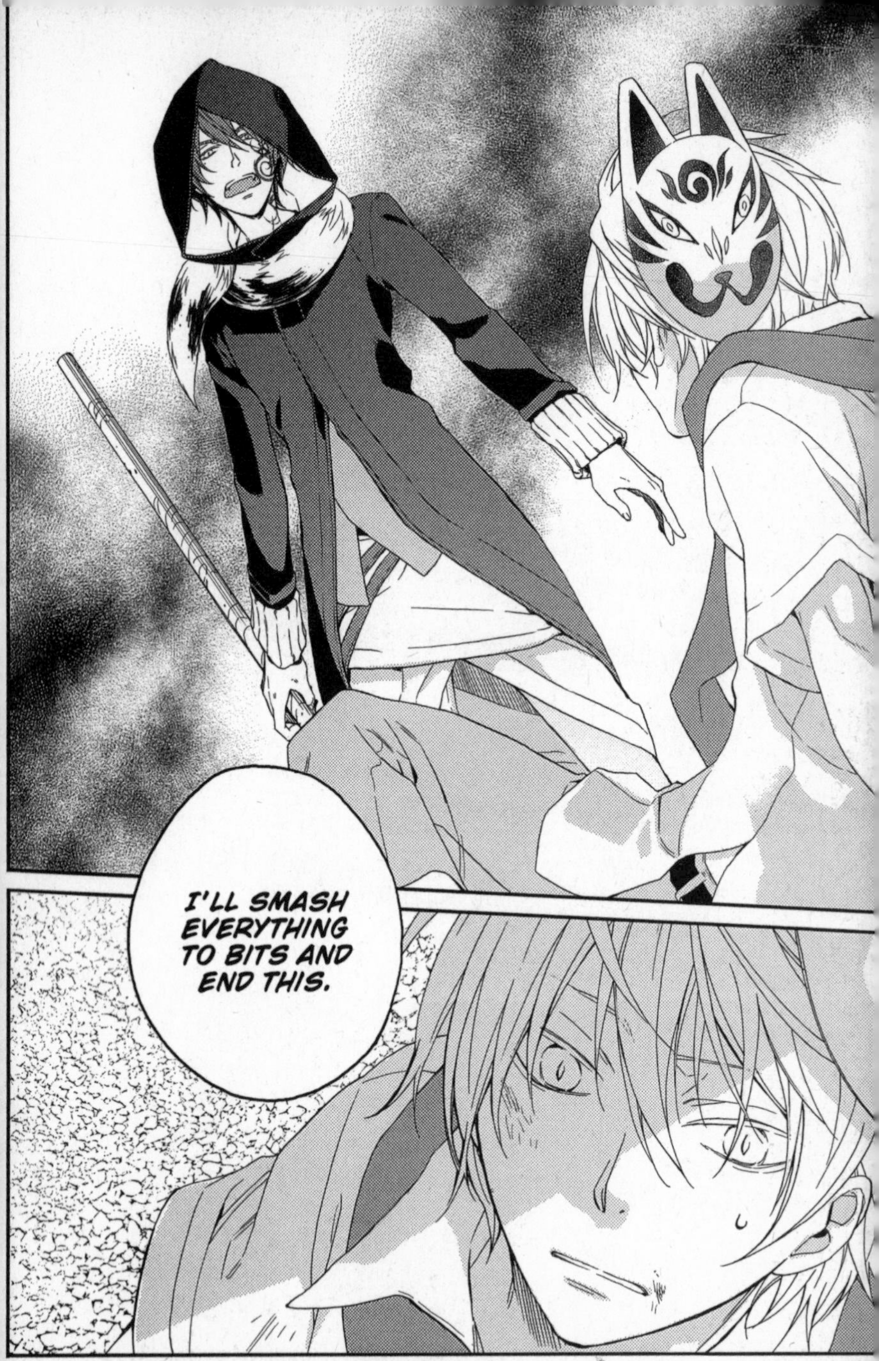
I'LL SMASH EVERYTHING TO BITS AND END THIS.

Of the Red,
the Light,
and the
Ayakashi

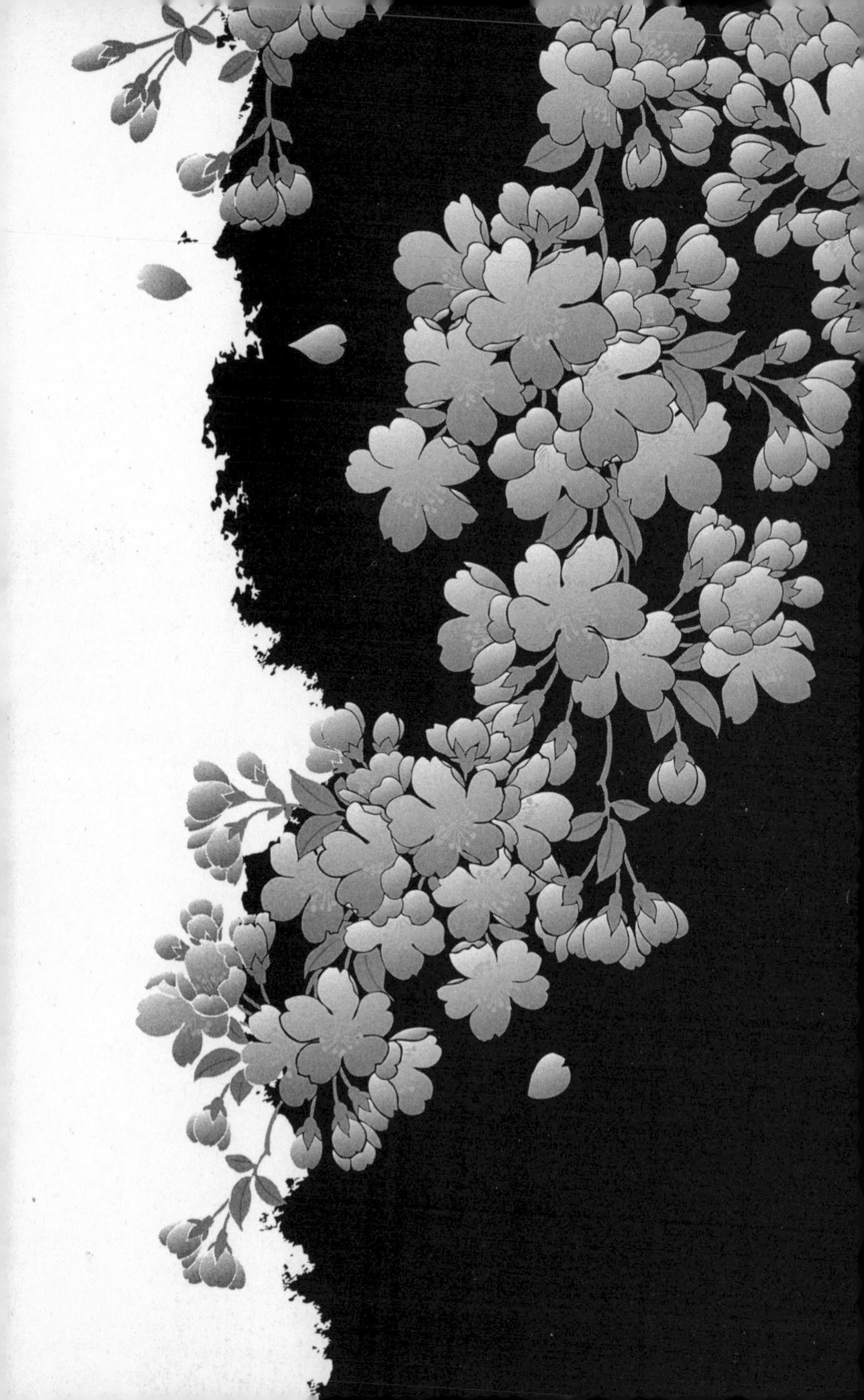

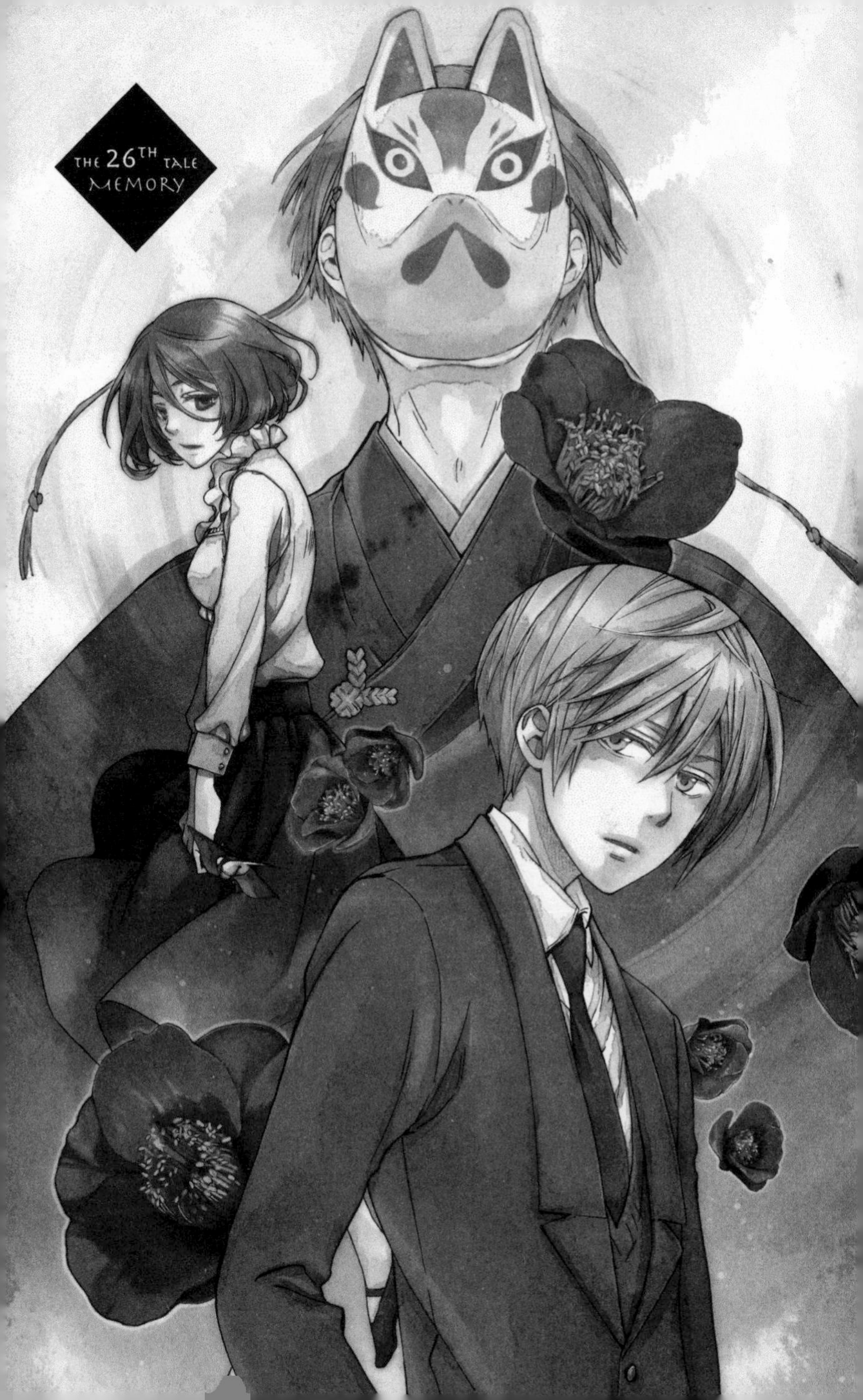
THE 26TH TALE
MEMORY

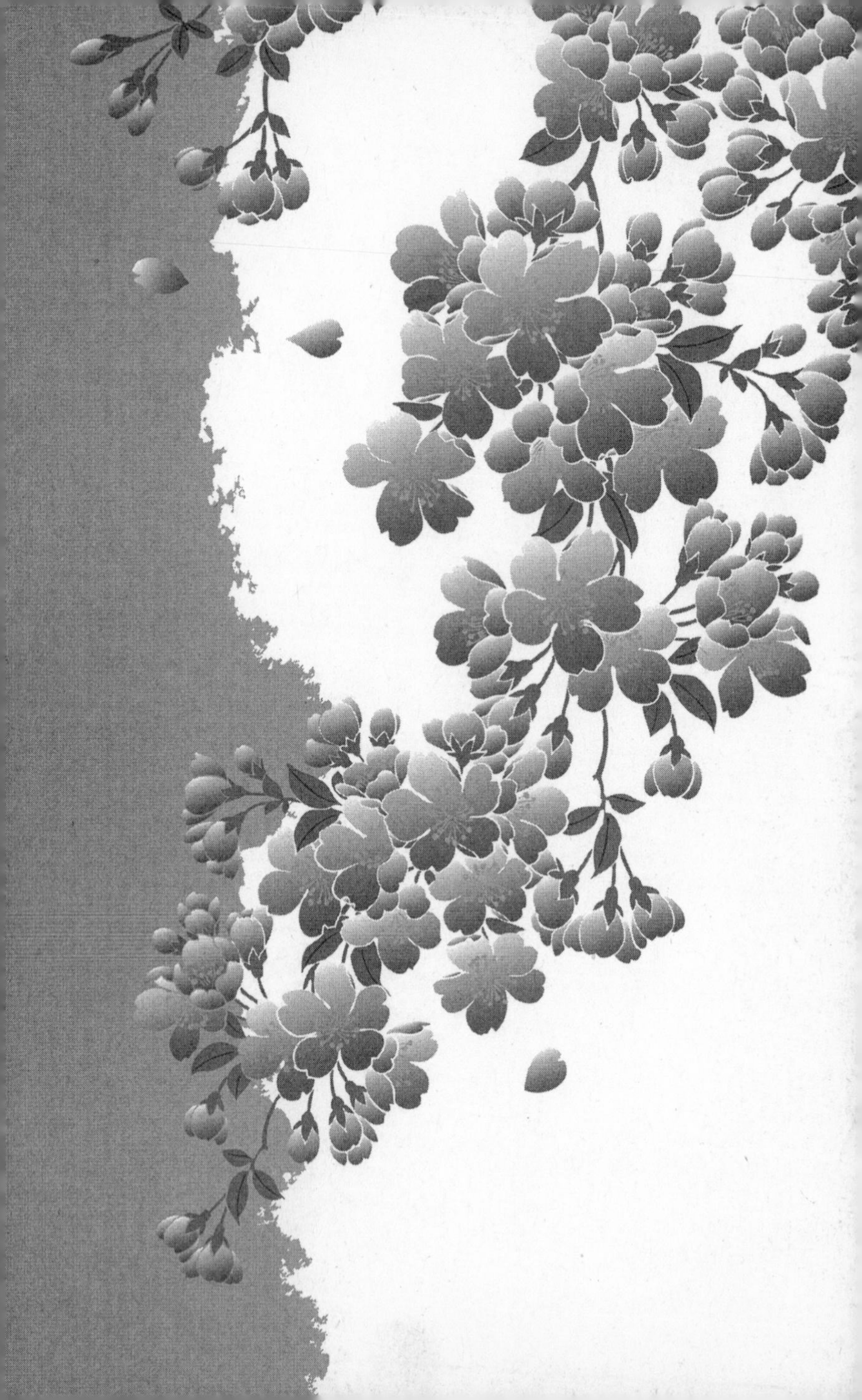

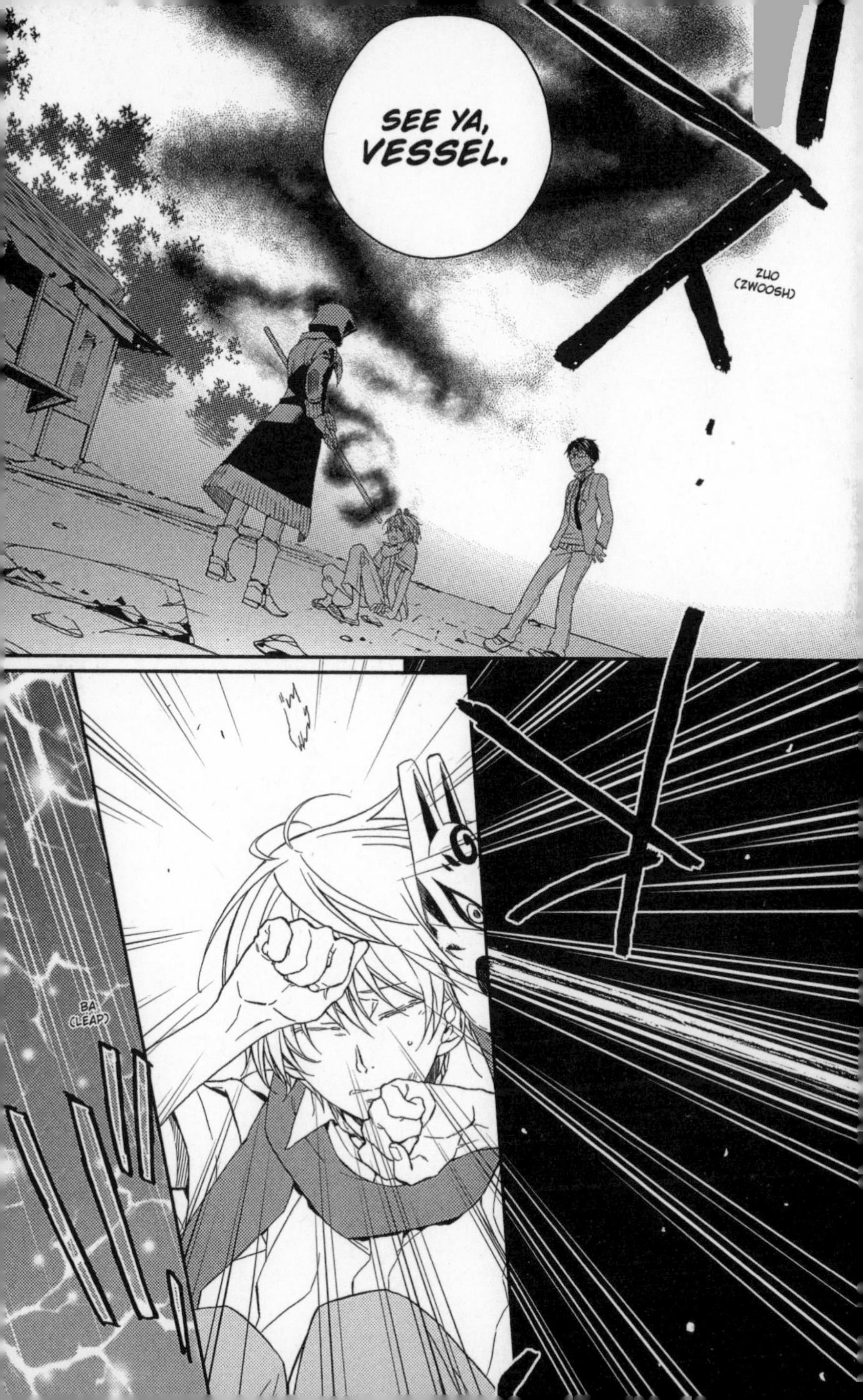
SEE YA, VESSEL.
ZUO (ZWOOSH)
BA (LEAP)

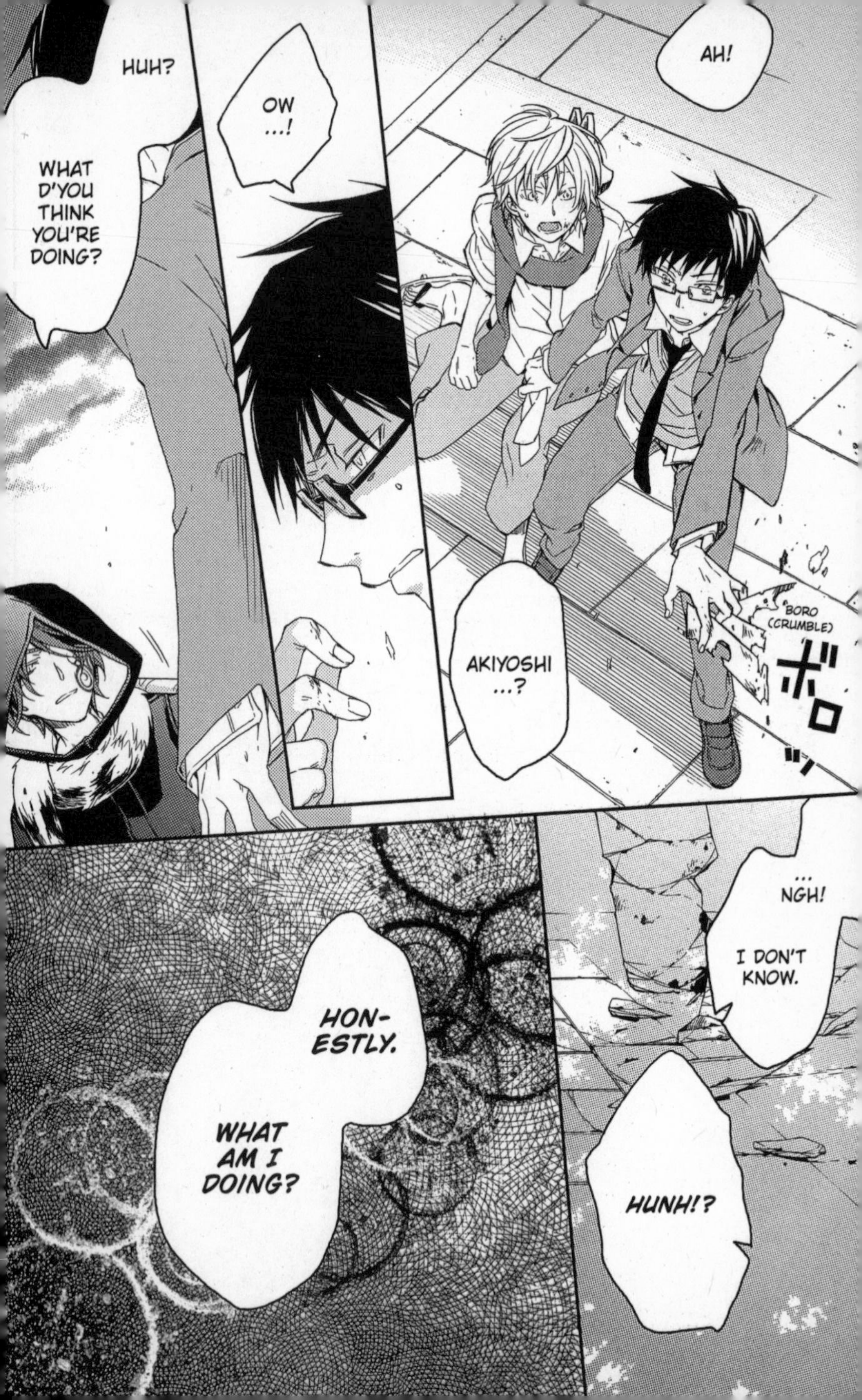
AH!
BORO (CRUMBLE)
ボロッ
AKIYOSHI ...?
OW ...!
HUH?
WHAT D'YOU THINK YOU'RE DOING?
... NGH!
I DON'T KNOW.
HUNH!?
HON-ESTLY.
WHAT AM I DOING?

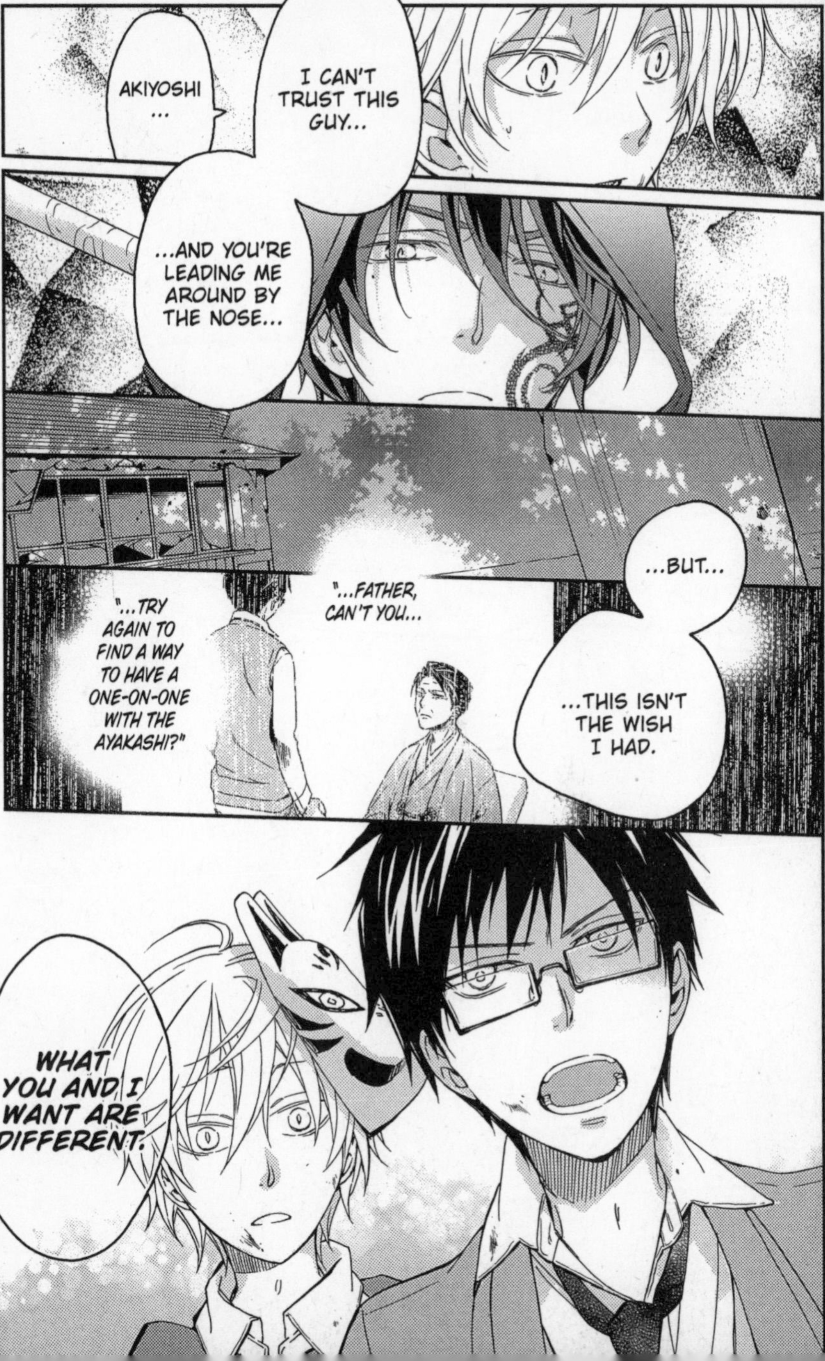
I CAN'T TRUST THIS GUY...
AKIYOSHI ...
...AND YOU'RE LEADING ME AROUND BY THE NOSE...
...BUT...
...THIS ISN'T THE WISH I HAD.
"...FATHER, CAN'T YOU...
"...TRY AGAIN TO FIND A WAY TO HAVE A ONE-ON-ONE WITH THE AYAKASHI?"
WHAT YOU AND I WANT ARE DIFFERENT.

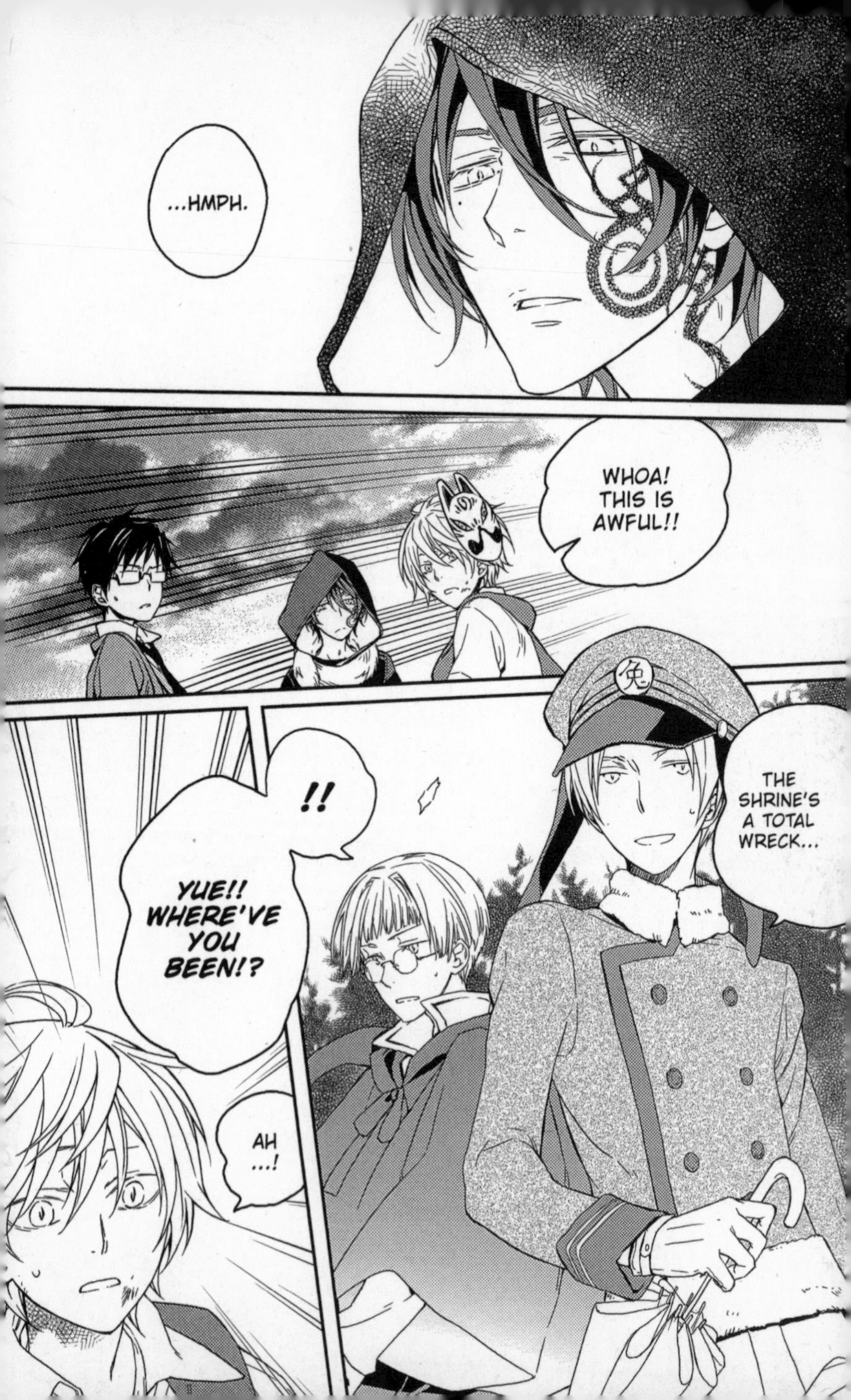
...HMPH.
WHOA! THIS IS AWFUL!!
THE SHRINE'S A TOTAL WRECK...
!!
YUE!! WHERE'VE YOU BEEN!?
AH ...!

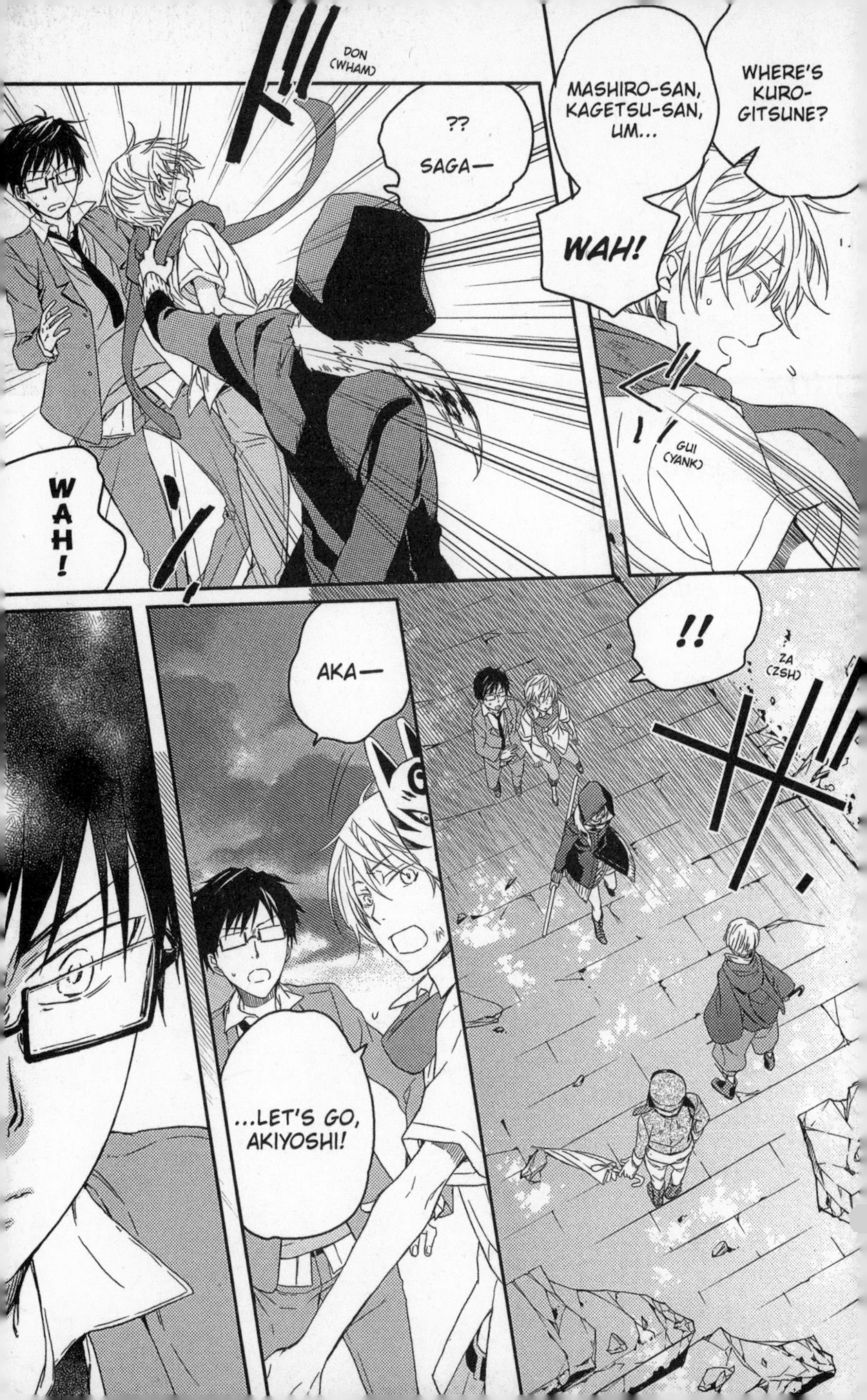
WHERE'S KURO-GITSUNE?
MASHIRO-SAN, KAGETSU-SAN, UM...
WAH!
GUI (YANK)
DON (WHAM)
?? SAGA—
WAH!
ZA (ZSH)
!!
AKA—
...LET'S GO, AKIYOSHI!

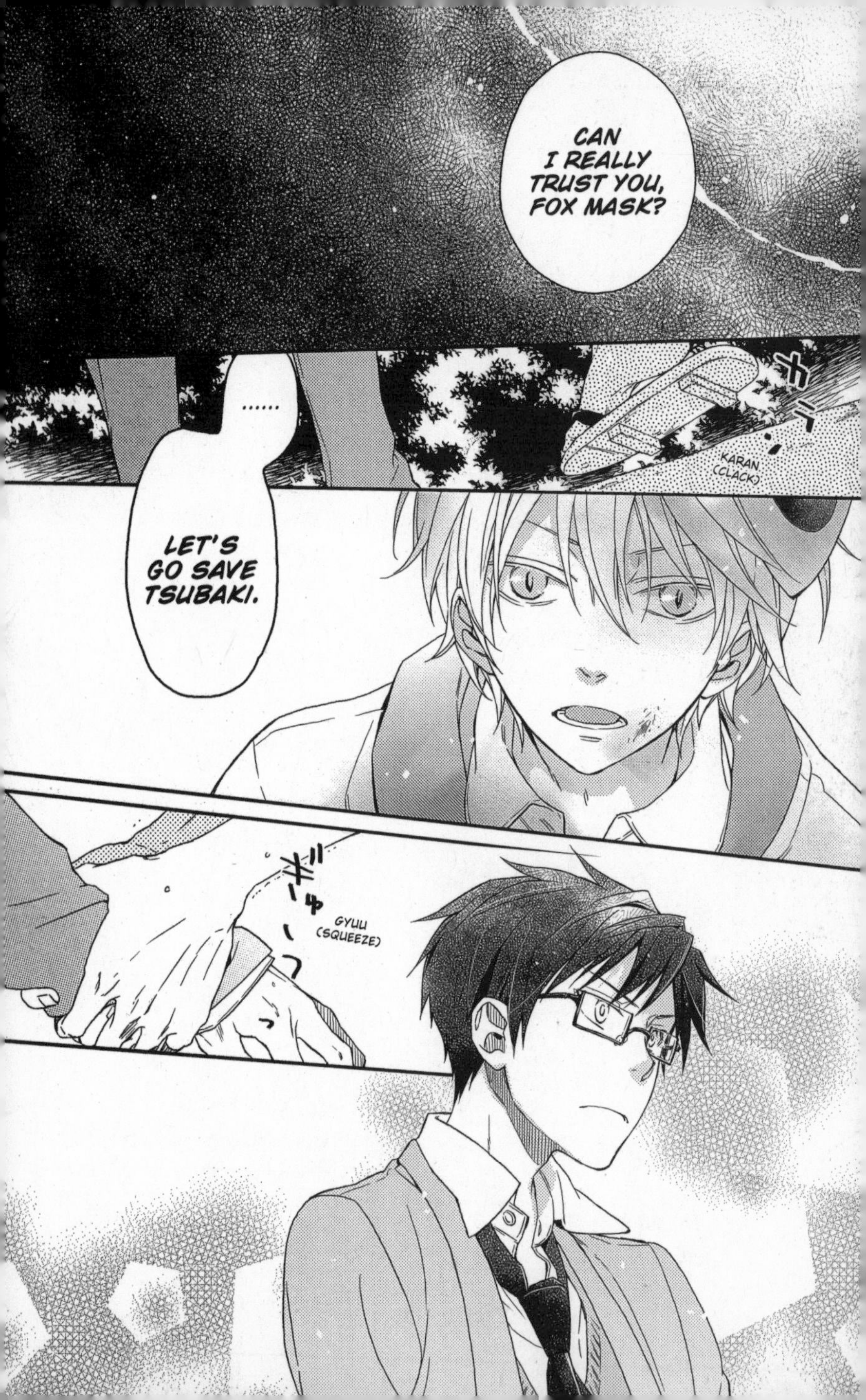
CAN I REALLY TRUST YOU, FOX MASK?
KARAN (CLACK)
……
LET'S GO SAVE TSUBAKI.
GYUU (SQUEEZE)

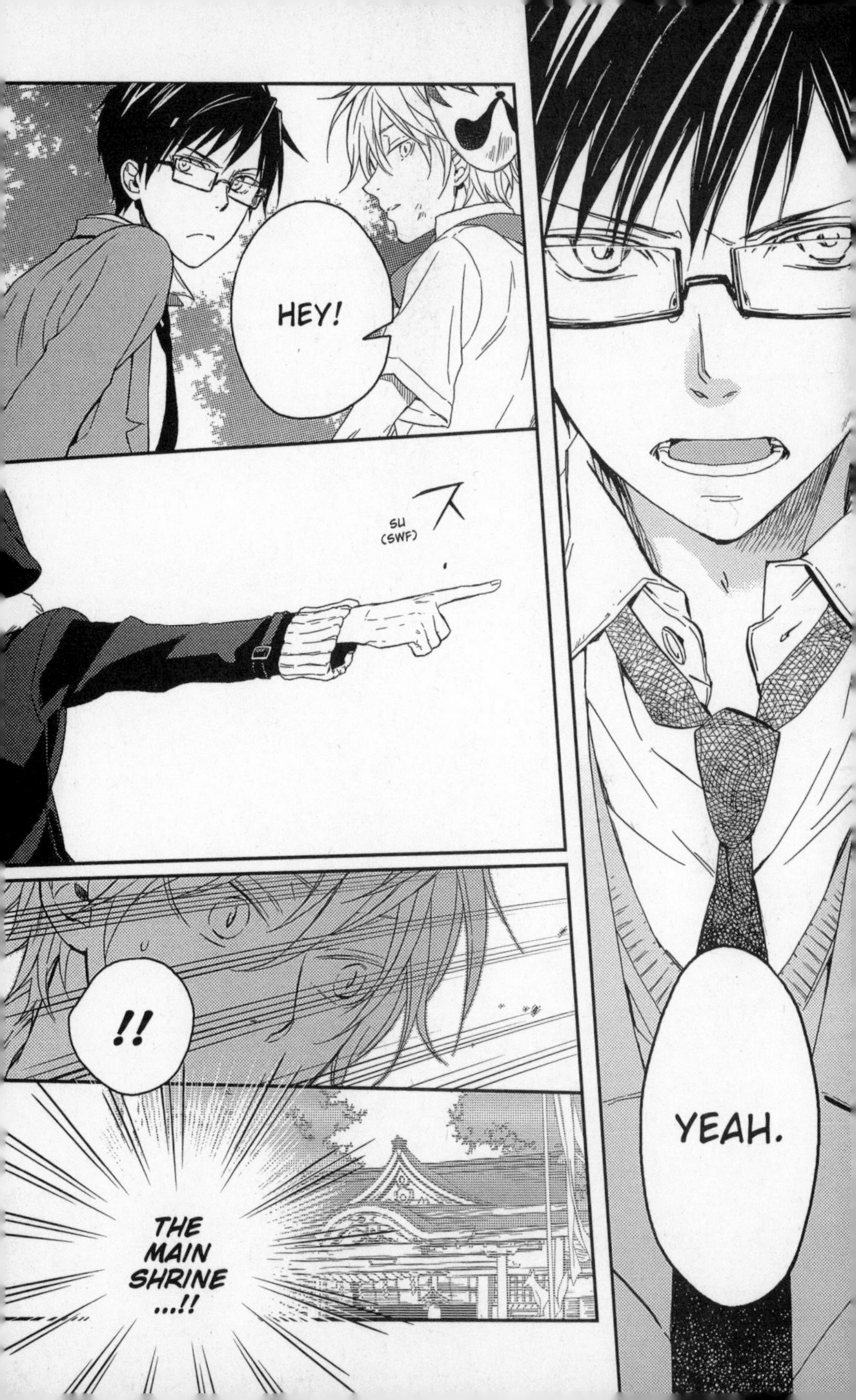
YEAH.
HEY!
SU
(SWF)
!!
THE MAIN SHRINE ...!!

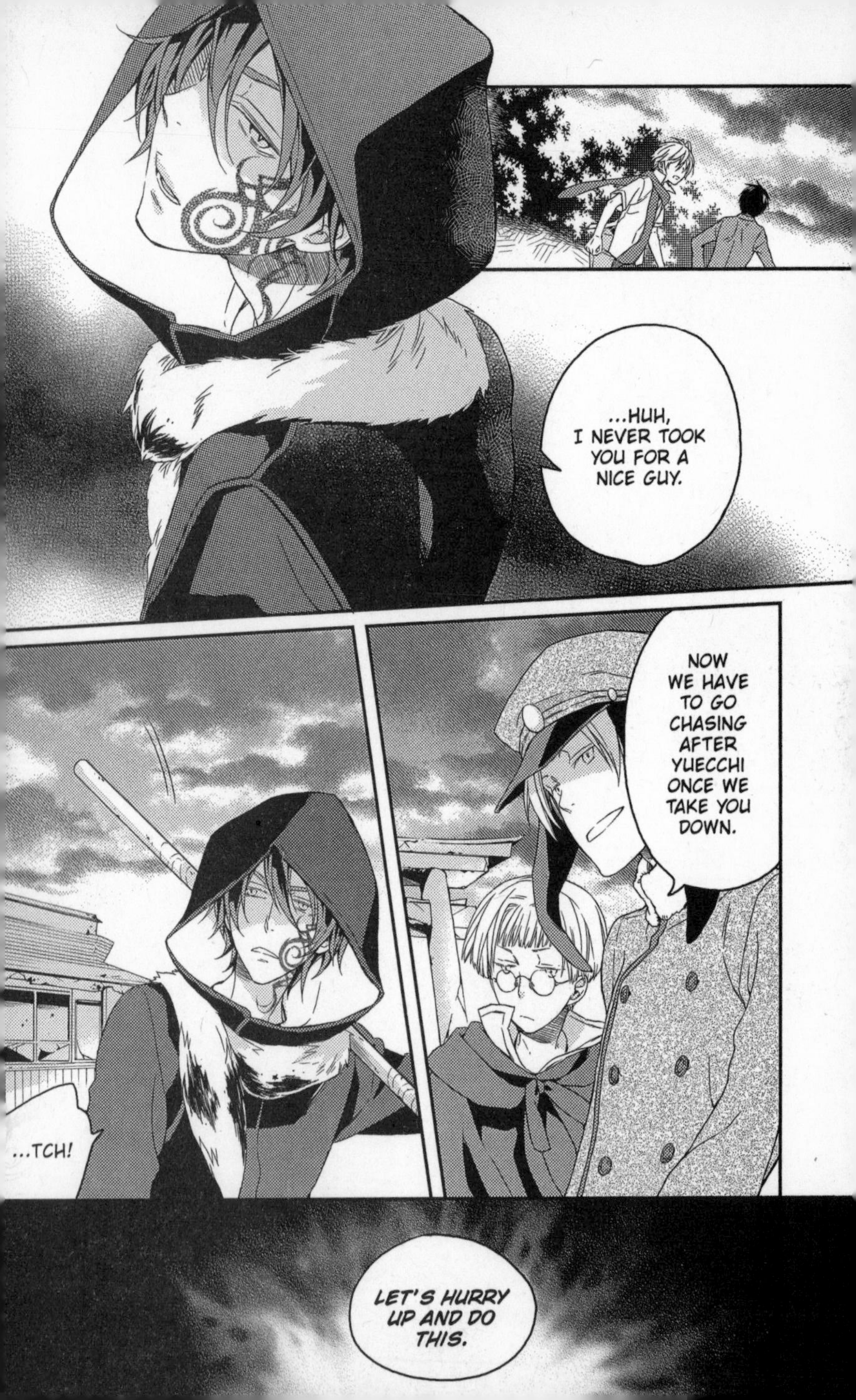
...HUH, I NEVER TOOK YOU FOR A NICE GUY.
NOW WE HAVE TO GO CHASING AFTER YUECCHI ONCE WE TAKE YOU DOWN.
...TCH!
LET'S HURRY UP AND DO THIS.

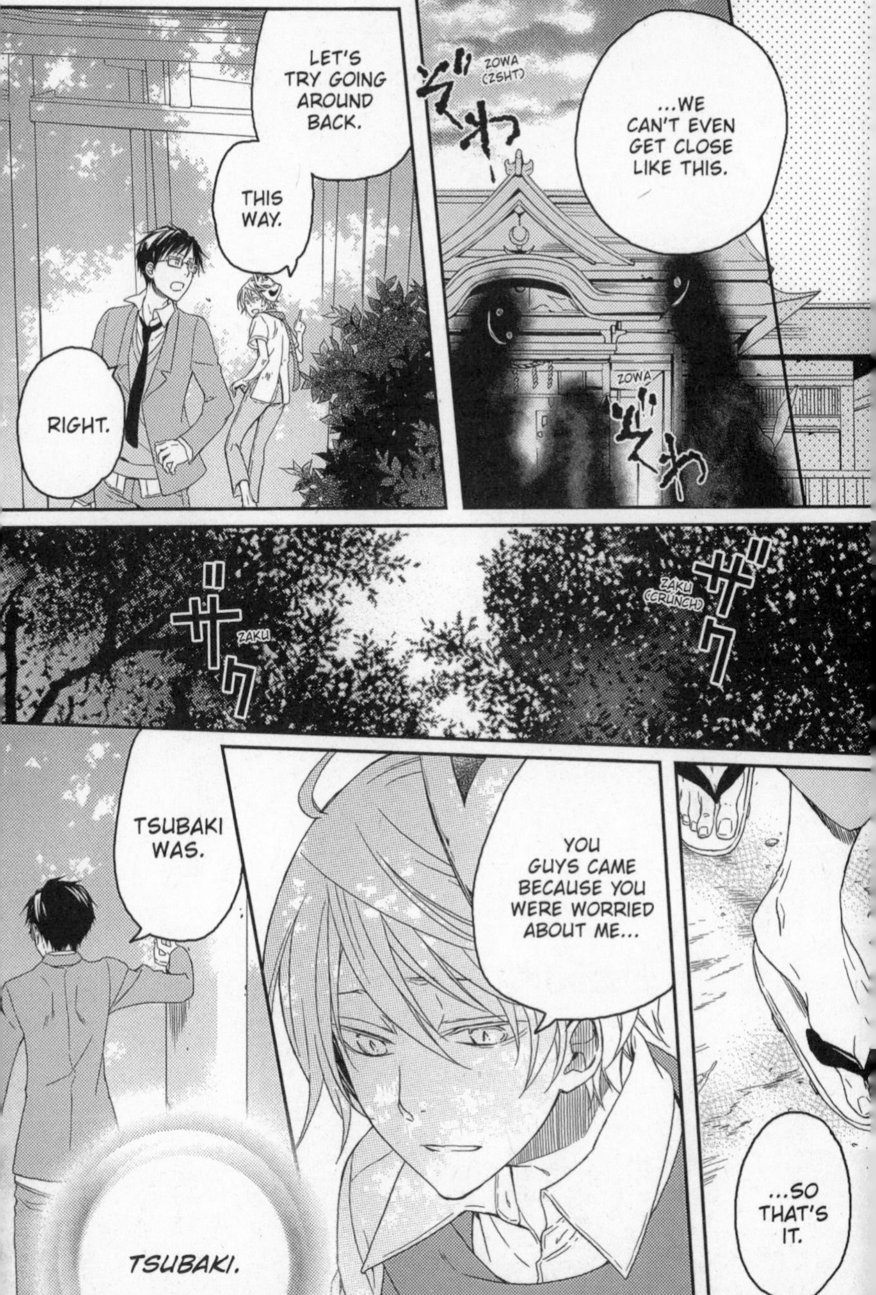
ZOWA (ZSHT)
...WE CAN'T EVEN GET CLOSE LIKE THIS.
ZOWA
LET'S TRY GOING AROUND BACK.
THIS WAY.
RIGHT.
ZAKU (CRUNCH)
ZAKU
...SO THAT'S IT.
YOU GUYS CAME BECAUSE YOU WERE WORRIED ABOUT ME...
TSUBAKI WAS.
TSUBAKI.

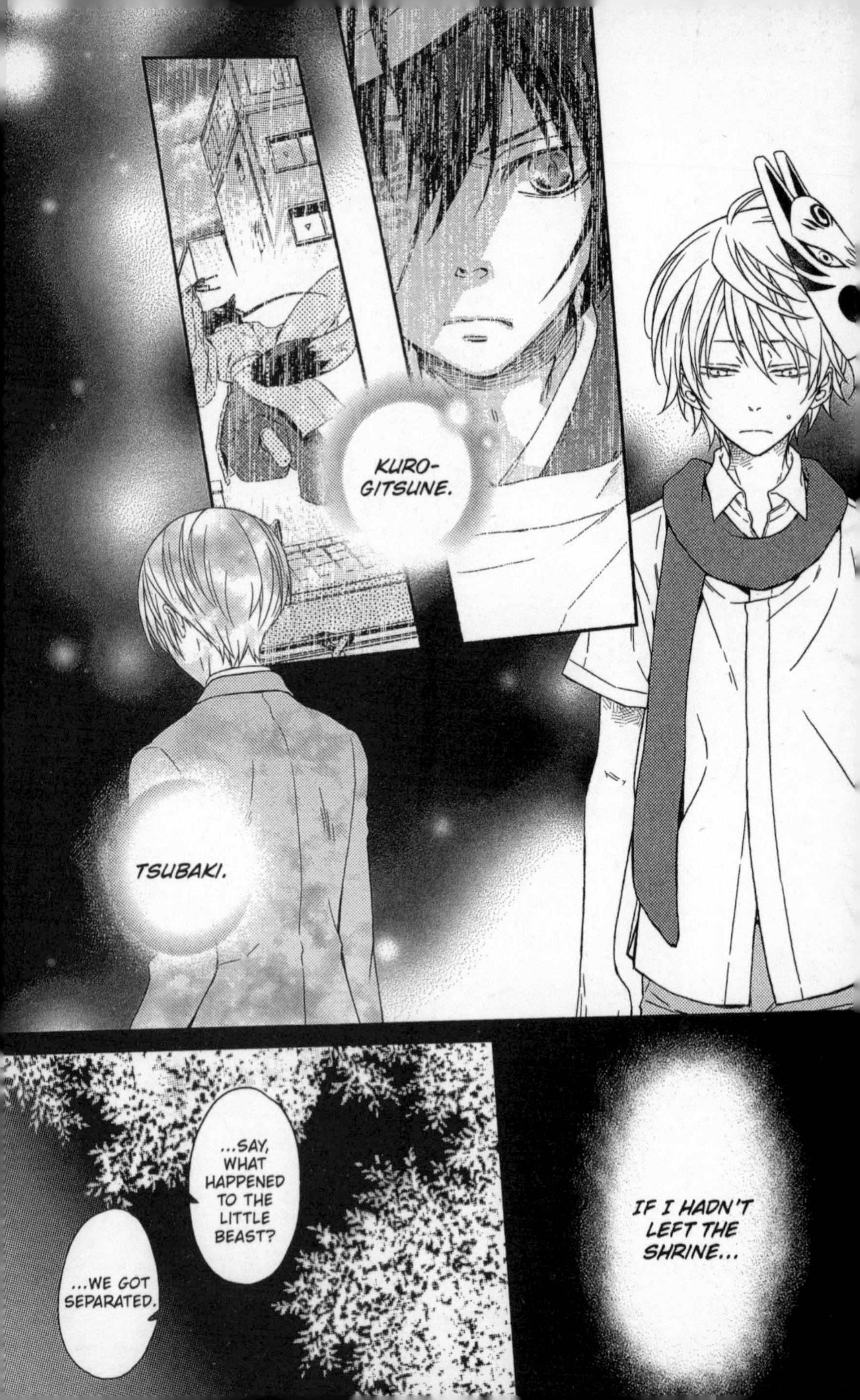
KURO-GITSUNE.
TSUBAKI.
IF I HADN'T LEFT THE SHRINE...
...SAY, WHAT HAPPENED TO THE LITTLE BEAST?
...WE GOT SEPARATED.

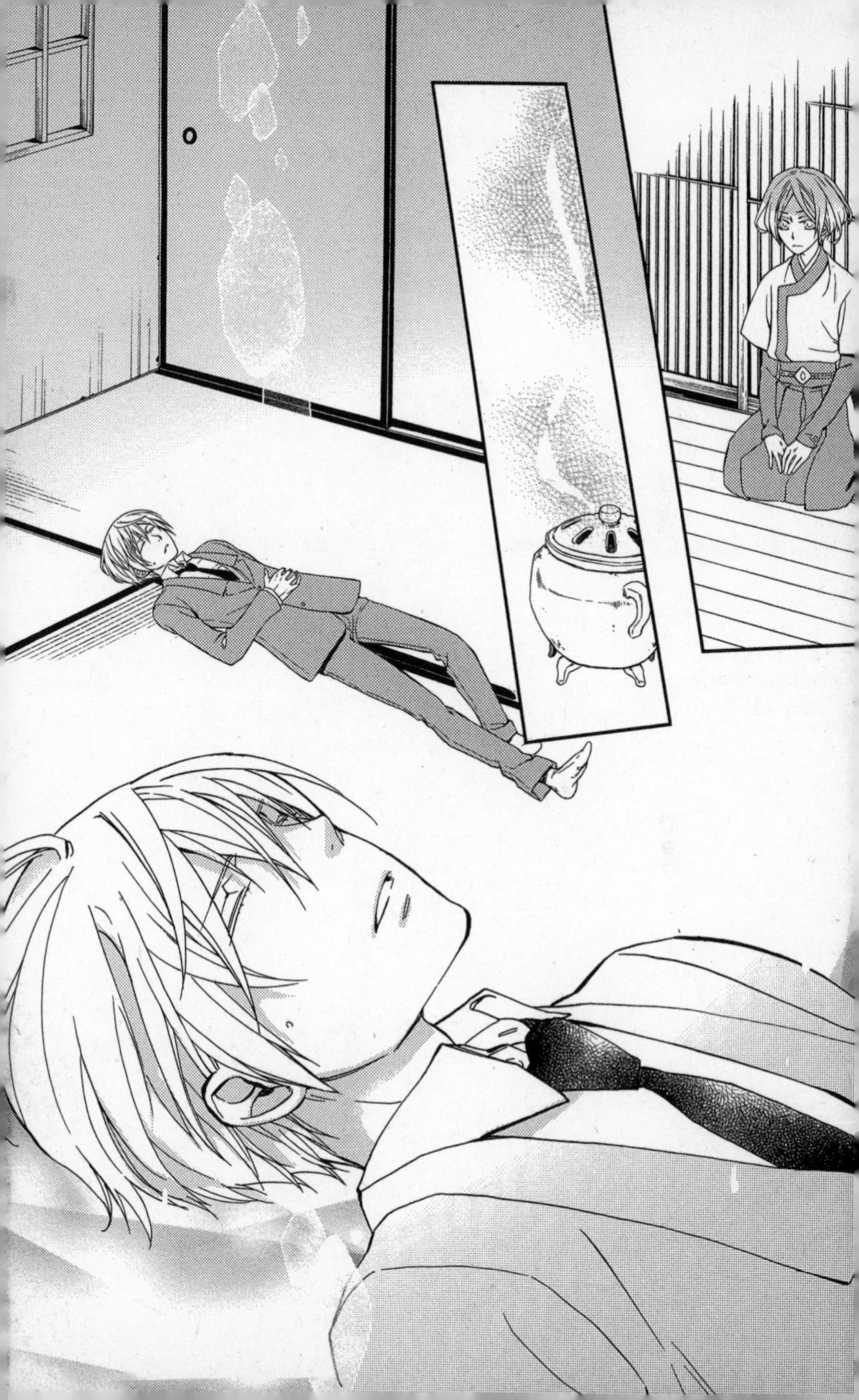

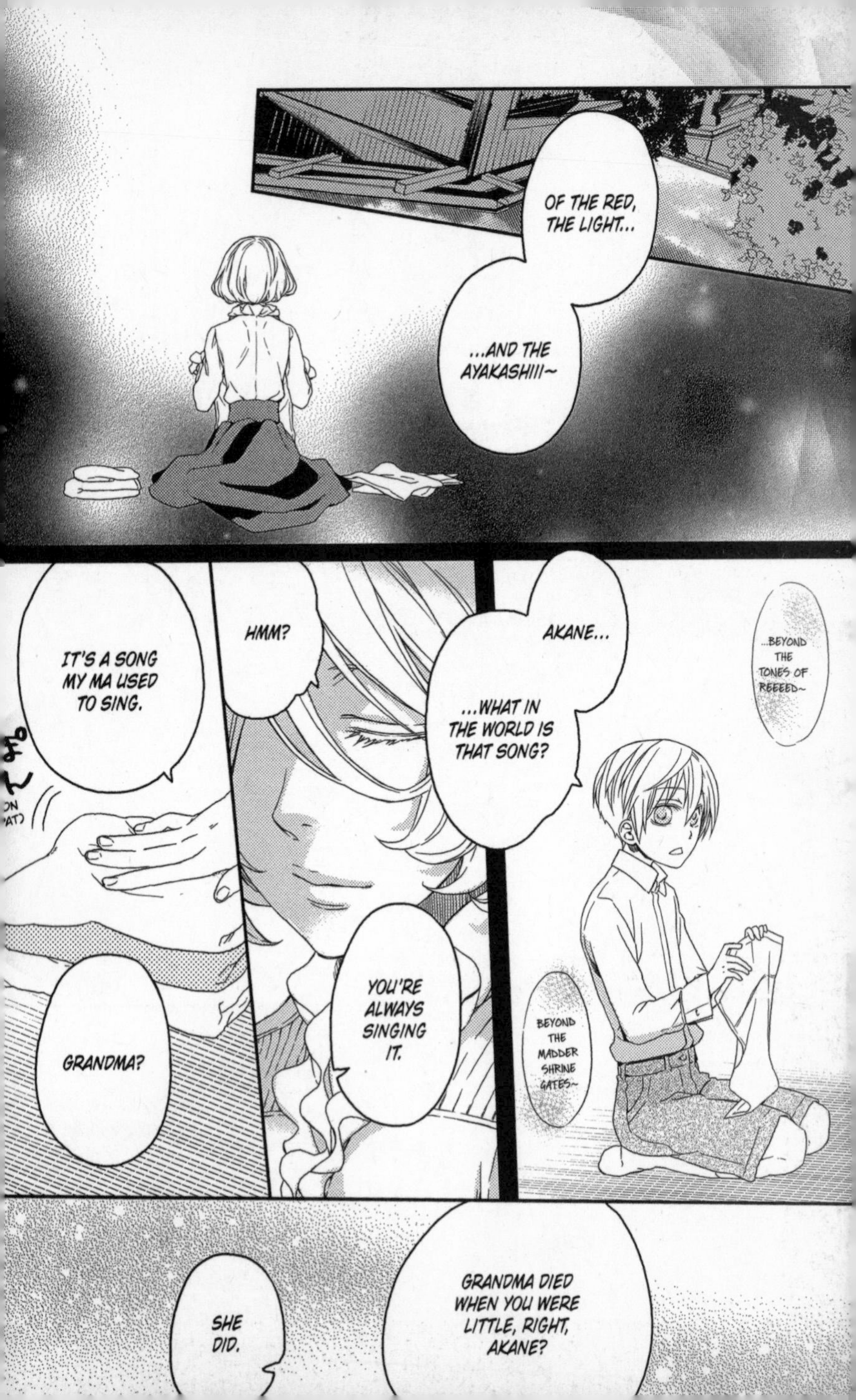

OF THE RED, THE LIGHT...
...AND THE AYAKASHIII~
...BEYOND THE TONES OF REEEED~
AKANE...
...WHAT IN THE WORLD IS THAT SONG?
BEYOND THE MADDER SHRINE GATES~
HMM?
YOU'RE ALWAYS SINGING IT.
IT'S A SONG MY MA USED TO SING.
GRANDMA?
GRANDMA DIED WHEN YOU WERE LITTLE, RIGHT, AKANE?
SHE DID.

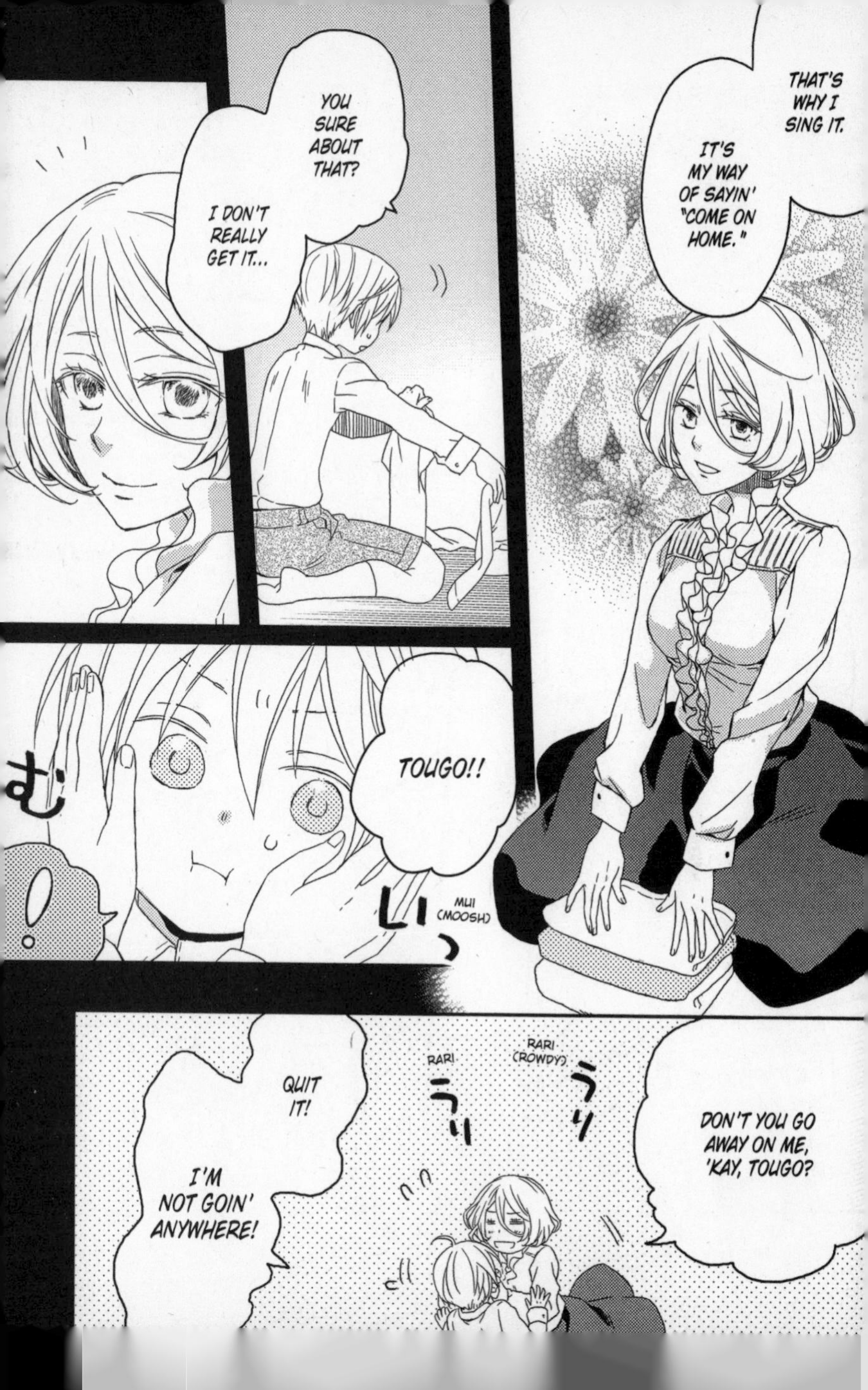
THAT'S WHY I SING IT.
IT'S MY WAY OF SAYIN' "COME ON HOME."
YOU SURE ABOUT THAT?
I DON'T REALLY GET IT...
TOUGO!!
MUI (MOOSH)
DON'T YOU GO AWAY ON ME, 'KAY, TOUGO?
RARI (ROWDY)
RARI
QUIT IT!
I'M NOT GOIN' ANYWHERE!

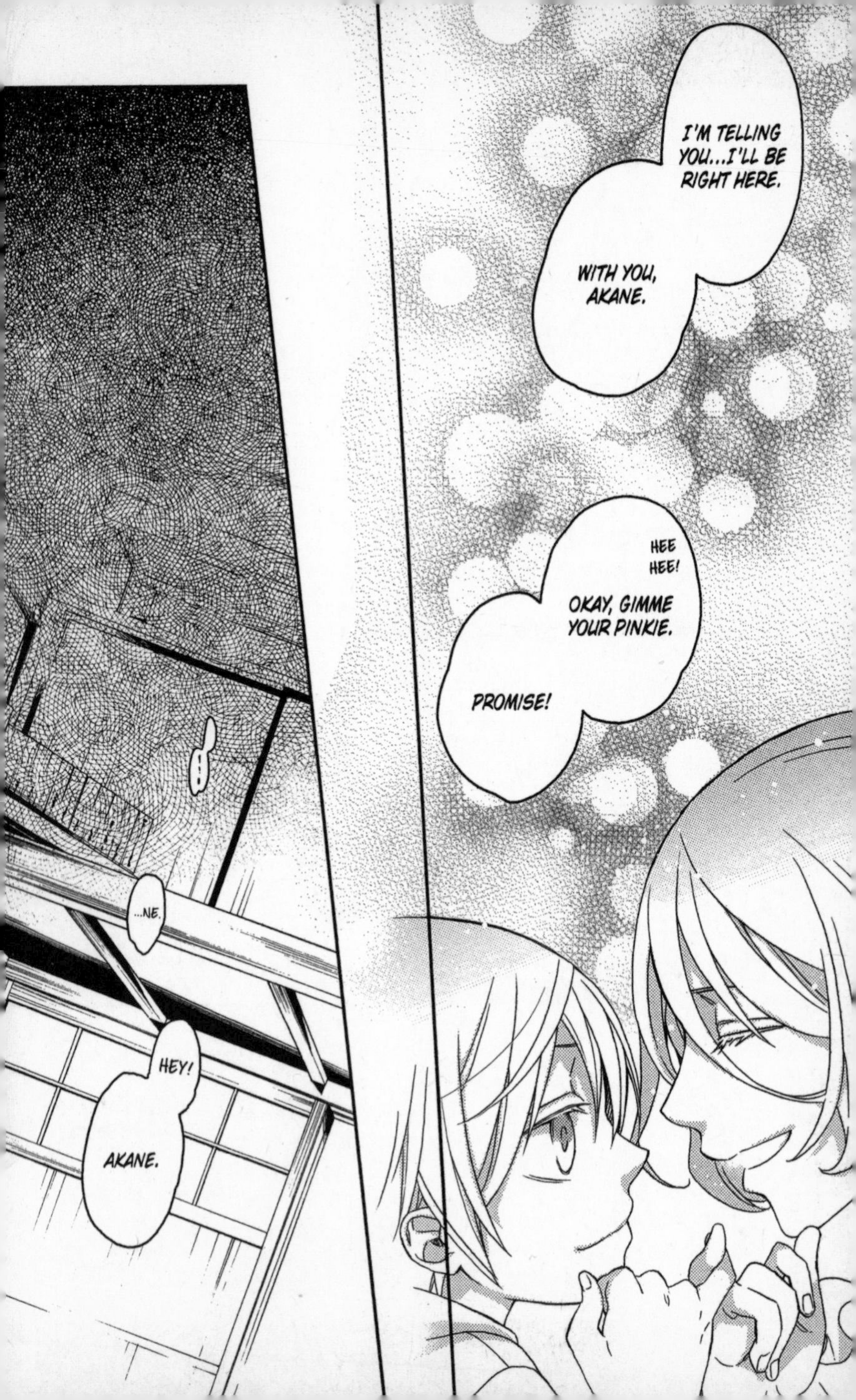
I'M TELLING YOU...I'LL BE RIGHT HERE.
WITH YOU, AKANE.
HEE HEE!
OKAY, GIMME YOUR PINKIE.
PROMISE!
...
...NE.
HEY!
AKANE.

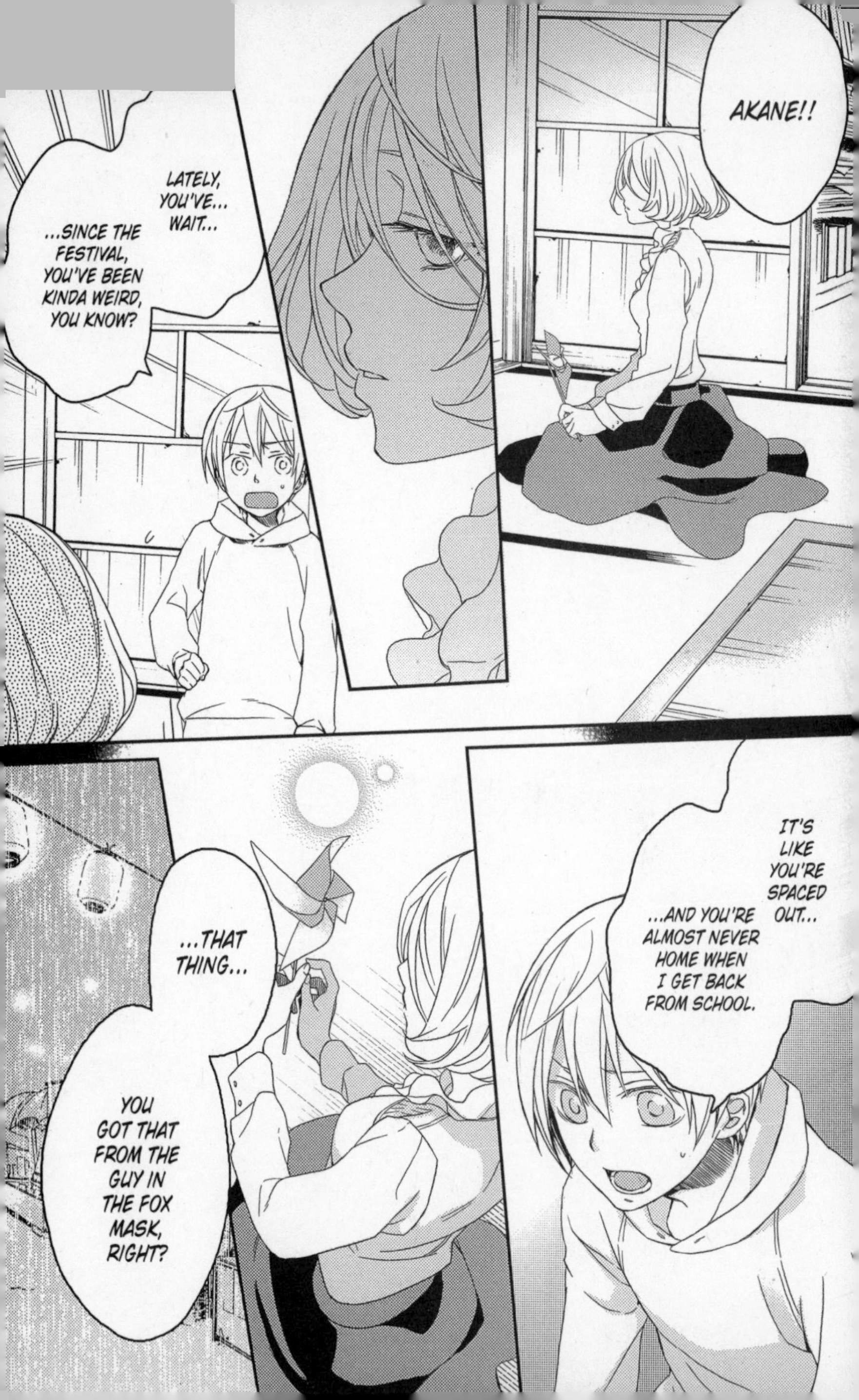
AKANE!!
LATELY, YOU'VE... WAIT...
...SINCE THE FESTIVAL, YOU'VE BEEN KINDA WEIRD, YOU KNOW?
IT'S LIKE YOU'RE SPACED OUT...
...AND YOU'RE ALMOST NEVER HOME WHEN I GET BACK FROM SCHOOL.
...THAT THING...
YOU GOT THAT FROM THE GUY IN THE FOX MASK, RIGHT?

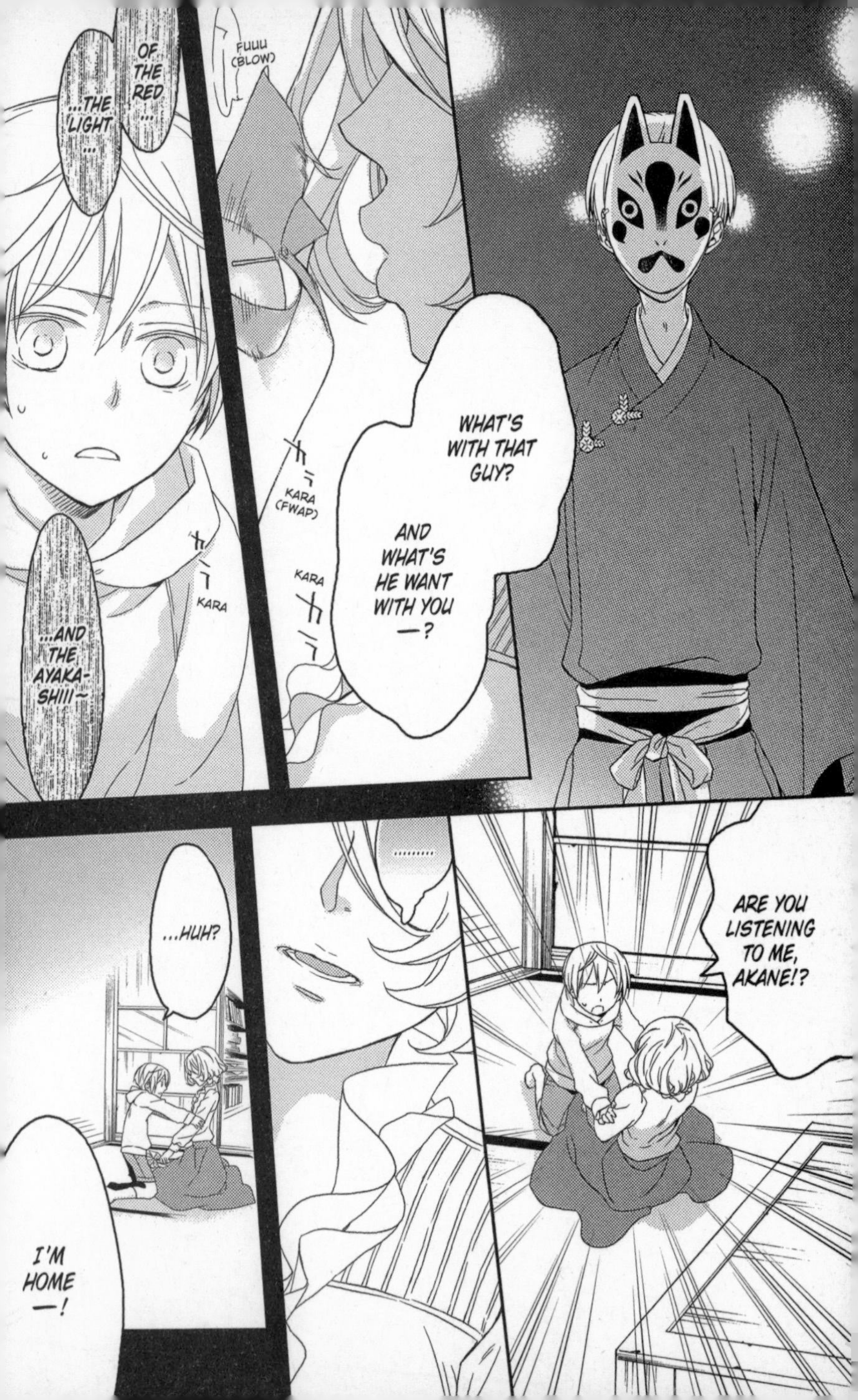
FUUU (BLOW)
WHAT'S WITH THAT GUY?
AND WHAT'S HE WANT WITH YOU —?
KARA (FWAP)
KARA
...THE LIGHT...
OF THE RED...
KARA
...AND THE AYAKASHIII~
ARE YOU LISTENING TO ME, AKANE!?
....
...HUH?
I'M HOME —!

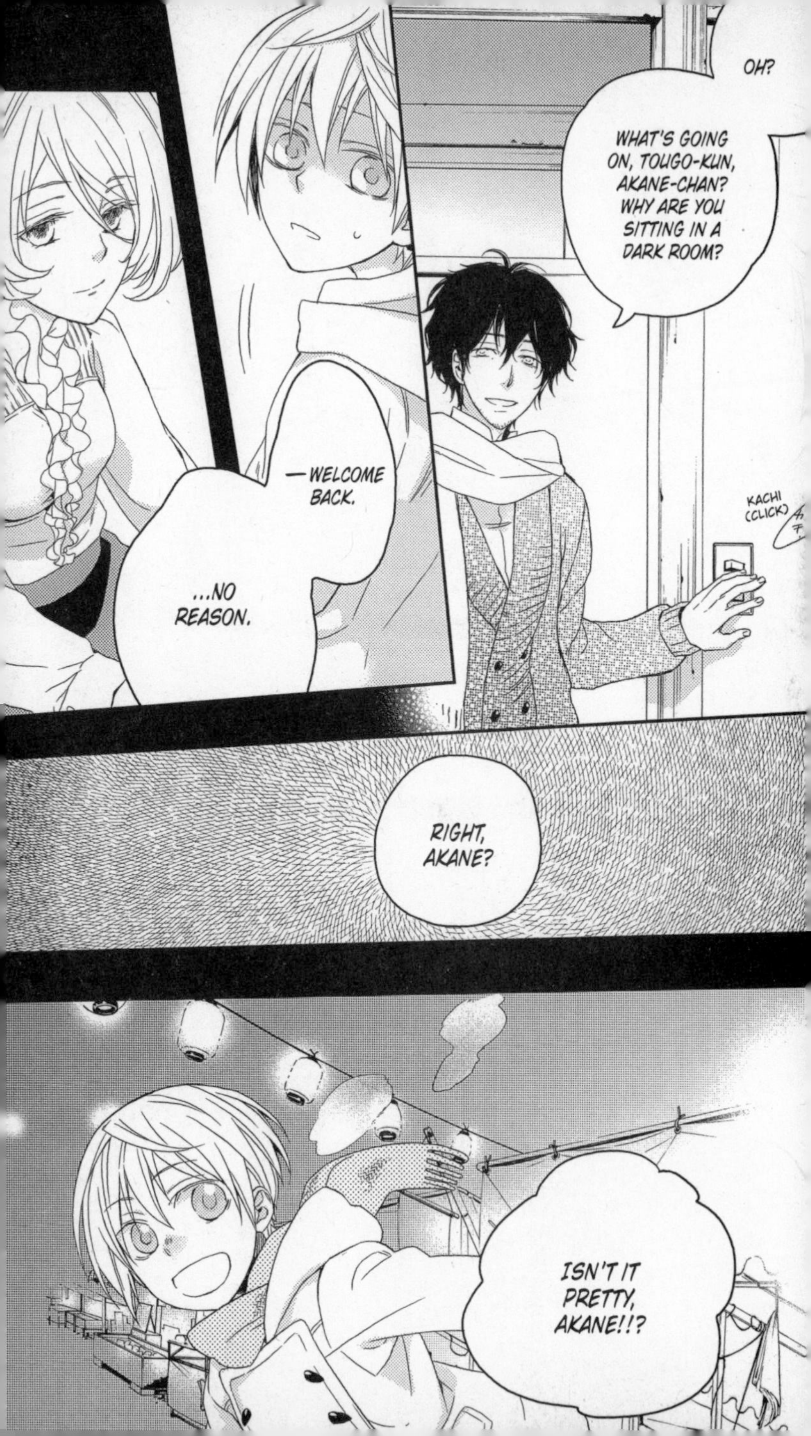
OH?
WHAT'S GOING ON, TOUGO-KUN, AKANE-CHAN? WHY ARE YOU SITTING IN A DARK ROOM?
KACHI (CLICK)
—WELCOME BACK.
...NO REASON.
RIGHT, AKANE?
ISN'T IT PRETTY, AKANE!!?

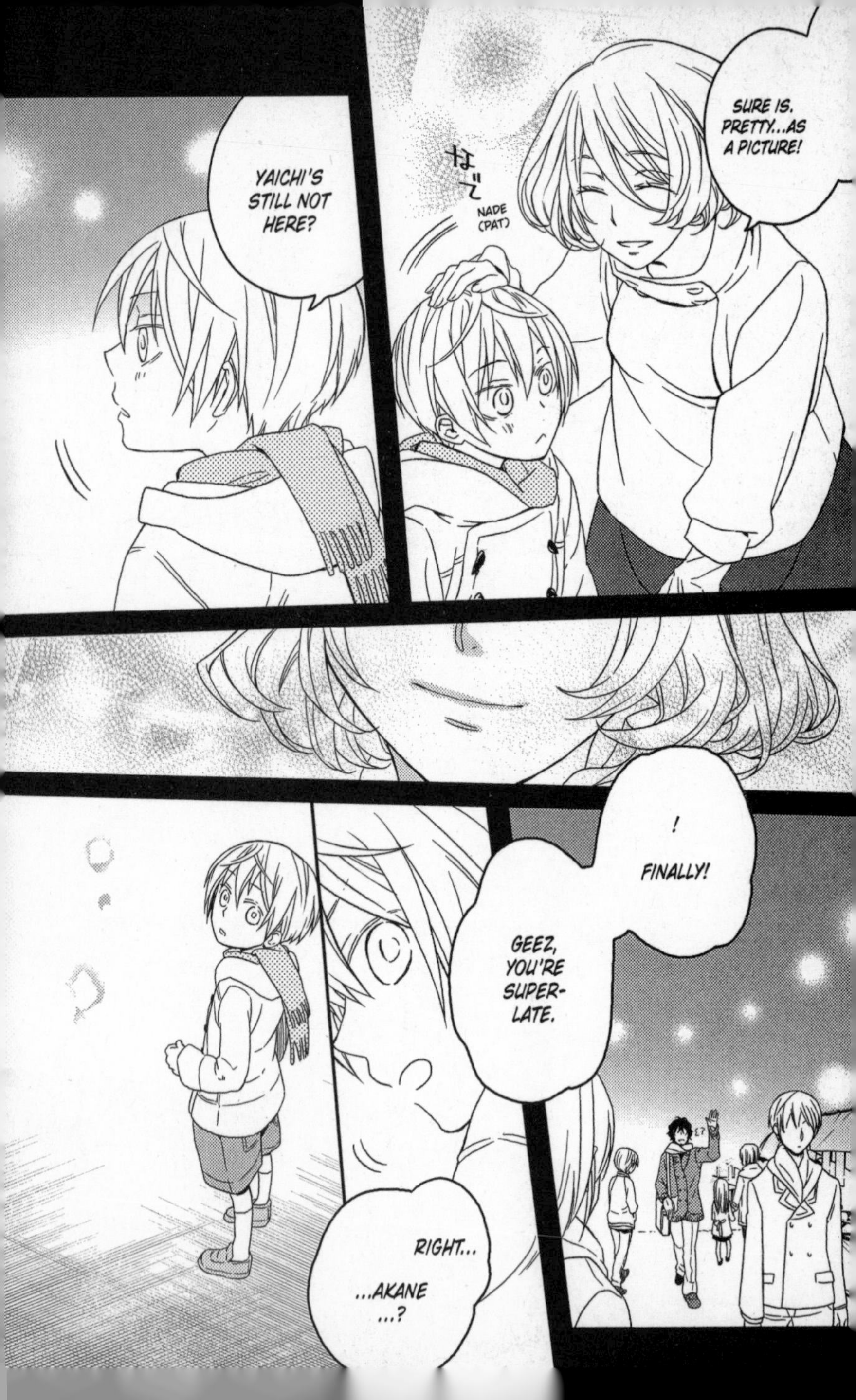
SURE IS. PRETTY...AS A PICTURE!
なで
NADE (PAT)
YAICHI'S STILL NOT HERE?
!
FINALLY!
GEEZ, YOU'RE SUPER-LATE.
RIGHT...
...AKANE ...?

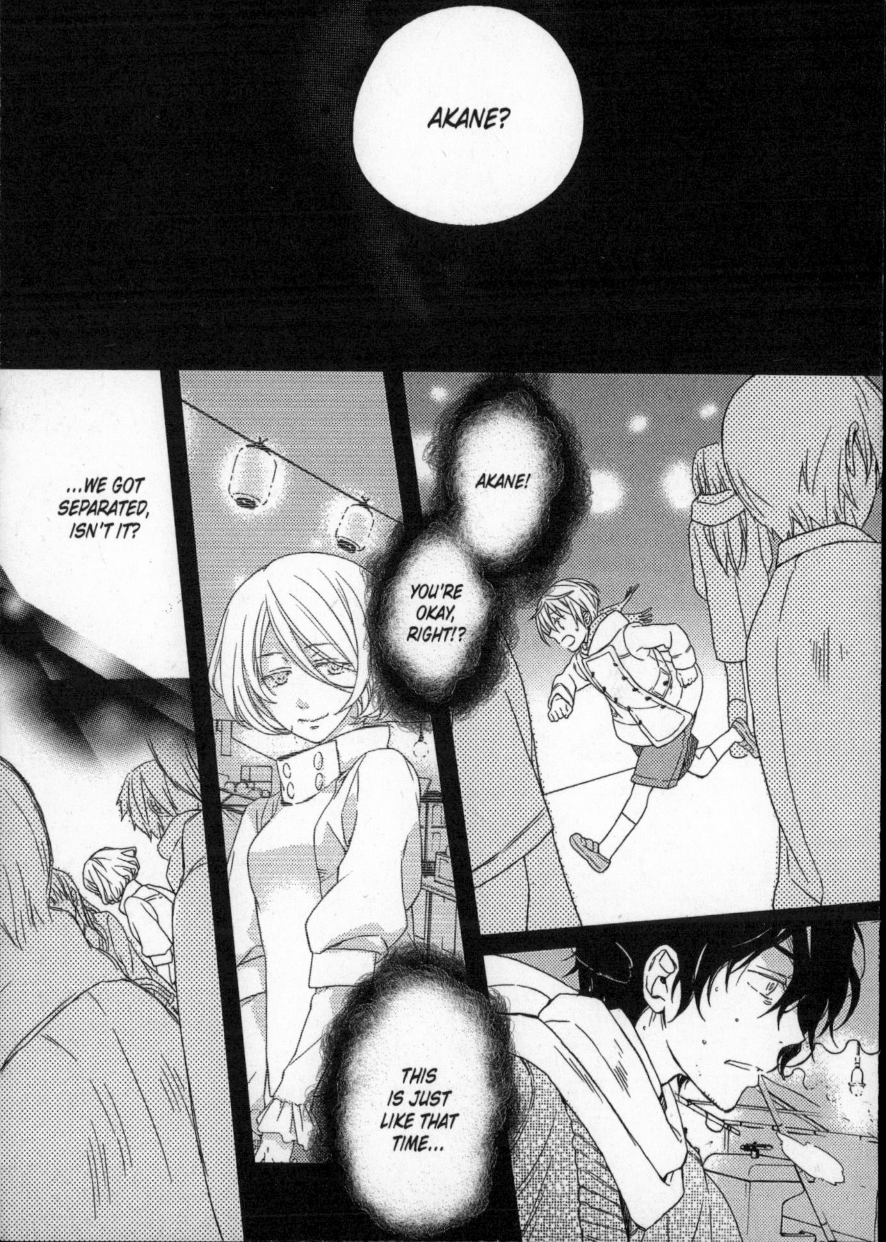
AKANE?
AKANE!
YOU'RE OKAY, RIGHT!?
THIS IS JUST LIKE THAT TIME...
...WE GOT SEPARATED, ISN'T IT?

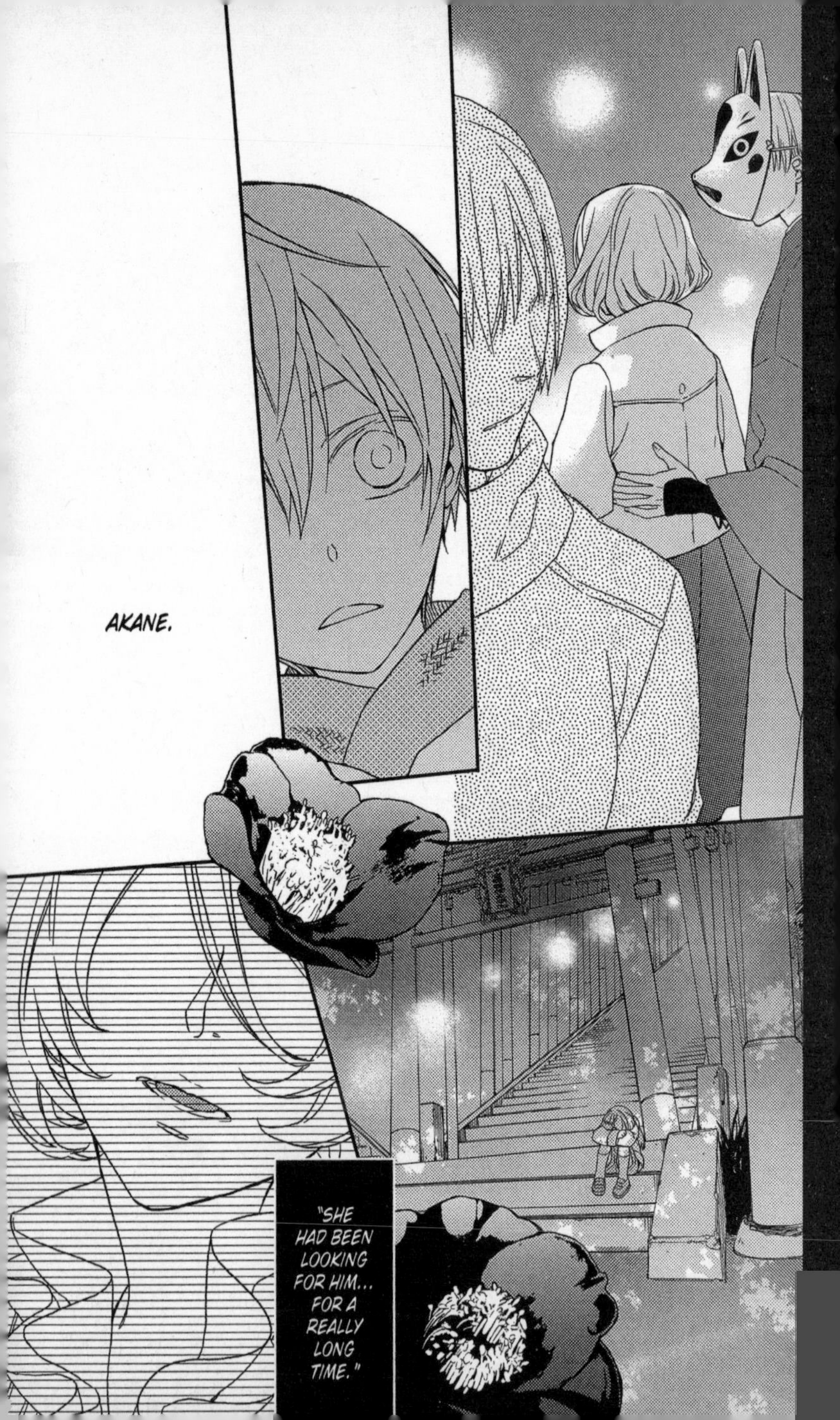
AKANE.
"SHE HAD BEEN LOOKING FOR HIM... FOR A REALLY LONG TIME."

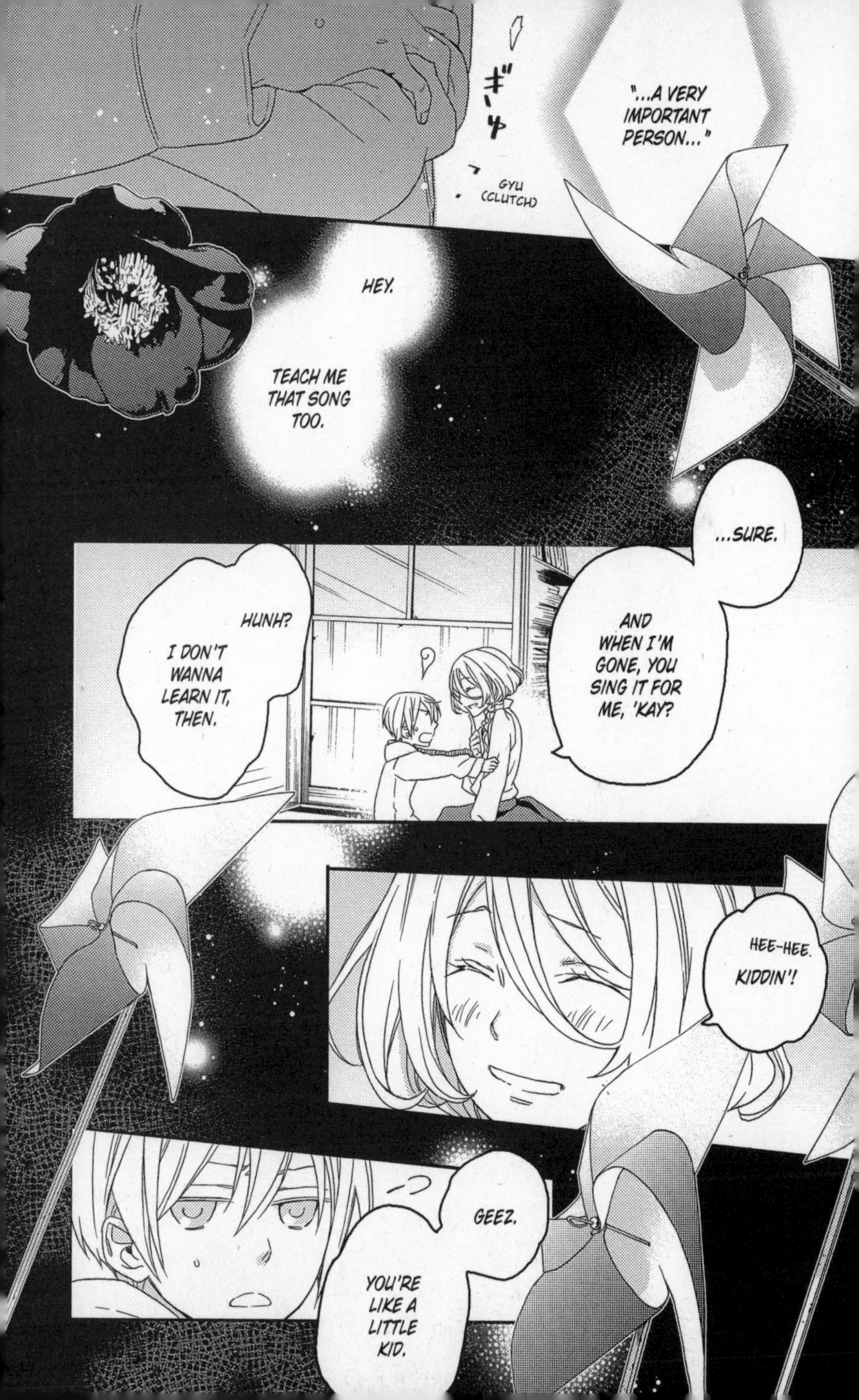
"...A VERY IMPORTANT PERSON..."
ギュ
GYU (CLUTCH)
HEY.
TEACH ME THAT SONG TOO.
...SURE.
AND WHEN I'M GONE, YOU SING IT FOR ME, 'KAY?
HUNH?
I DON'T WANNA LEARN IT, THEN.
HEE-HEE.
KIDDIN'!
GEEZ.
YOU'RE LIKE A LITTLE KID.

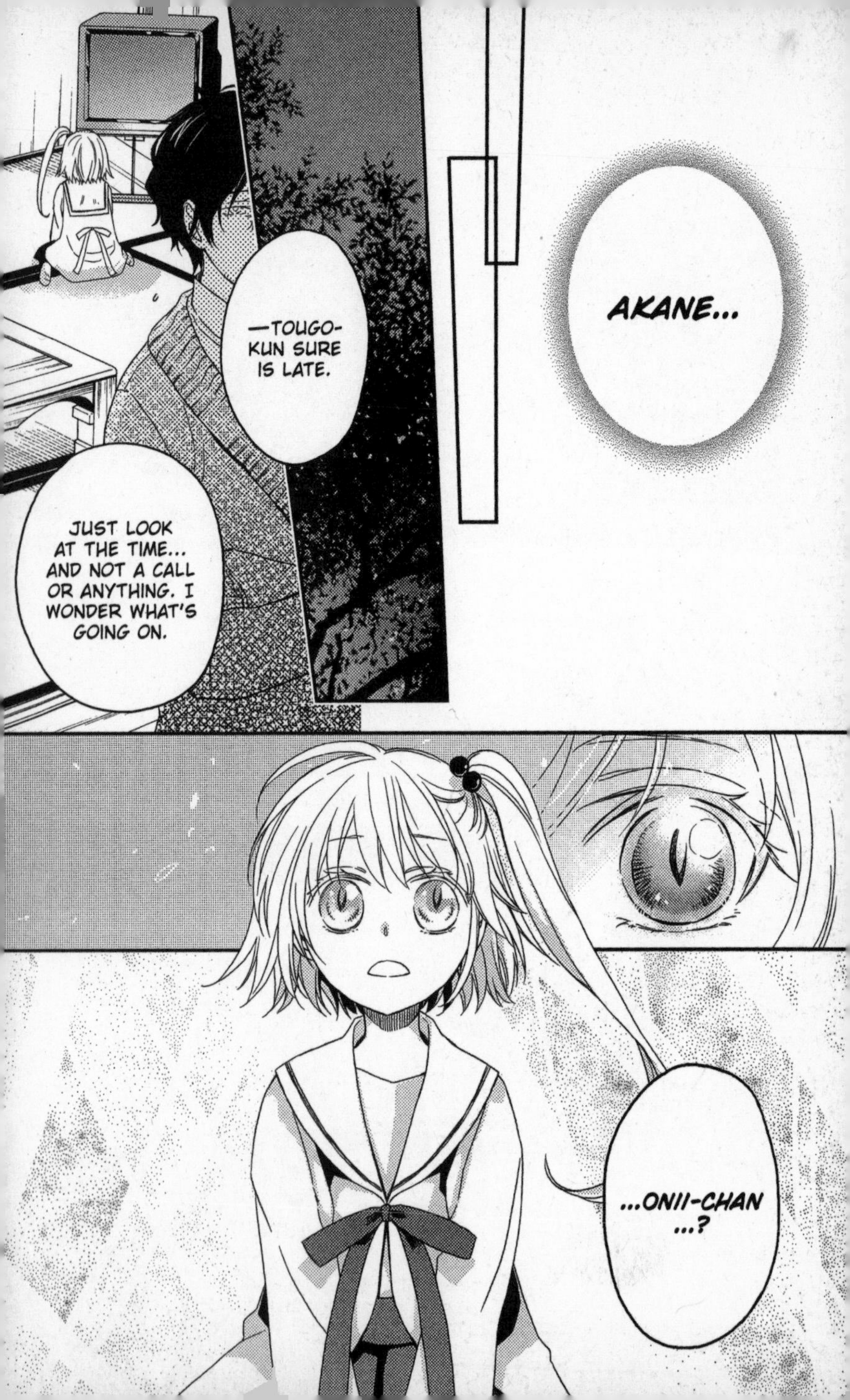
AKANE...
—TOUGO-KUN SURE IS LATE.
JUST LOOK AT THE TIME... AND NOT A CALL OR ANYTHING. I WONDER WHAT'S GOING ON.
...ONII-CHAN ...?

Of the Red,
the Light,
and the
Ayakashi

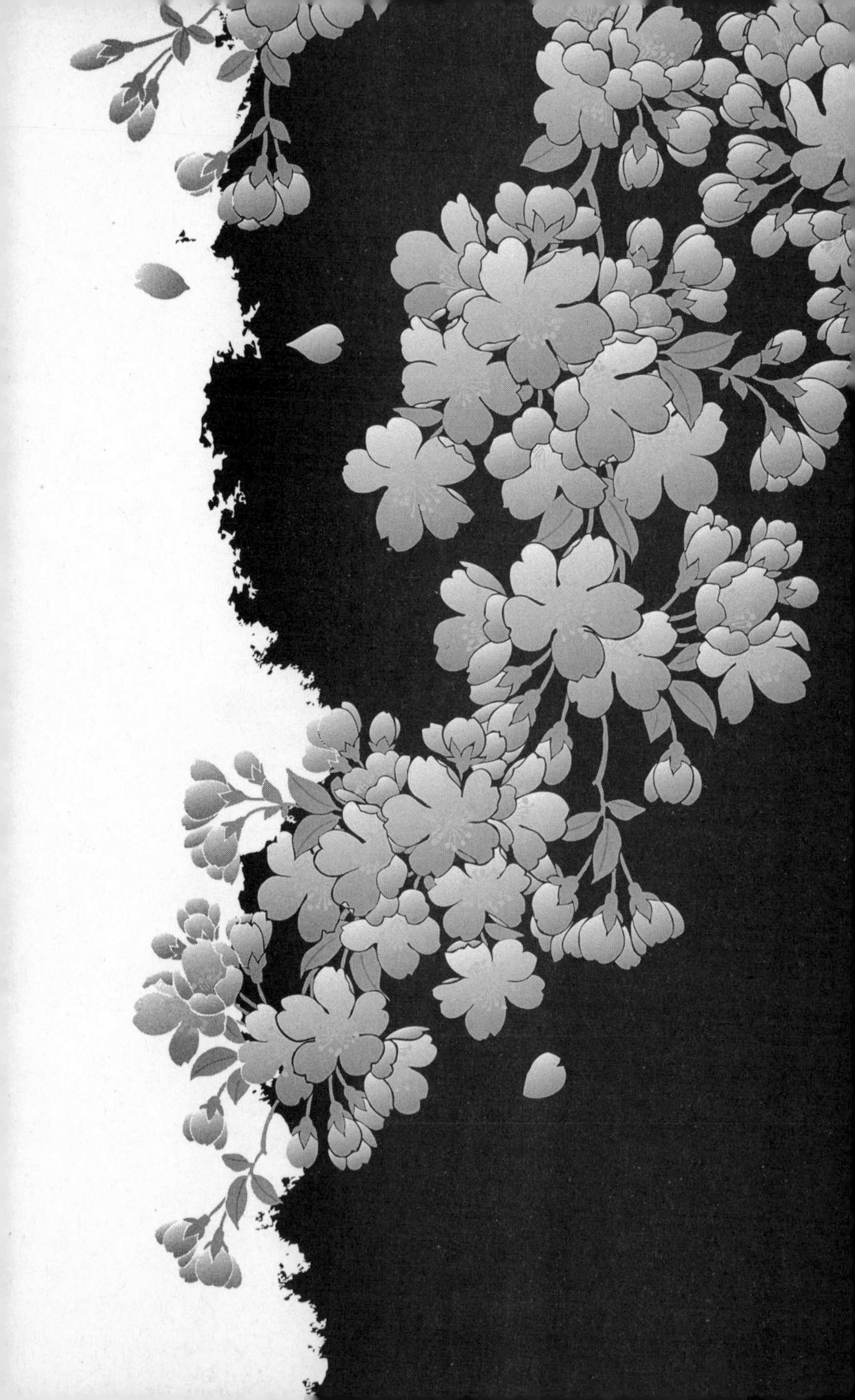

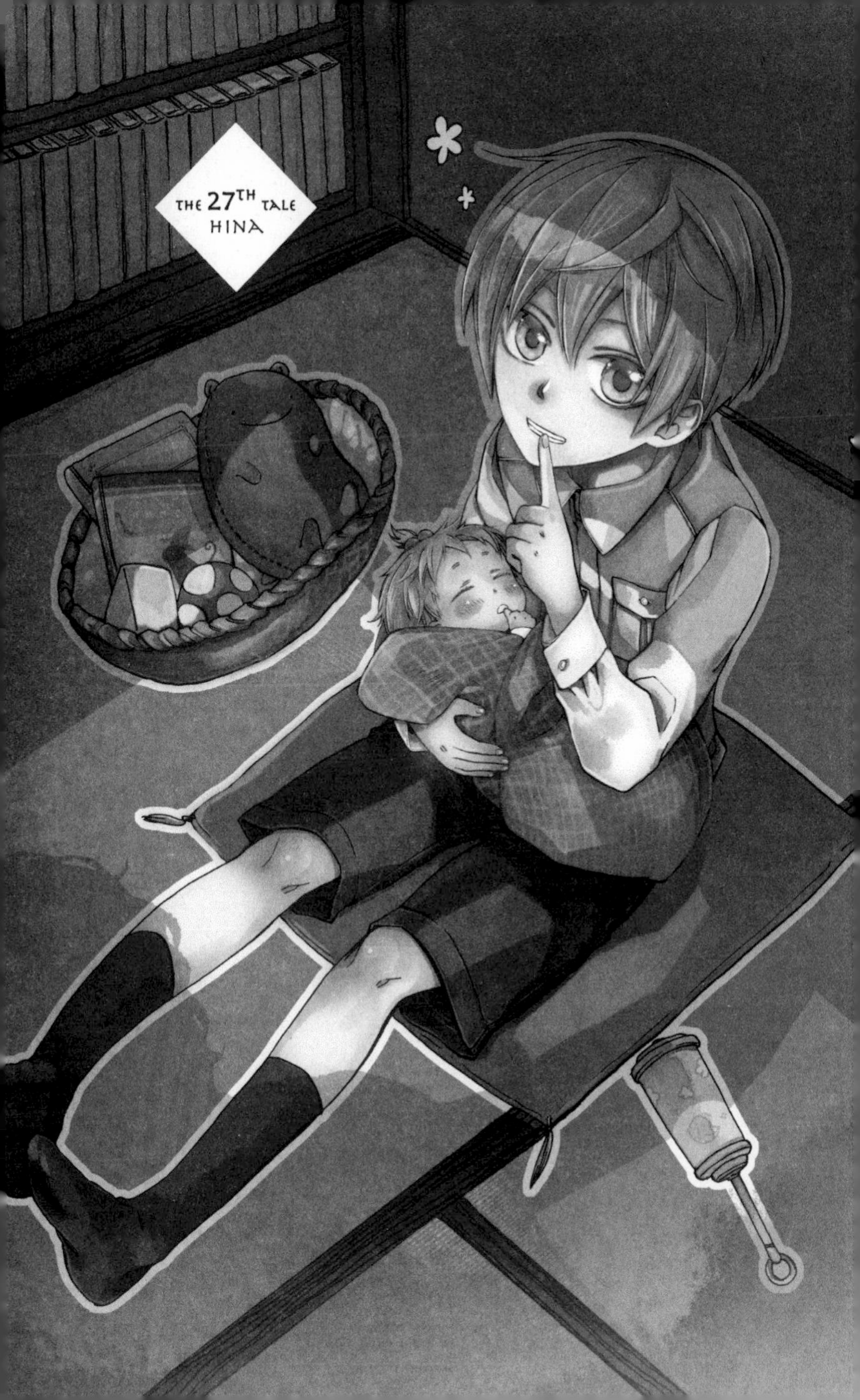
THE 27TH TALE
HINA

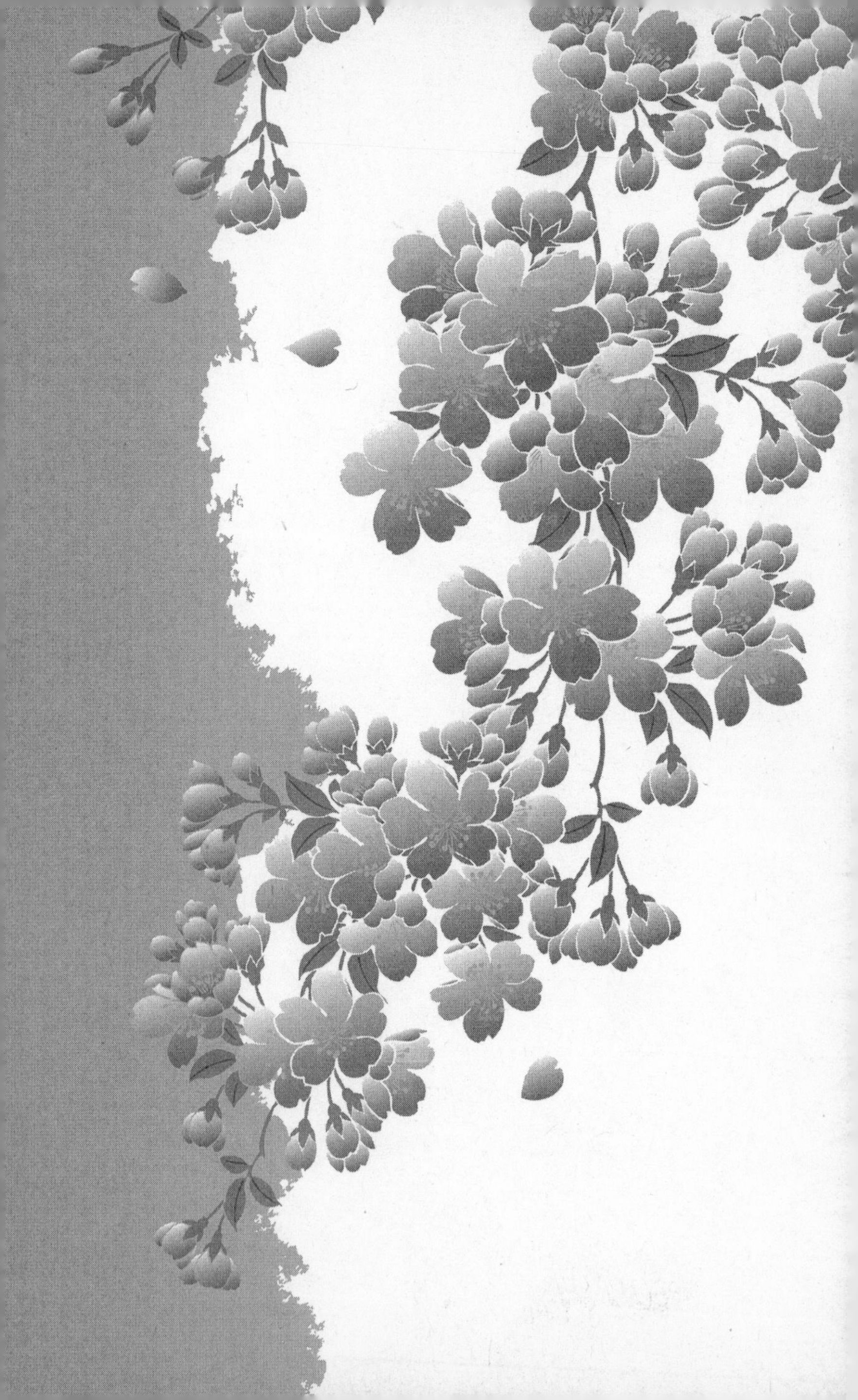

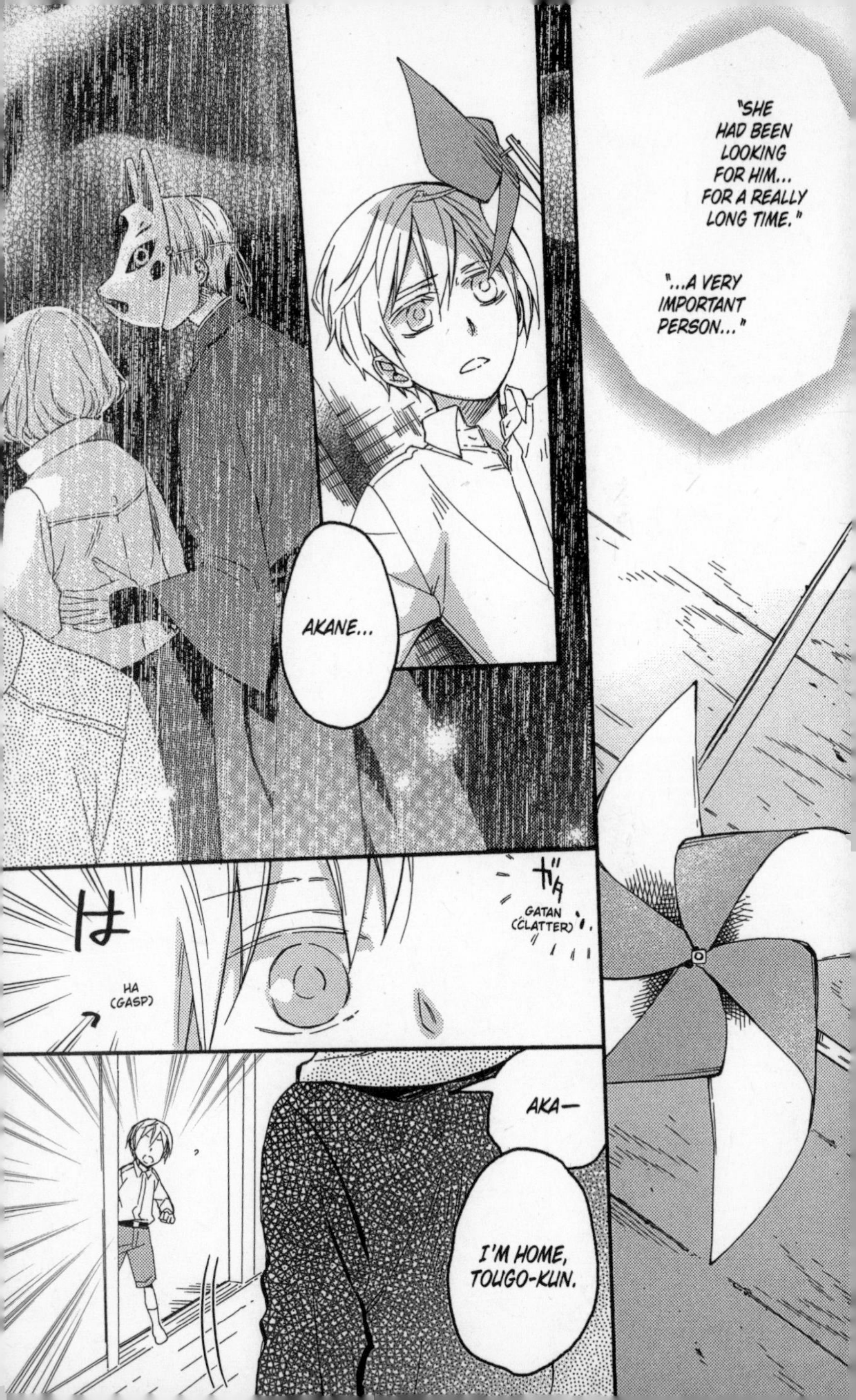
"SHE HAD BEEN LOOKING FOR HIM... FOR A REALLY LONG TIME."
"...A VERY IMPORTANT PERSON..."
AKANE...
ガタ
GATAN (CLATTER)
は
HA (GASP)
AKA—
I'M HOME, TOUGO-KUN.

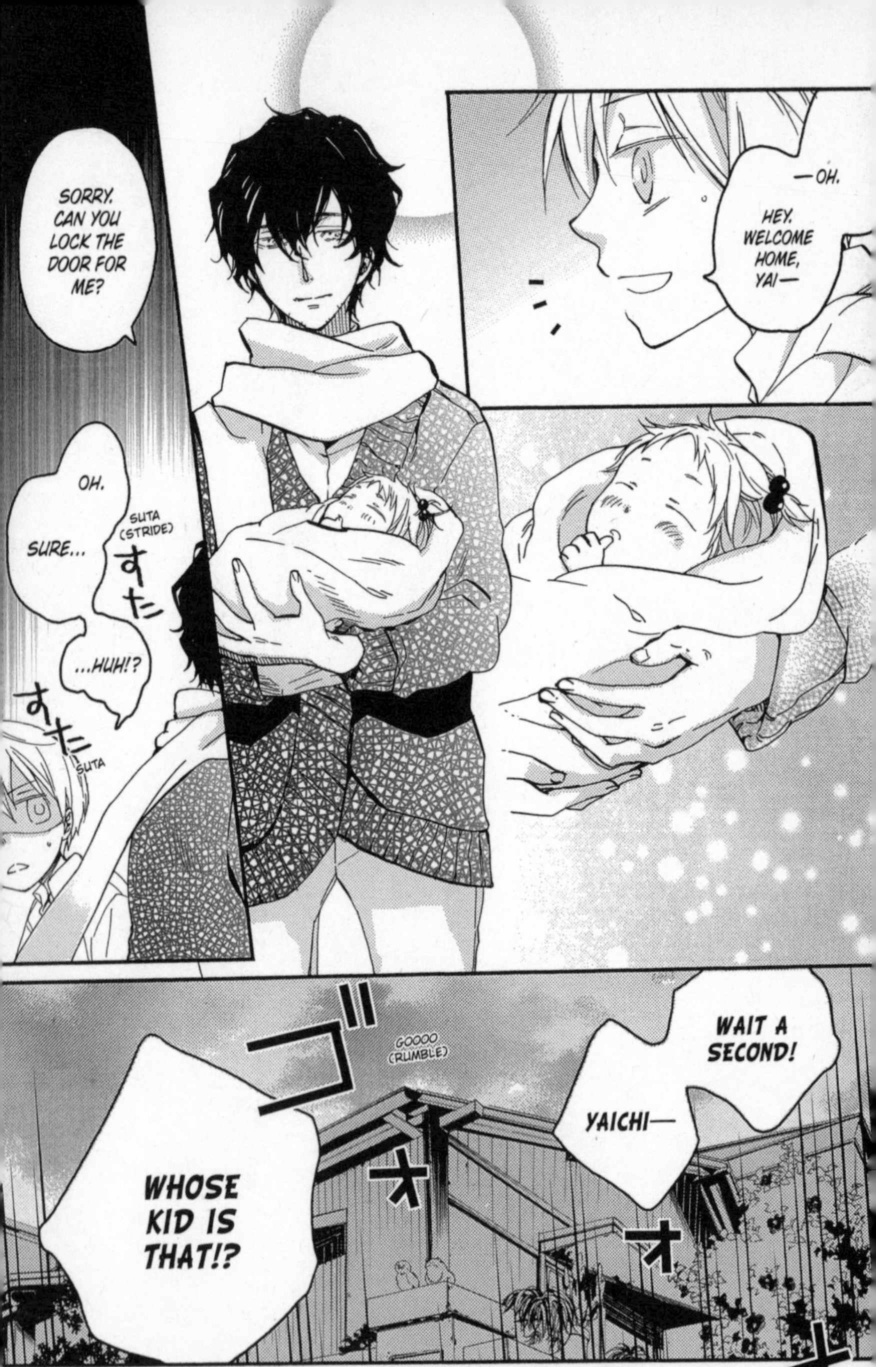
—OH.
HEY. WELCOME HOME, YAI—
SORRY. CAN YOU LOCK THE DOOR FOR ME?
OH.
SURE...
SUTA (STRIDE)
すた
...HUH!?
すた
SUTA
WAIT A SECOND!
YAICHI—
ゴォォォ
GOOOO (RUMBLE)
WHOSE KID IS THAT!?

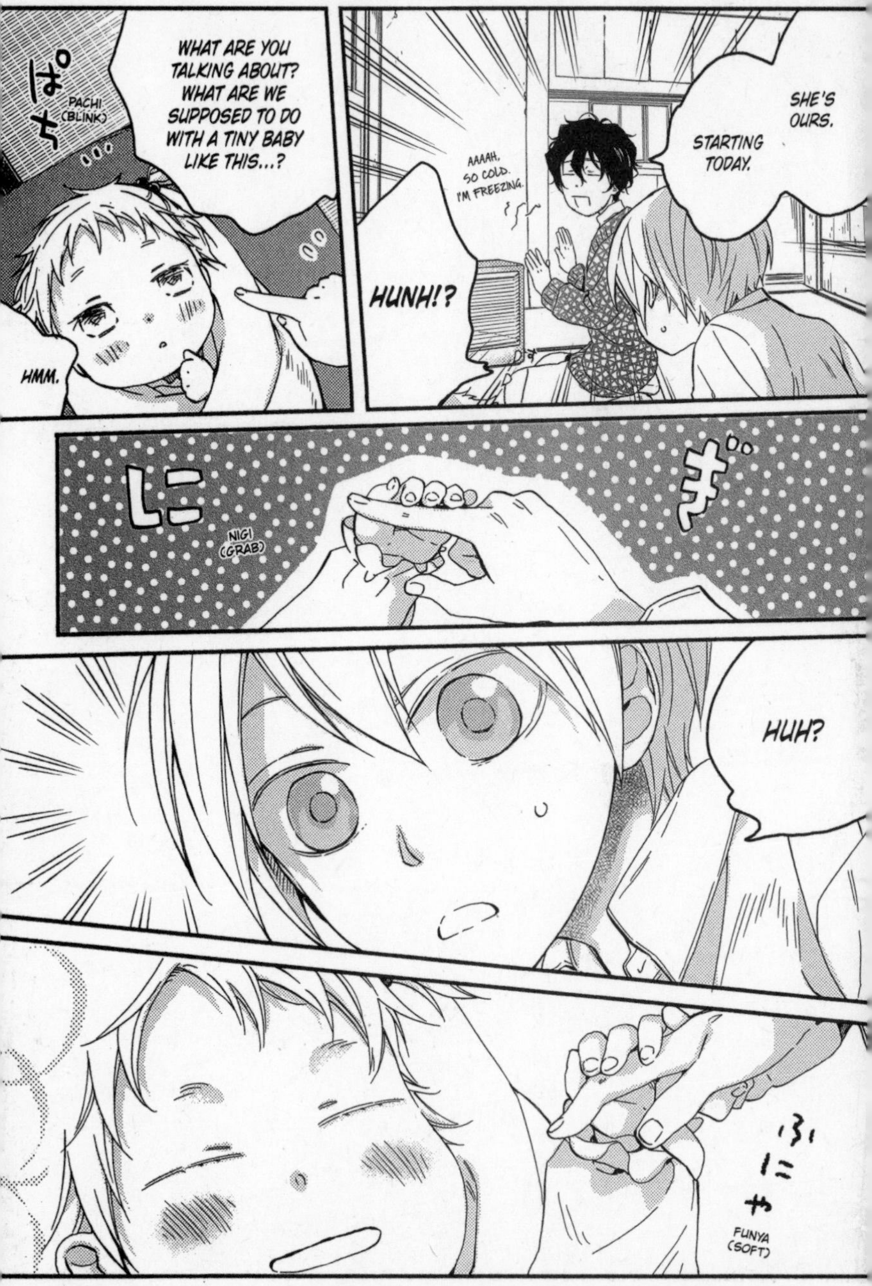
SHE'S OURS. STARTING TODAY.
AAAAH, SO COLD. I'M FREEZING.
HUNH!?
WHAT ARE YOU TALKING ABOUT? WHAT ARE WE SUPPOSED TO DO WITH A TINY BABY LIKE THIS...?
ぱち
PACHI (BLINK)
HMM.
にぎ
NIGI (GRAB)
HUH?
ふにゃ
FUNYA (SOFT)

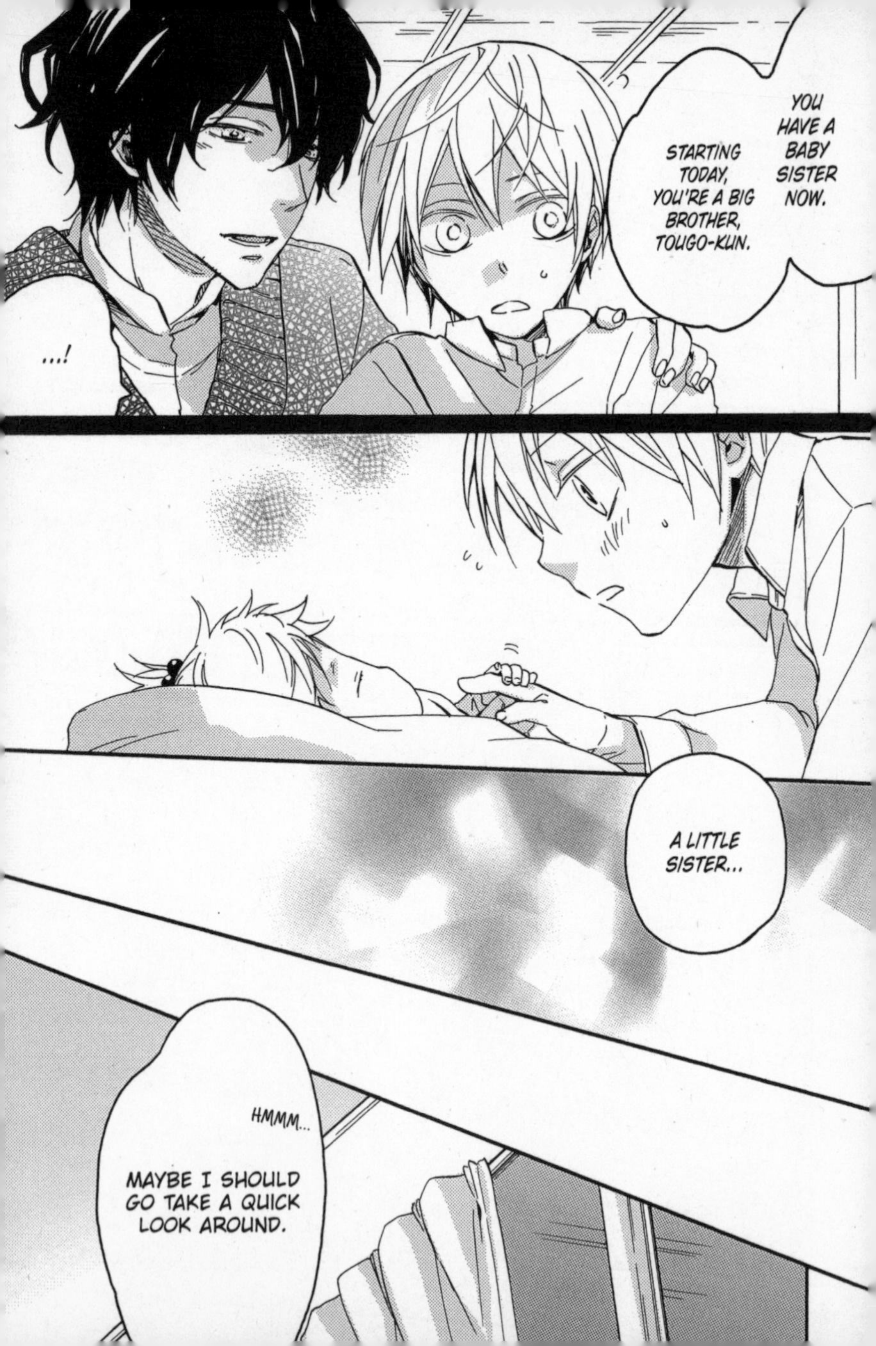
STARTING TODAY, YOU'RE A BIG BROTHER, TOUGO-KUN.
YOU HAVE A BABY SISTER NOW.
...!
A LITTLE SISTER...
HMMM...
MAYBE I SHOULD GO TAKE A QUICK LOOK AROUND.

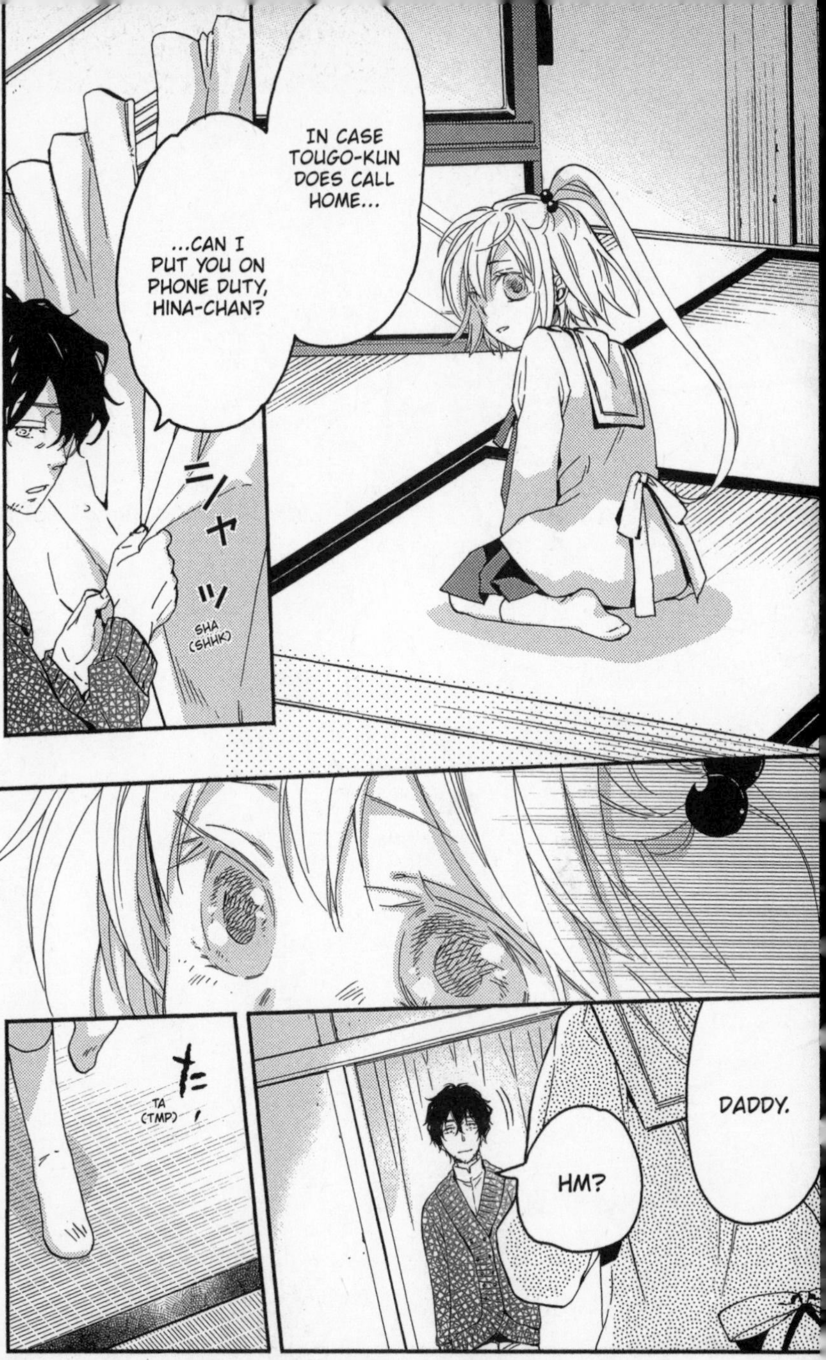
IN CASE TOUGO-KUN DOES CALL HOME...
...CAN I PUT YOU ON PHONE DUTY, HINA-CHAN?
SHA (SHHK)
DADDY.
HM?
TA (TMP)

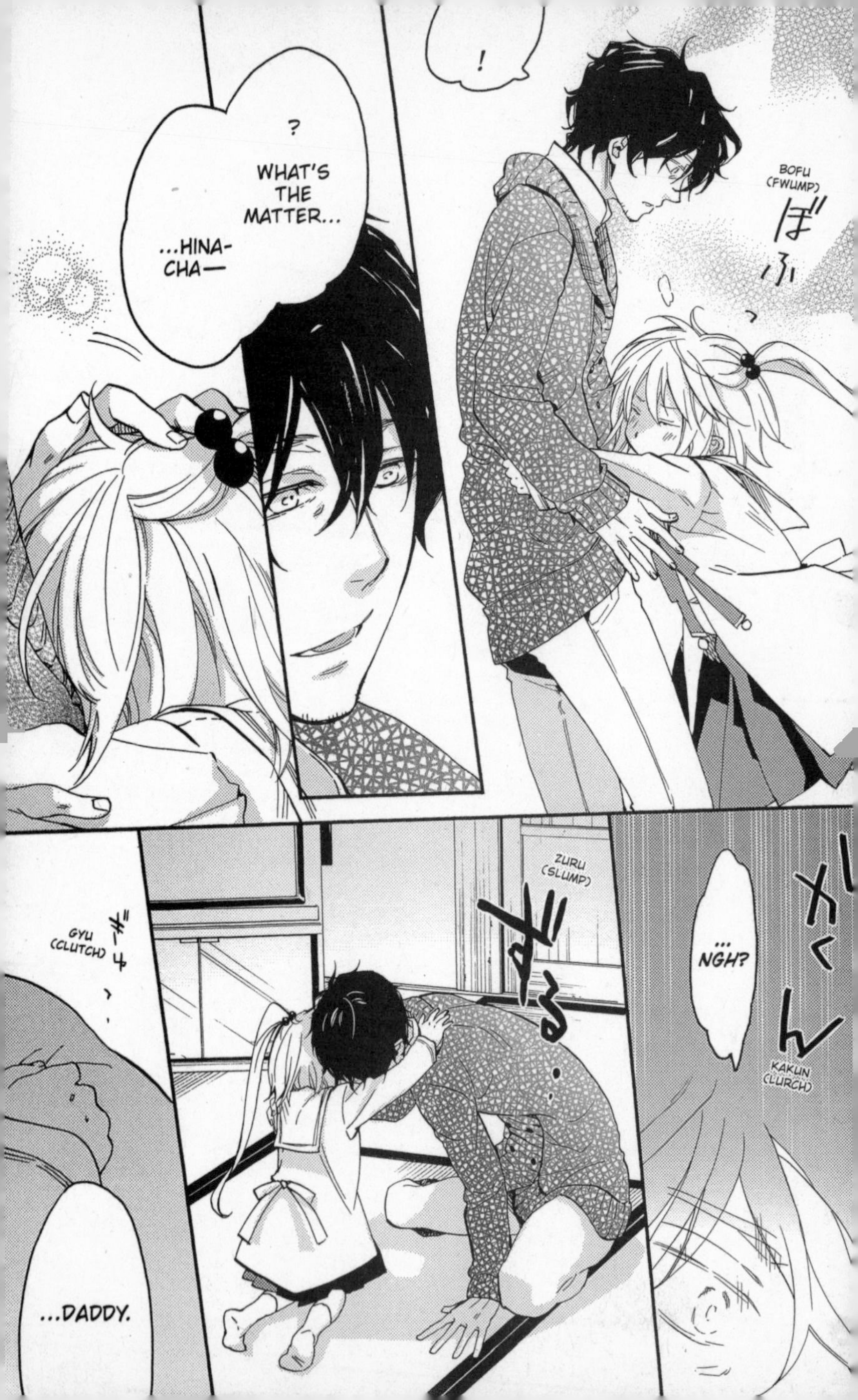
!
BOFU (FWUMP)
ぼふっ
?
WHAT'S THE MATTER...
...HINA-CHA—
...NGH?
がくん
KAKUN (LURCH)
ZURU (SLUMP)
ずる
GYU (CLUTCH)
ぎゅ
...DADDY.

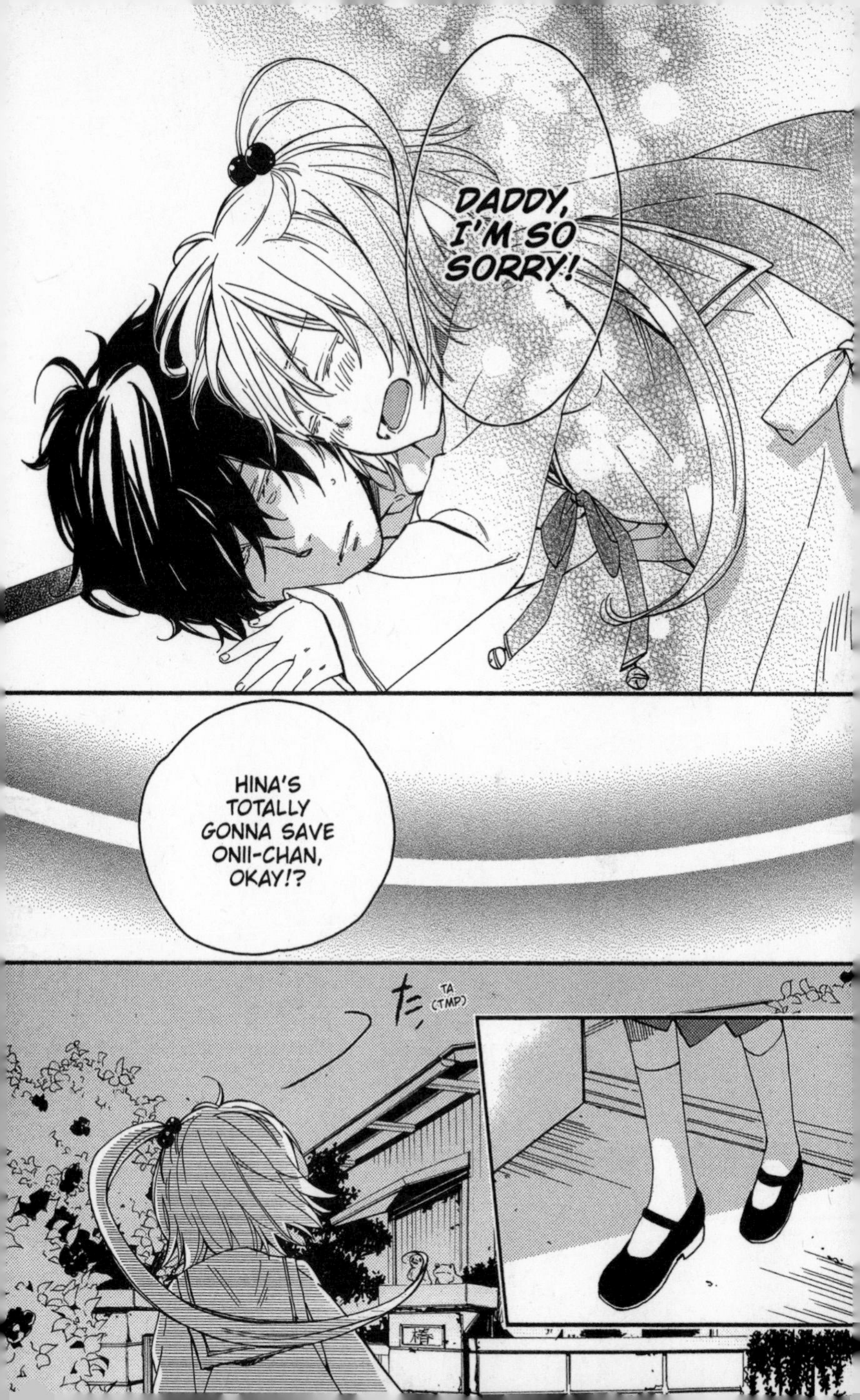
DADDY, I'M SO SORRY!
HINA'S TOTALLY GONNA SAVE ONII-CHAN, OKAY!?
た
TA (TMP)

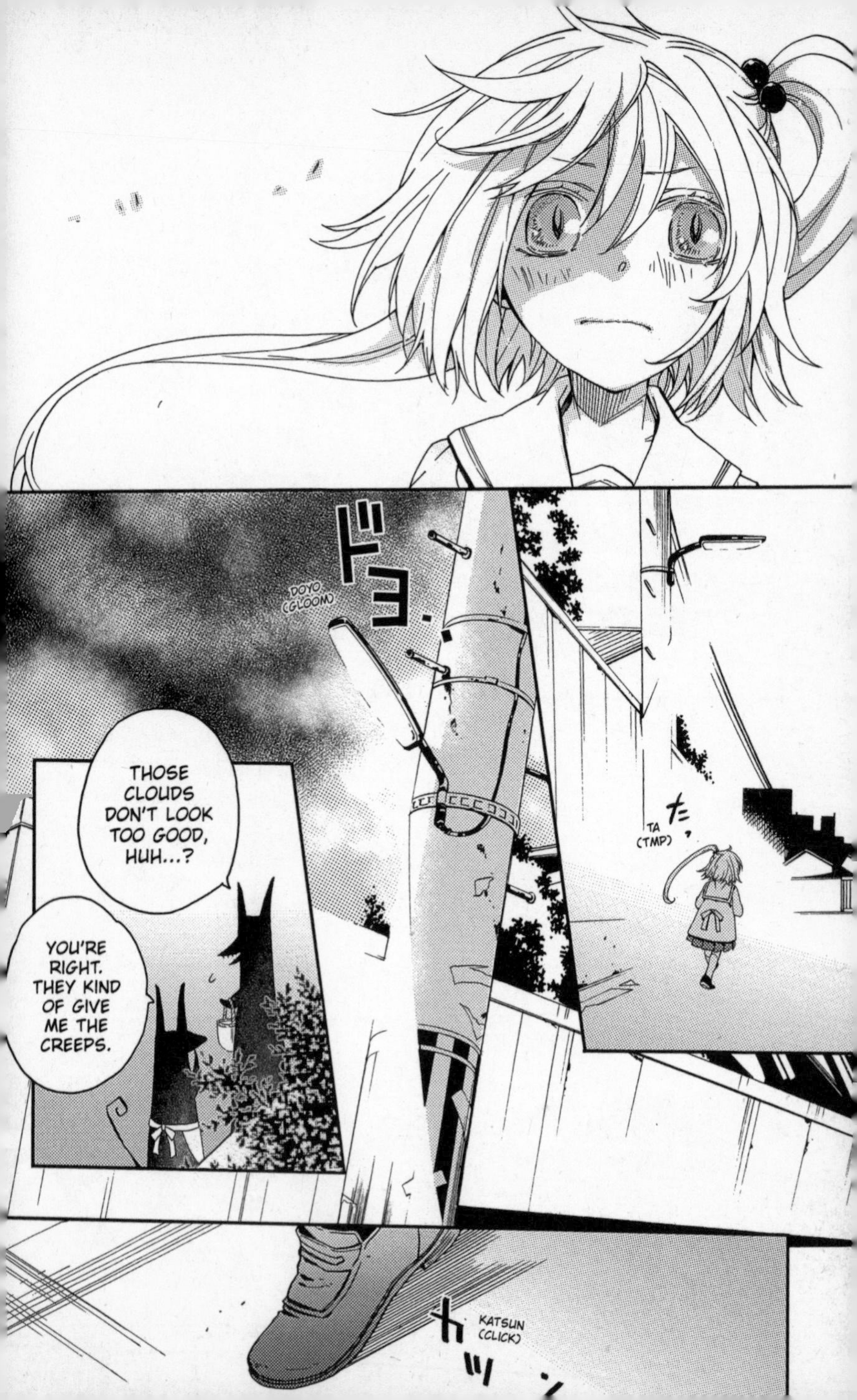
DOYO (GLOOM)
TA (TMP)
THOSE CLOUDS DON'T LOOK TOO GOOD, HUH...?
YOU'RE RIGHT. THEY KIND OF GIVE ME THE CREEPS.
KATSUN (CLICK)

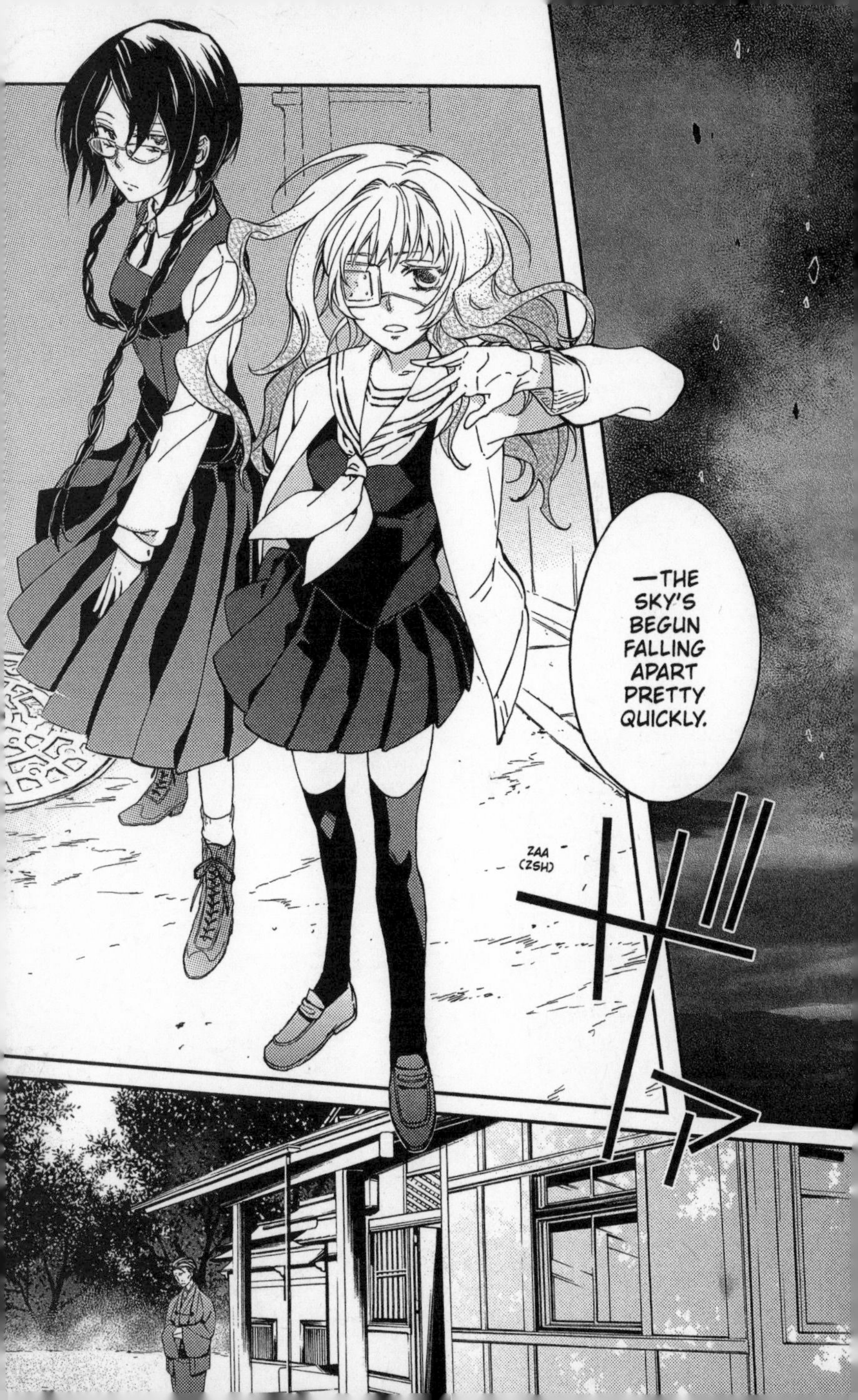
—THE SKY'S BEGUN FALLING APART PRETTY QUICKLY.
ZAA (ZSH)

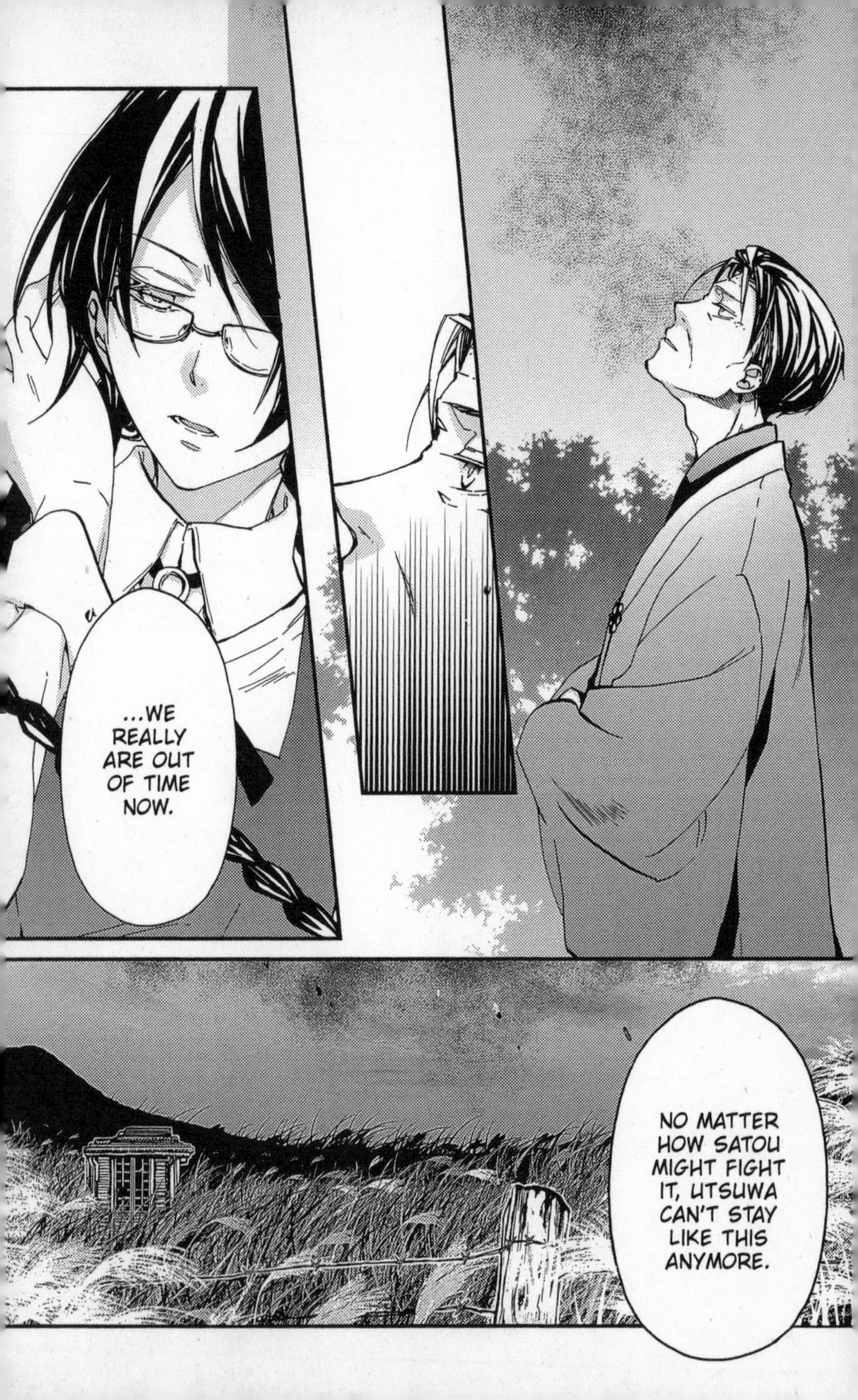
...WE REALLY ARE OUT OF TIME NOW.
NO MATTER HOW SATOU MIGHT FIGHT IT, UTSUWA CAN'T STAY LIKE THIS ANYMORE.

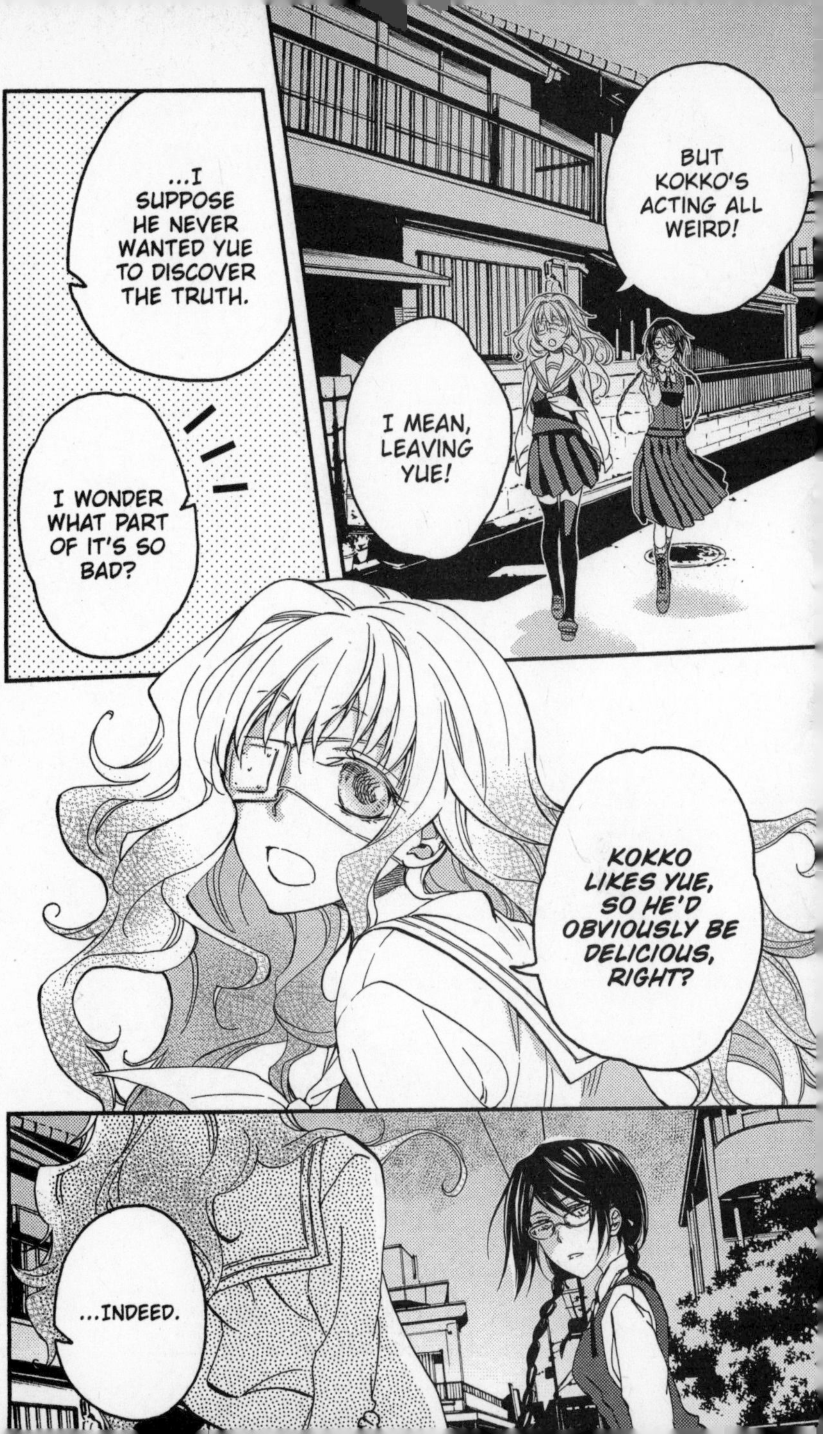
BUT KOKKO'S ACTING ALL WEIRD!
I MEAN, LEAVING YUE!
...I SUPPOSE HE NEVER WANTED YUE TO DISCOVER THE TRUTH.
I WONDER WHAT PART OF IT'S SO BAD?
KOKKO LIKES YUE, SO HE'D OBVIOUSLY BE DELICIOUS, RIGHT?
...INDEED.

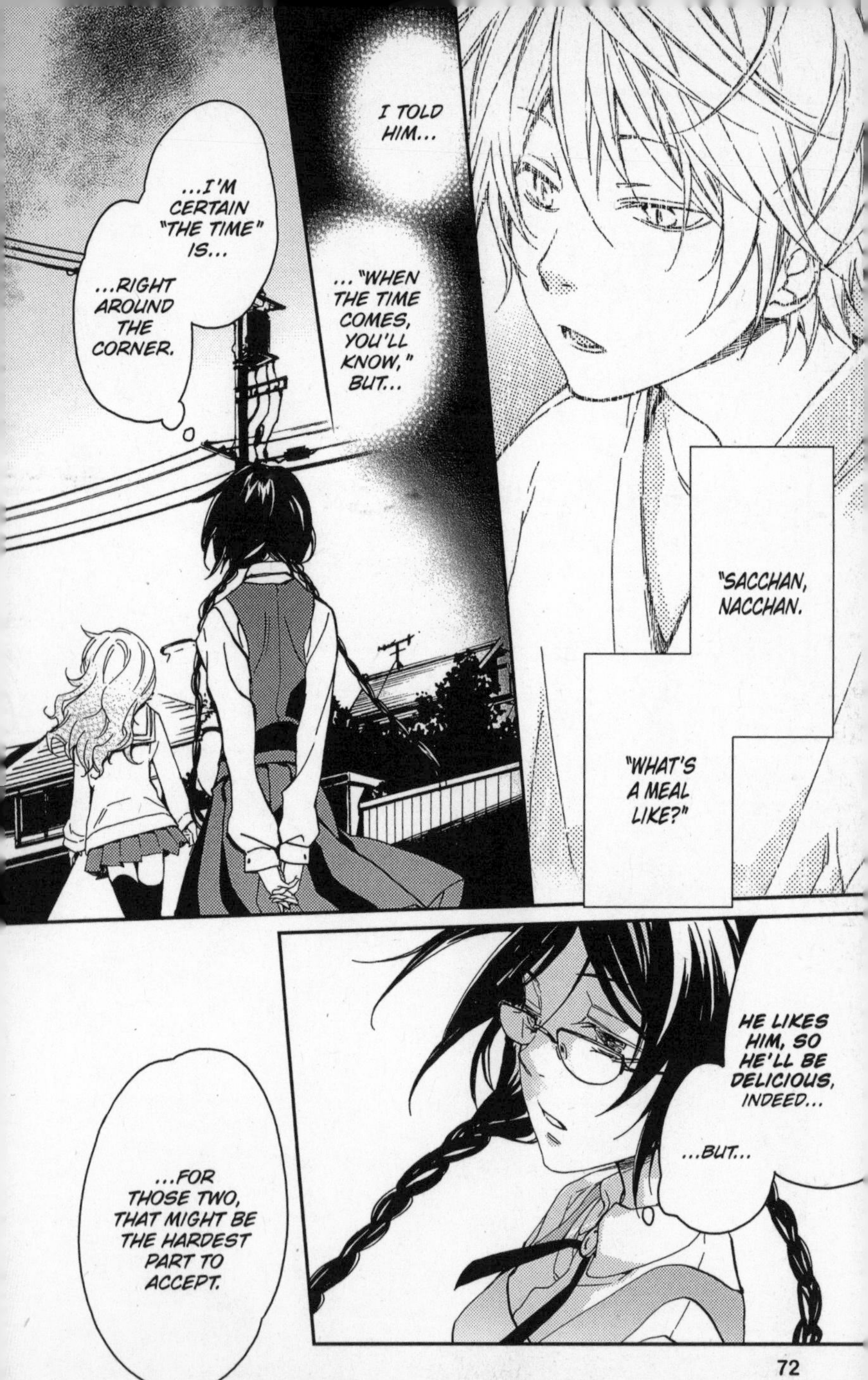
"SACCHAN, NACCHAN.
"WHAT'S A MEAL LIKE?"
I TOLD HIM...
..."WHEN THE TIME COMES, YOU'LL KNOW," BUT...
...I'M CERTAIN "THE TIME" IS...
...RIGHT AROUND THE CORNER.
HE LIKES HIM, SO HE'LL BE DELICIOUS, INDEED...
...BUT...
...FOR THOSE TWO, THAT MIGHT BE THE HARDEST PART TO ACCEPT.

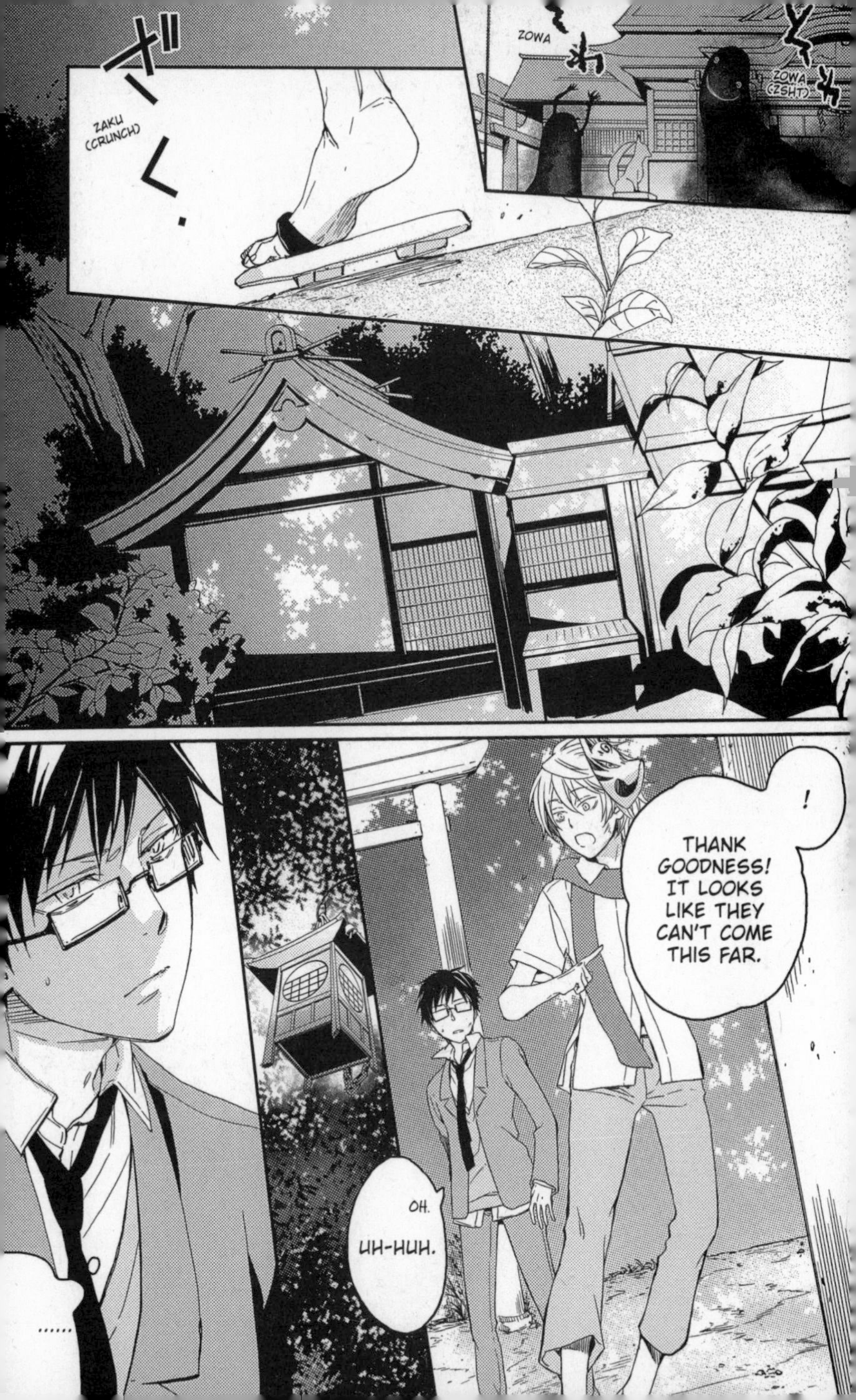
ZOWA
ZOWA (ZSHT)
ZAKU (CRUNCH)
!
THANK GOODNESS! IT LOOKS LIKE THEY CAN'T COME THIS FAR.
OH.
UH-HUH.
......

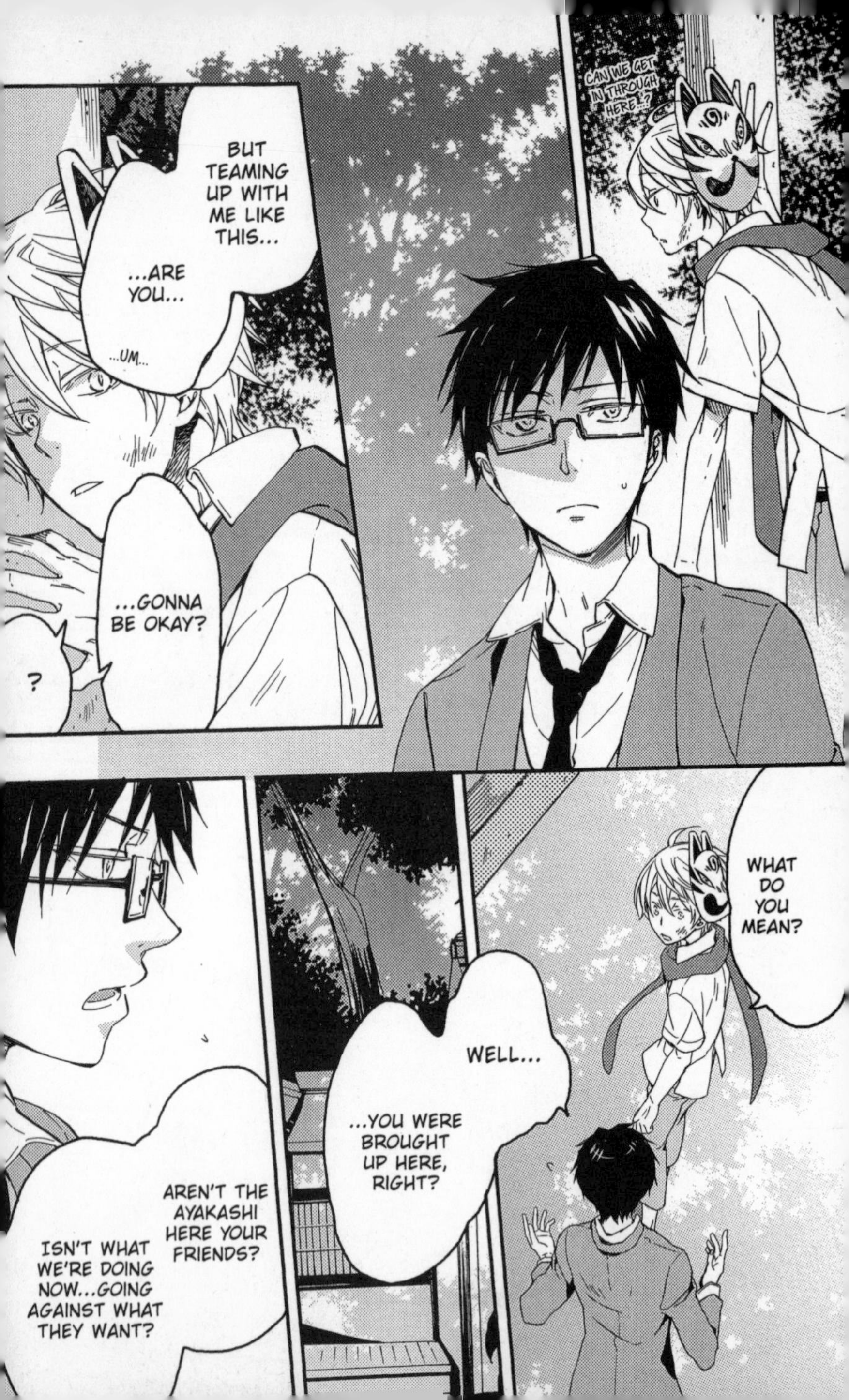
CAN WE GET IN THROUGH HERE...?
BUT TEAMING UP WITH ME LIKE THIS...
...ARE YOU...
...UM...
...GONNA BE OKAY?
?
WHAT DO YOU MEAN?
WELL...
...YOU WERE BROUGHT UP HERE, RIGHT?
AREN'T THE AYAKASHI HERE YOUR FRIENDS?
ISN'T WHAT WE'RE DOING NOW...GOING AGAINST WHAT THEY WANT?

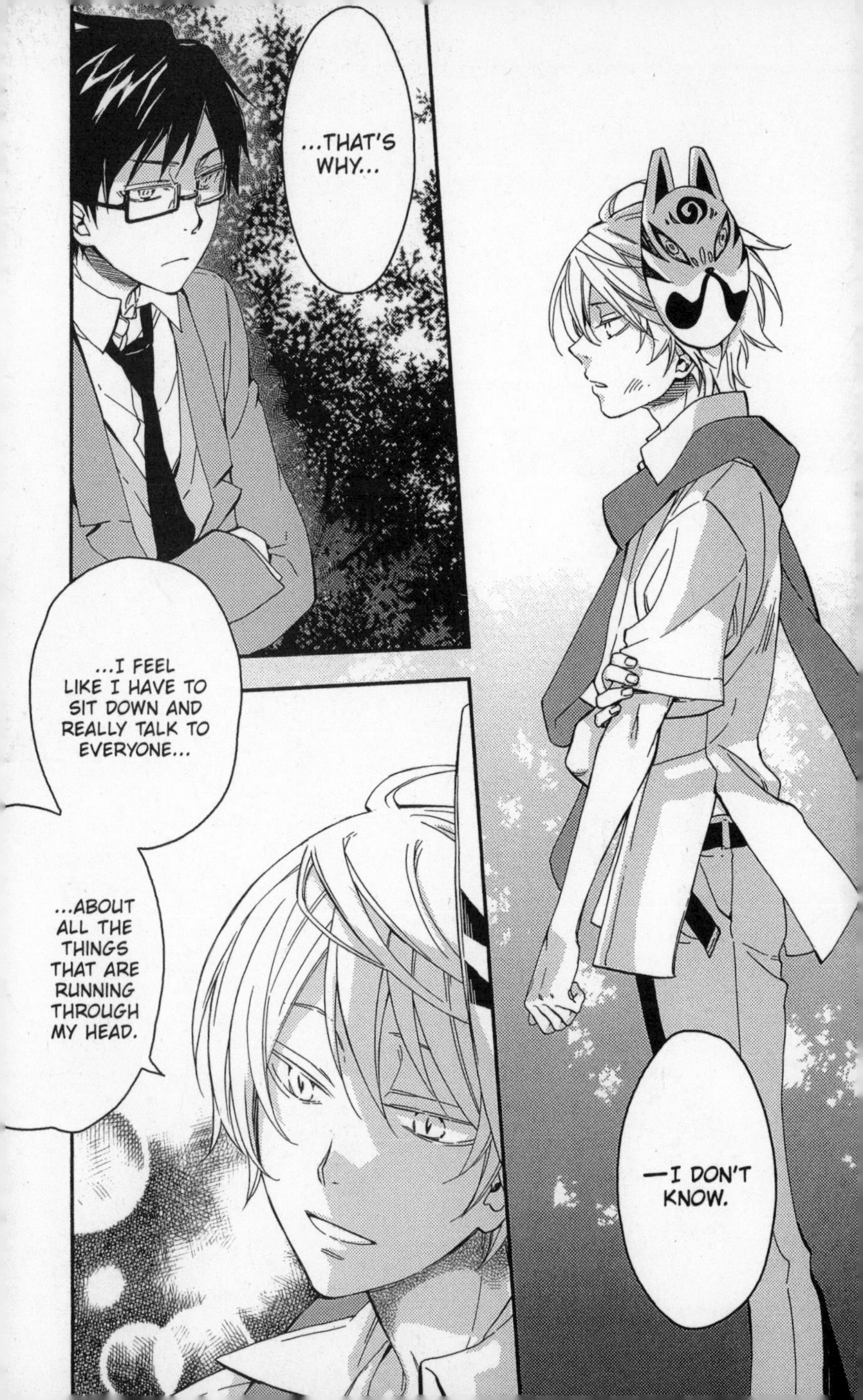
—I DON'T KNOW.
...THAT'S WHY...
...I FEEL LIKE I HAVE TO SIT DOWN AND REALLY TALK TO EVERYONE...
...ABOUT ALL THE THINGS THAT ARE RUNNING THROUGH MY HEAD.

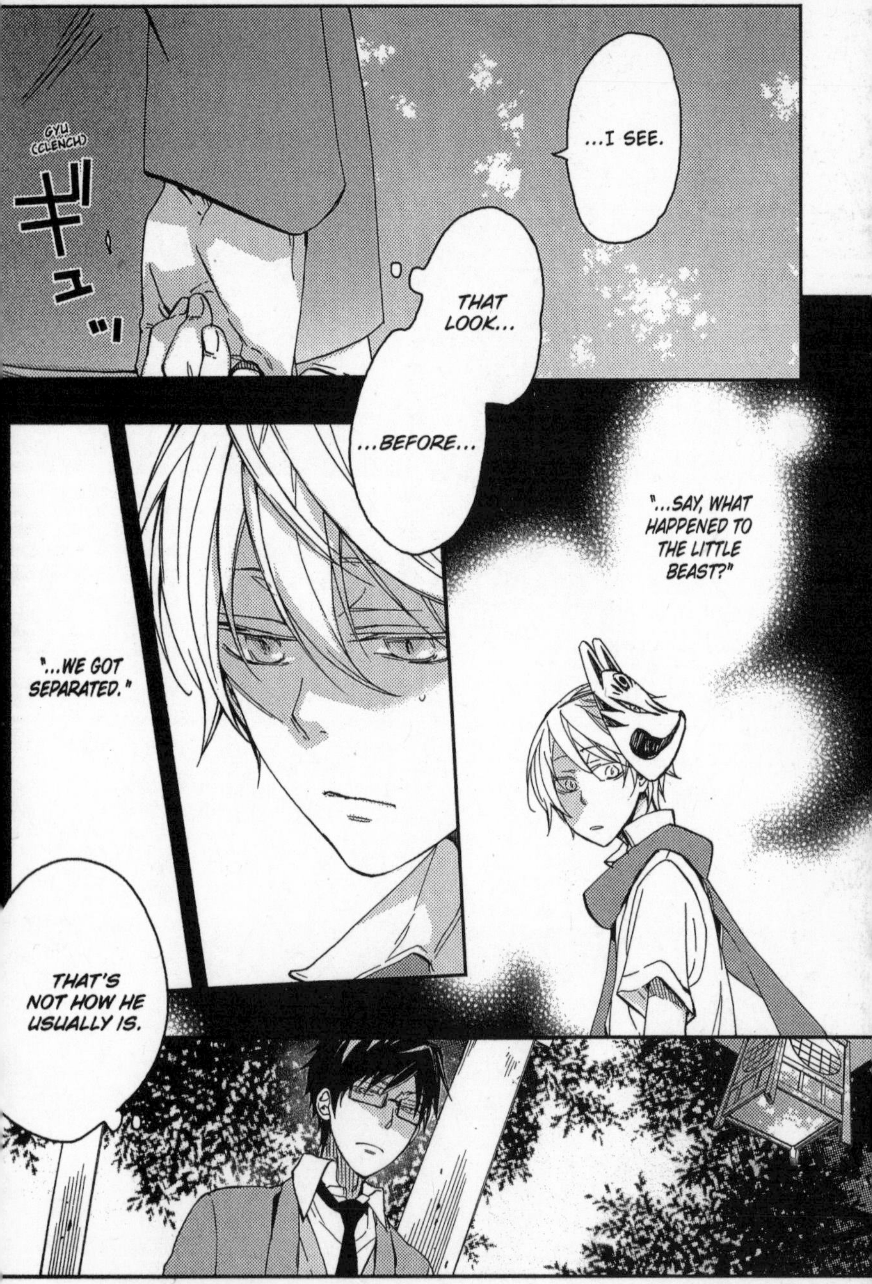
...I SEE.
THAT LOOK...
...BEFORE...
GYU (CLENCH)
ギュッ
"...SAY, WHAT HAPPENED TO THE LITTLE BEAST?"
"...WE GOT SEPARATED."
THAT'S NOT HOW HE USUALLY IS.

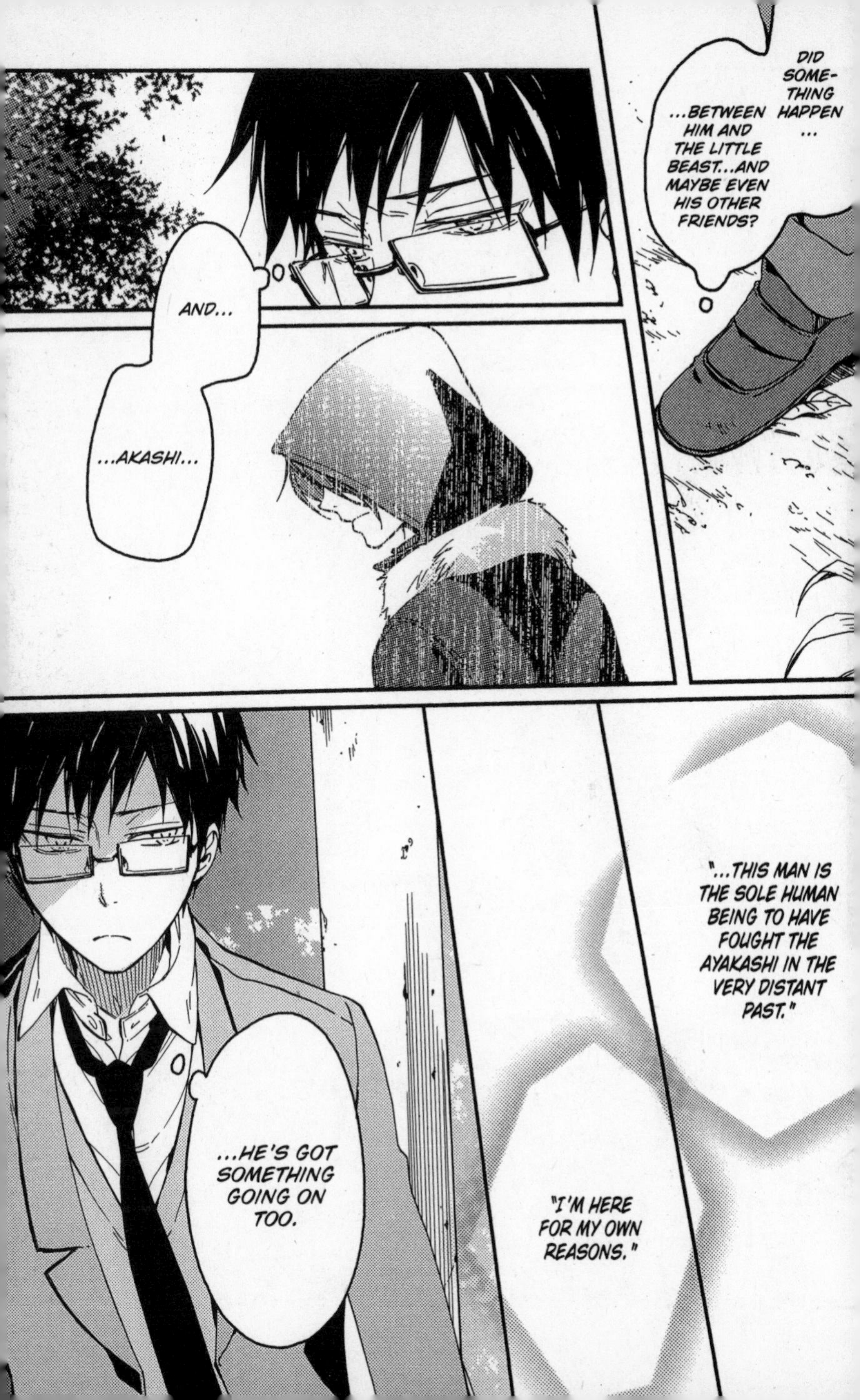
DID SOMETHING HAPPEN... ...BETWEEN HIM AND THE LITTLE BEAST...AND MAYBE EVEN HIS OTHER FRIENDS?
AND...
...AKASHI...
"...THIS MAN IS THE SOLE HUMAN BEING TO HAVE FOUGHT THE AYAKASHI IN THE VERY DISTANT PAST."
"I'M HERE FOR MY OWN REASONS."
...HE'S GOT SOMETHING GOING ON TOO.

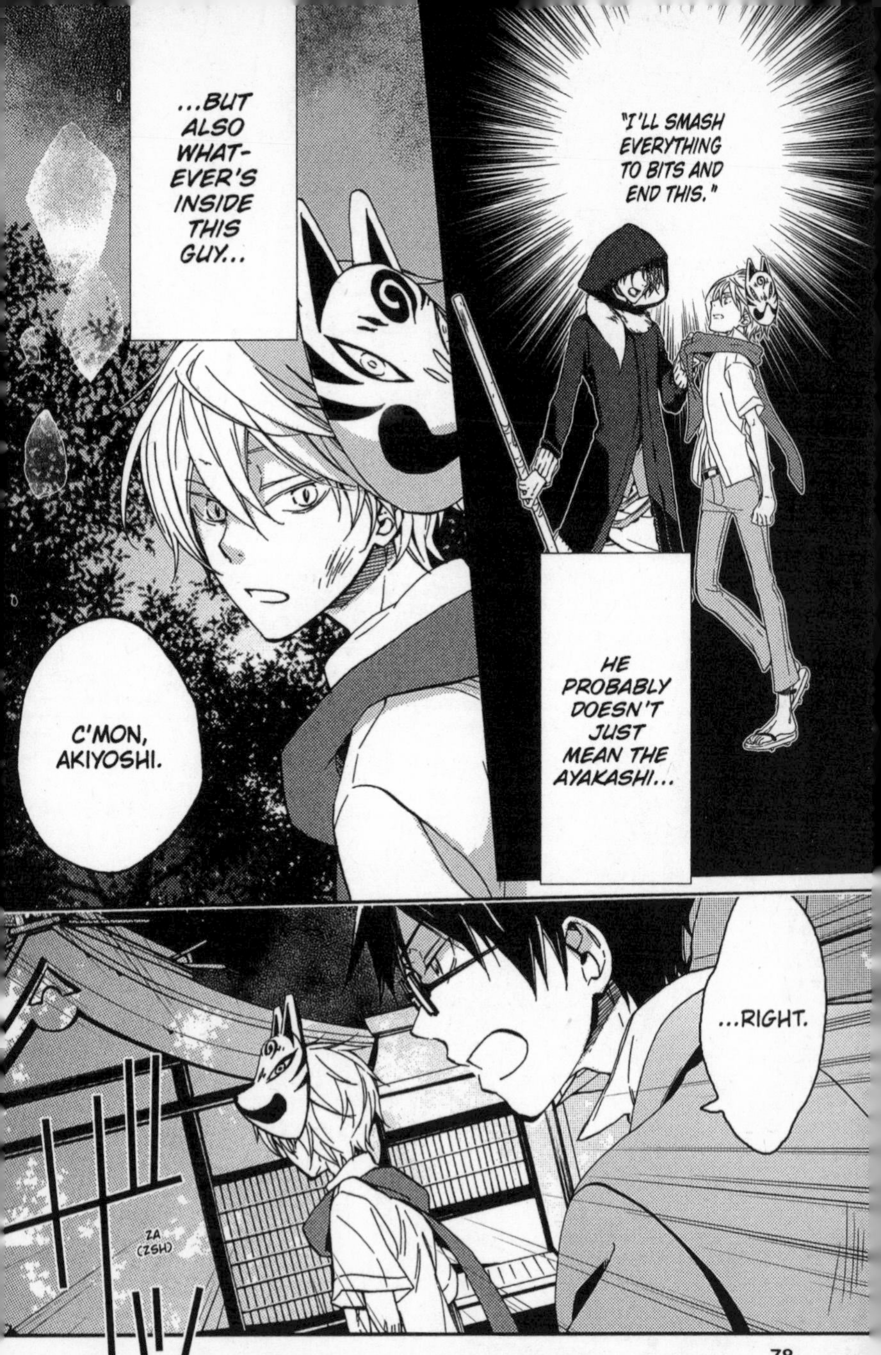
"I'LL SMASH EVERYTHING TO BITS AND END THIS."
HE PROBABLY DOESN'T JUST MEAN THE AYAKASHI...
...BUT ALSO WHAT-EVER'S INSIDE THIS GUY...
C'MON, AKIYOSHI.
...RIGHT.
ZA (ZSH)

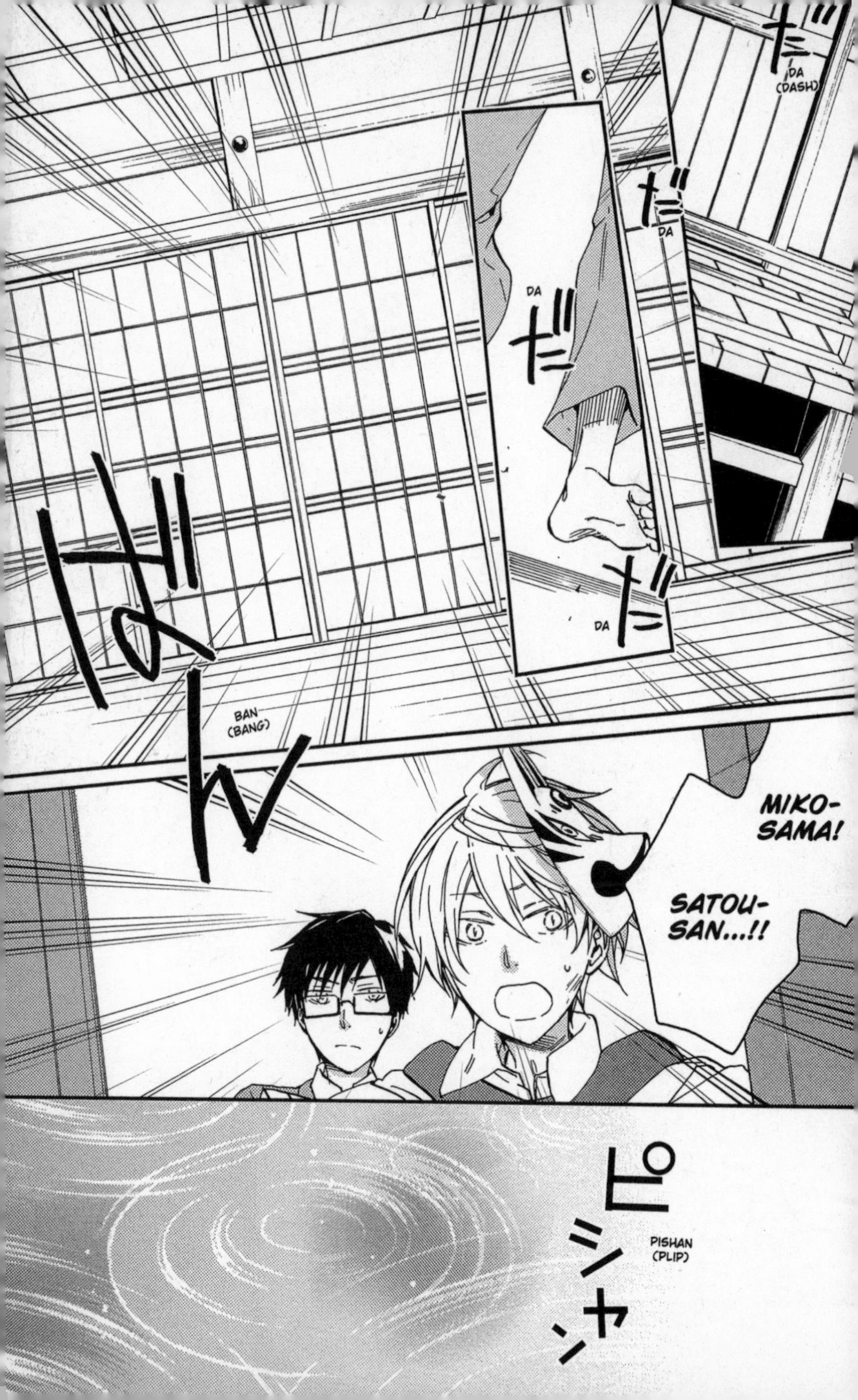
だ
DA
(DASH)
だ
DA
DA
だ
だ
DA
ばん
BAN
(BANG)
MIKO-SAMA!
SATOU-SAN...!!
ピシャン
PISHAN
(PLIP)

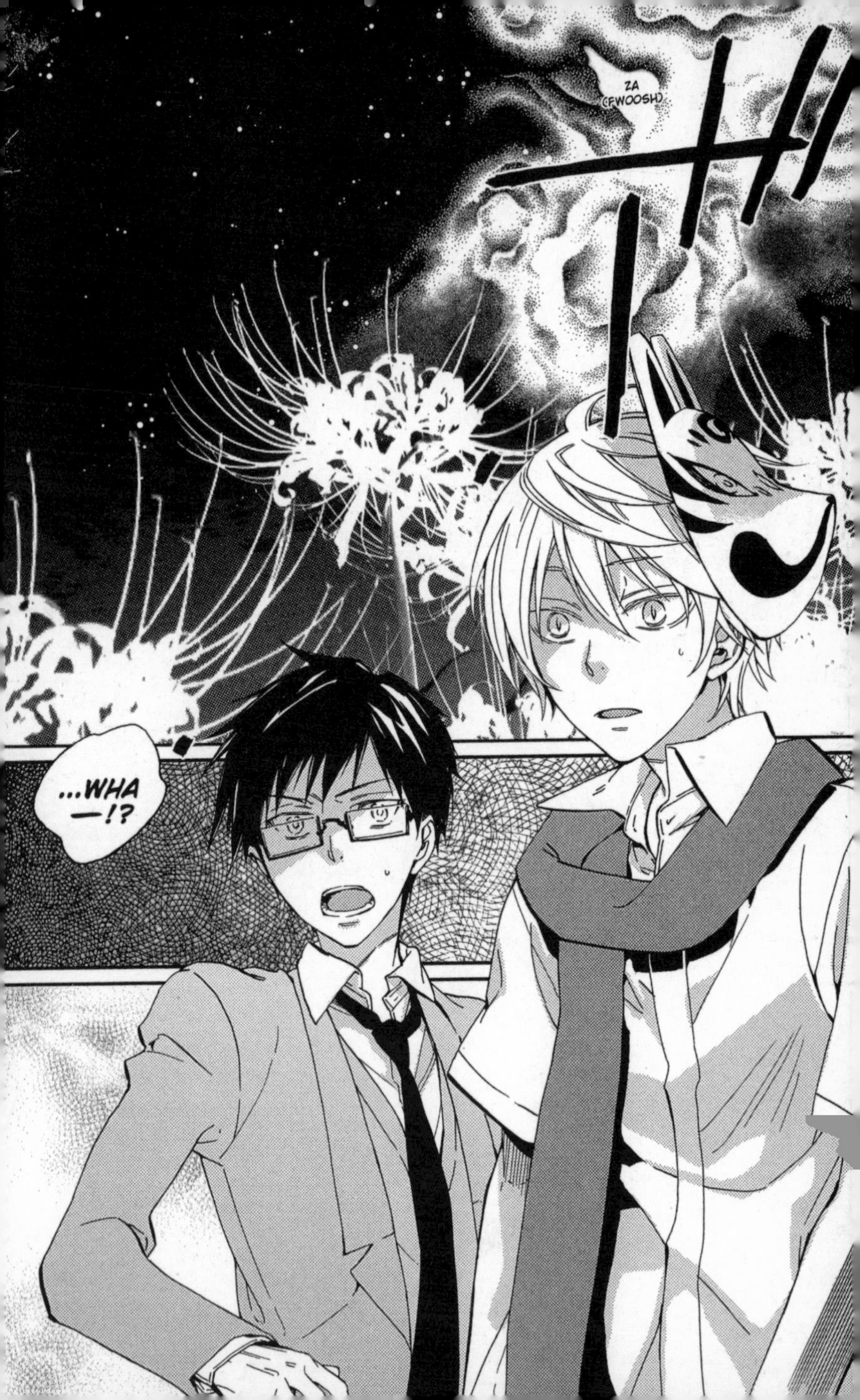
ZA (FWOOSH)
...WHA—!?

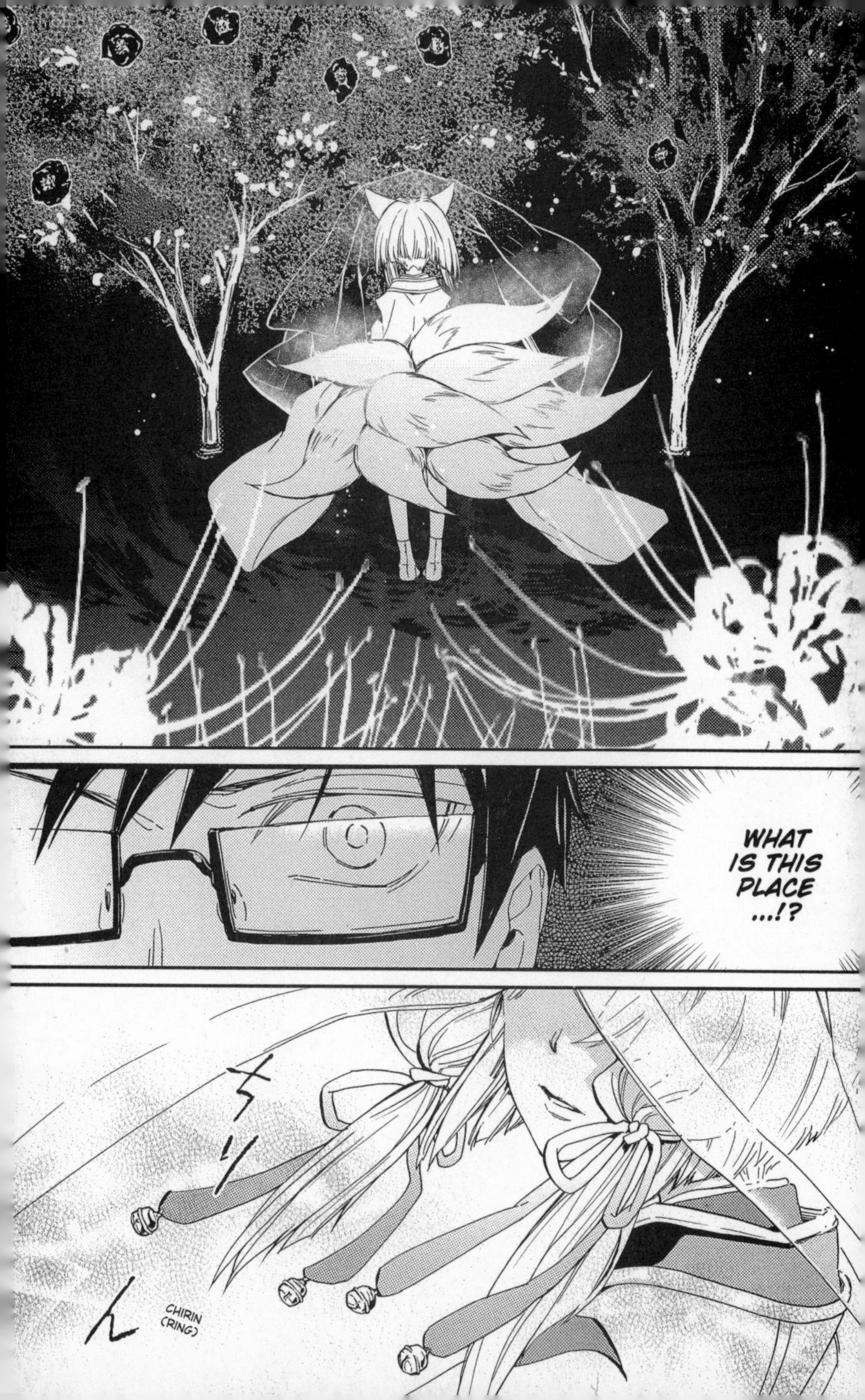
WHAT IS THIS PLACE ...!?
ちりーん
CHIRIN (RING)

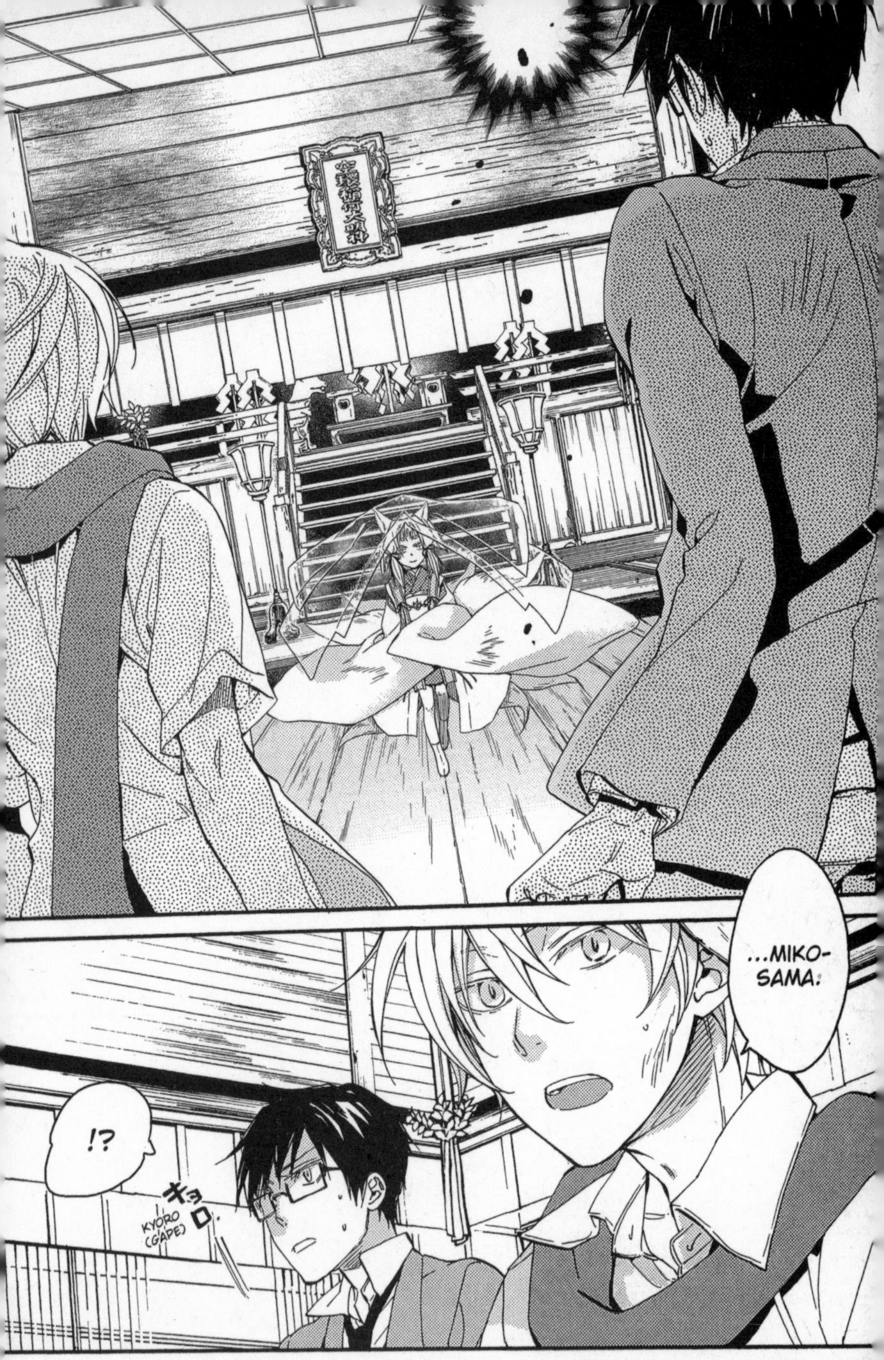
...MIKO-SAMA.
!?
キョロ
KYORO (GAPE)

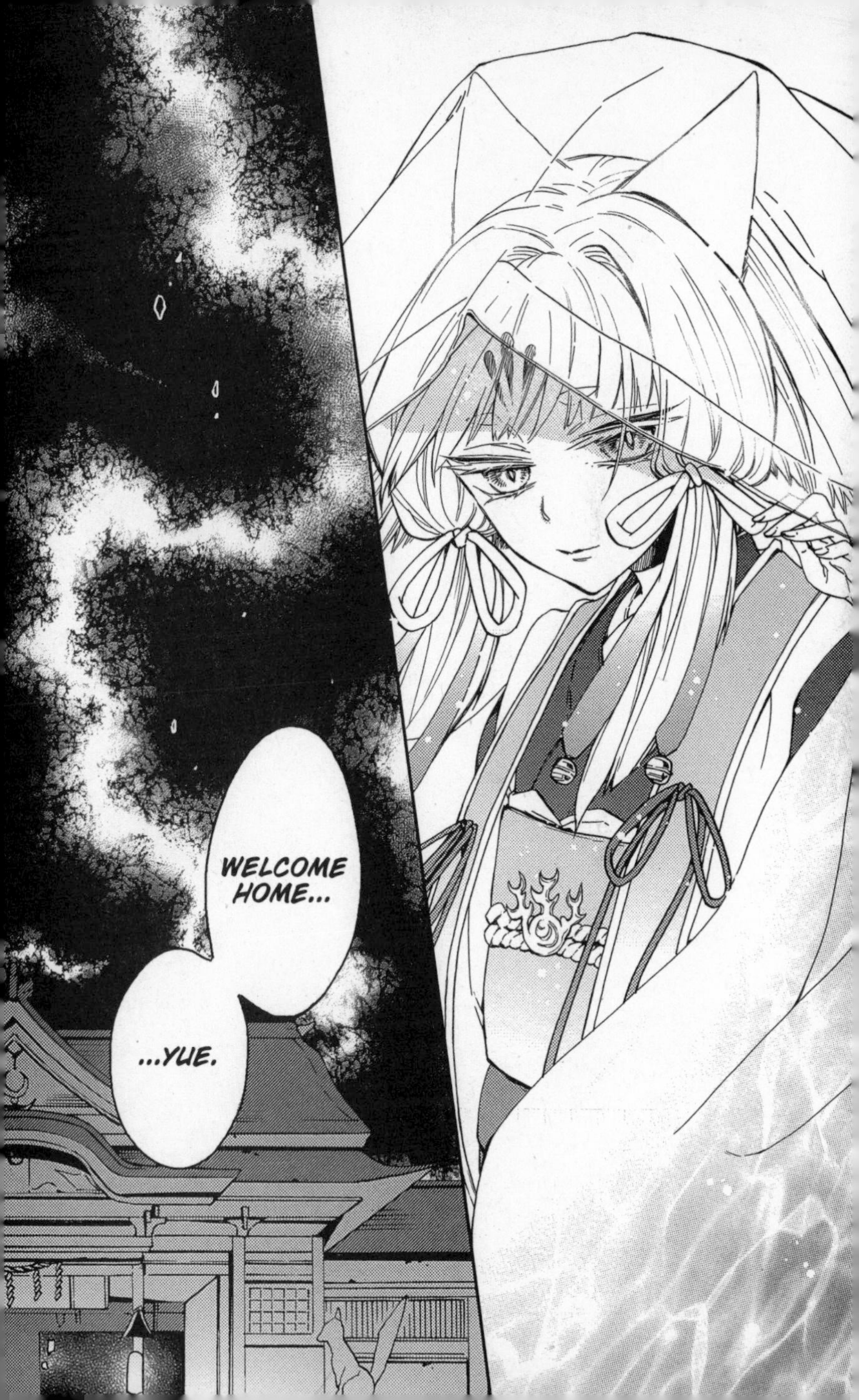
WELCOME HOME...
...YUE.

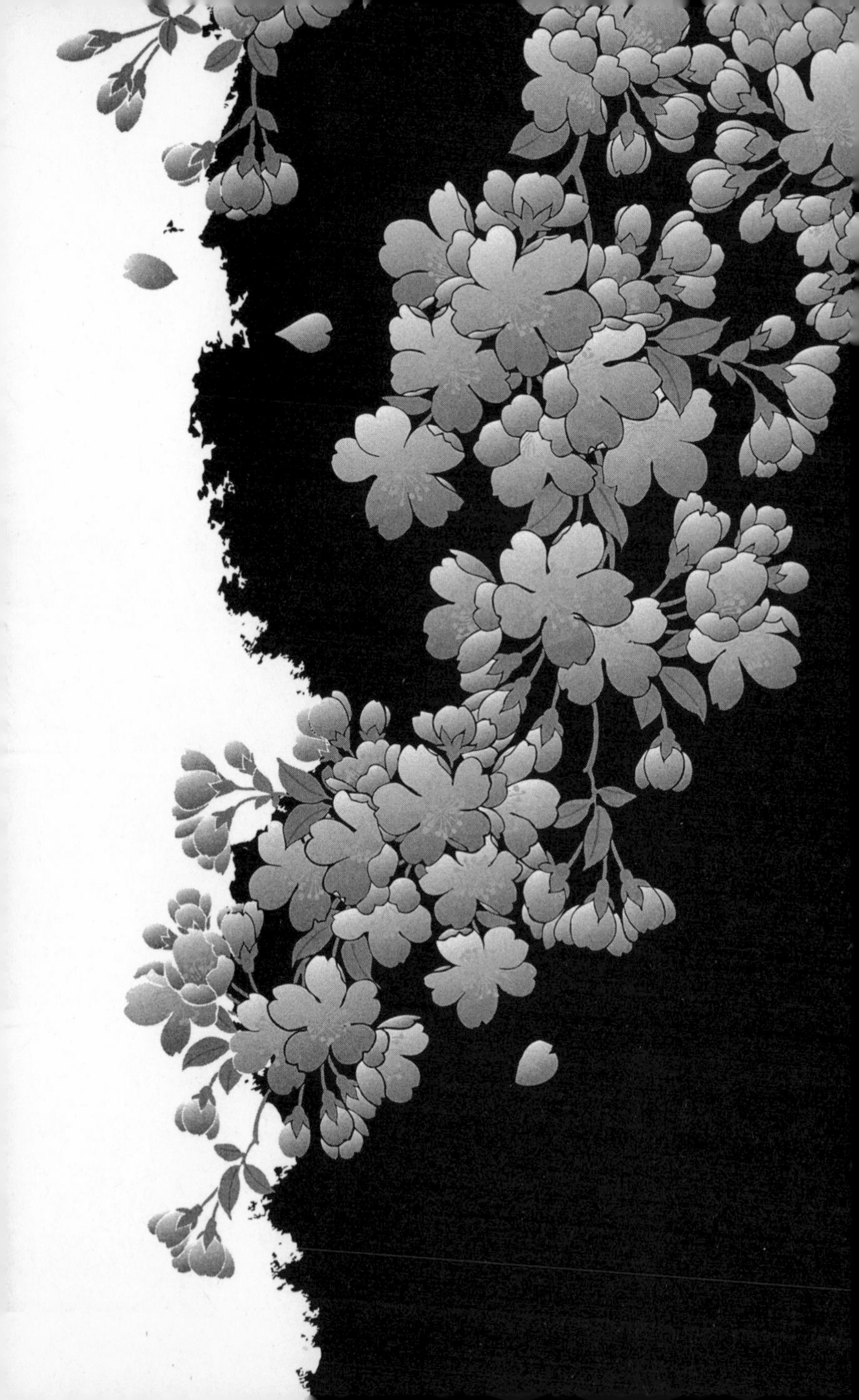

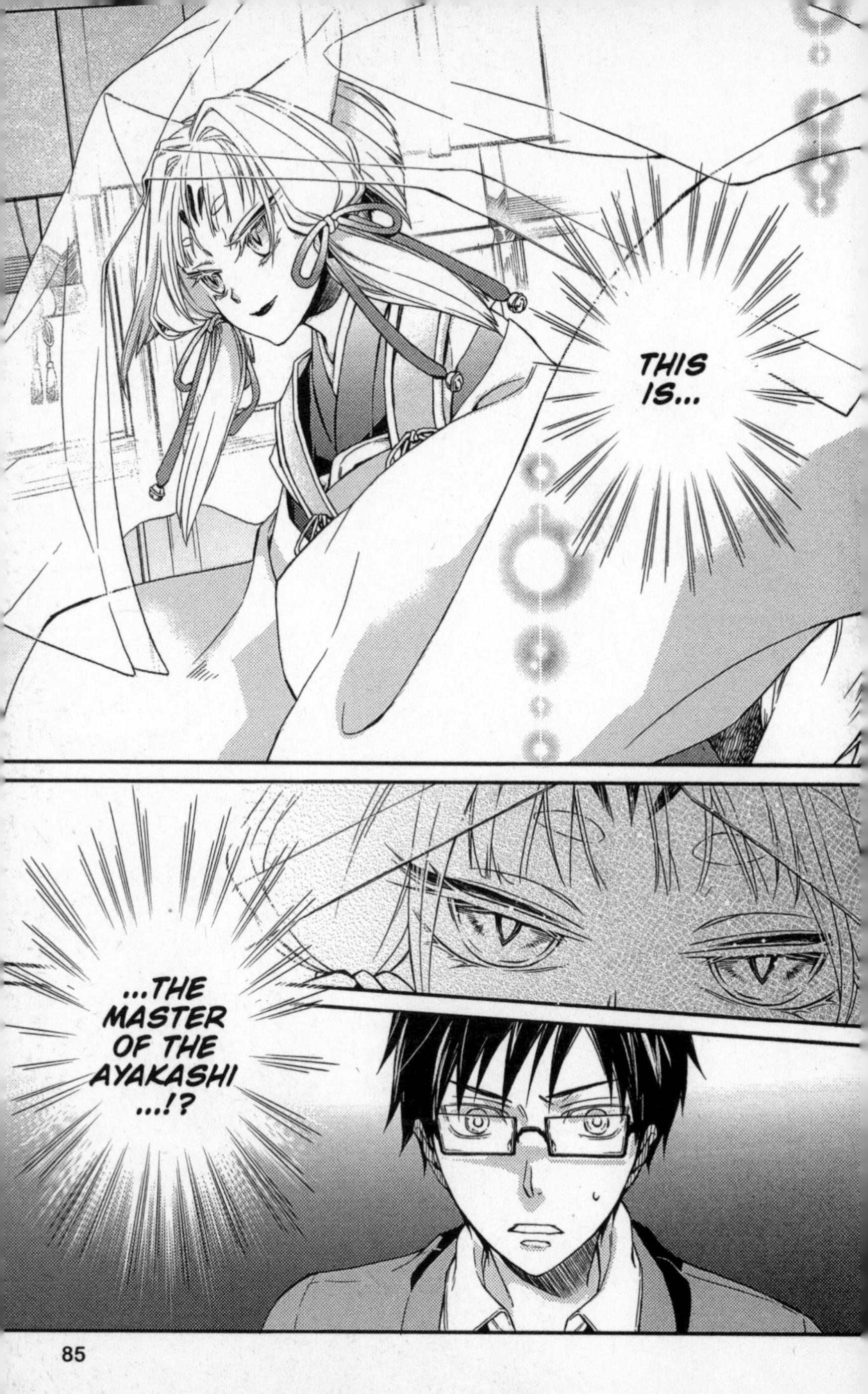
THIS IS...
...THE MASTER OF THE AYAKASHI ...!?

THE 28TH TALE
HOMECOMING

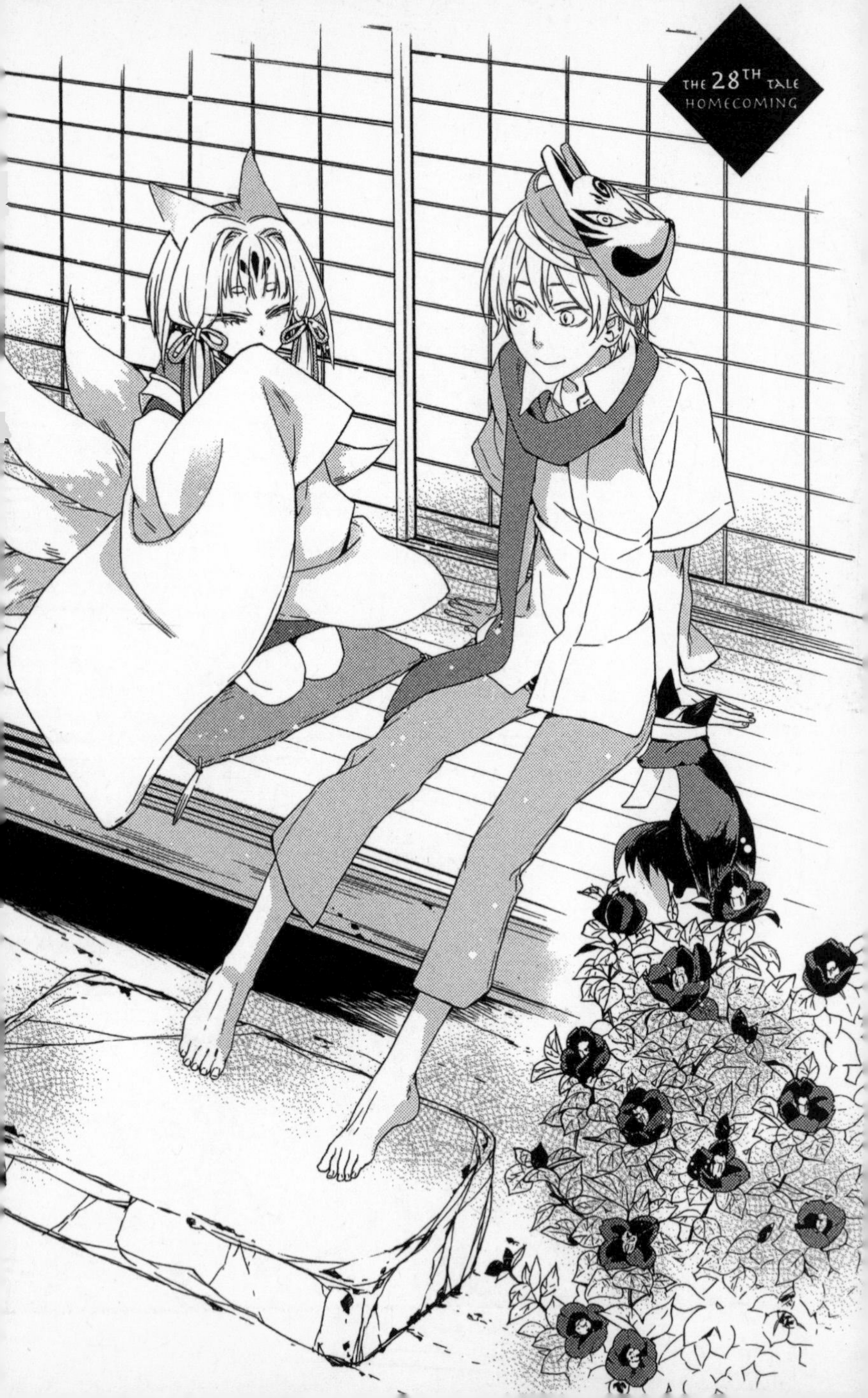

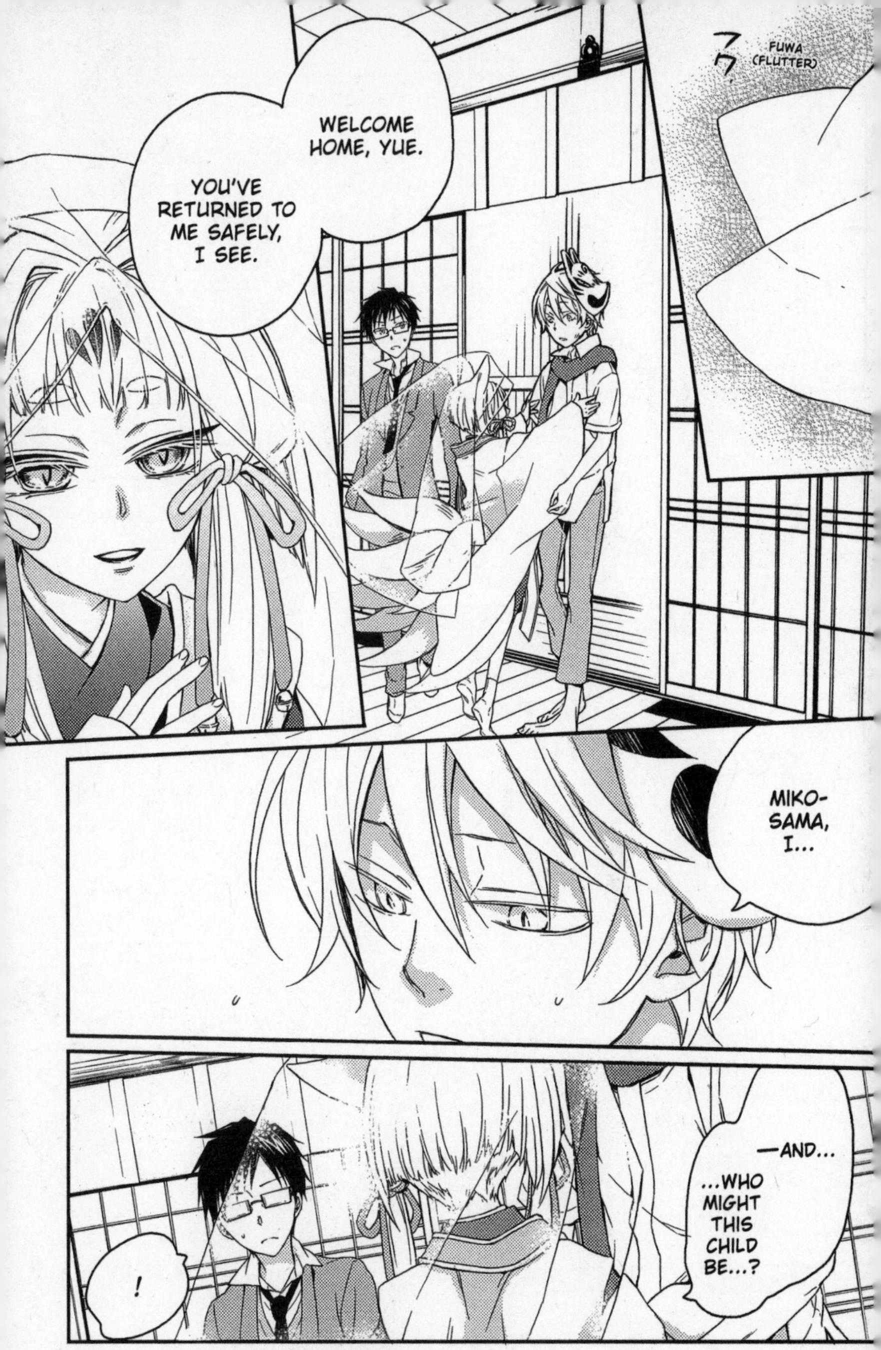
FUWA (FLUTTER)
WELCOME HOME, YUE.
YOU'VE RETURNED TO ME SAFELY, I SEE.
MIKO-SAMA, I...
—AND...
...WHO MIGHT THIS CHILD BE...?
!

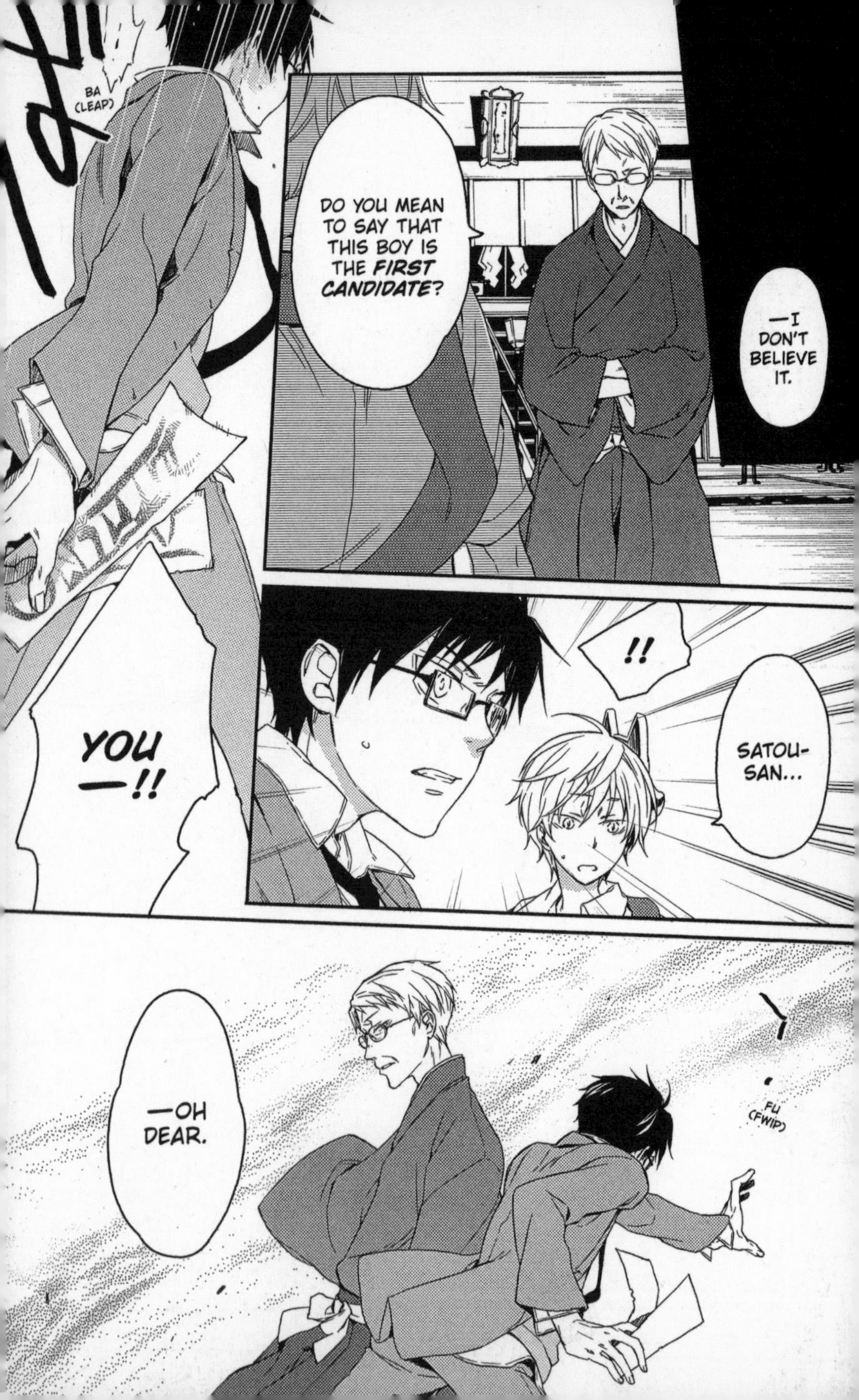
DO YOU MEAN TO SAY THAT THIS BOY IS THE *FIRST CANDIDATE*?
—I DON'T BELIEVE IT.
!!
SATOU-SAN...
BA (LEAP)
YOU—!!
FU (FWIP)
—OH DEAR.

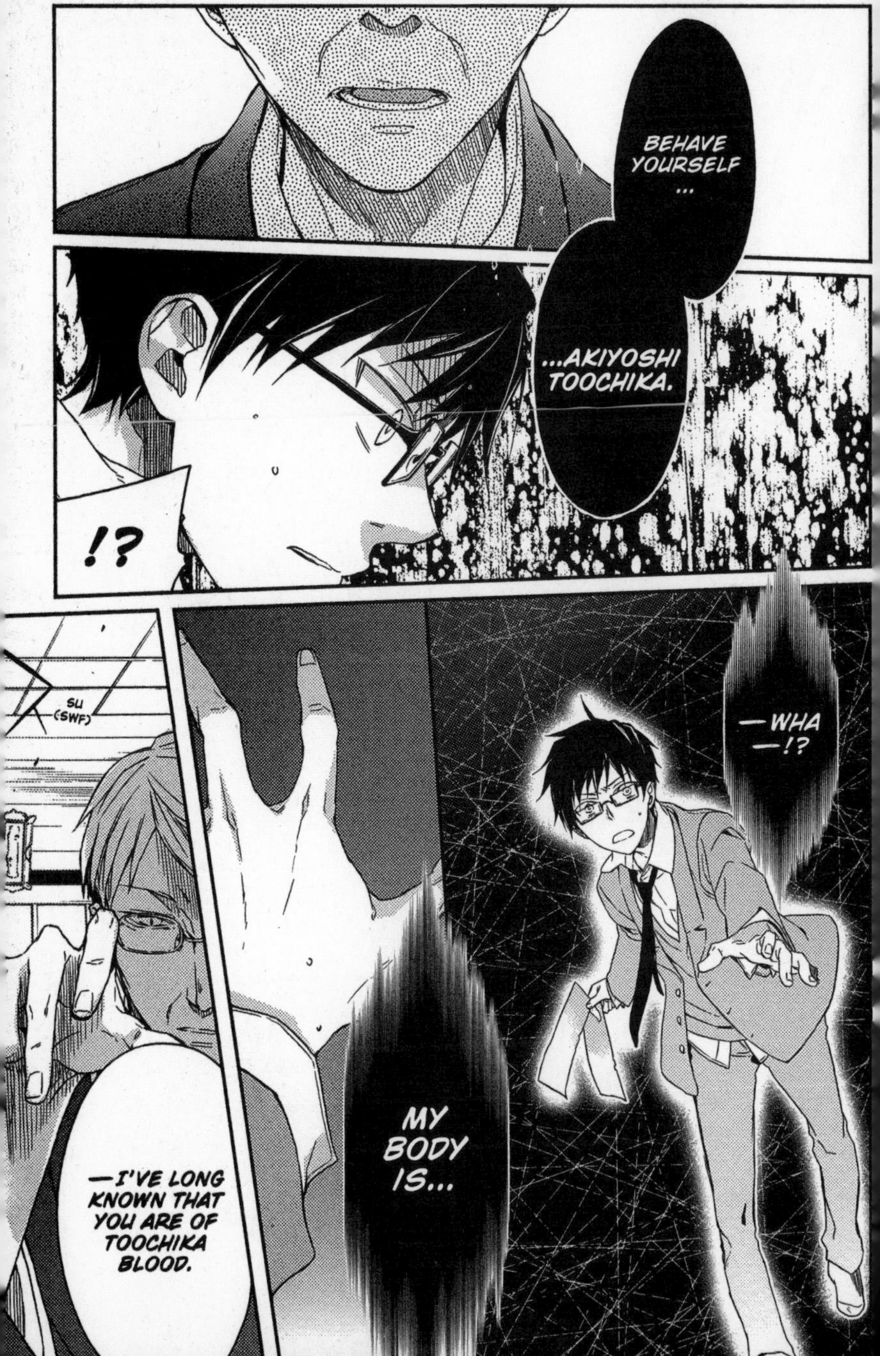
BEHAVE YOURSELF ...
...AKIYOSHI TOOCHIKA.
!?
—WHA —!?
MY BODY IS...
SU (SWF)
—I'VE LONG KNOWN THAT YOU ARE OF TOOCHIKA BLOOD.

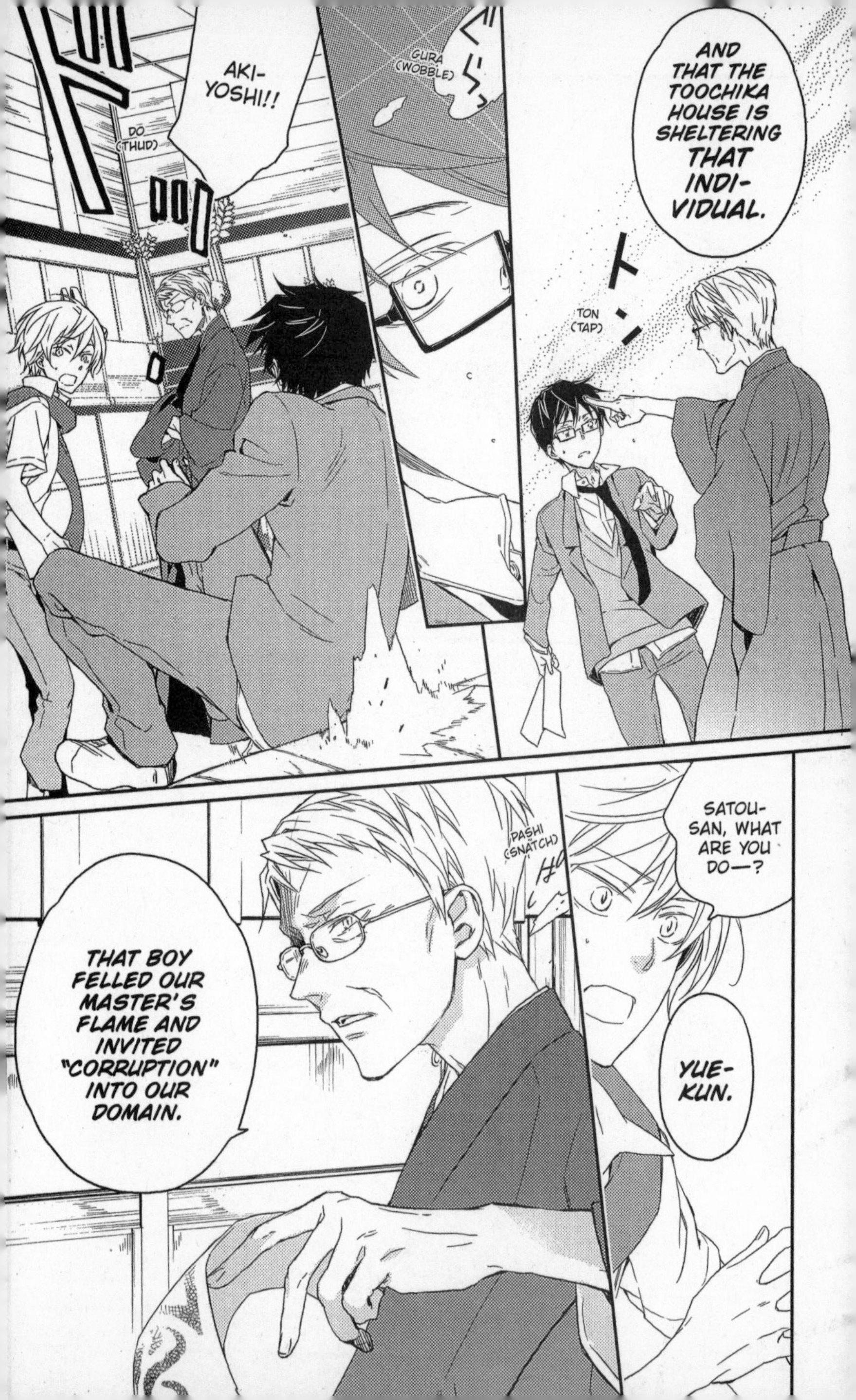
AND THAT THE TOOCHIKA HOUSE IS SHELTERING THAT INDIVIDUAL.
TON (TAP)
GURA (WOBBLE)
AKI-YOSHI!!
DO (THUD)
SATOU-SAN, WHAT ARE YOU DO—?
PASHI (SNATCH)
YUE-KUN.
THAT BOY FELLED OUR MASTER'S FLAME AND INVITED "CORRUPTION" INTO OUR DOMAIN.

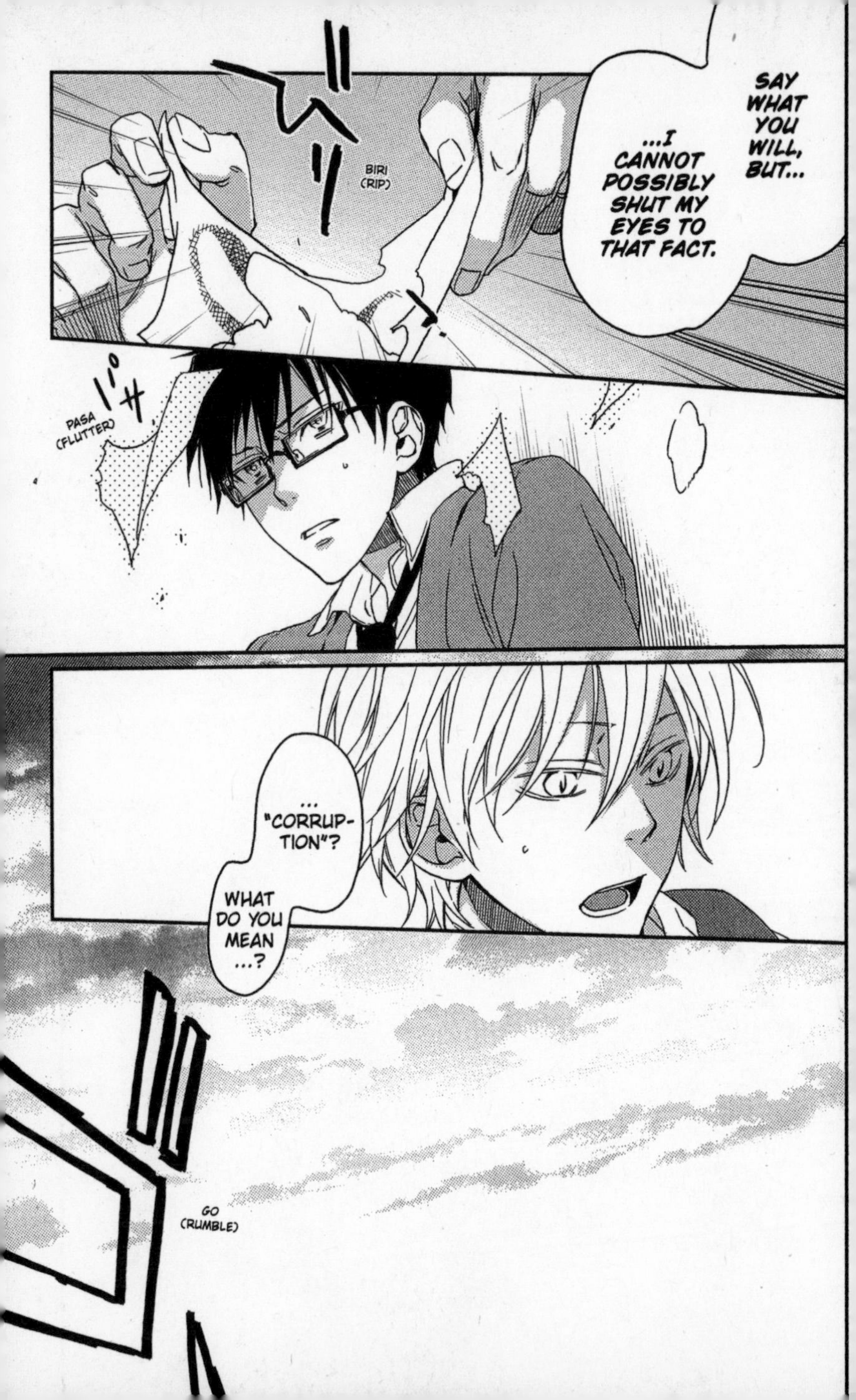

SAY WHAT YOU WILL, BUT...
...I CANNOT POSSIBLY SHUT MY EYES TO THAT FACT.
BIRI (RIP)
PASA (FLUTTER)
... "CORRUPTION"?
WHAT DO YOU MEAN ...?
GO (RUMBLE)

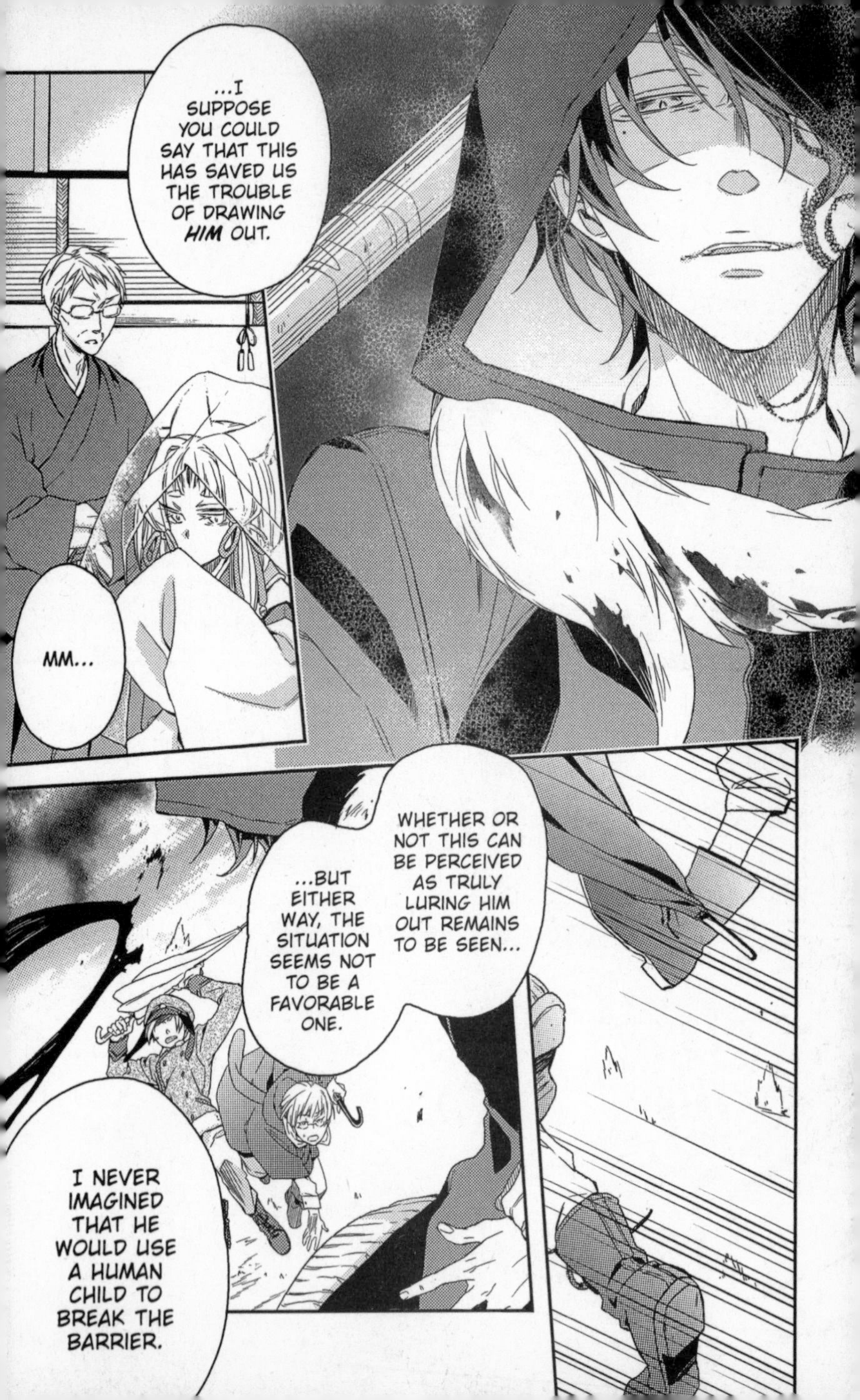
...I SUPPOSE YOU COULD SAY THAT THIS HAS SAVED US THE TROUBLE OF DRAWING *HIM* OUT.
MM...
WHETHER OR NOT THIS CAN BE PERCEIVED AS TRULY LURING HIM OUT REMAINS TO BE SEEN...
...BUT EITHER WAY, THE SITUATION SEEMS NOT TO BE A FAVORABLE ONE.
I NEVER IMAGINED THAT HE WOULD USE A HUMAN CHILD TO BREAK THE BARRIER.

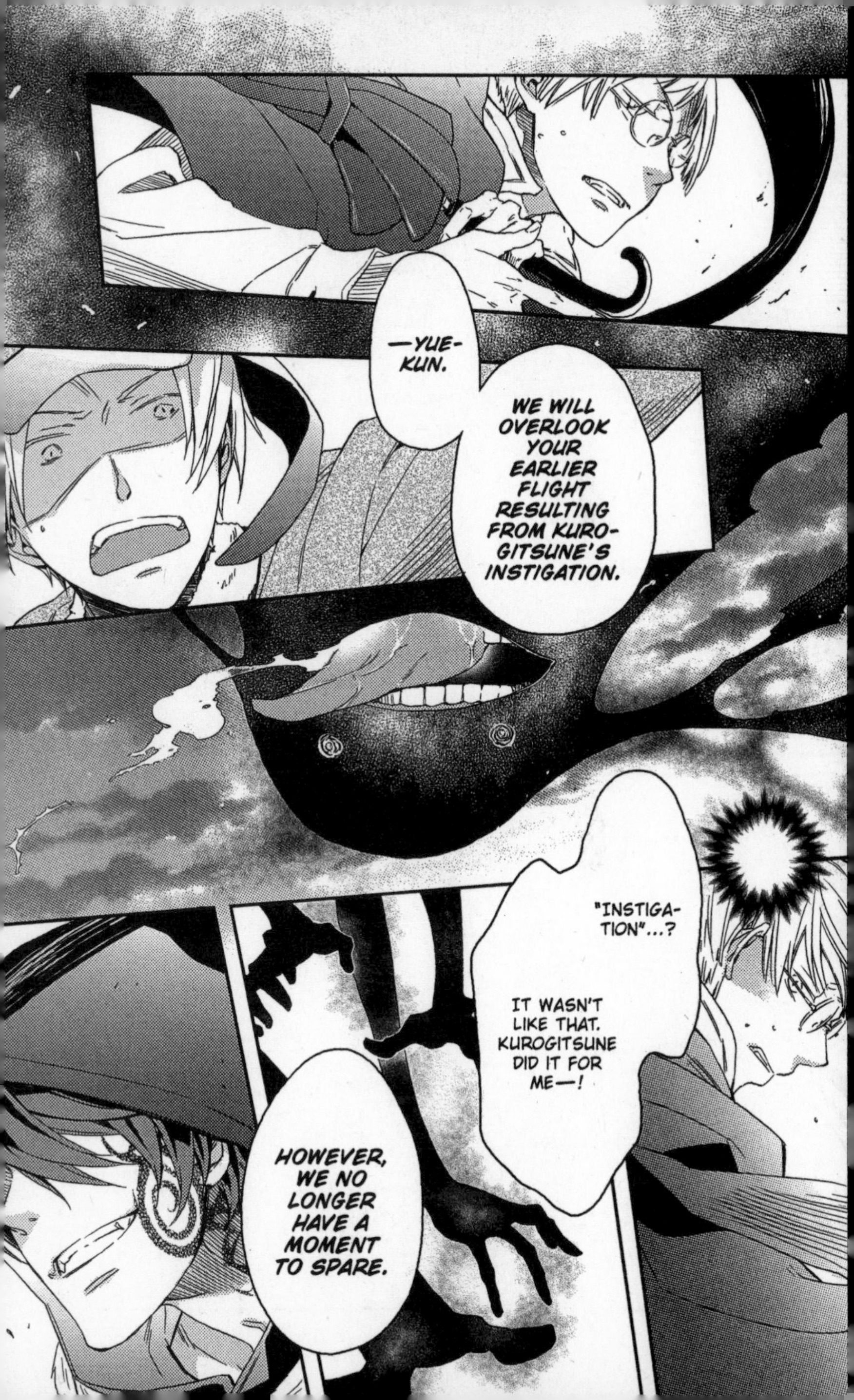
—YUE-KUN.
WE WILL OVERLOOK YOUR EARLIER FLIGHT RESULTING FROM KURO-GITSUNE'S INSTIGATION.
"INSTIGA-TION"...?
IT WASN'T LIKE THAT. KUROGITSUNE DID IT FOR ME—!
HOWEVER, WE NO LONGER HAVE A MOMENT TO SPARE.

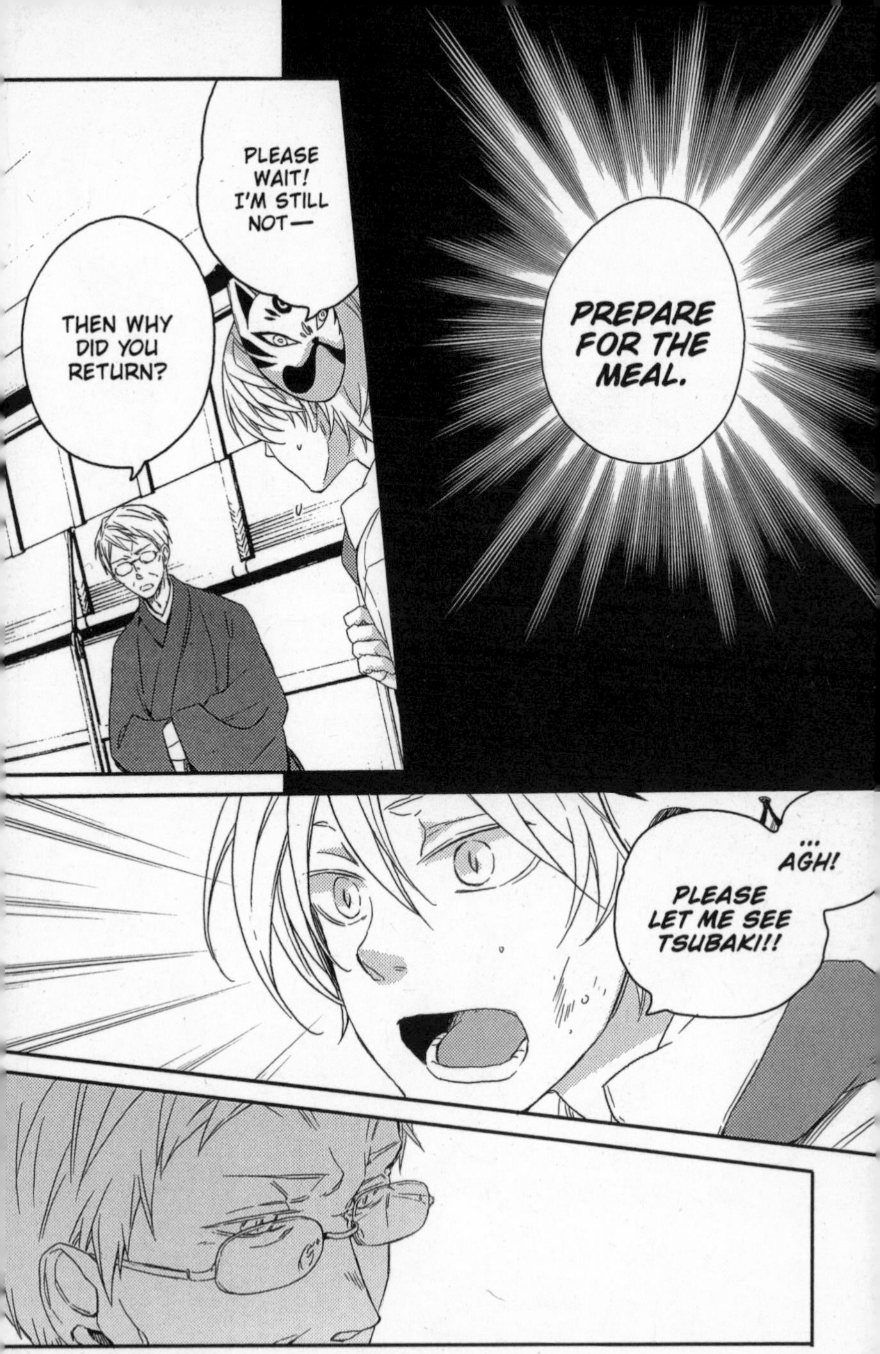
PREPARE FOR THE MEAL.
PLEASE WAIT! I'M STILL NOT—
THEN WHY DID YOU RETURN?
... AGH!
PLEASE LET ME SEE TSUBAKI!!

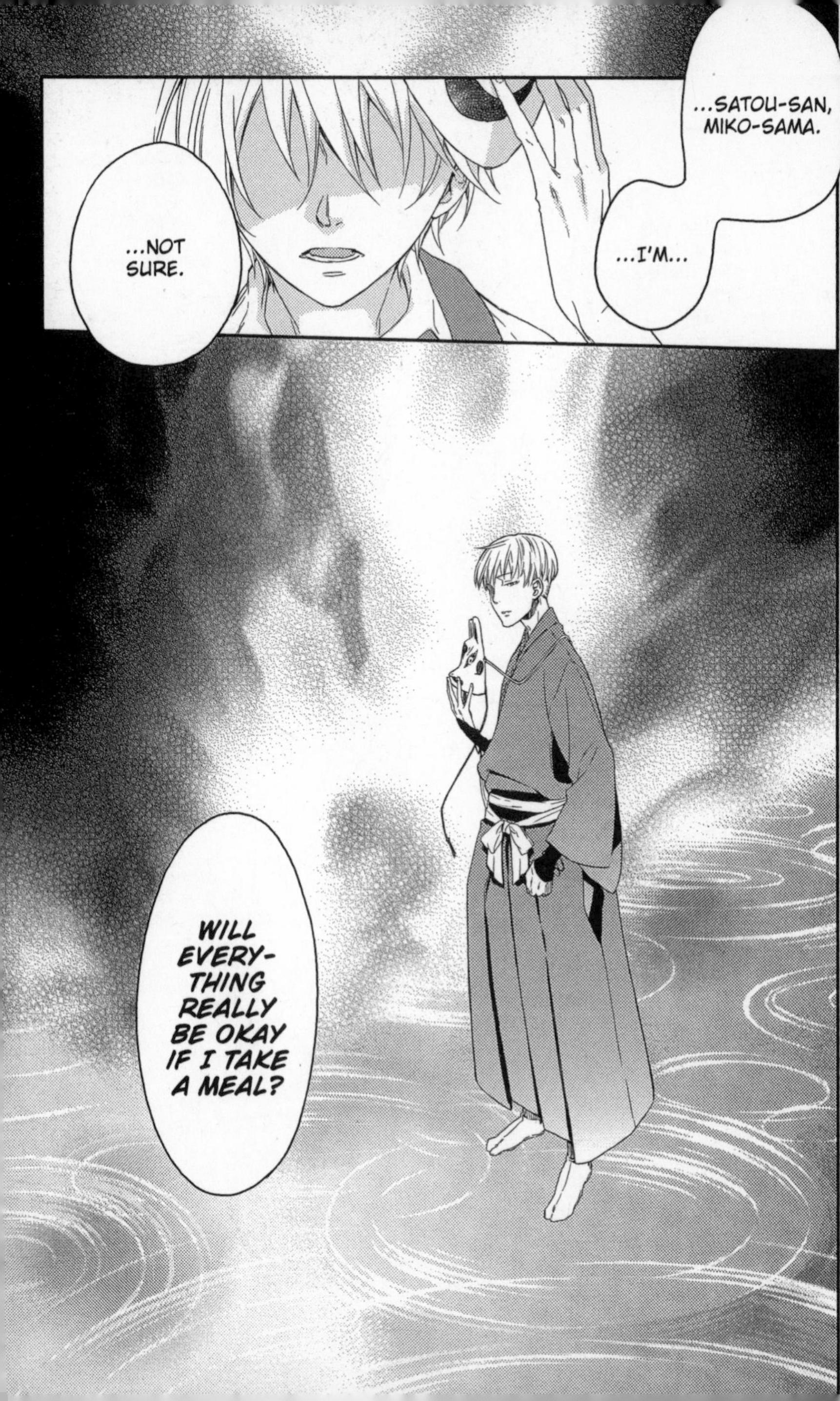
...SATOU-SAN, MIKO-SAMA.
...I'M...
...NOT SURE.
WILL EVERY-THING REALLY BE OKAY IF I TAKE A MEAL?

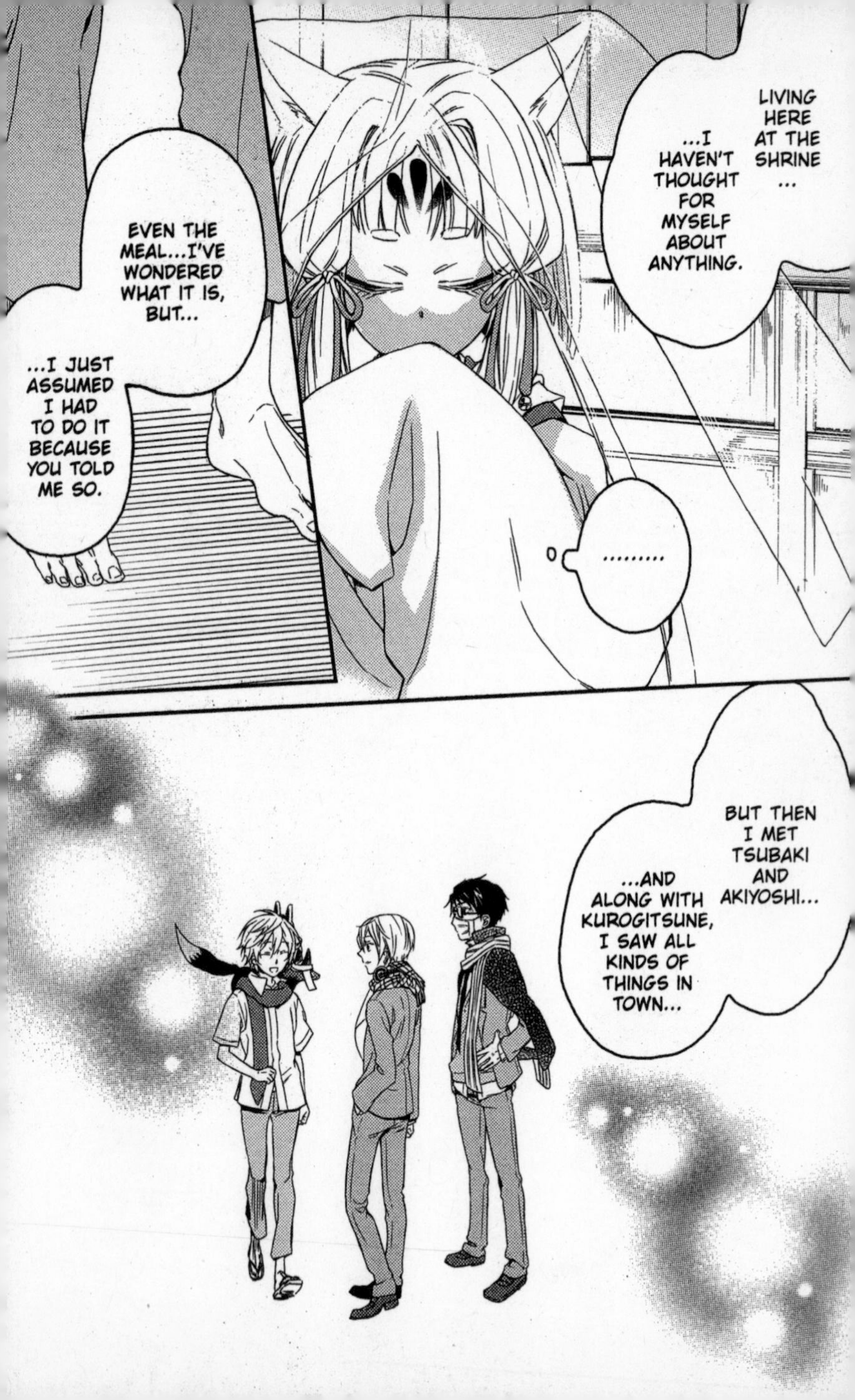
LIVING HERE AT THE SHRINE ...
...I HAVEN'T THOUGHT FOR MYSELF ABOUT ANYTHING.
....
EVEN THE MEAL...I'VE WONDERED WHAT IT IS, BUT...
...I JUST ASSUMED I HAD TO DO IT BECAUSE YOU TOLD ME SO.
BUT THEN I MET TSUBAKI AND AKIYOSHI...
...AND ALONG WITH KUROGITSUNE, I SAW ALL KINDS OF THINGS IN TOWN...

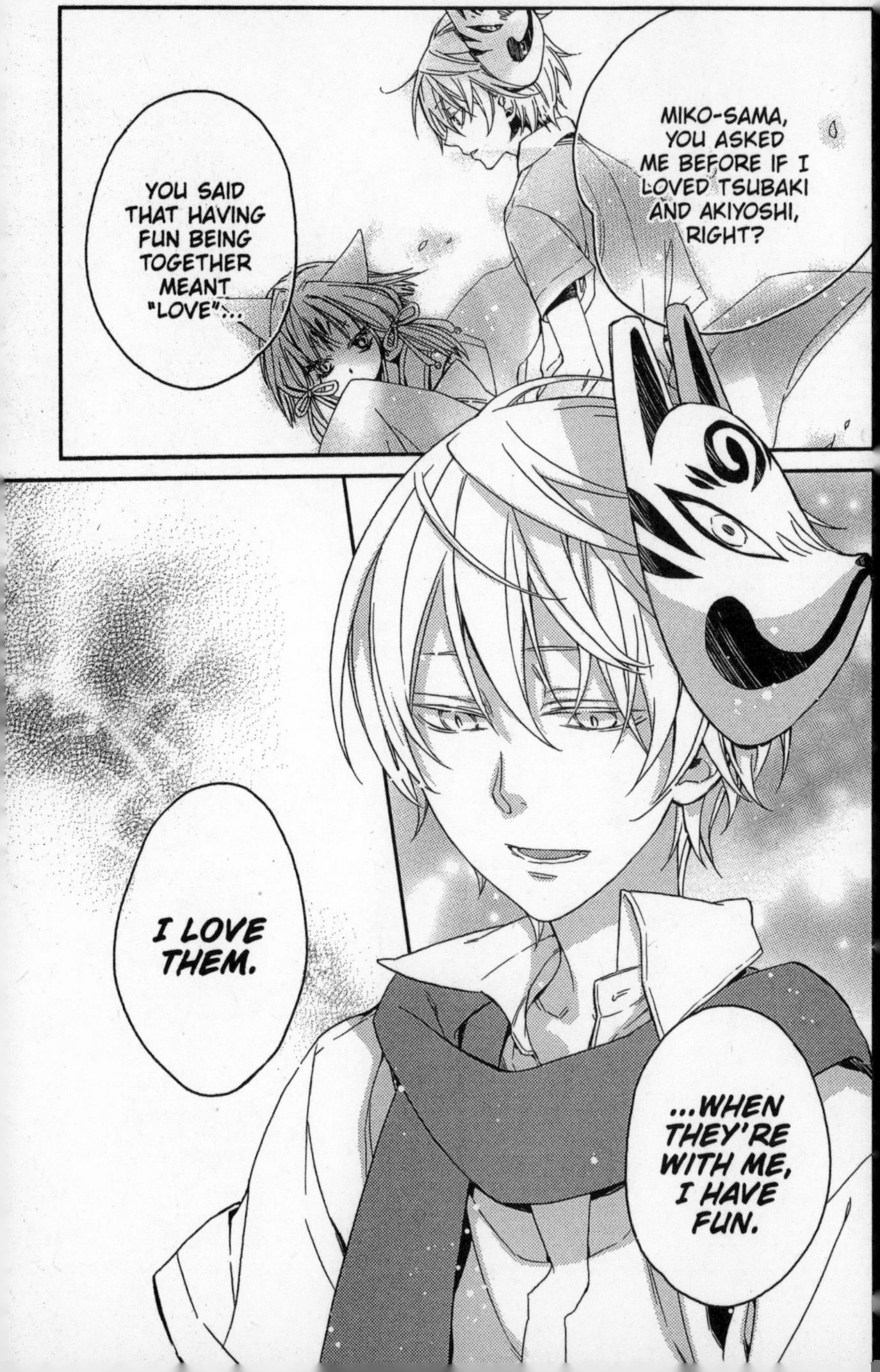
MIKO-SAMA, YOU ASKED ME BEFORE IF I LOVED TSUBAKI AND AKIYOSHI, RIGHT?
YOU SAID THAT HAVING FUN BEING TOGETHER MEANT "LOVE"...
...WHEN THEY'RE WITH ME, I HAVE FUN.
I LOVE THEM.

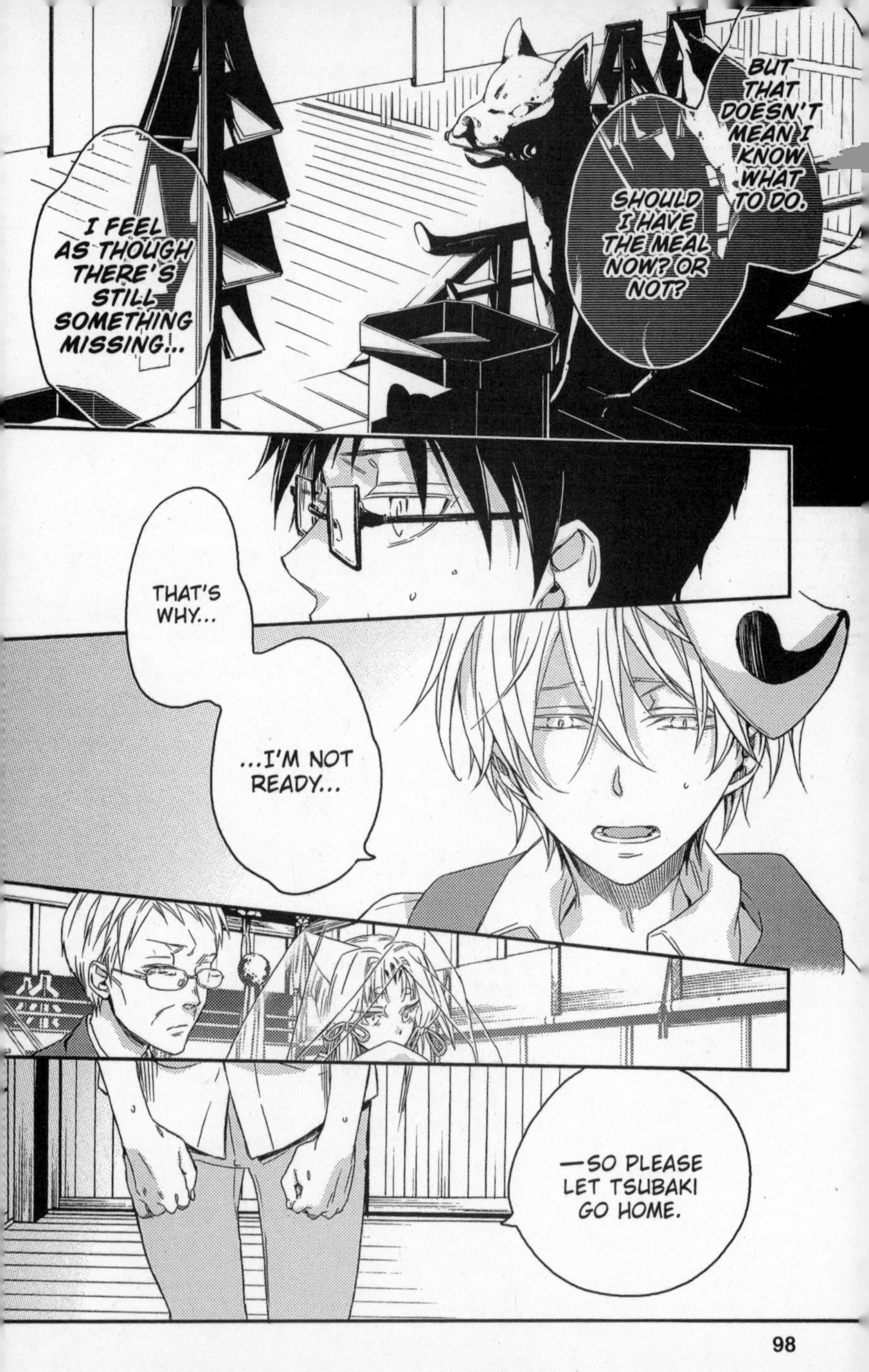
BUT THAT DOESN'T MEAN I KNOW WHAT TO DO.
SHOULD I HAVE THE MEAL NOW? OR NOT?
I FEEL AS THOUGH THERE'S STILL SOMETHING MISSING...
THAT'S WHY...
...I'M NOT READY...
—SO PLEASE LET TSUBAKI GO HOME.

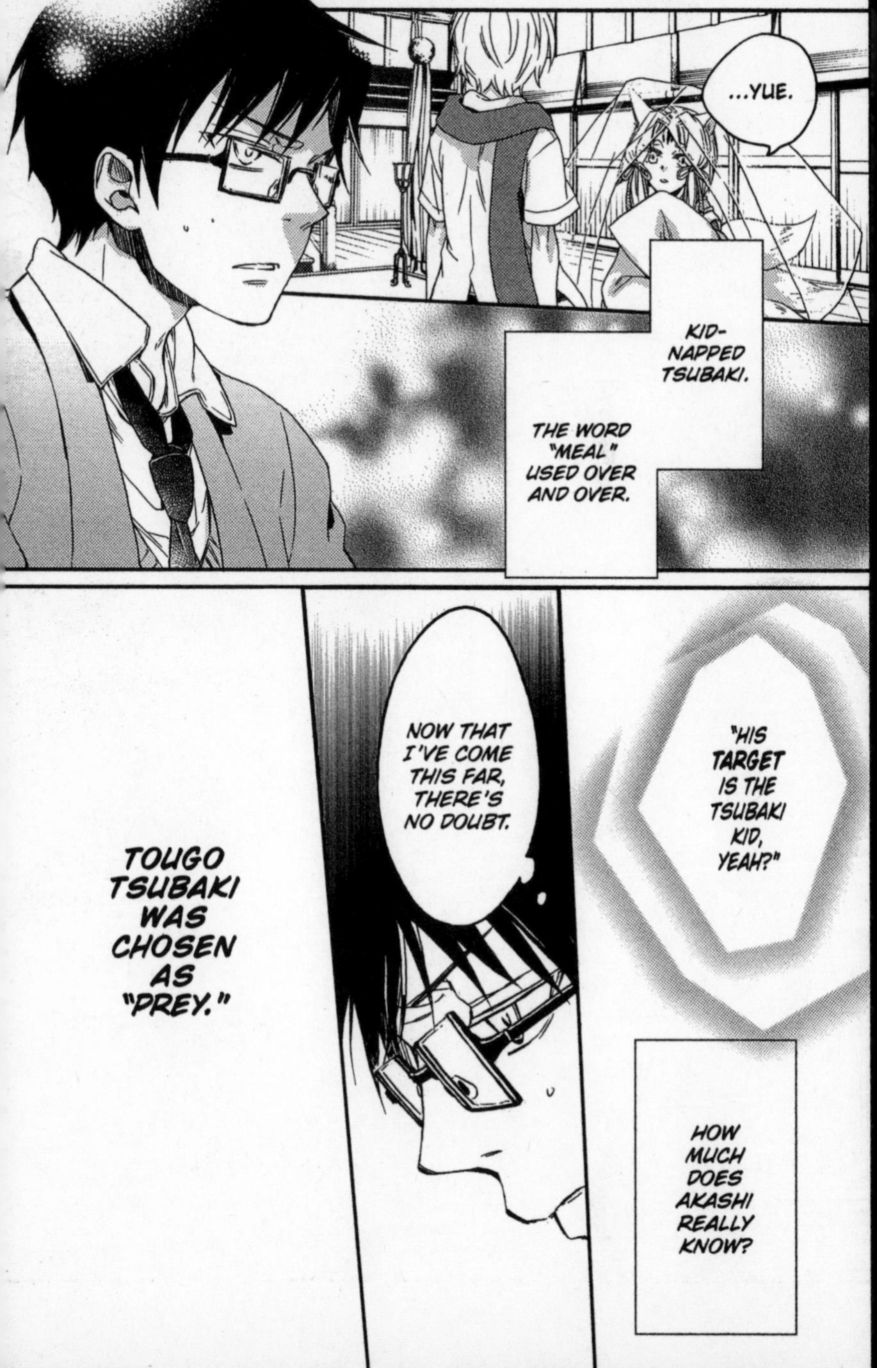
...YUE.
KID-NAPPED TSUBAKI.
THE WORD "MEAL" USED OVER AND OVER.
"HIS TARGET IS THE TSUBAKI KID, YEAH?"
HOW MUCH DOES AKASHI REALLY KNOW?
NOW THAT I'VE COME THIS FAR, THERE'S NO DOUBT.
TOUGO TSUBAKI WAS CHOSEN AS "PREY."

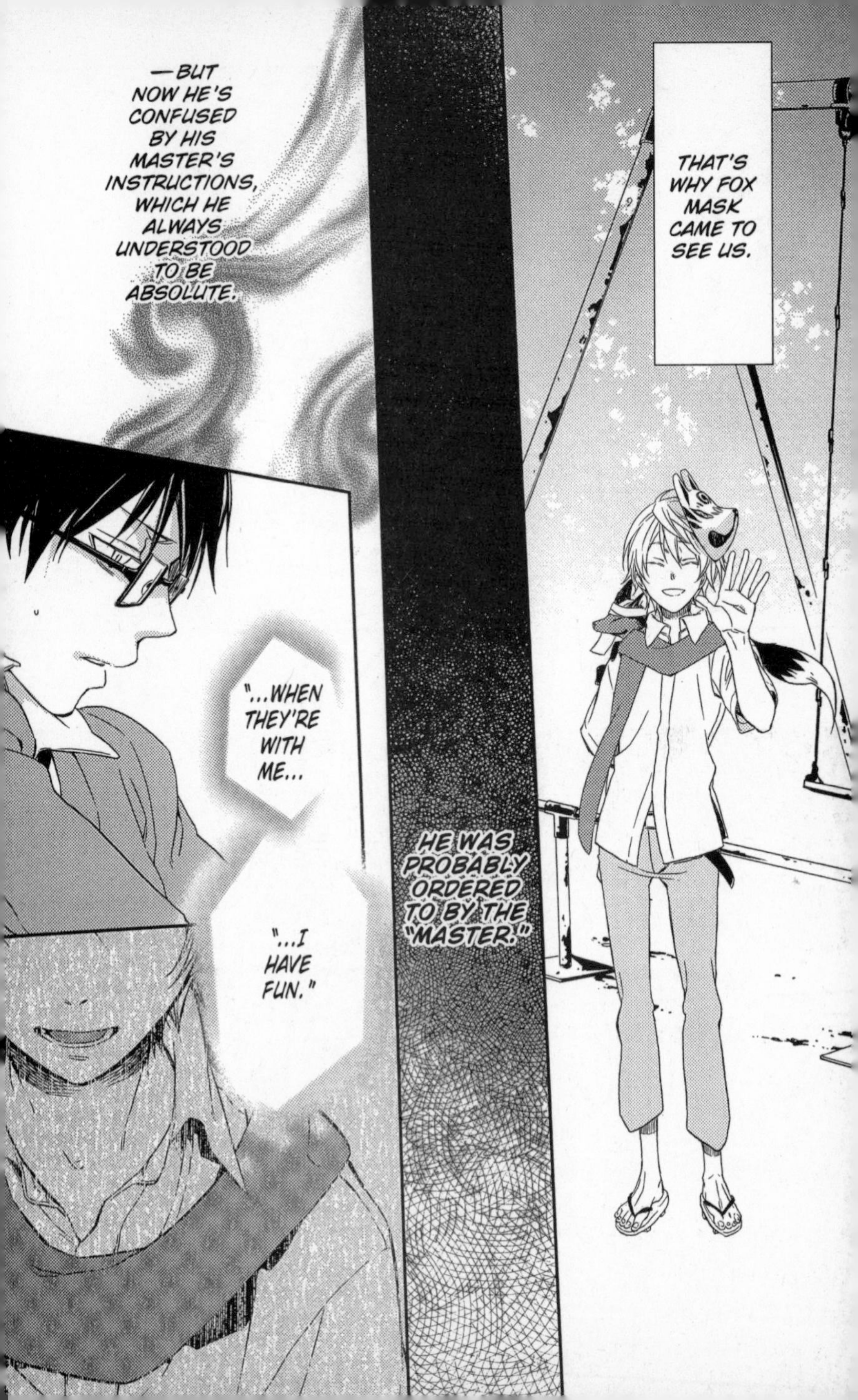
THAT'S WHY FOX MASK CAME TO SEE US.
HE WAS PROBABLY ORDERED TO BY THE "MASTER."
—BUT NOW HE'S CONFUSED BY HIS MASTER'S INSTRUCTIONS, WHICH HE ALWAYS UNDERSTOOD TO BE ABSOLUTE.
"...WHEN THEY'RE WITH ME...
"...I HAVE FUN."

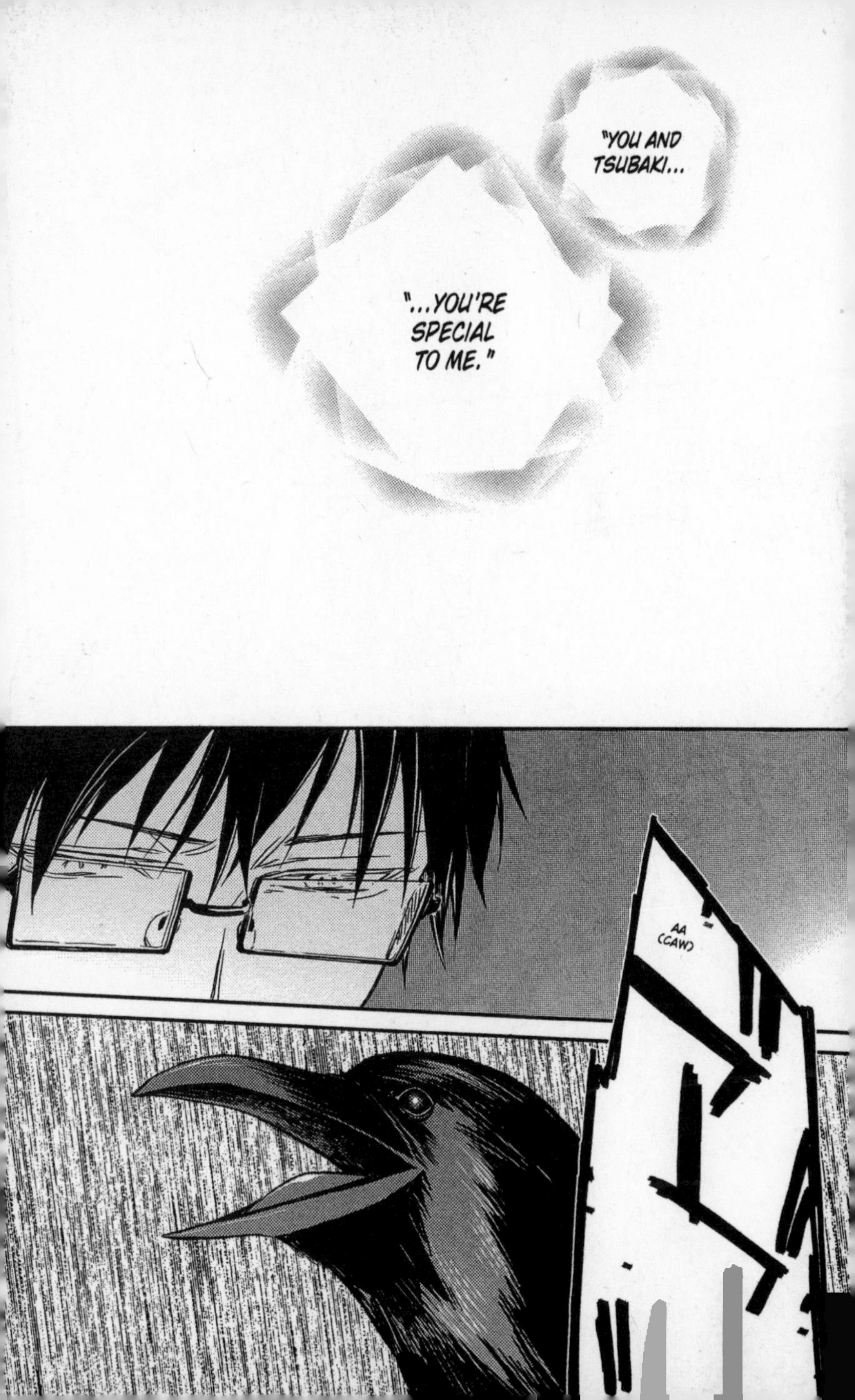
"YOU AND TSUBAKI...
"...YOU'RE SPECIAL TO ME."
AA (CAW)

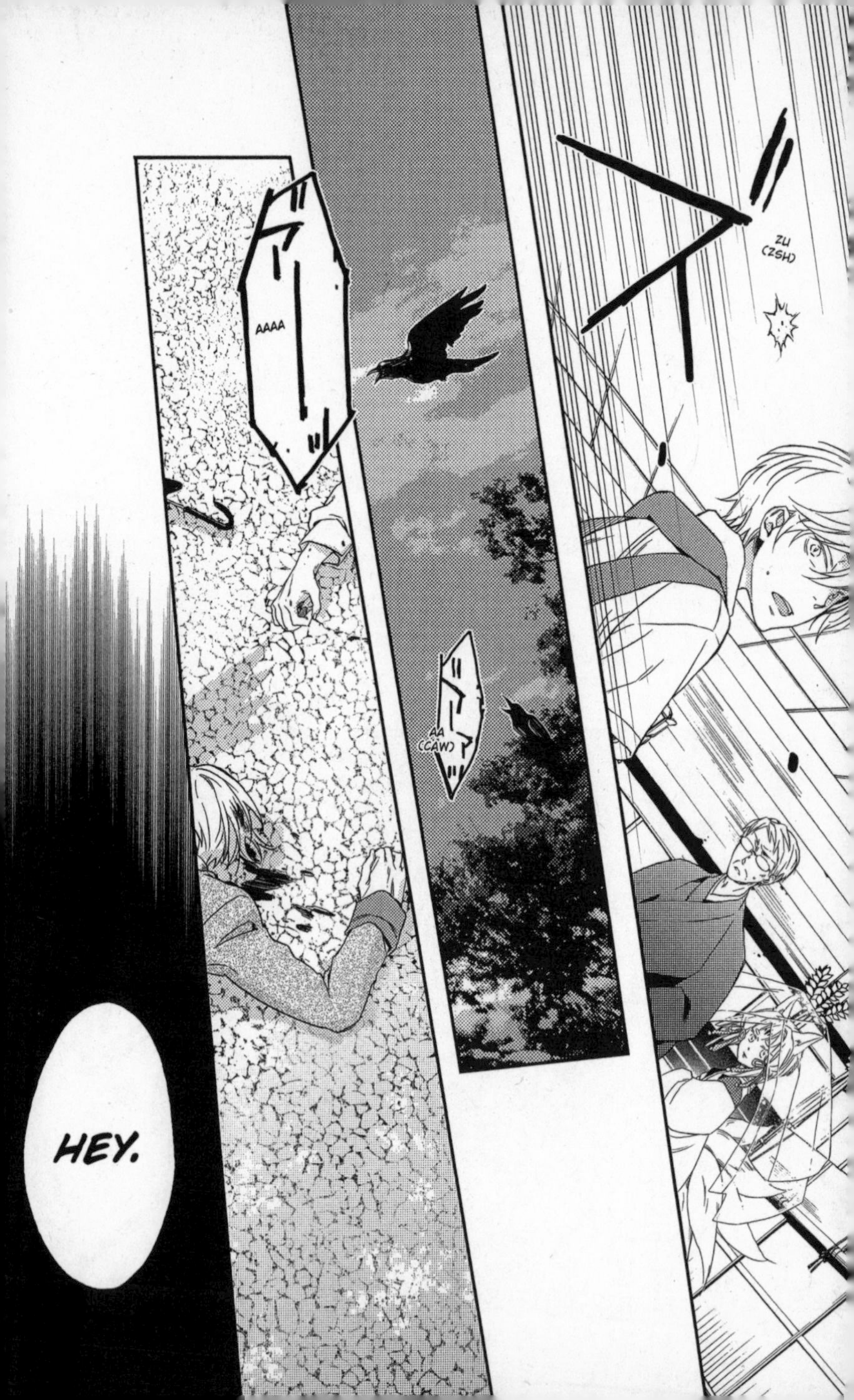
ZU (ZSH)
AA (CAW)
AAAA
HEY.

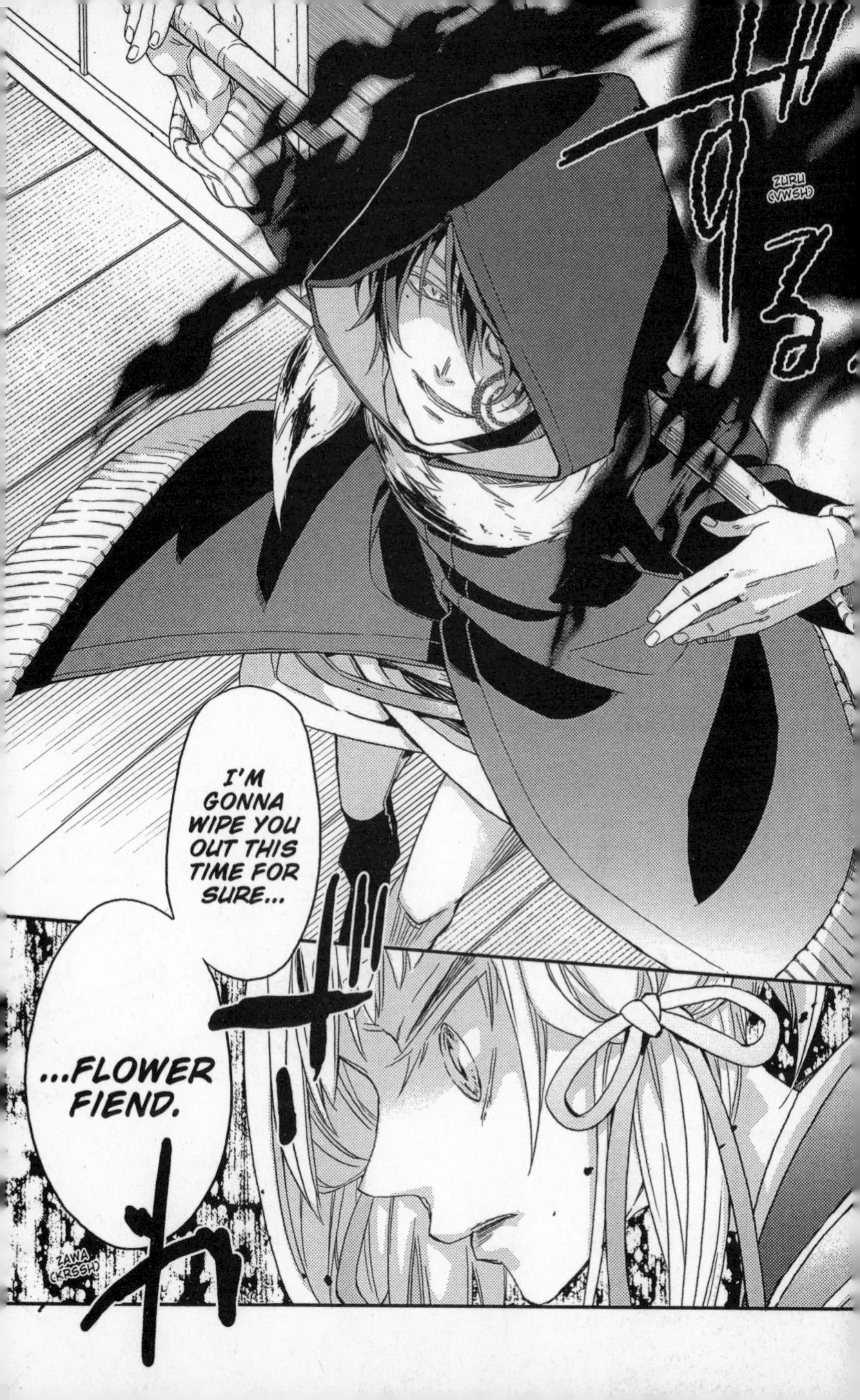
ZURU (VWSH)
I'M GONNA WIPE YOU OUT THIS TIME FOR SURE...
...FLOWER FIEND.
ZAWA (KRSSH)

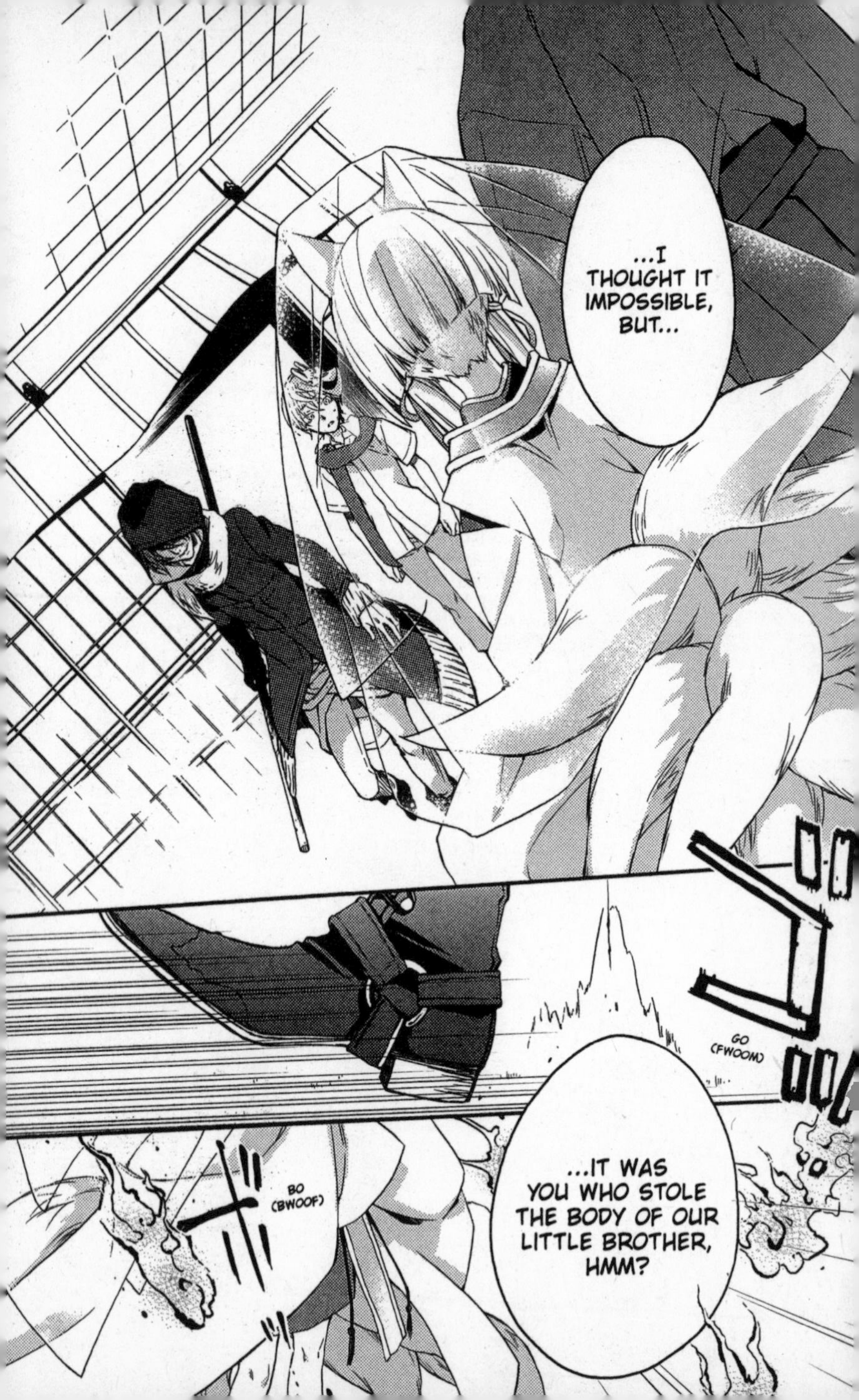
...I THOUGHT IT IMPOSSIBLE, BUT...
GO (FWOOM)
...IT WAS YOU WHO STOLE THE BODY OF OUR LITTLE BROTHER, HMM?
BO (BWOOF)

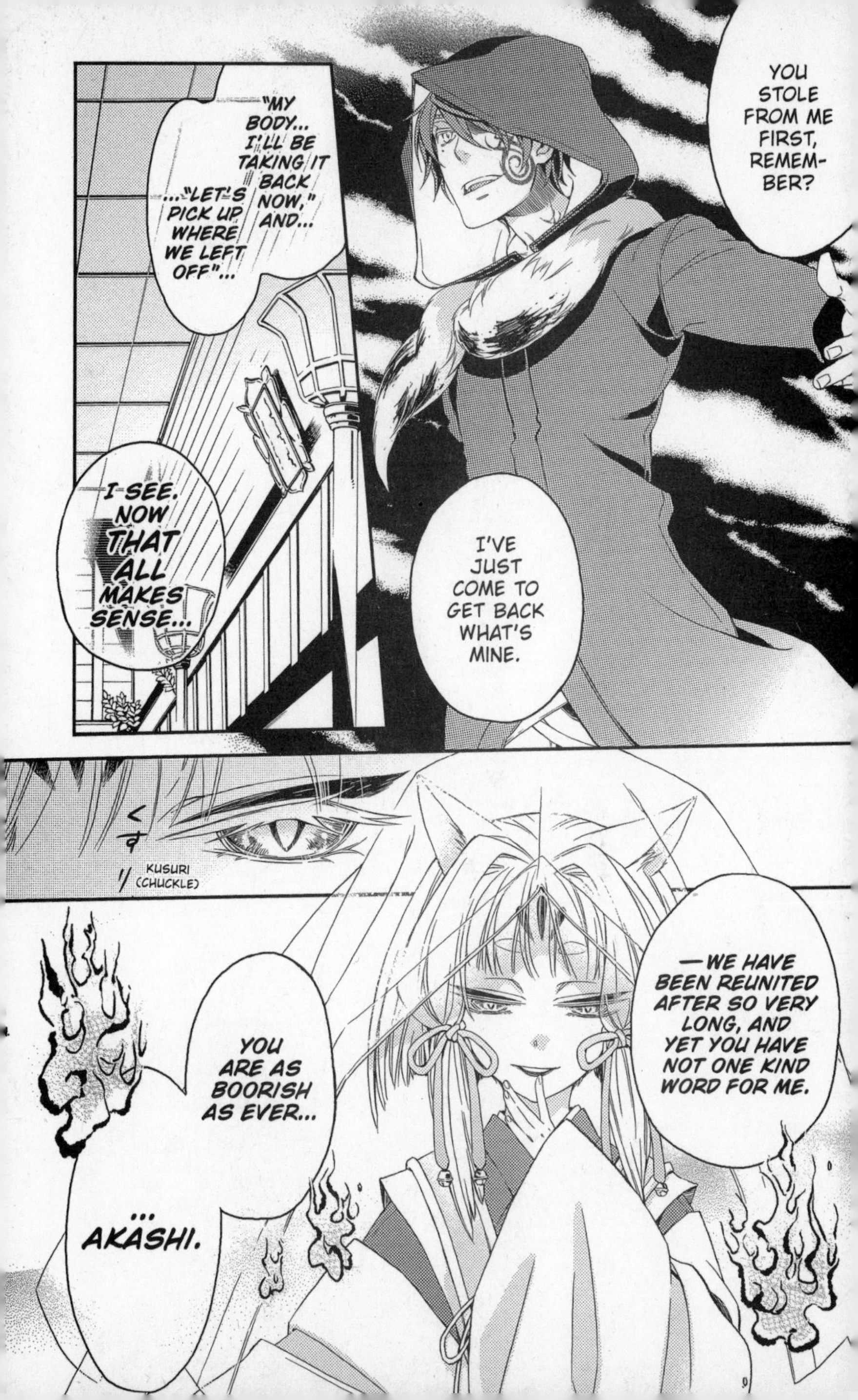
YOU STOLE FROM ME FIRST, REMEMBER?
I'VE JUST COME TO GET BACK WHAT'S MINE.
"MY BODY... I'LL BE TAKING IT BACK NOW," AND... ..."LET'S PICK UP WHERE WE LEFT OFF"...
I SEE. NOW THAT ALL MAKES SENSE...
くすり
KUSURI (CHUCKLE)
—WE HAVE BEEN REUNITED AFTER SO VERY LONG, AND YET YOU HAVE NOT ONE KIND WORD FOR ME.
YOU ARE AS BOORISH AS EVER...
...AKASHI.

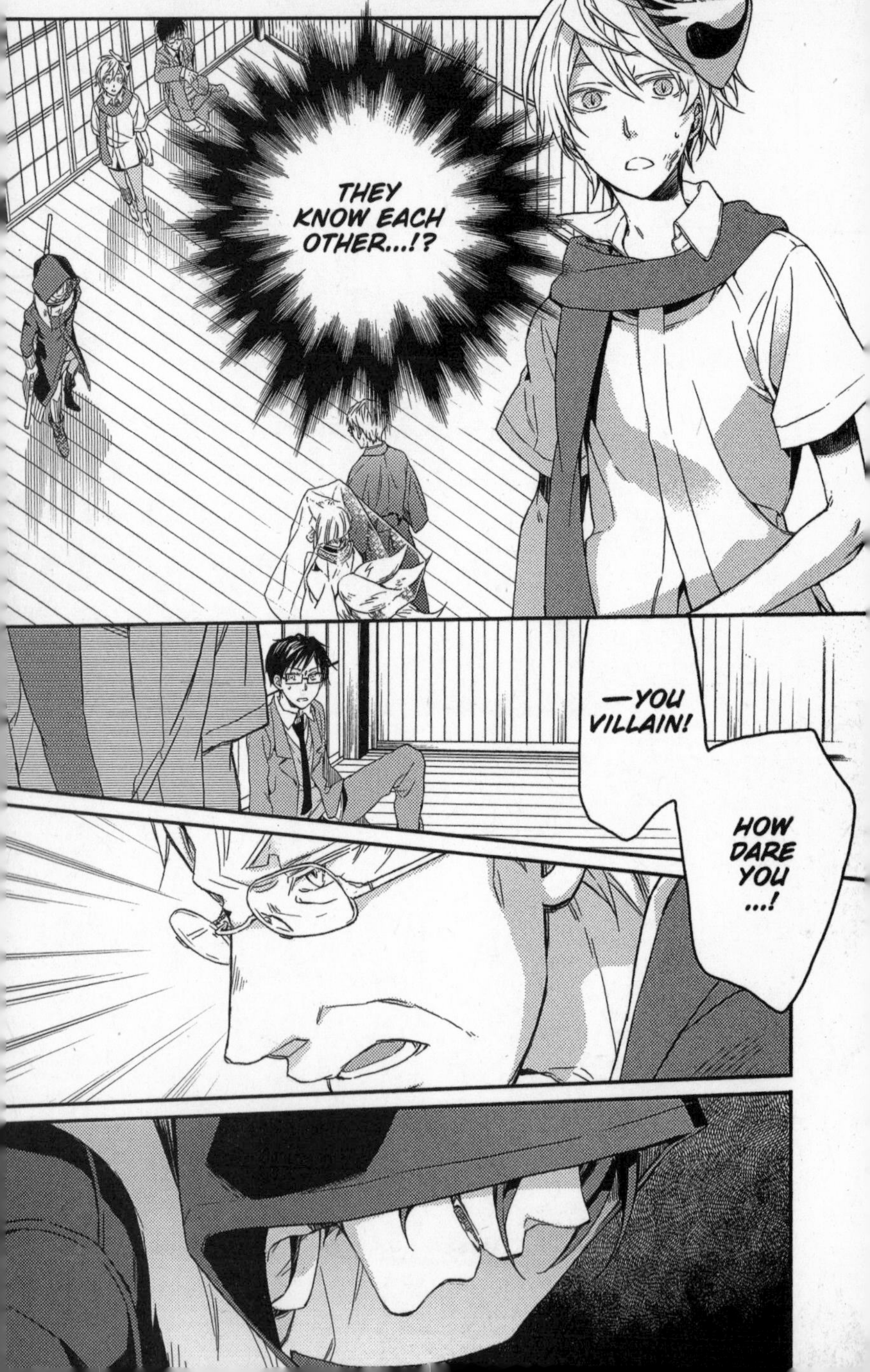
THEY KNOW EACH OTHER...!?
—YOU VILLAIN!
HOW DARE YOU ...!

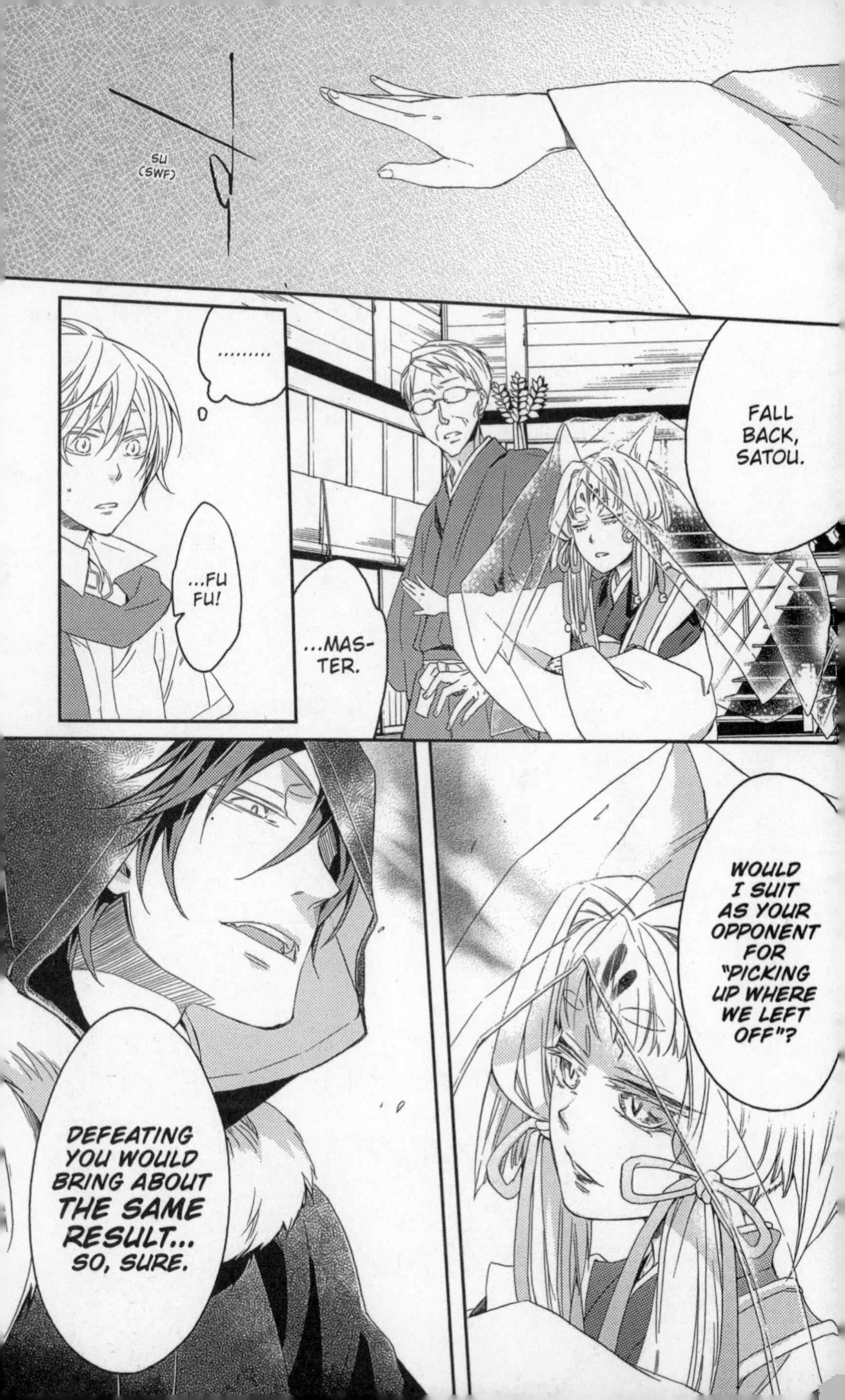
SU (SWF)
FALL BACK, SATOU.
...MAS-TER.
....
...FU FU!
WOULD I SUIT AS YOUR OPPONENT FOR "PICKING UP WHERE WE LEFT OFF"?
DEFEATING YOU WOULD BRING ABOUT THE SAME RESULT... SO, SURE.

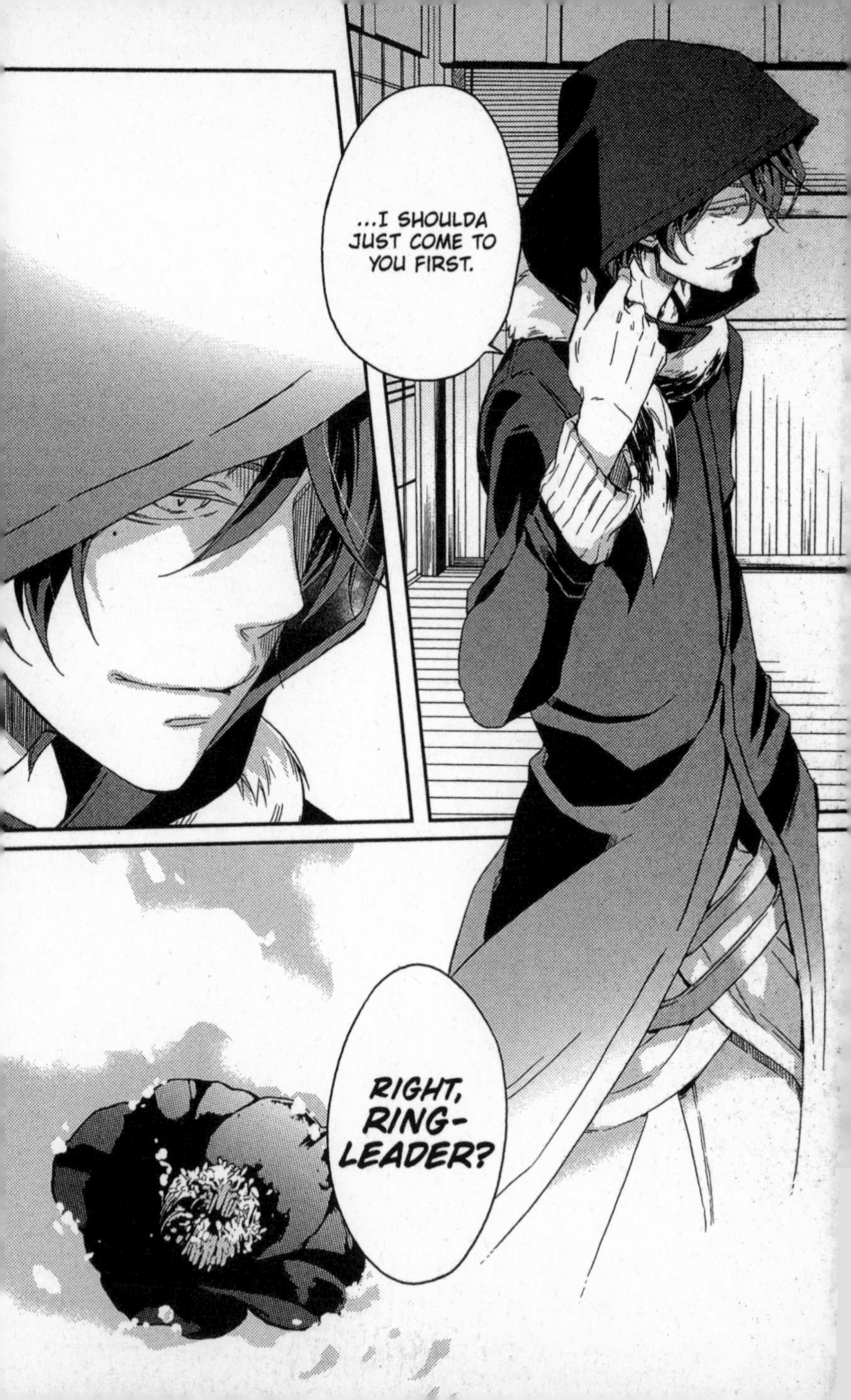
...I SHOULDA JUST COME TO YOU FIRST.
RIGHT, RING-LEADER?

Of the Red,
the Light,
and the
Ayakashi

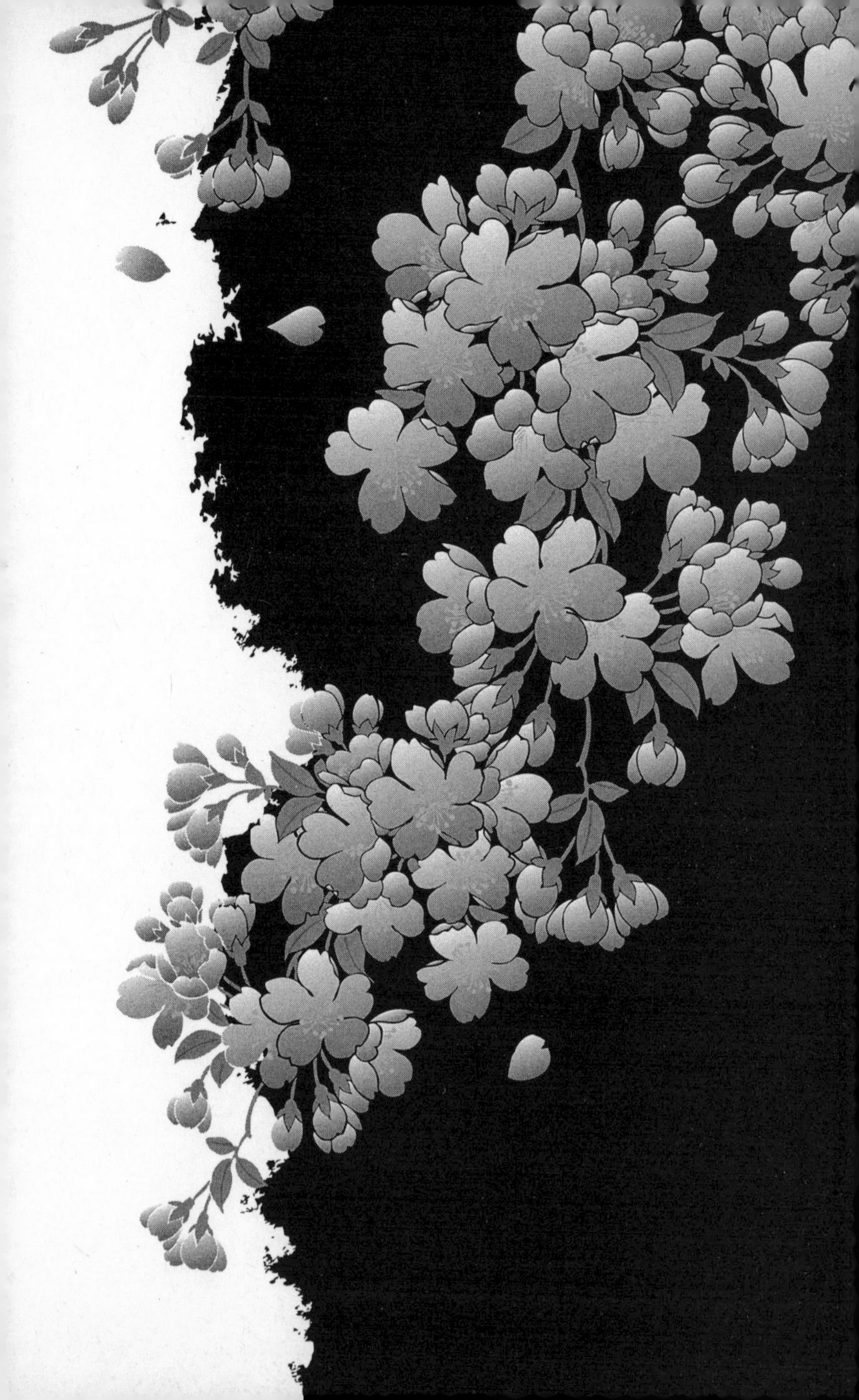

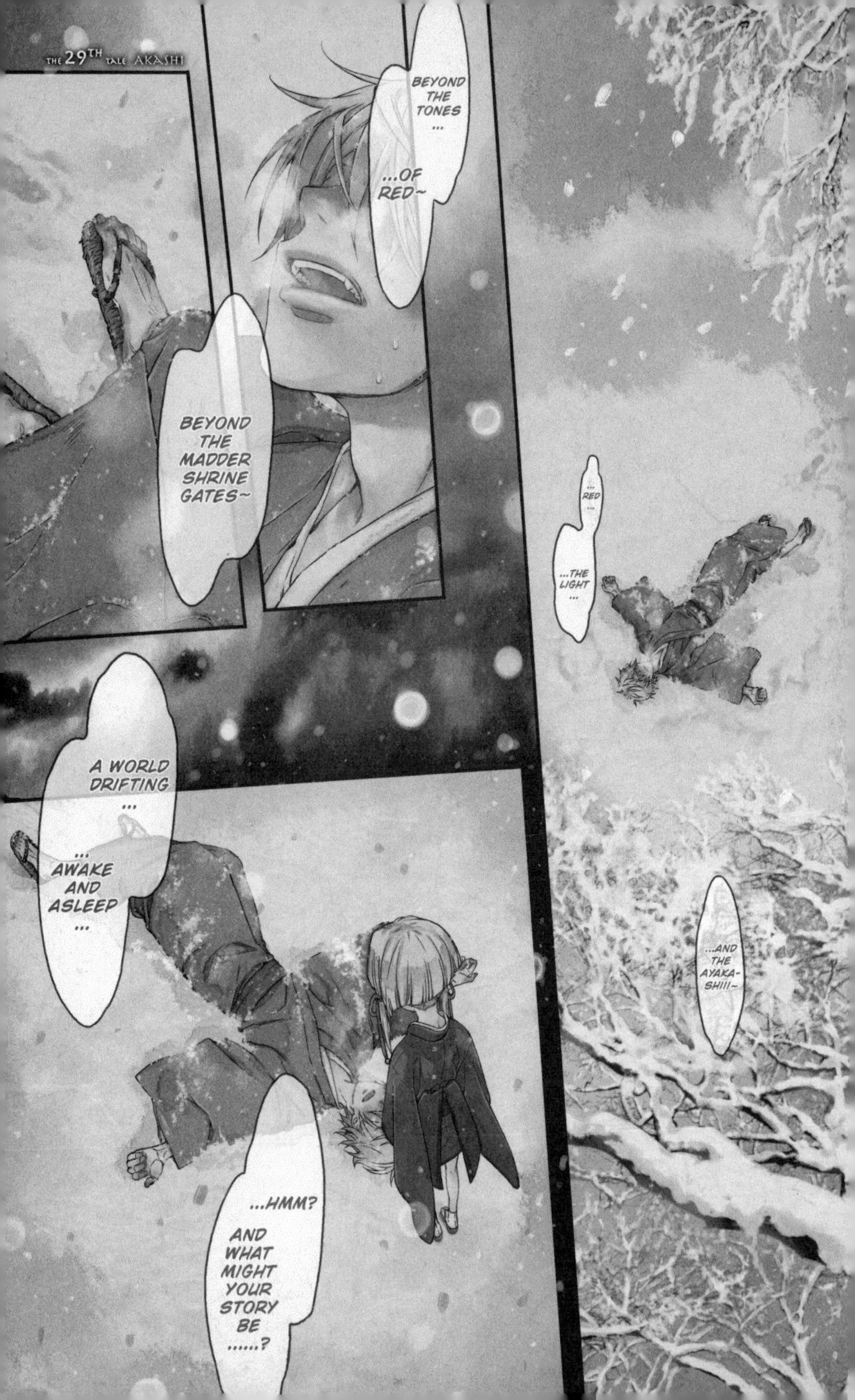
...RED...
...THE LIGHT...
...AND THE AYAKA-SHIII~
BEYOND THE TONES...
...OF RED~
BEYOND THE MADDER SHRINE GATES~
A WORLD DRIFTING...
...AWAKE AND ASLEEP...
...HMM?
AND WHAT MIGHT YOUR STORY BE ......?

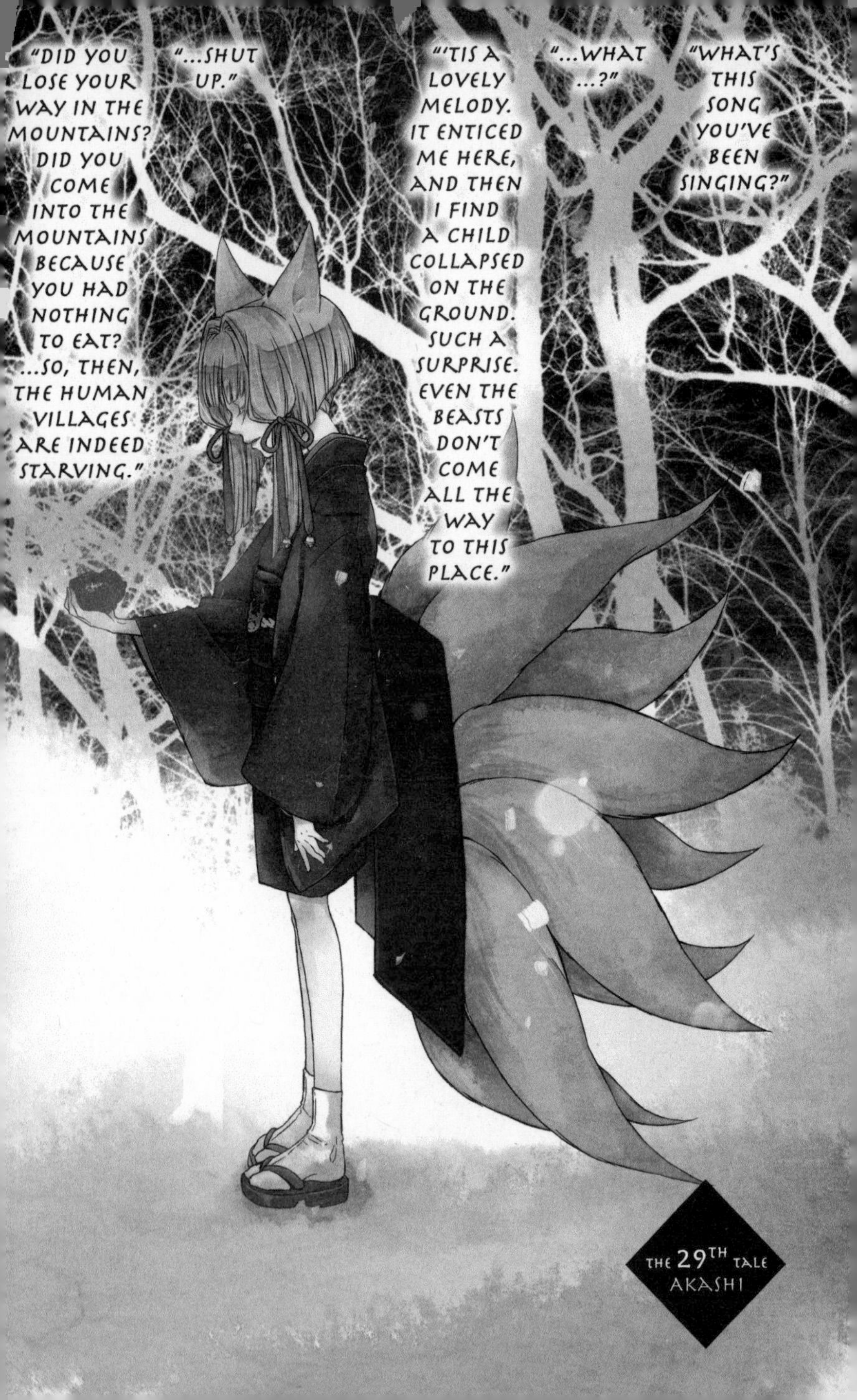
"WHAT'S THIS SONG YOU'VE BEEN SINGING?"
"...WHAT ...?"
"'TIS A LOVELY MELODY. IT ENTICED ME HERE, AND THEN I FIND A CHILD COLLAPSED ON THE GROUND. SUCH A SURPRISE. EVEN THE BEASTS DON'T COME ALL THE WAY TO THIS PLACE."
"...SHUT UP."
"DID YOU LOSE YOUR WAY IN THE MOUNTAINS? DID YOU COME INTO THE MOUNTAINS BECAUSE YOU HAD NOTHING TO EAT? ...SO, THEN, THE HUMAN VILLAGES ARE INDEED STARVING."
THE 29TH TALE
AKASHI

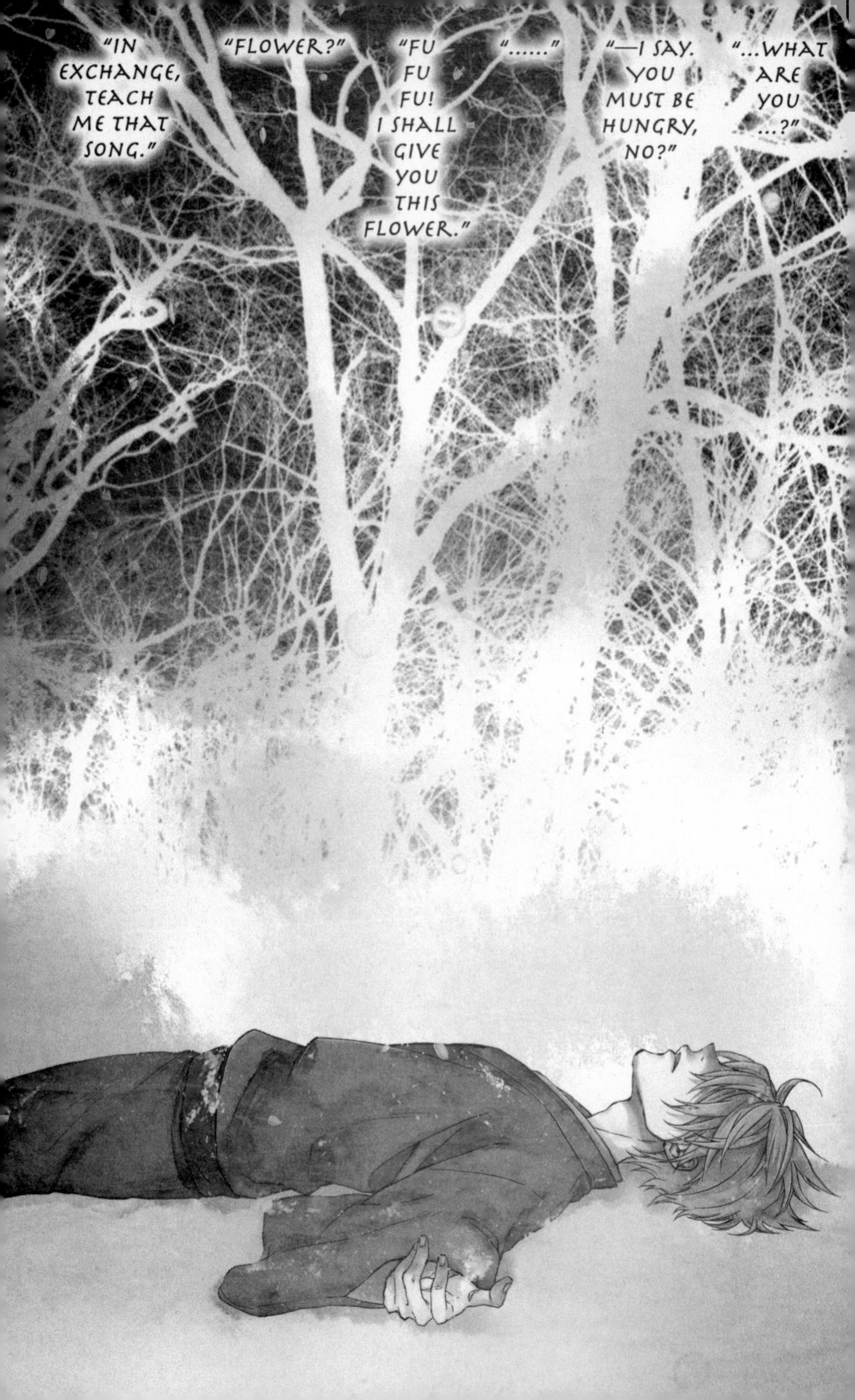
"...WHAT ARE YOU ...?"
"—I SAY. YOU MUST BE HUNGRY, NO?"
"......"
"FU FU FU! I SHALL GIVE YOU THIS FLOWER."
"FLOWER?"
"IN EXCHANGE, TEACH ME THAT SONG."

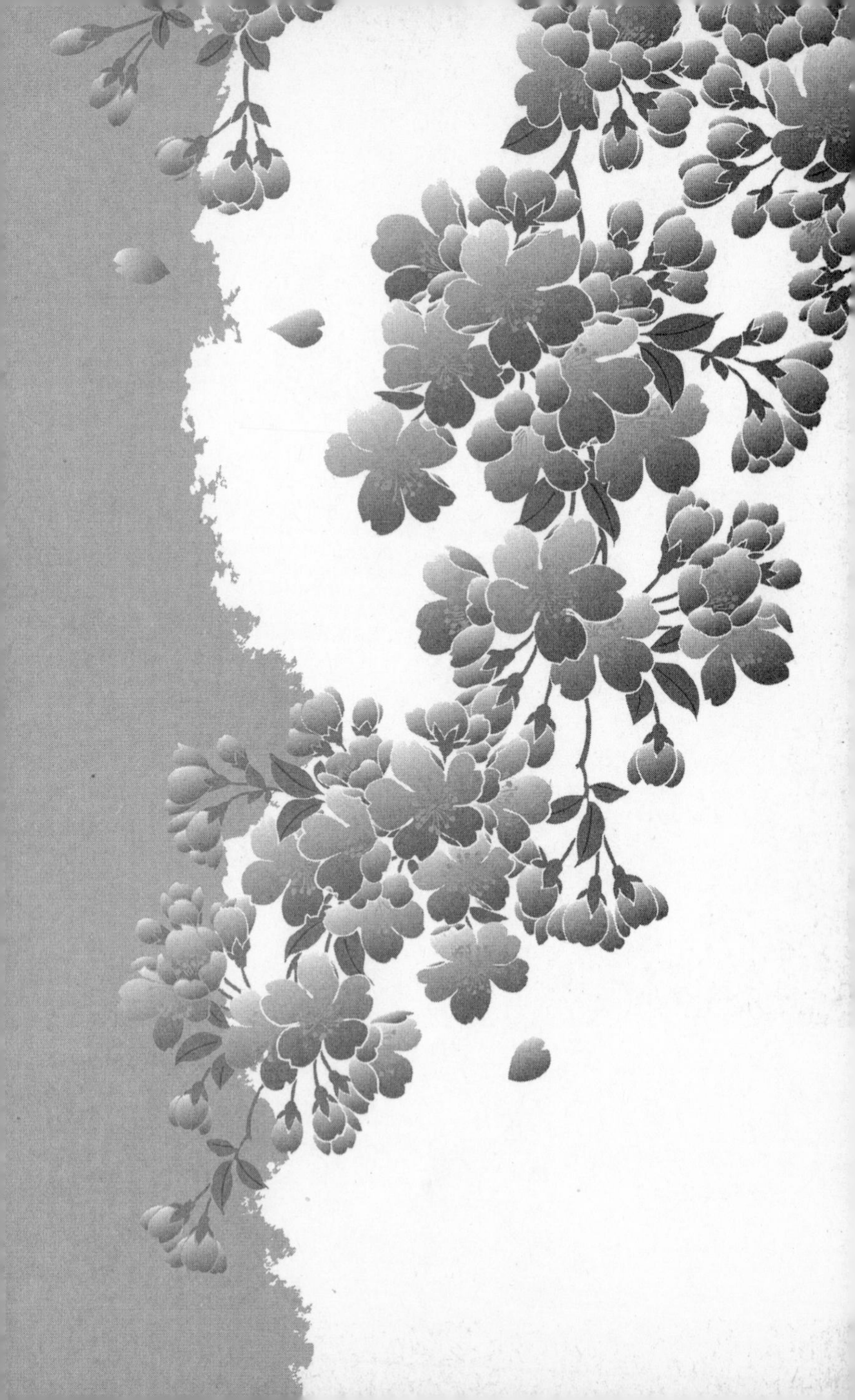

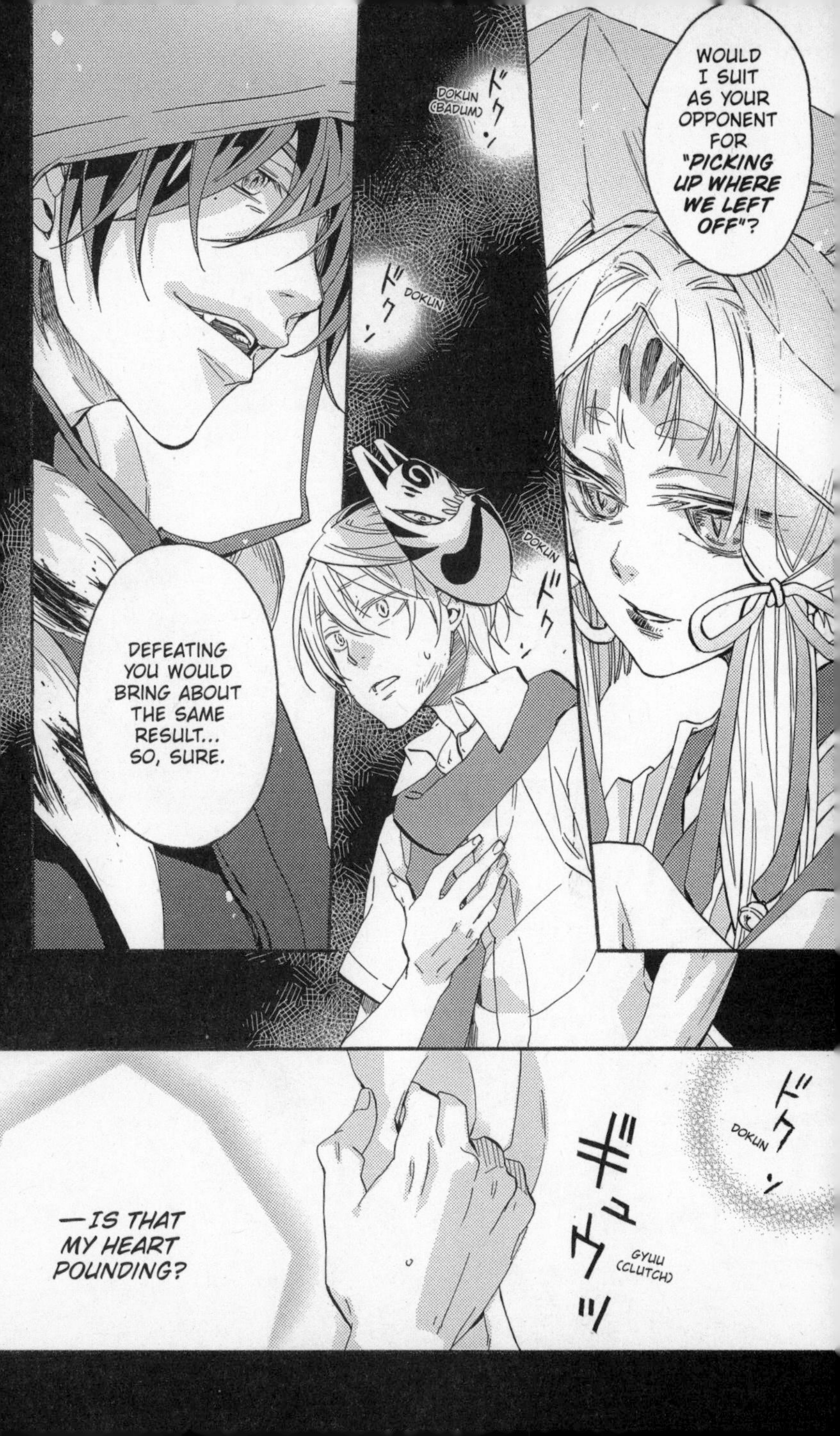
WOULD I SUIT AS YOUR OPPONENT FOR "PICKING UP WHERE WE LEFT OFF"?
ドクン
DOKUN (BADUM)
ドクン
DOKUN
ドクン
DOKUN
DEFEATING YOU WOULD BRING ABOUT THE SAME RESULT... SO, SURE.
ドクン
DOKUN
ギュウッ
GYUU (CLUTCH)
—IS THAT MY HEART POUNDING?

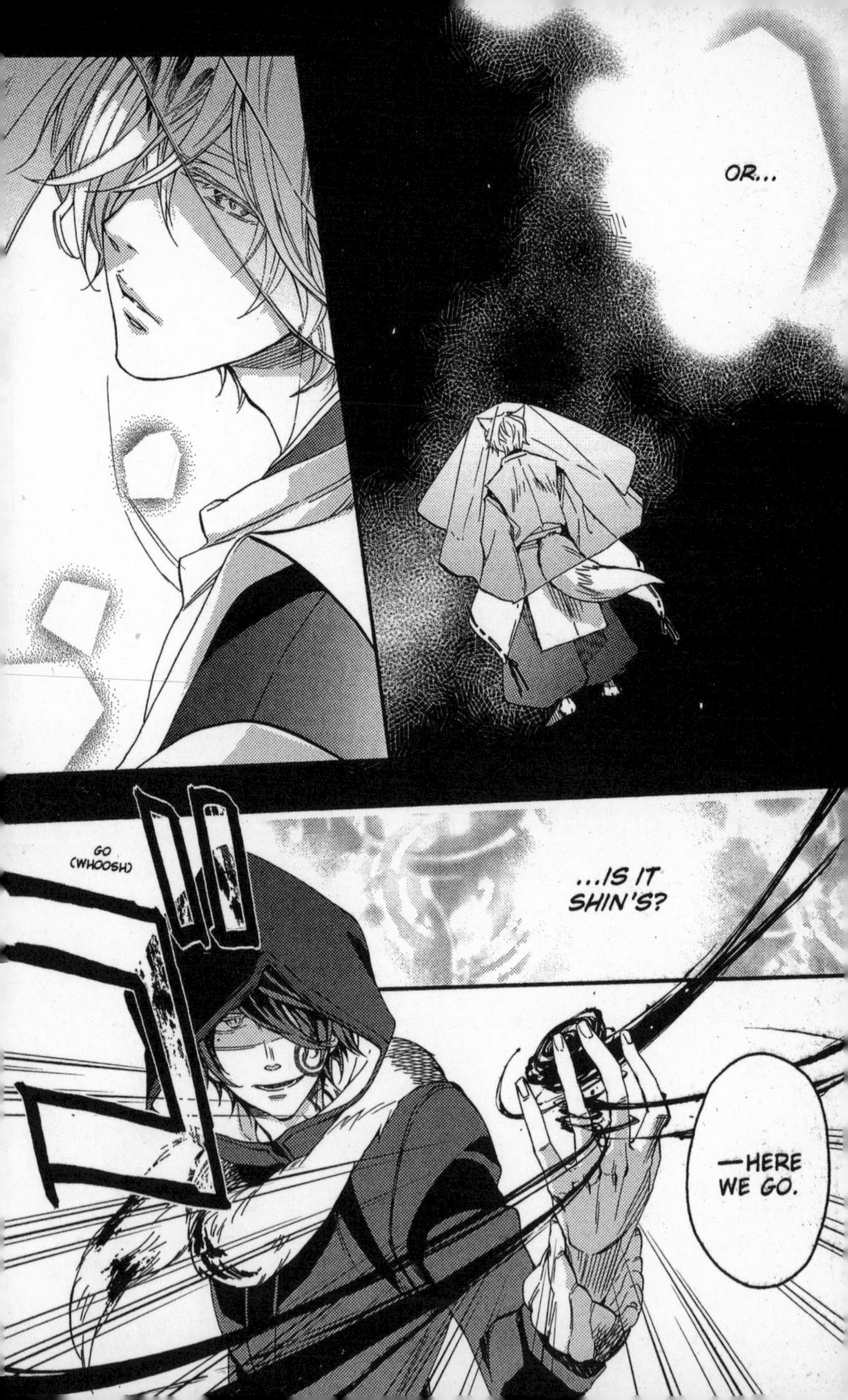
OR...
...IS IT SHIN'S?
—HERE WE GO.
GO (WHOOSH)

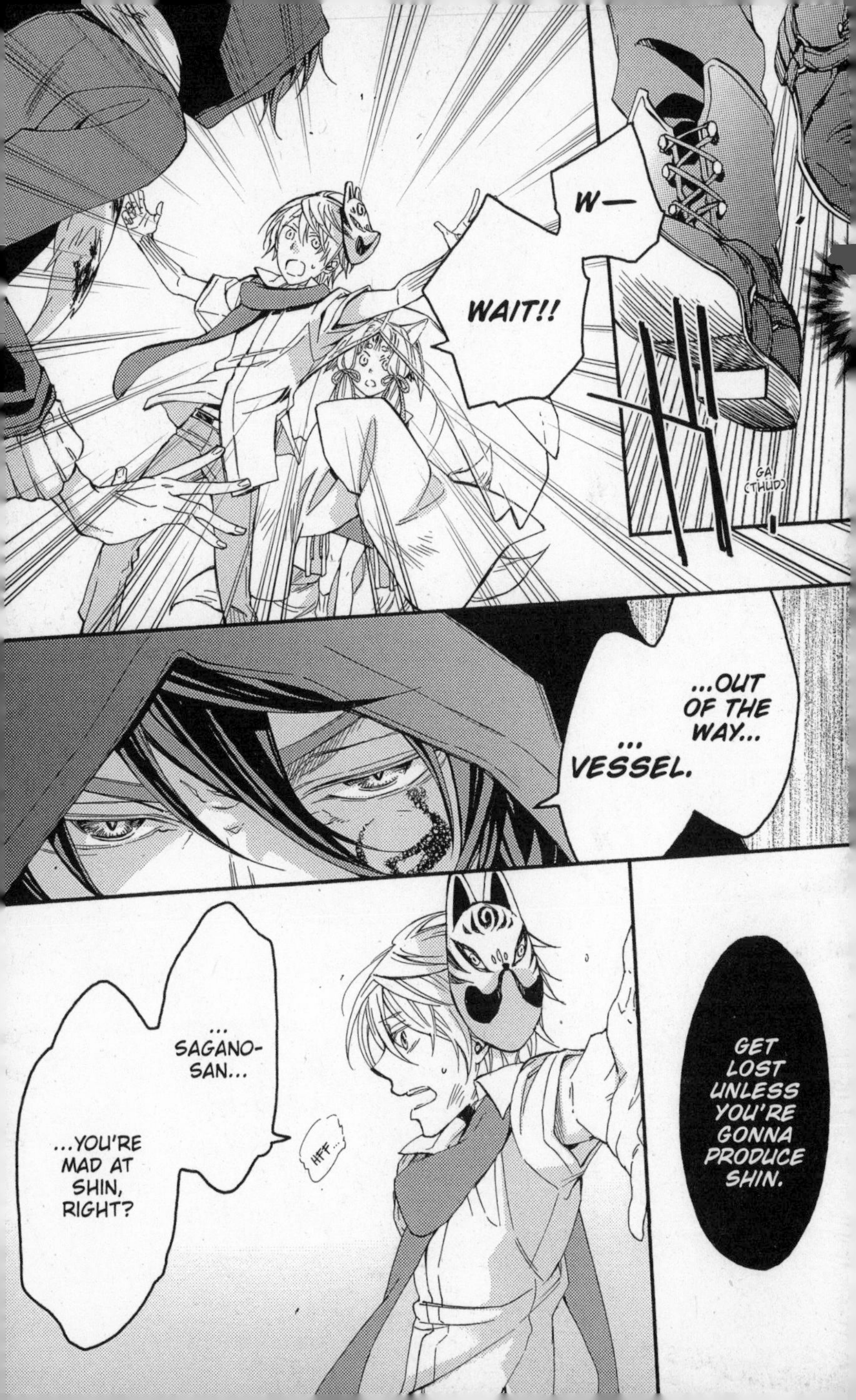
W—
WAIT!!
GA (THUD)
...OUT OF THE WAY...
... VESSEL.
GET LOST UNLESS YOU'RE GONNA PRODUCE SHIN.
HFF...
... SAGANO-SAN...
...YOU'RE MAD AT SHIN, RIGHT?

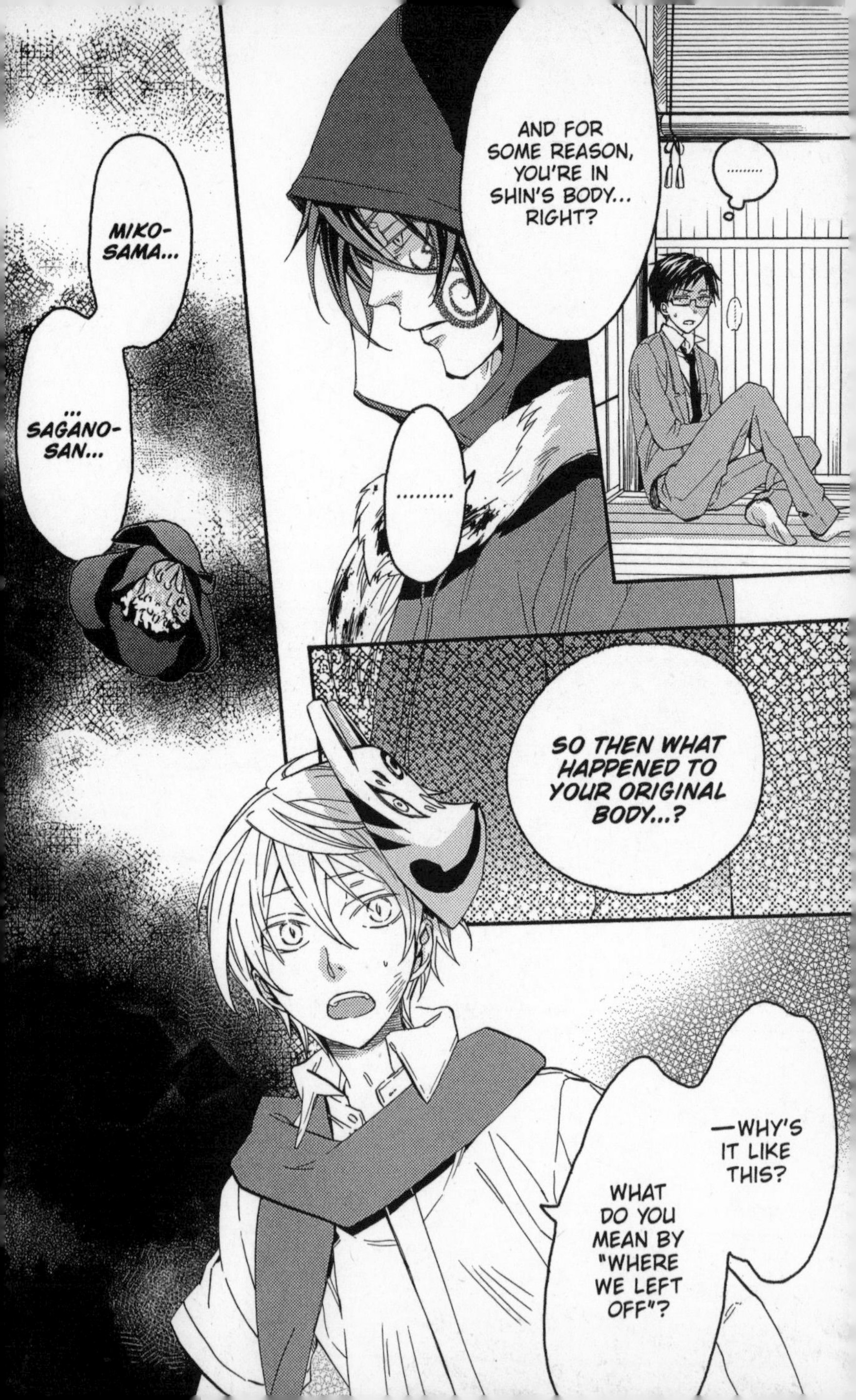
....
AND FOR SOME REASON, YOU'RE IN SHIN'S BODY... RIGHT?
....
SO THEN WHAT HAPPENED TO YOUR ORIGINAL BODY...?
—WHY'S IT LIKE THIS?
WHAT DO YOU MEAN BY "WHERE WE LEFT OFF"?
MIKO-SAMA...
...SAGANO-SAN...

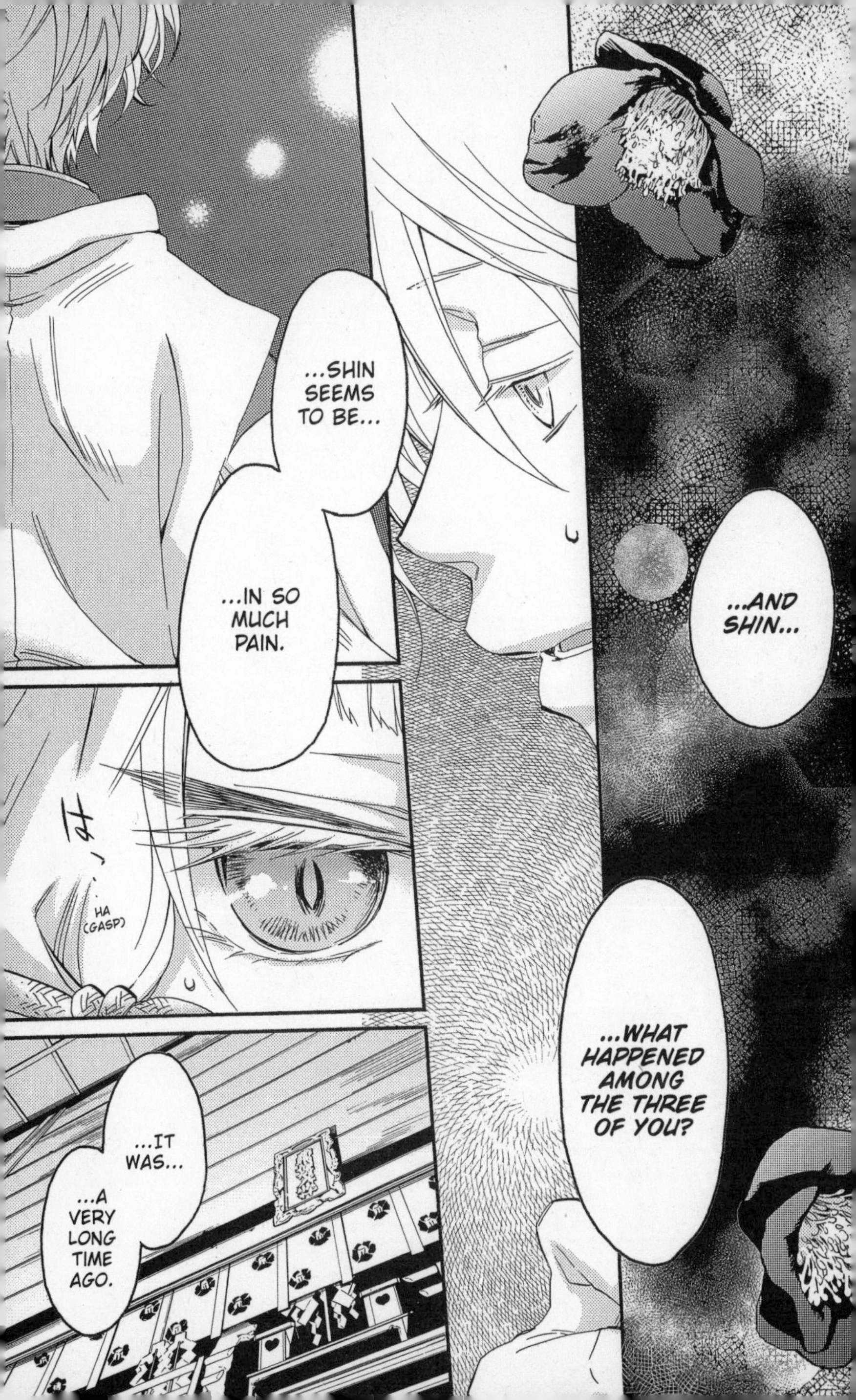
...AND SHIN...
...WHAT HAPPENED AMONG THE THREE OF YOU?
...SHIN SEEMS TO BE...
...IN SO MUCH PAIN.
HA (GASP)
...IT WAS...
...A VERY LONG TIME AGO.

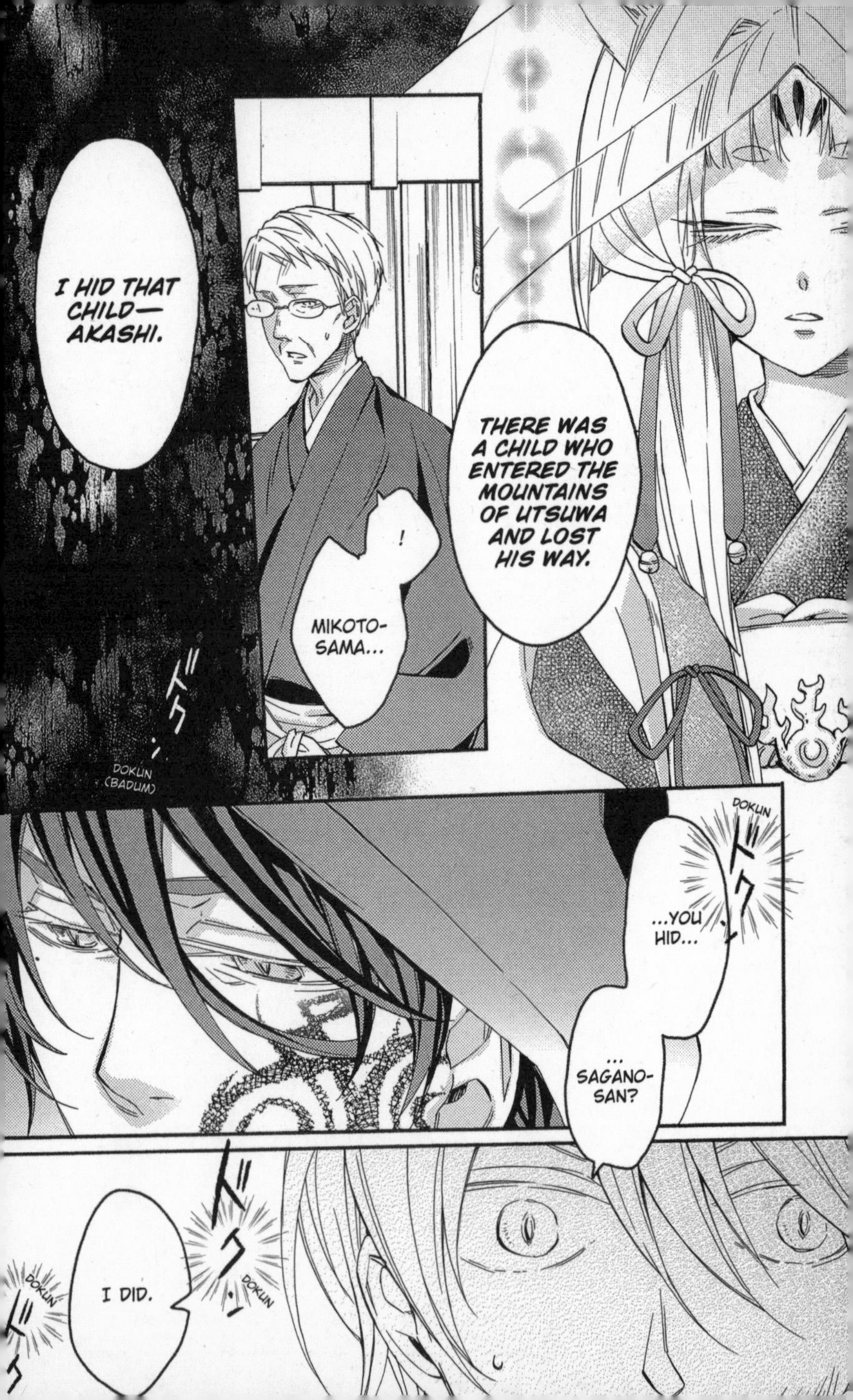
THERE WAS A CHILD WHO ENTERED THE MOUNTAINS OF UTSUWA AND LOST HIS WAY.
!
MIKOTO-SAMA...
I HID THAT CHILD—AKASHI.
DOKUN (BADUM)
DOKUN
...YOU HID...
...SAGANO-SAN?
DOKUN
I DID.
DOKUN

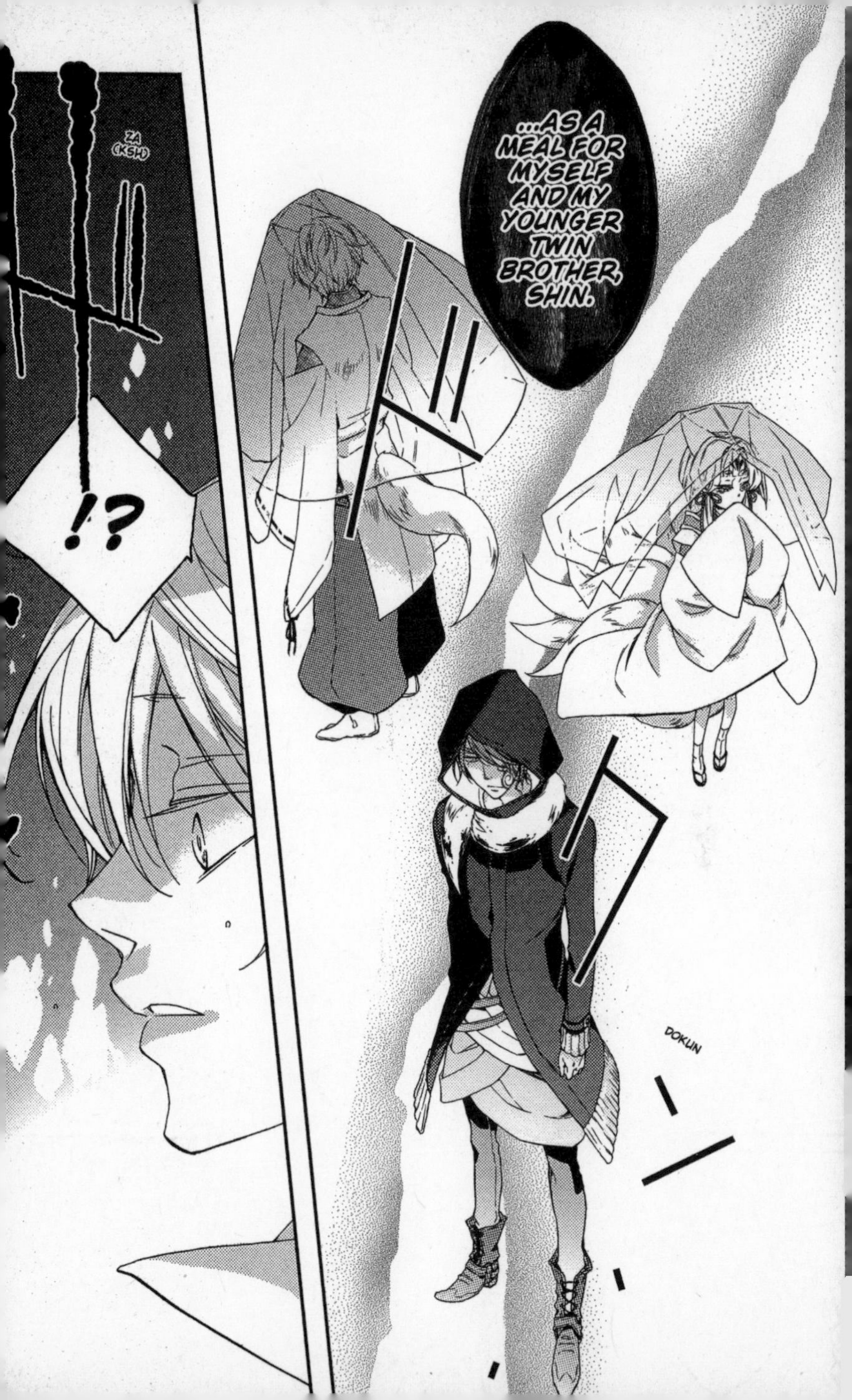
...AS A MEAL FOR MYSELF AND MY YOUNGER TWIN BROTHER, SHIN.
DOKUN
ZA (KSH)
!?

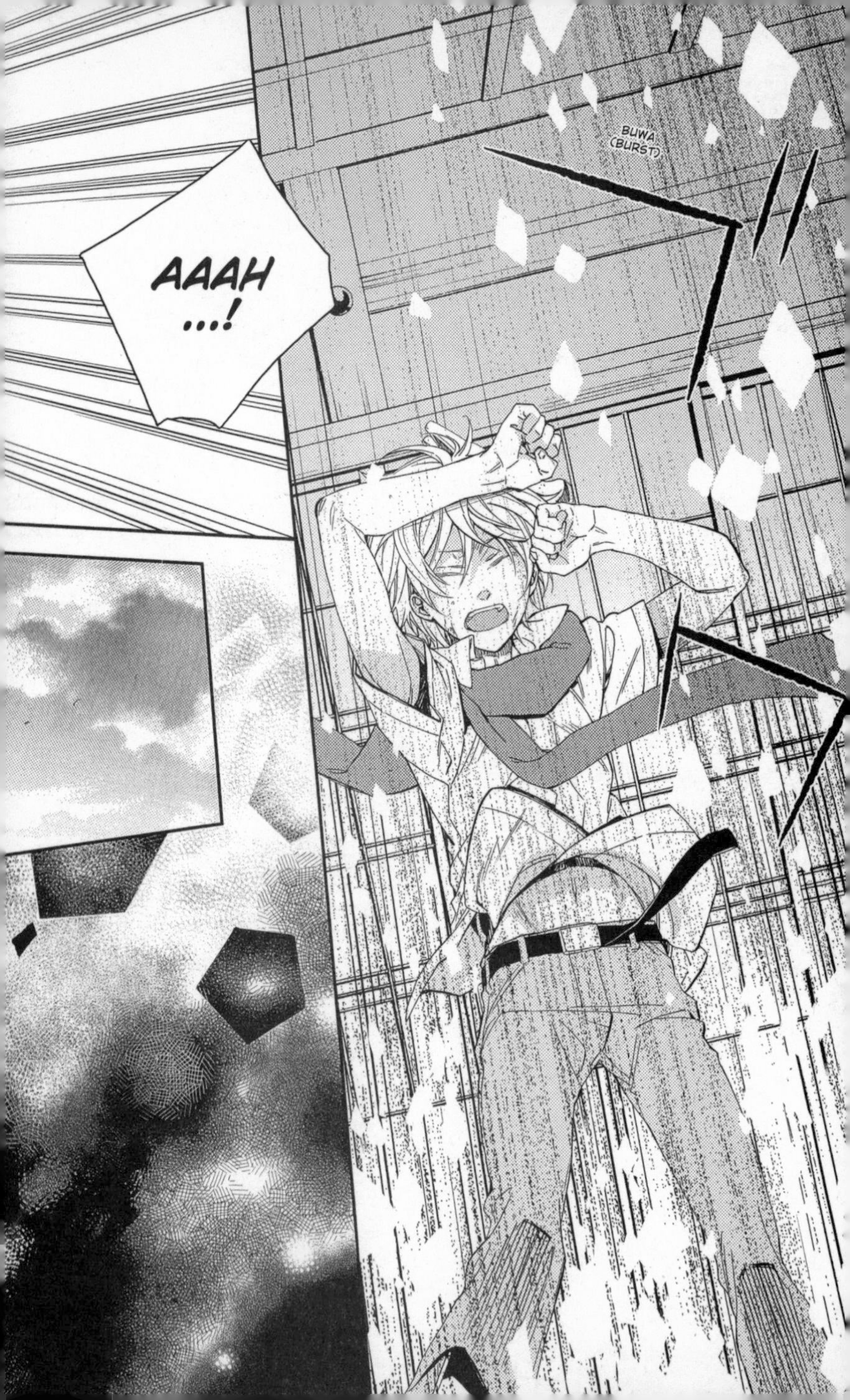
BUWA
(BURST)
AAAH ...!

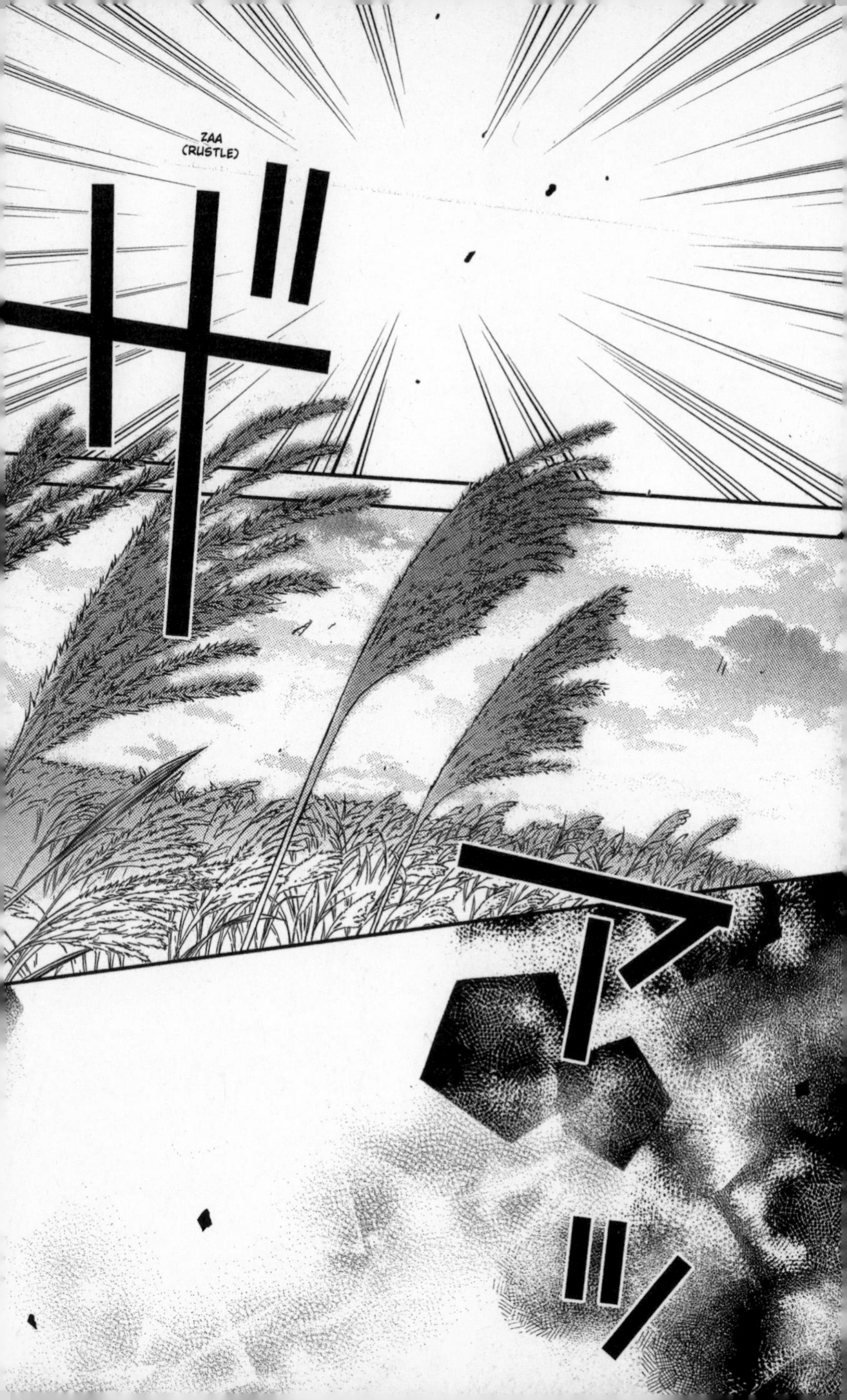
ZAA
(RUSTLE)

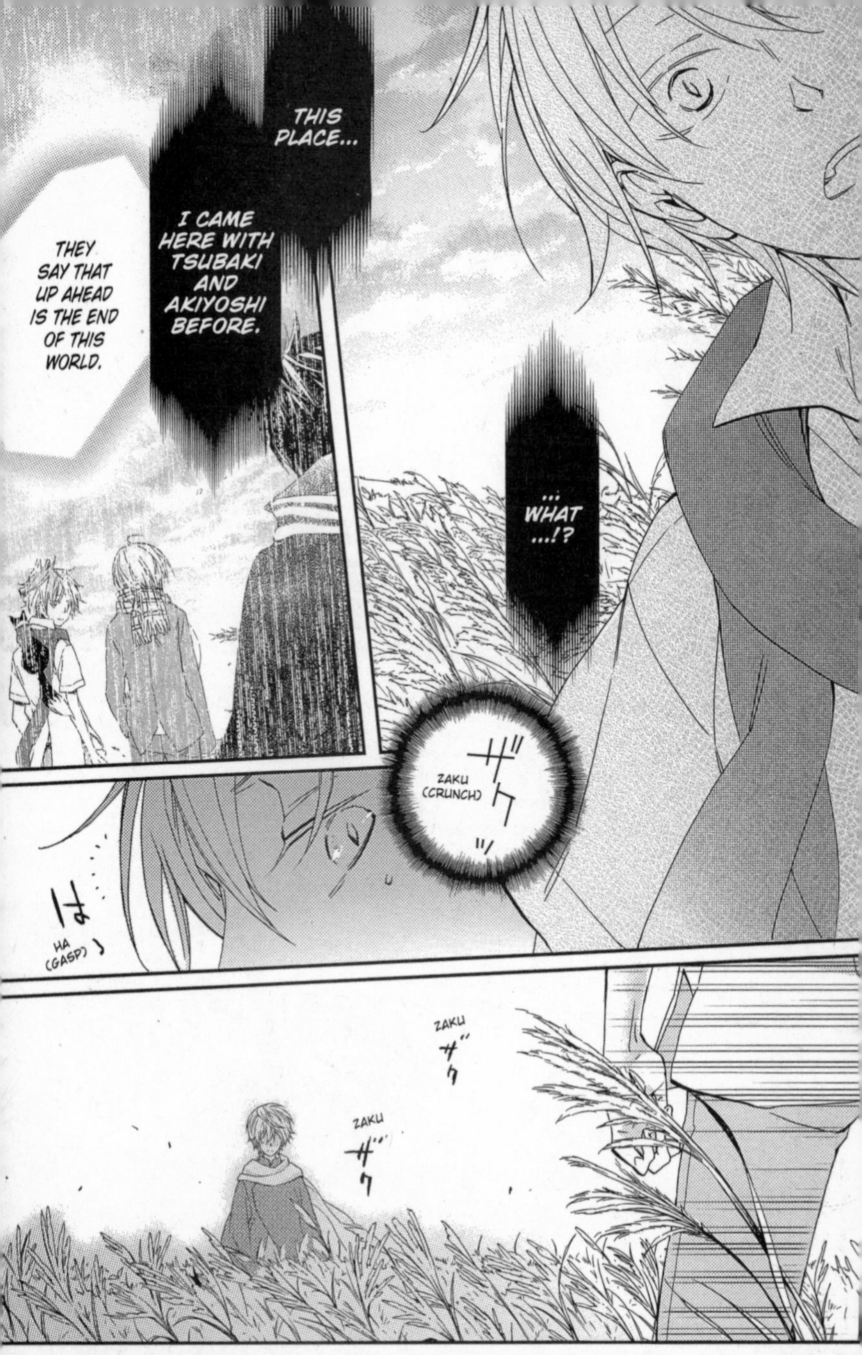
THIS PLACE...
I CAME HERE WITH TSUBAKI AND AKIYOSHI BEFORE.
THEY SAY THAT UP AHEAD IS THE END OF THIS WORLD.
...WHAT ...!?
ザクッ
ZAKU (CRUNCH)
は
HA (GASP)
ザク
ZAKU
ザク
ZAKU

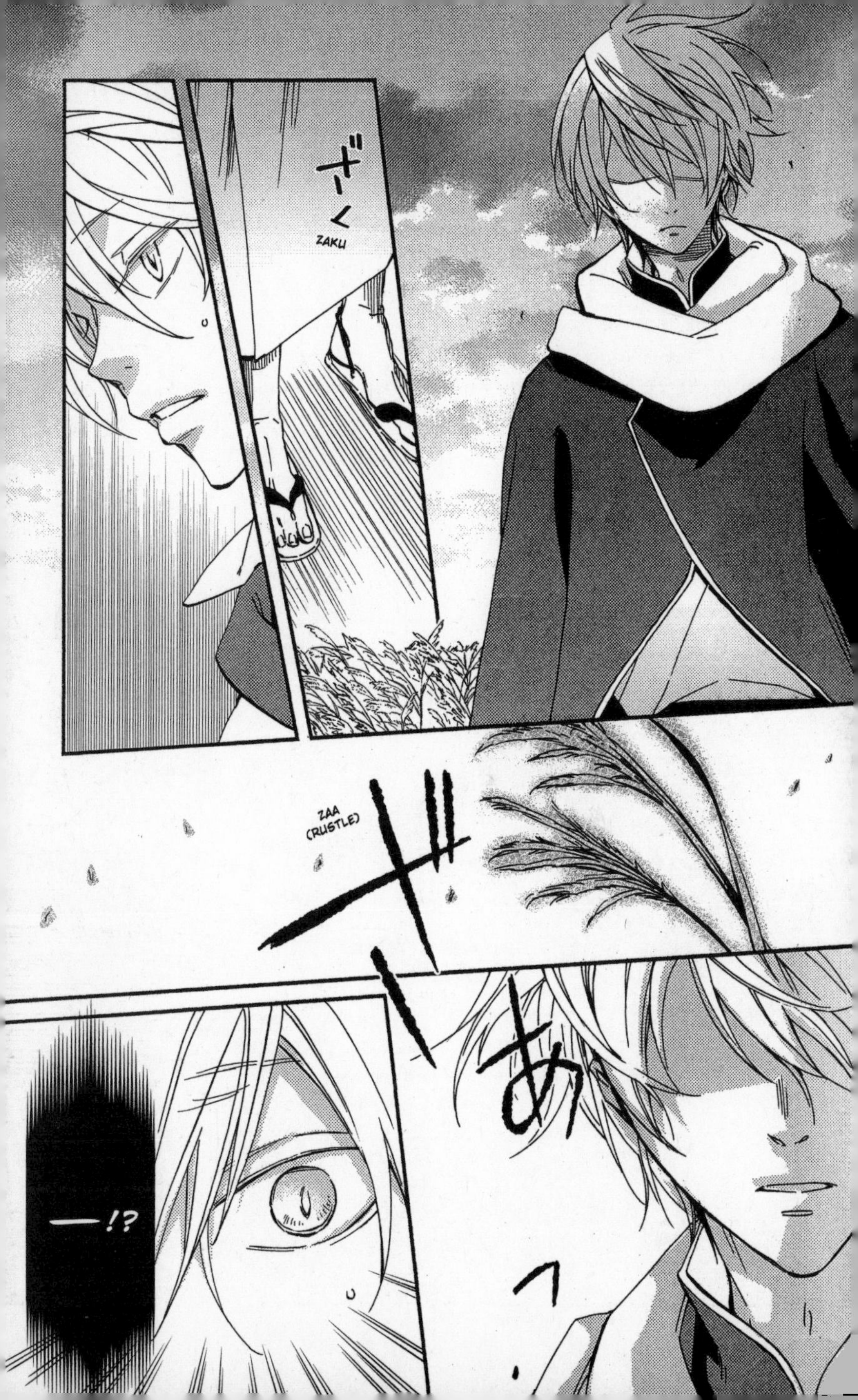
ザく
ZAKU
ザー
ZAA
(RUSTLE)
あっ
—!?

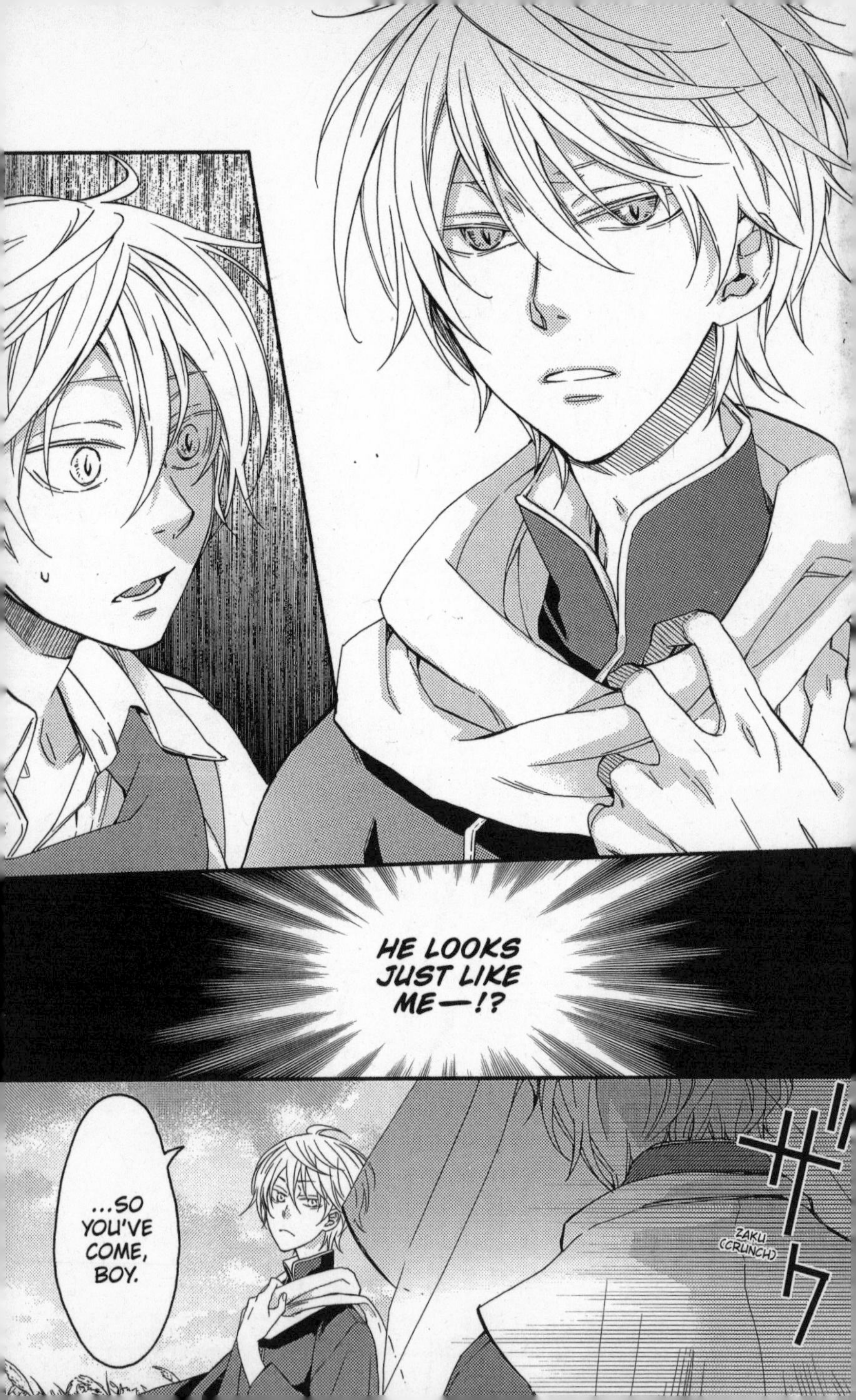
HE LOOKS JUST LIKE ME—!?
ZAKU (CRUNCH)
...SO YOU'VE COME, BOY.

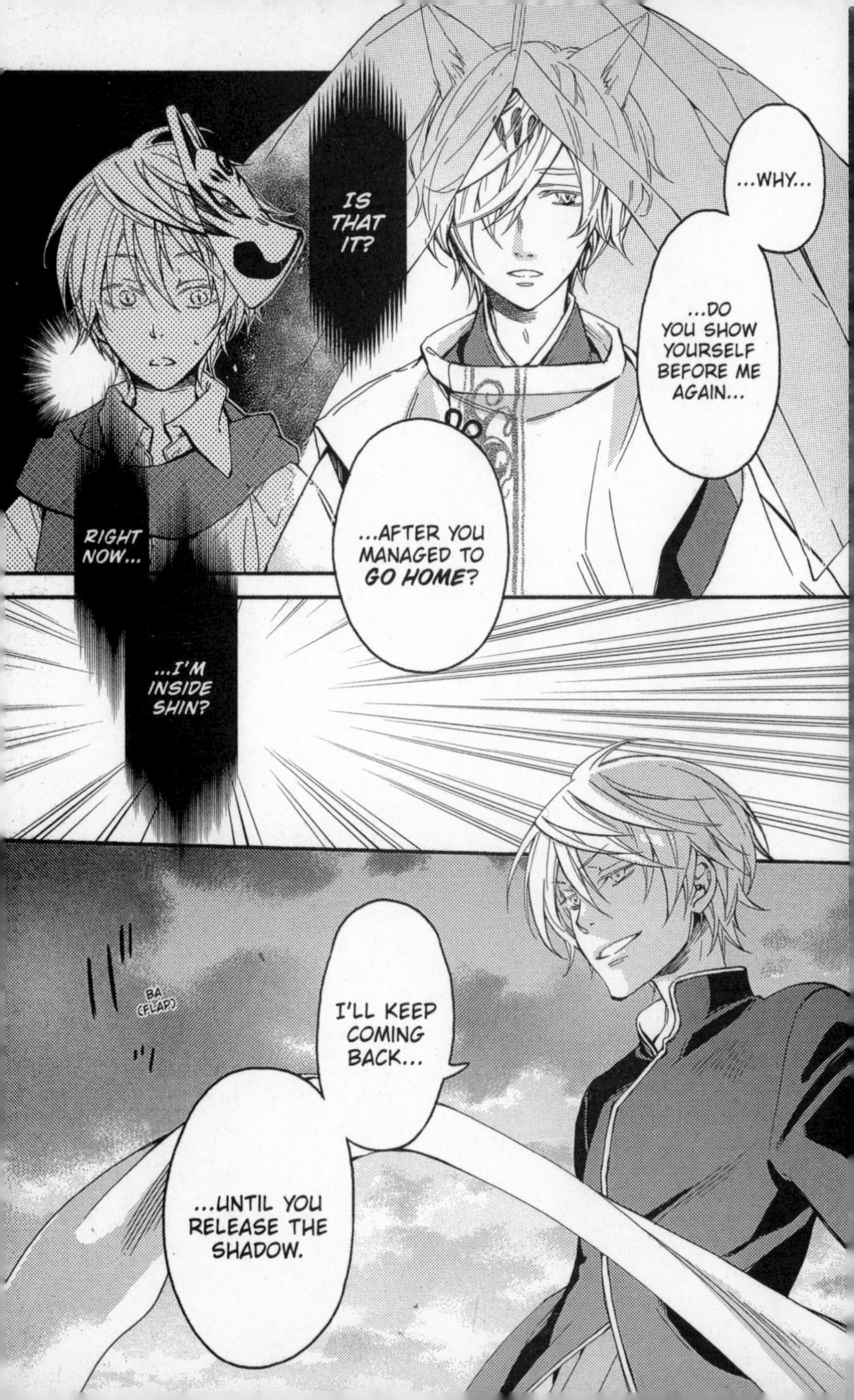
...WHY...
...DO YOU SHOW YOURSELF BEFORE ME AGAIN...
...AFTER YOU MANAGED TO GO HOME?
IS THAT IT?
RIGHT NOW...
...I'M INSIDE SHIN?
I'LL KEEP COMING BACK...
...UNTIL YOU RELEASE THE SHADOW.
BA (FLAP)

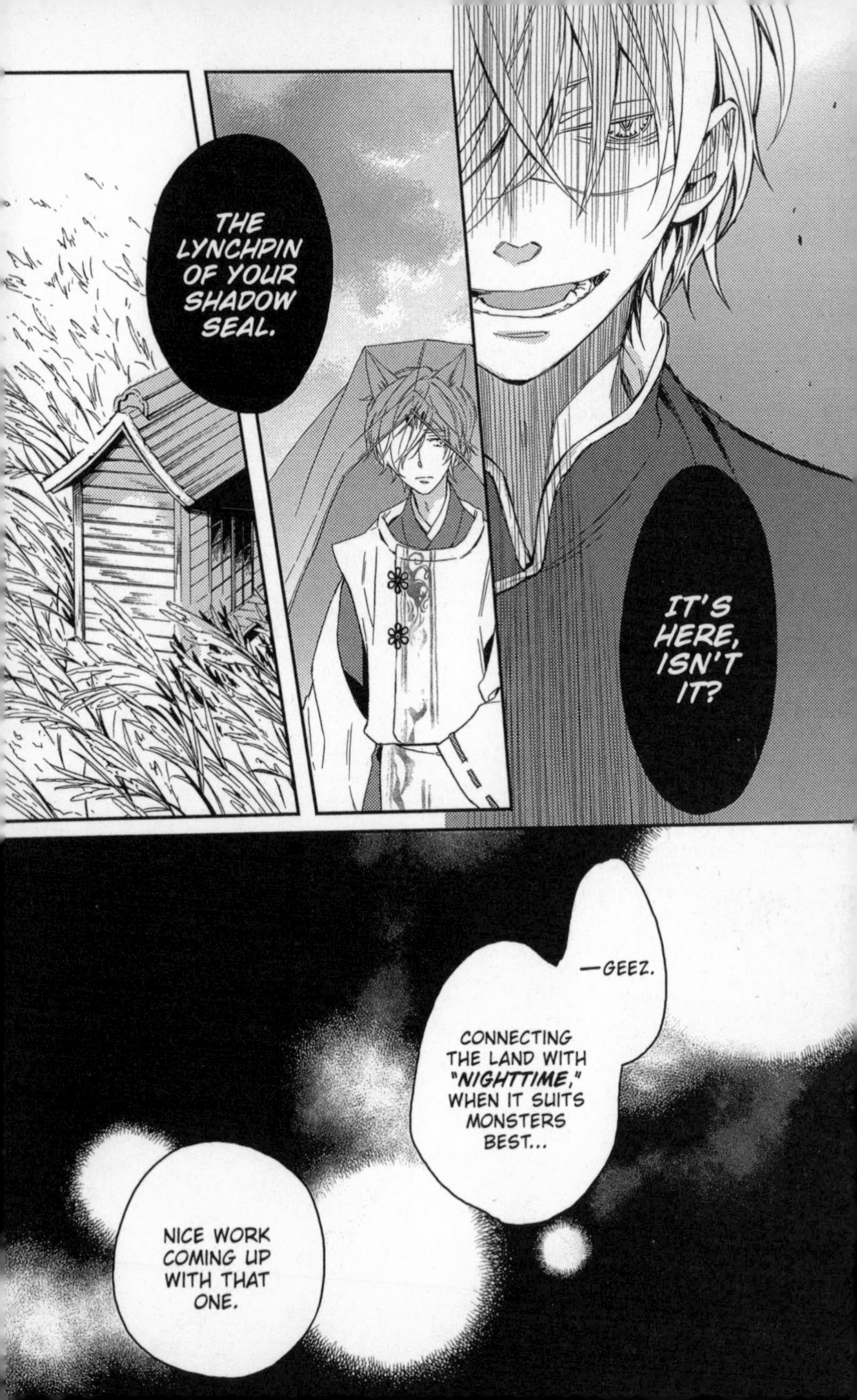
IT'S HERE, ISN'T IT?
THE LYNCHPIN OF YOUR SHADOW SEAL.
—GEEZ.
CONNECTING THE LAND WITH "NIGHTTIME," WHEN IT SUITS MONSTERS BEST...
NICE WORK COMING UP WITH THAT ONE.

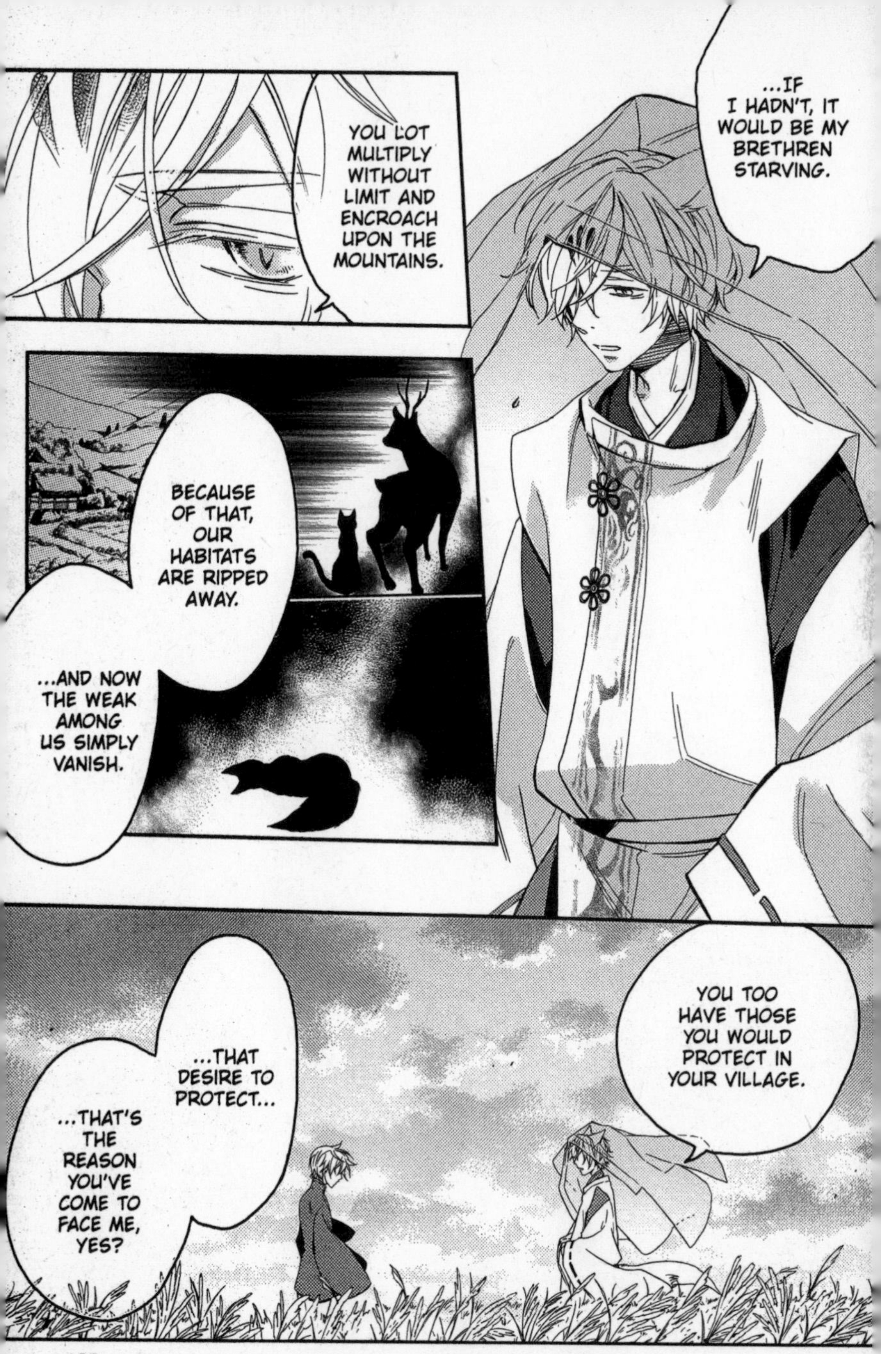
...IF I HADN'T, IT WOULD BE MY BRETHREN STARVING.
YOU LOT MULTIPLY WITHOUT LIMIT AND ENCROACH UPON THE MOUNTAINS.
BECAUSE OF THAT, OUR HABITATS ARE RIPPED AWAY.
...AND NOW THE WEAK AMONG US SIMPLY VANISH.
YOU TOO HAVE THOSE YOU WOULD PROTECT IN YOUR VILLAGE.
...THAT DESIRE TO PROTECT...
...THAT'S THE REASON YOU'VE COME TO FACE ME, YES?

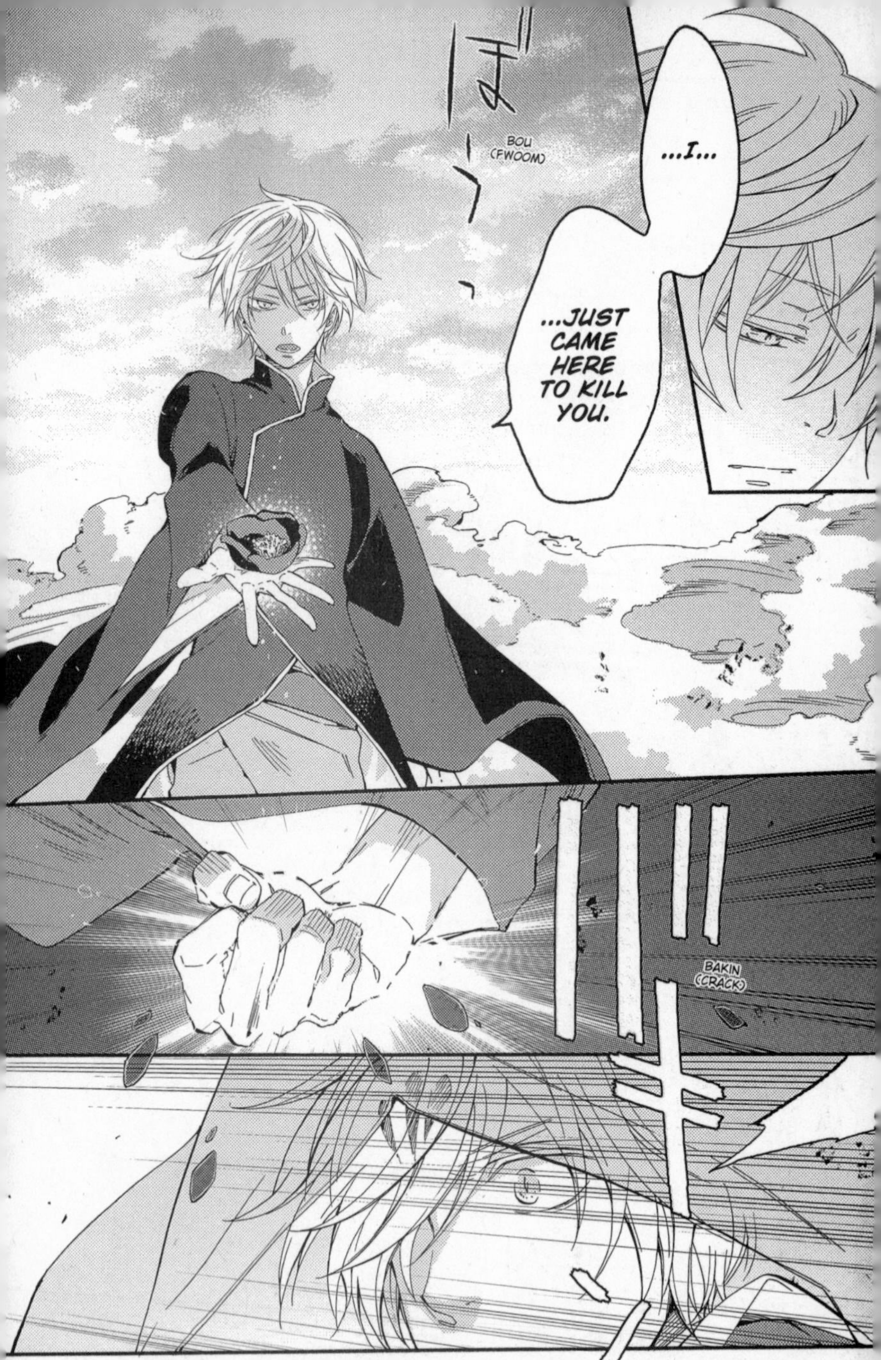
...I...
...JUST CAME HERE TO KILL YOU.
BOU (FWOOM)
BAKIN (CRACK)

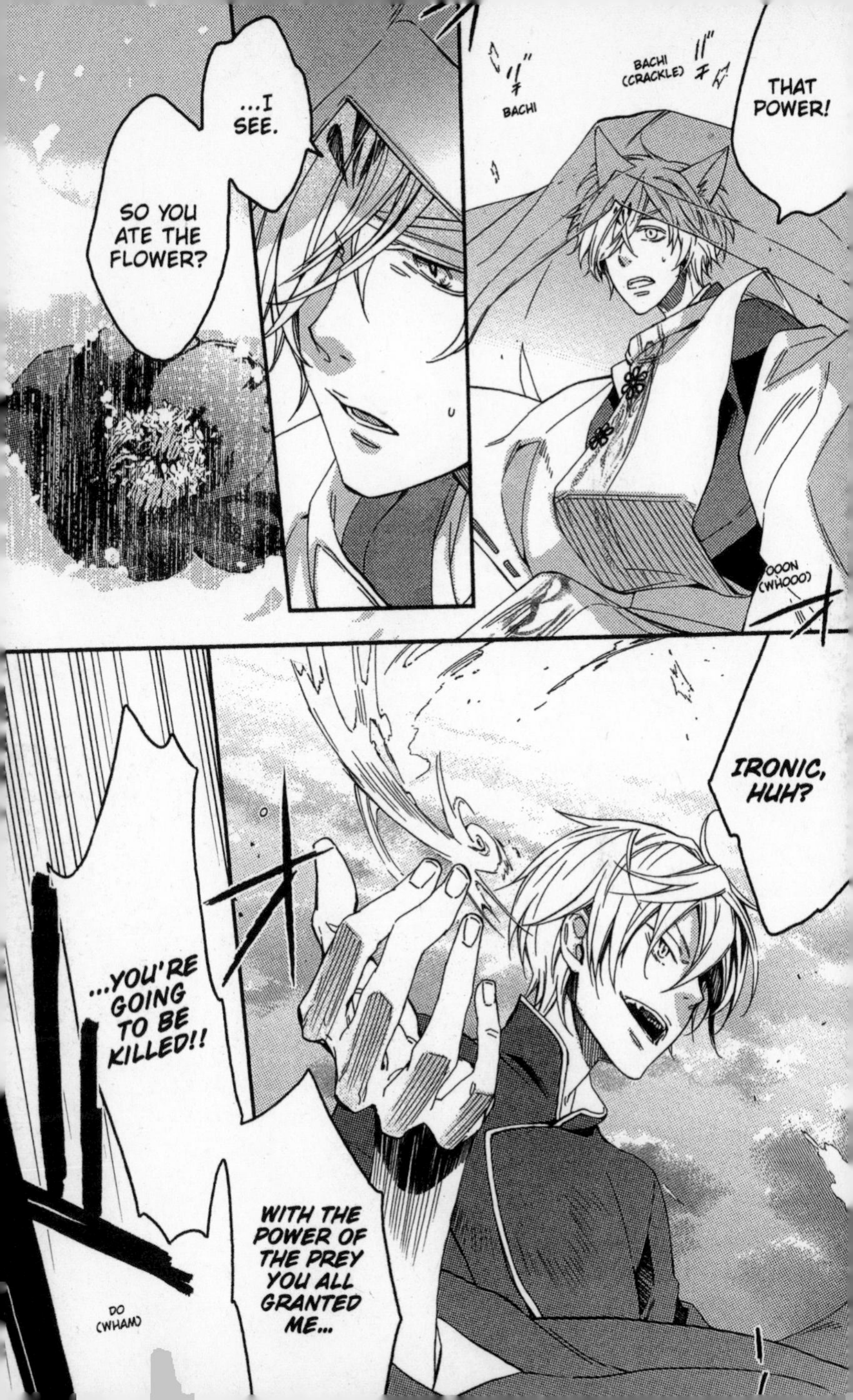
BACHI (CRACKLE)
BACHI
THAT POWER!
OOON (WHOOO)
...I SEE.
SO YOU ATE THE FLOWER?
IRONIC, HUH?
WITH THE POWER OF THE PREY YOU ALL GRANTED ME...
...YOU'RE GOING TO BE KILLED!!
DO (WHAM)

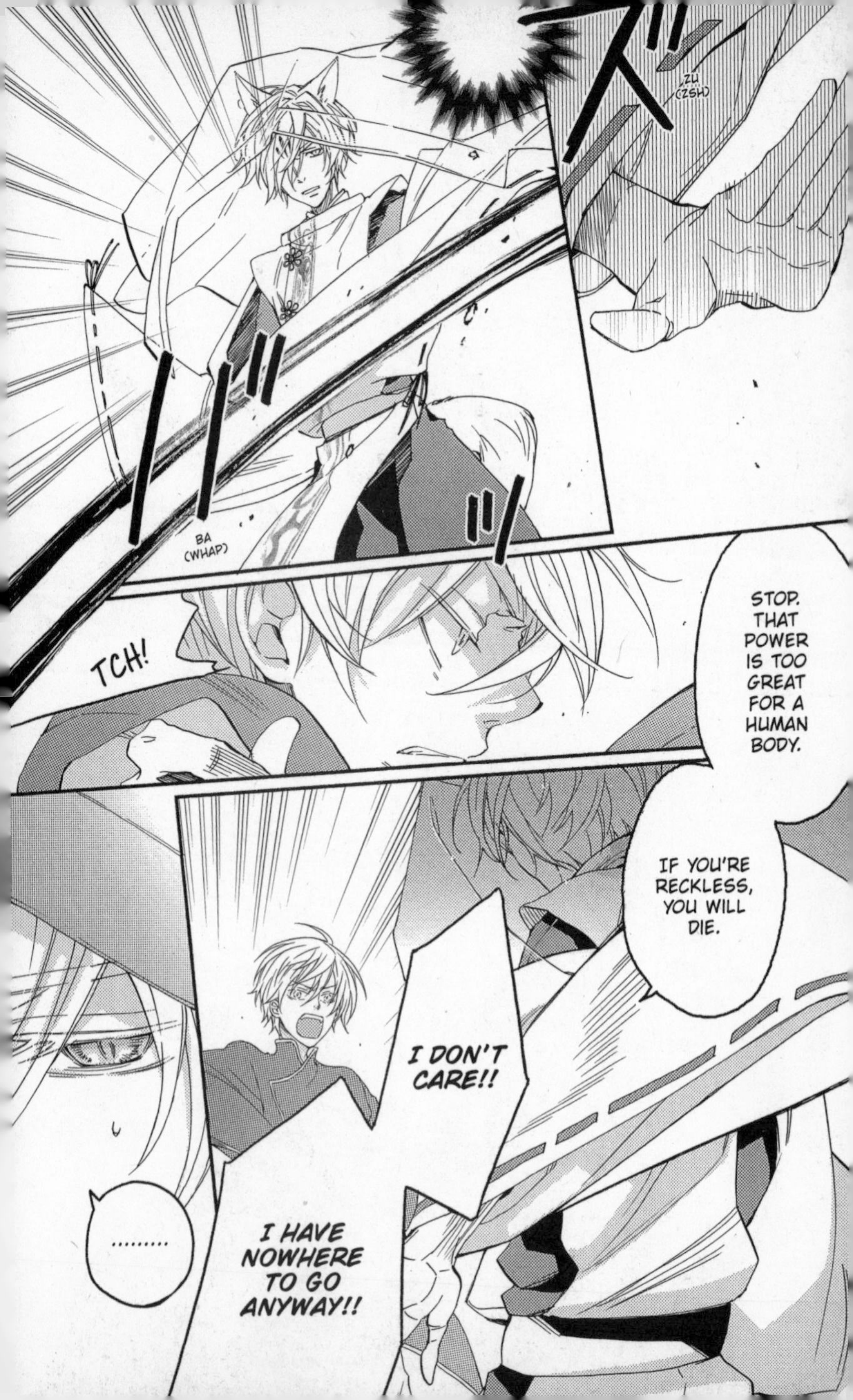
ZU (ZSH)
BA (WHAP)
STOP. THAT POWER IS TOO GREAT FOR A HUMAN BODY.
TCH!
IF YOU'RE RECKLESS, YOU WILL DIE.
I DON'T CARE!!
I HAVE NOWHERE TO GO ANYWAY!!
....

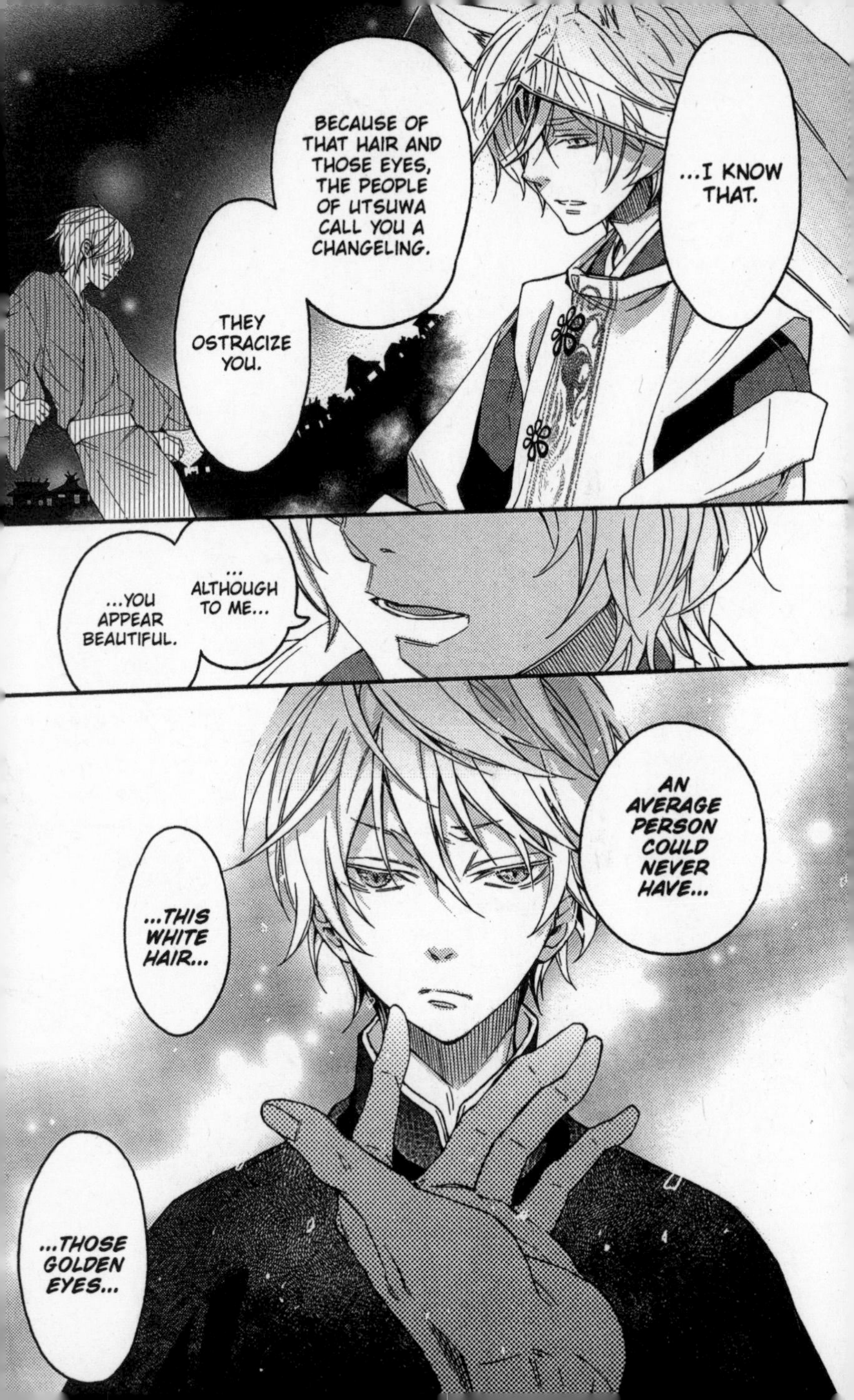
...I KNOW THAT.
BECAUSE OF THAT HAIR AND THOSE EYES, THE PEOPLE OF UTSUWA CALL YOU A CHANGELING.
THEY OSTRACIZE YOU.
... ALTHOUGH TO ME...
...YOU APPEAR BEAUTIFUL.
AN AVERAGE PERSON COULD NEVER HAVE...
...THIS WHITE HAIR...
...THOSE GOLDEN EYES...

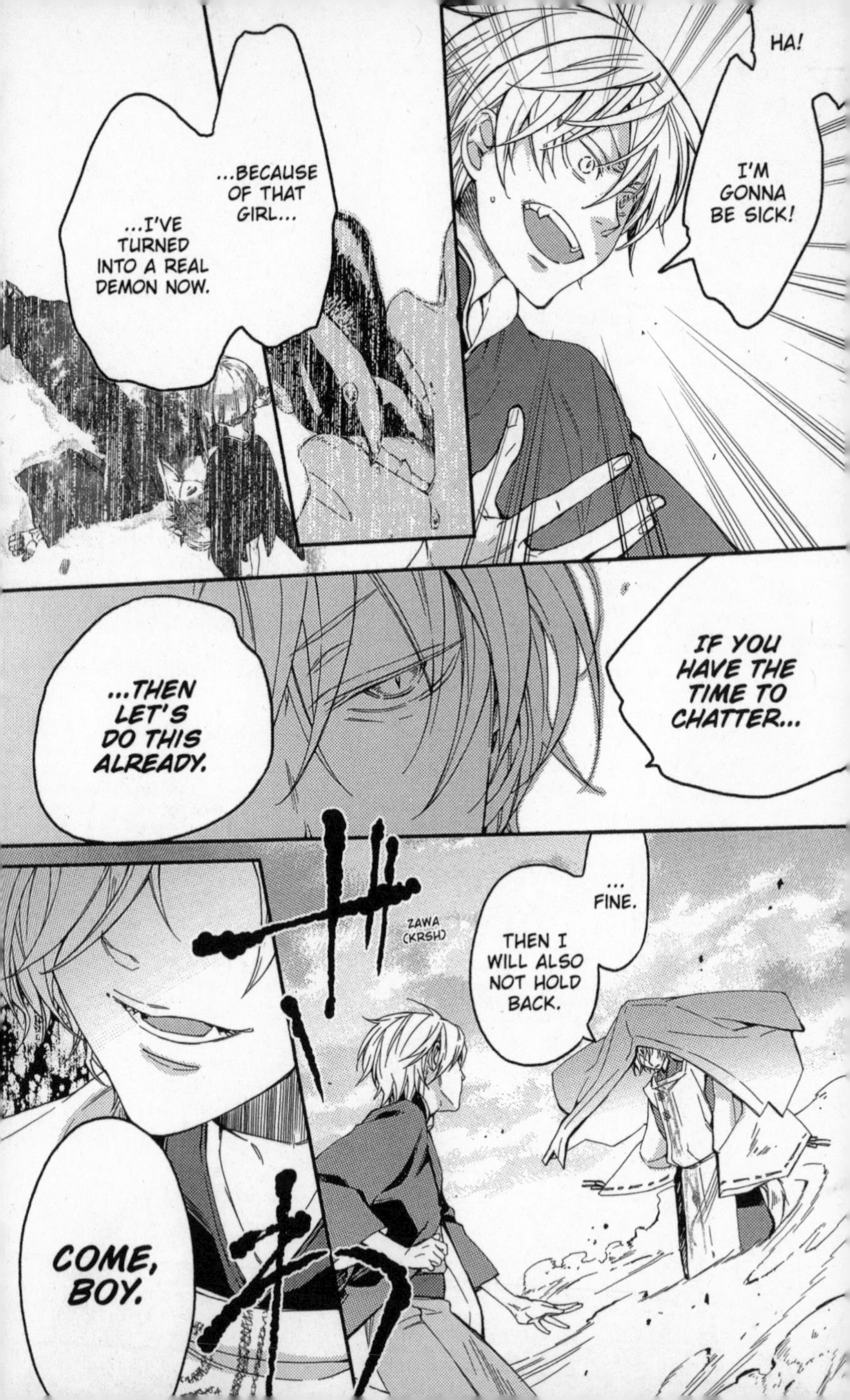
HA!
I'M GONNA BE SICK!
...BECAUSE OF THAT GIRL...
...I'VE TURNED INTO A REAL DEMON NOW.
IF YOU HAVE THE TIME TO CHATTER...
...THEN LET'S DO THIS ALREADY.
... FINE.
THEN I WILL ALSO NOT HOLD BACK.
ZAWA (KRSH)
COME, BOY.

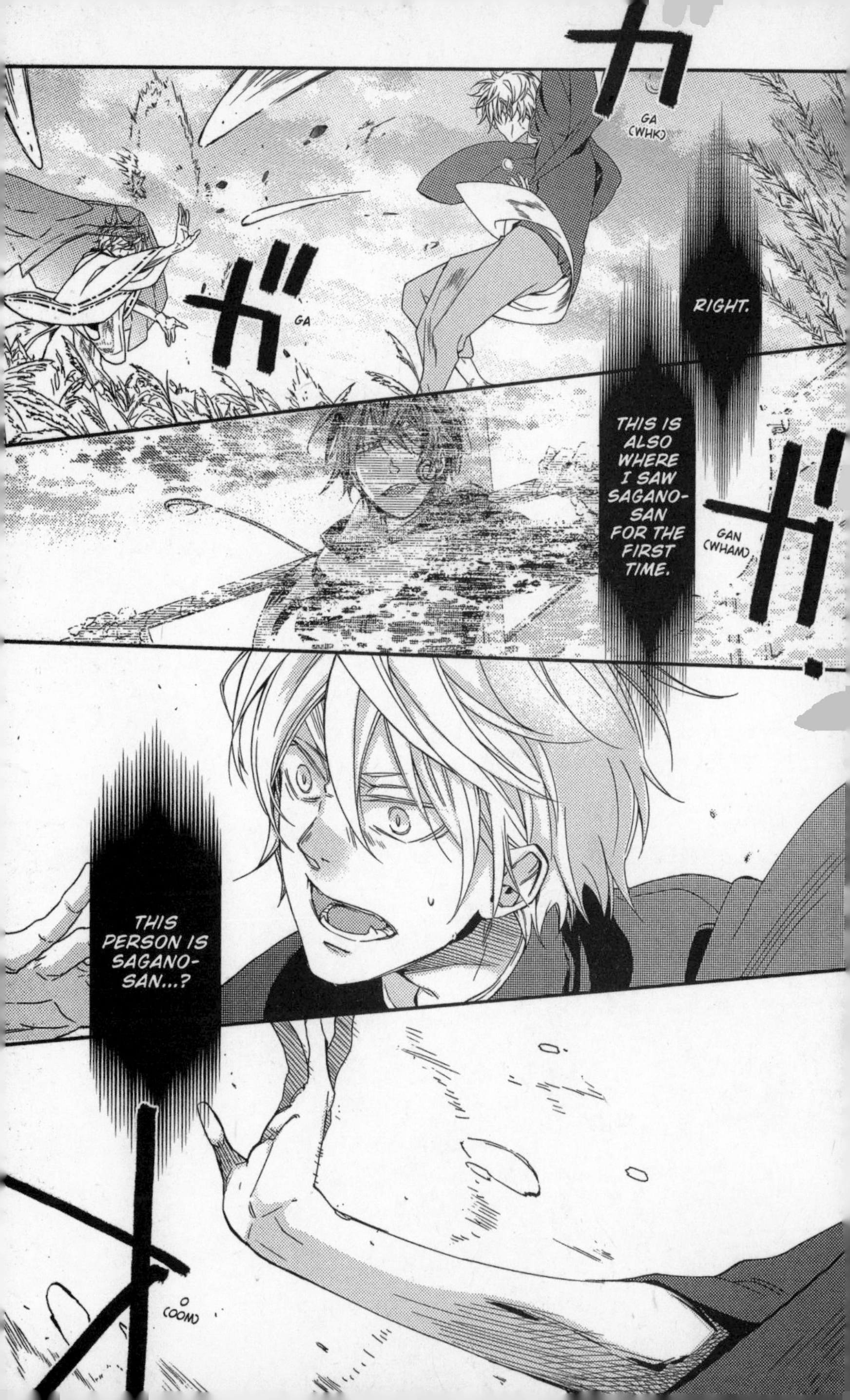
カ
GA (WHK)
RIGHT.
ガ
GA
ガ
GAN (WHAM)
THIS IS ALSO WHERE I SAW SAGANO-SAN FOR THE FIRST TIME.
THIS PERSON IS SAGANO-SAN...?
O (OOM)

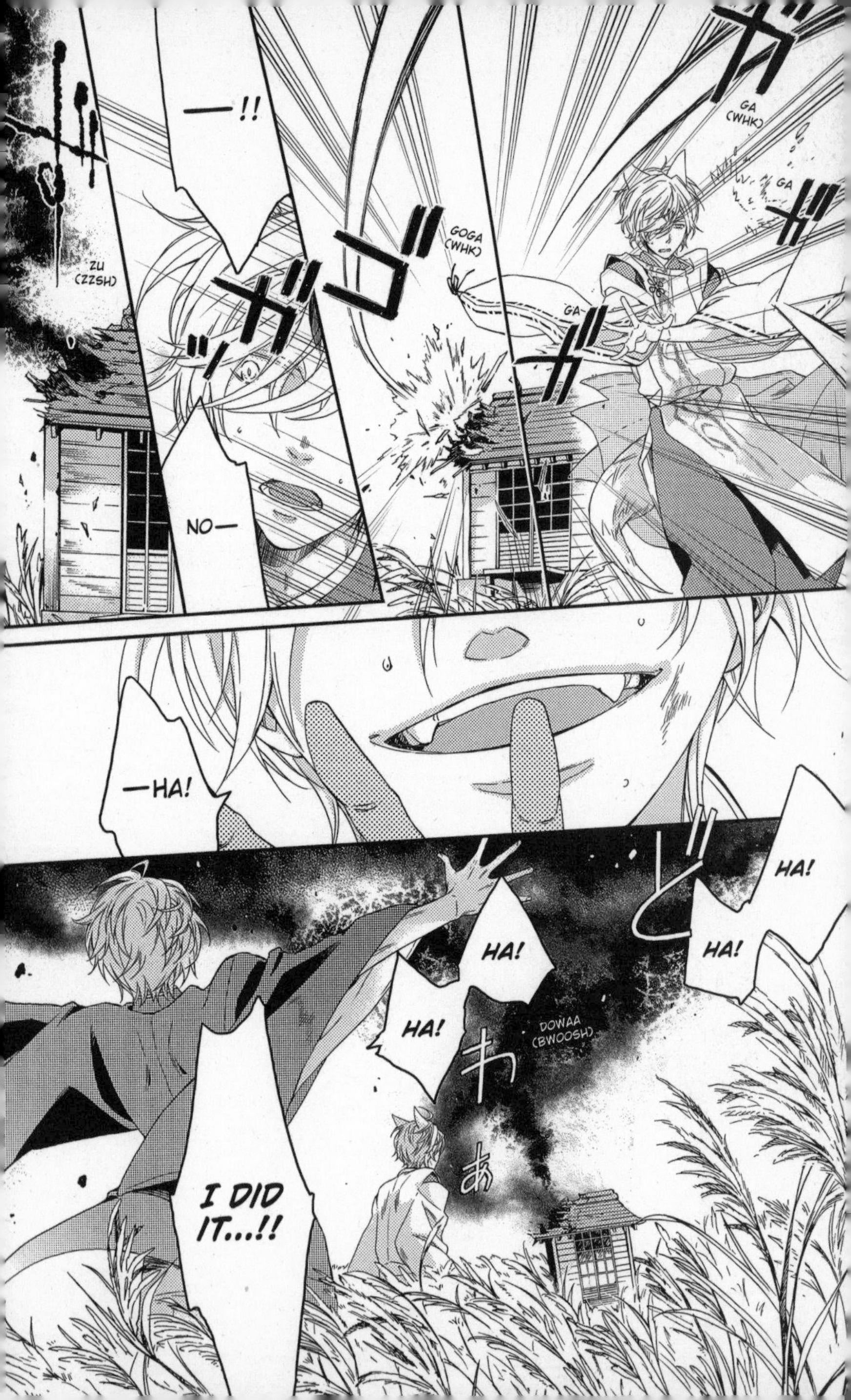
GA (WHK)
GA
GA-
GOGA (WHK)
—!!
NO—
ZU (ZZSH)
—HA!
HA!
HA!
HA!
HA!
DOWAA (BWOOSH)
I DID IT...!!

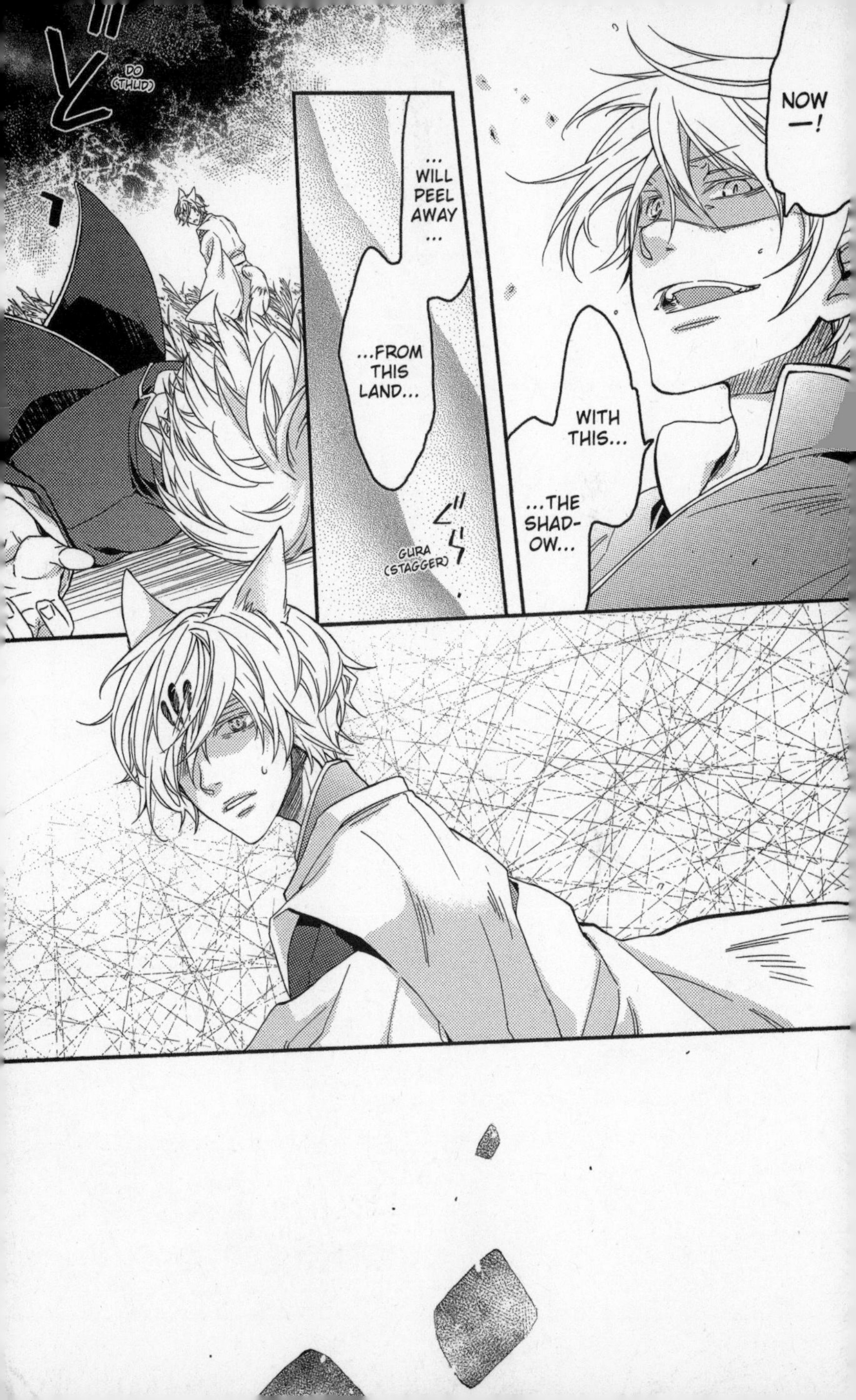
NOW—!
WITH THIS...
...THE SHADOW...
...WILL PEEL AWAY...
...FROM THIS LAND...
GURA (STAGGER)
DO (THUD)

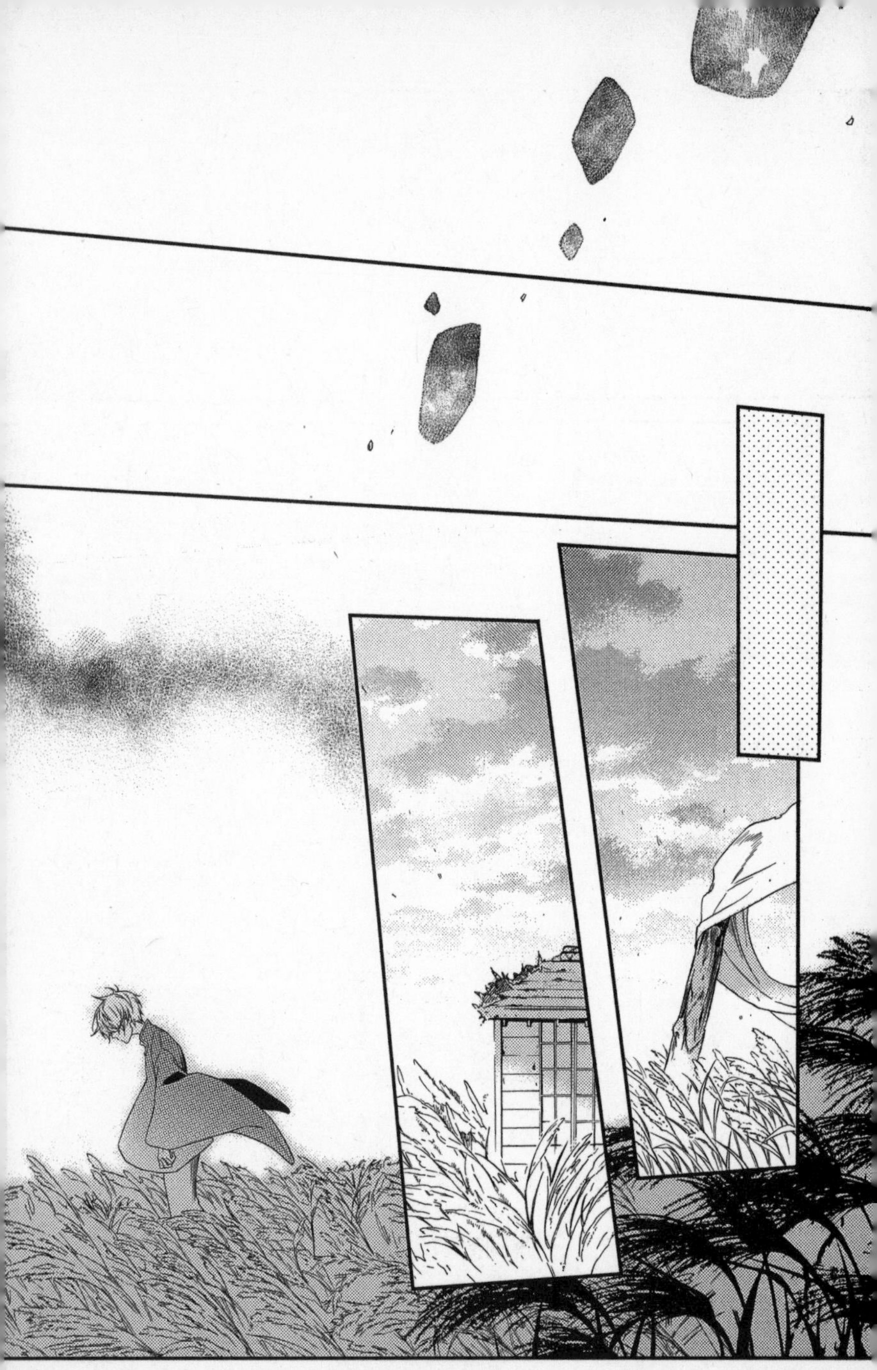

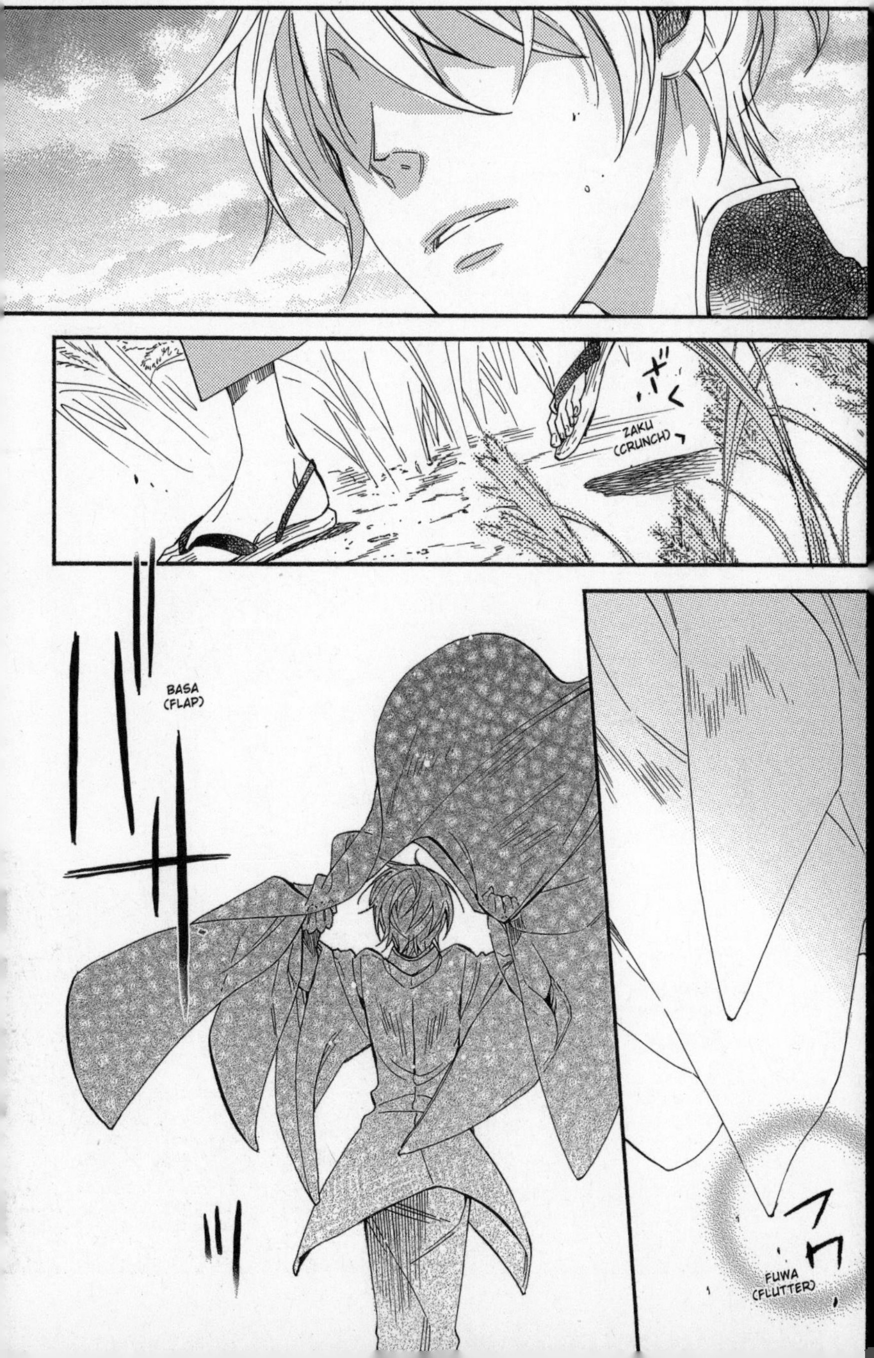
ザく
ZAKU (CRUNCH)
フワ
FUWA (FLUTTER)
バサ
BASA (FLAP)

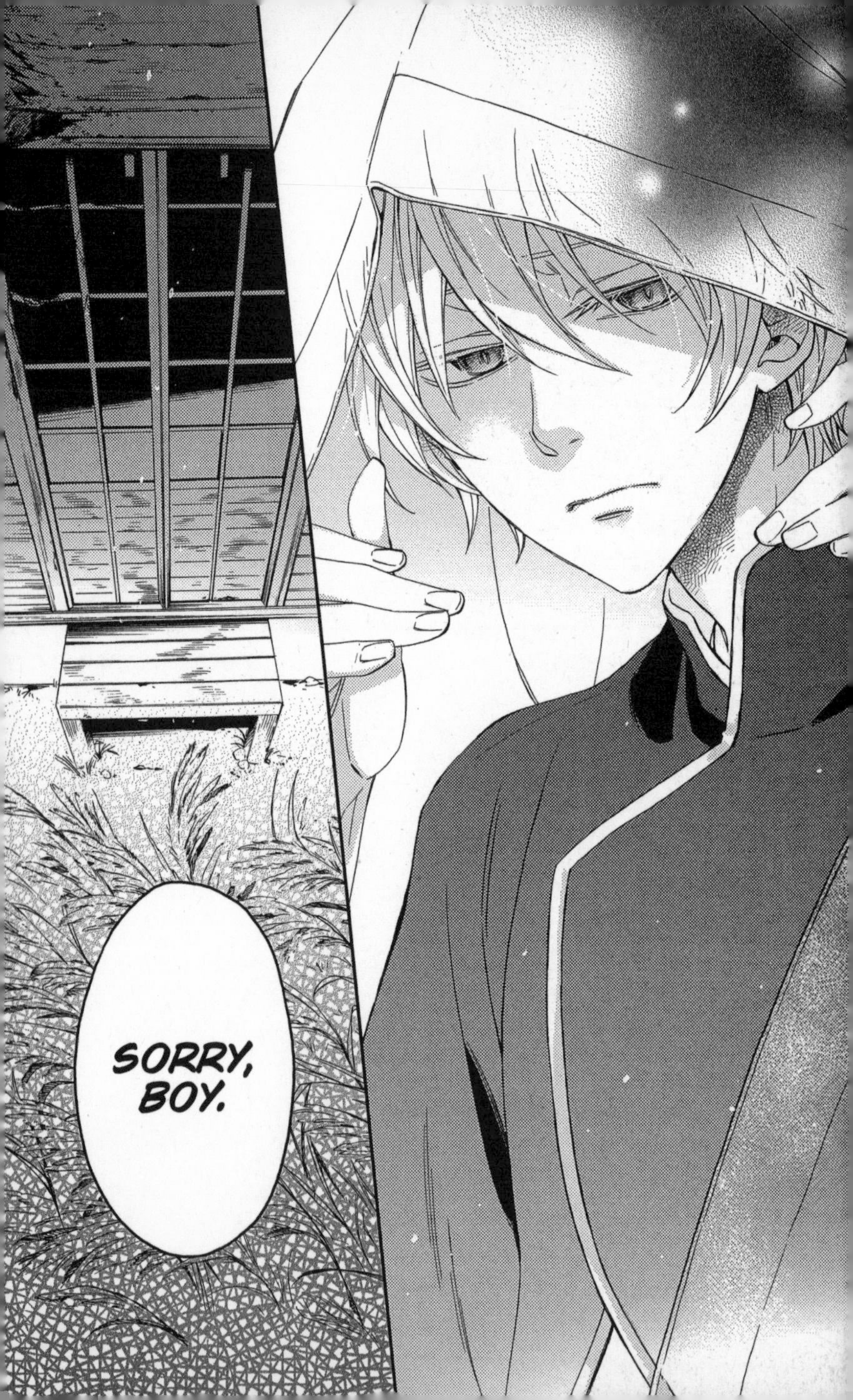
SORRY, BOY.

TO BE CONTINUED
IN VOLUME 7

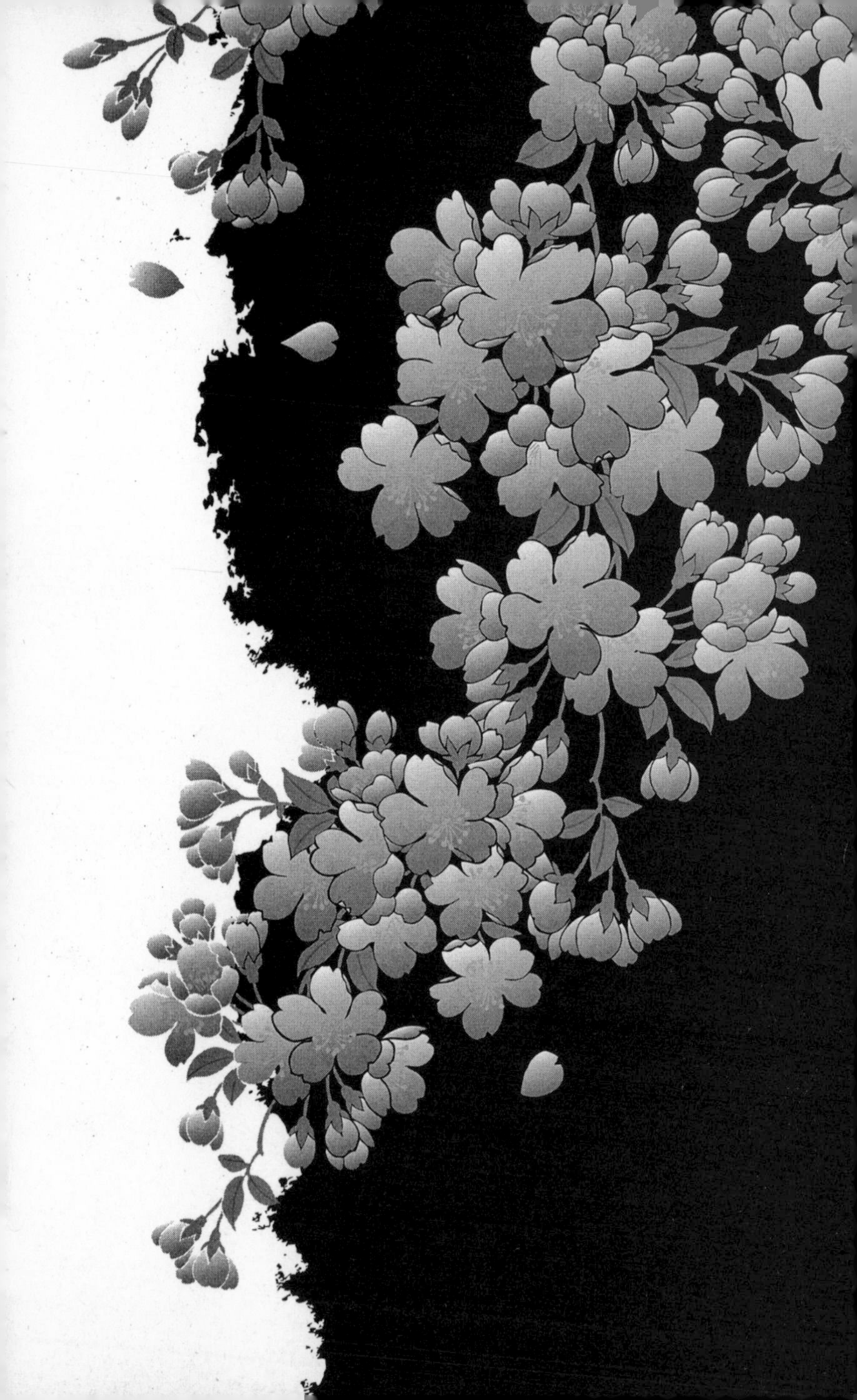

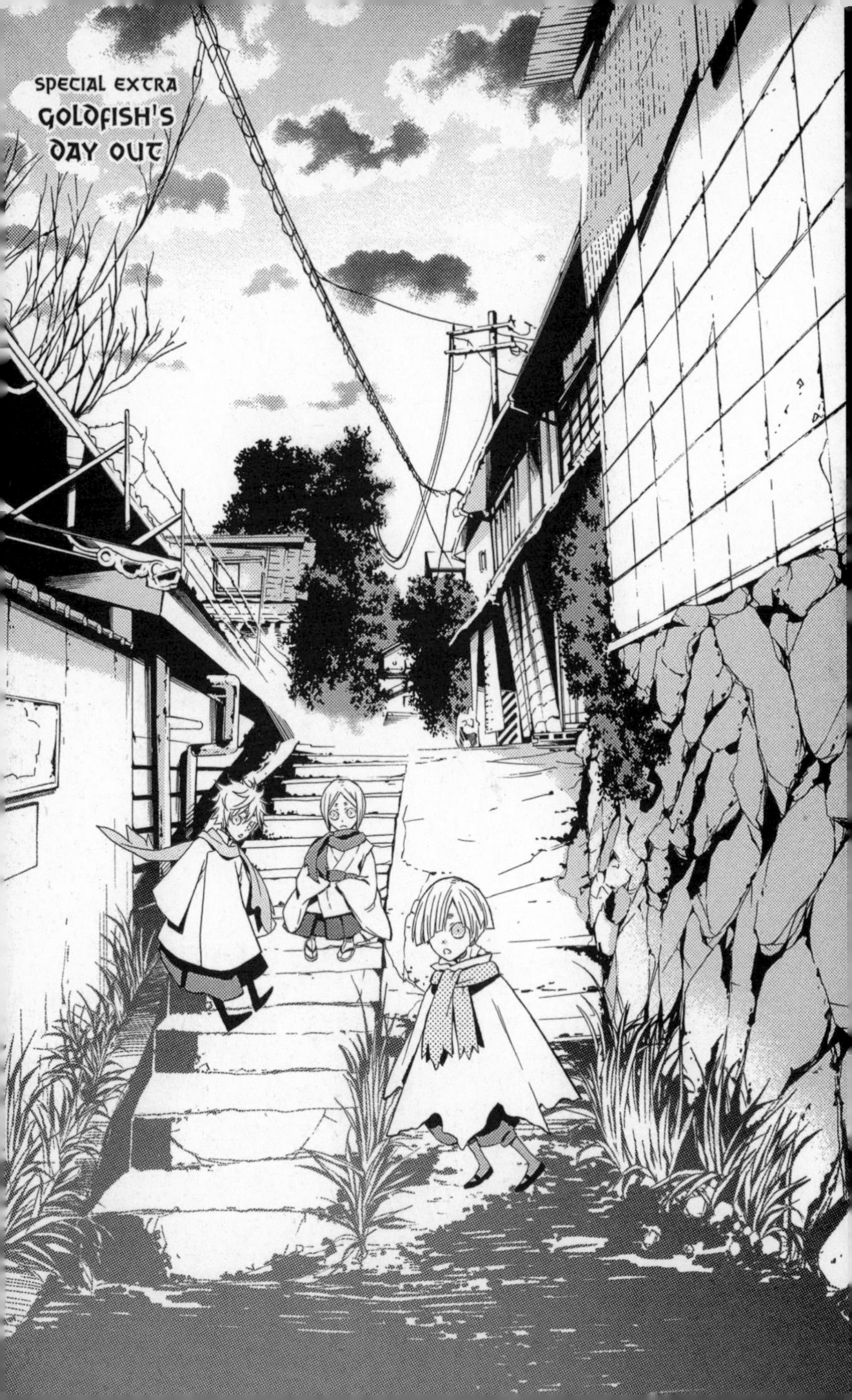
SPECIAL EXTRA
GOLDFISH'S DAY OUT

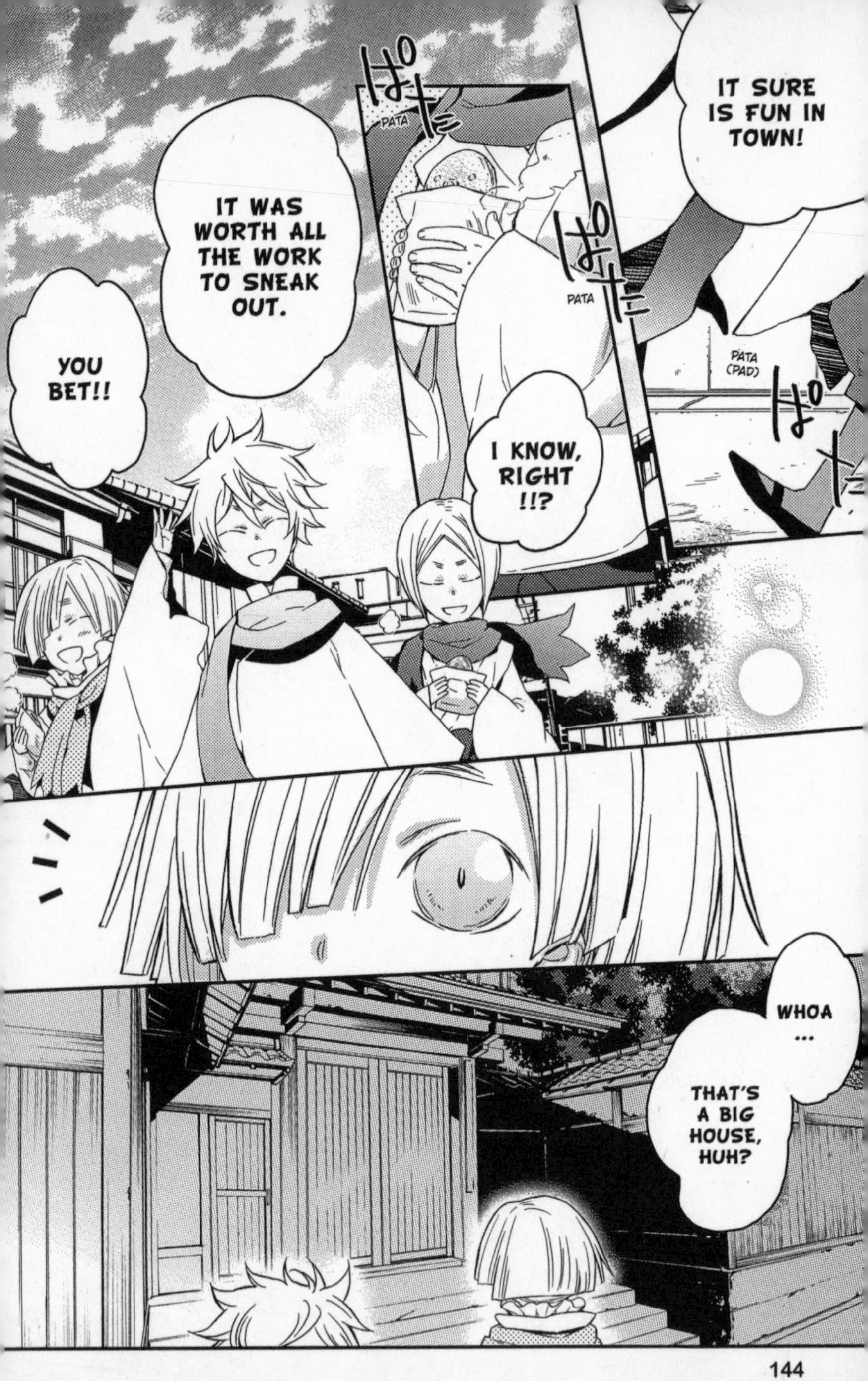
IT SURE IS FUN IN TOWN!
PATA (PAD)
PATA
PATA
IT WAS WORTH ALL THE WORK TO SNEAK OUT.
I KNOW, RIGHT!!?
YOU BET!!
WHOA...
THAT'S A BIG HOUSE, HUH?

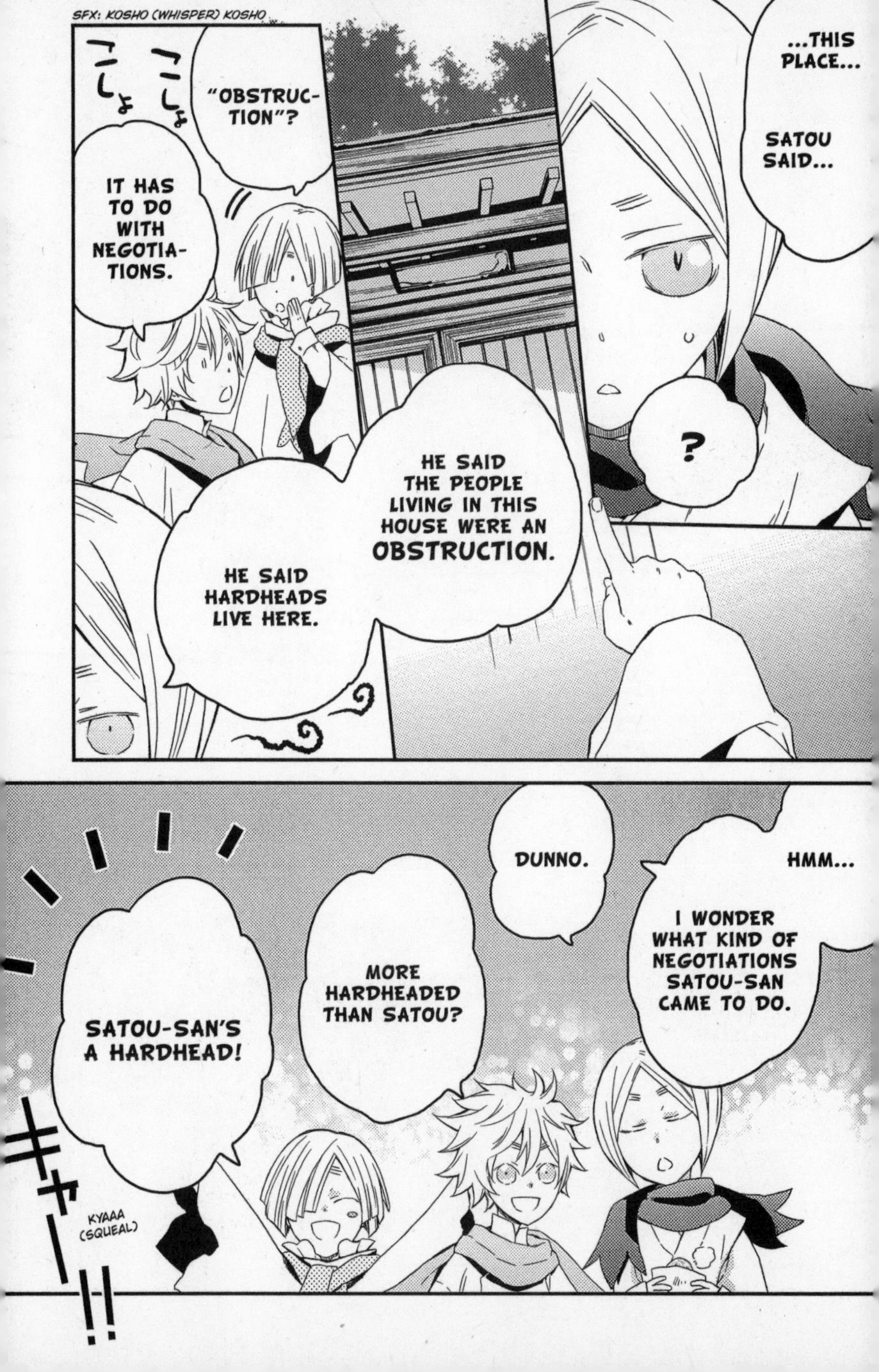
SFX: KOSHO (WHISPER) KOSHO
...THIS PLACE...
SATOU SAID...
?
HE SAID THE PEOPLE LIVING IN THIS HOUSE WERE AN OBSTRUCTION.
HE SAID HARDHEADS LIVE HERE.
"OBSTRUCTION"?
IT HAS TO DO WITH NEGOTIATIONS.
こしょこしょ
HMM...
I WONDER WHAT KIND OF NEGOTIATIONS SATOU-SAN CAME TO DO.
DUNNO.
MORE HARDHEADED THAN SATOU?
SATOU-SAN'S A HARDHEAD!
キャー!!
KYAAA (SQUEAL)

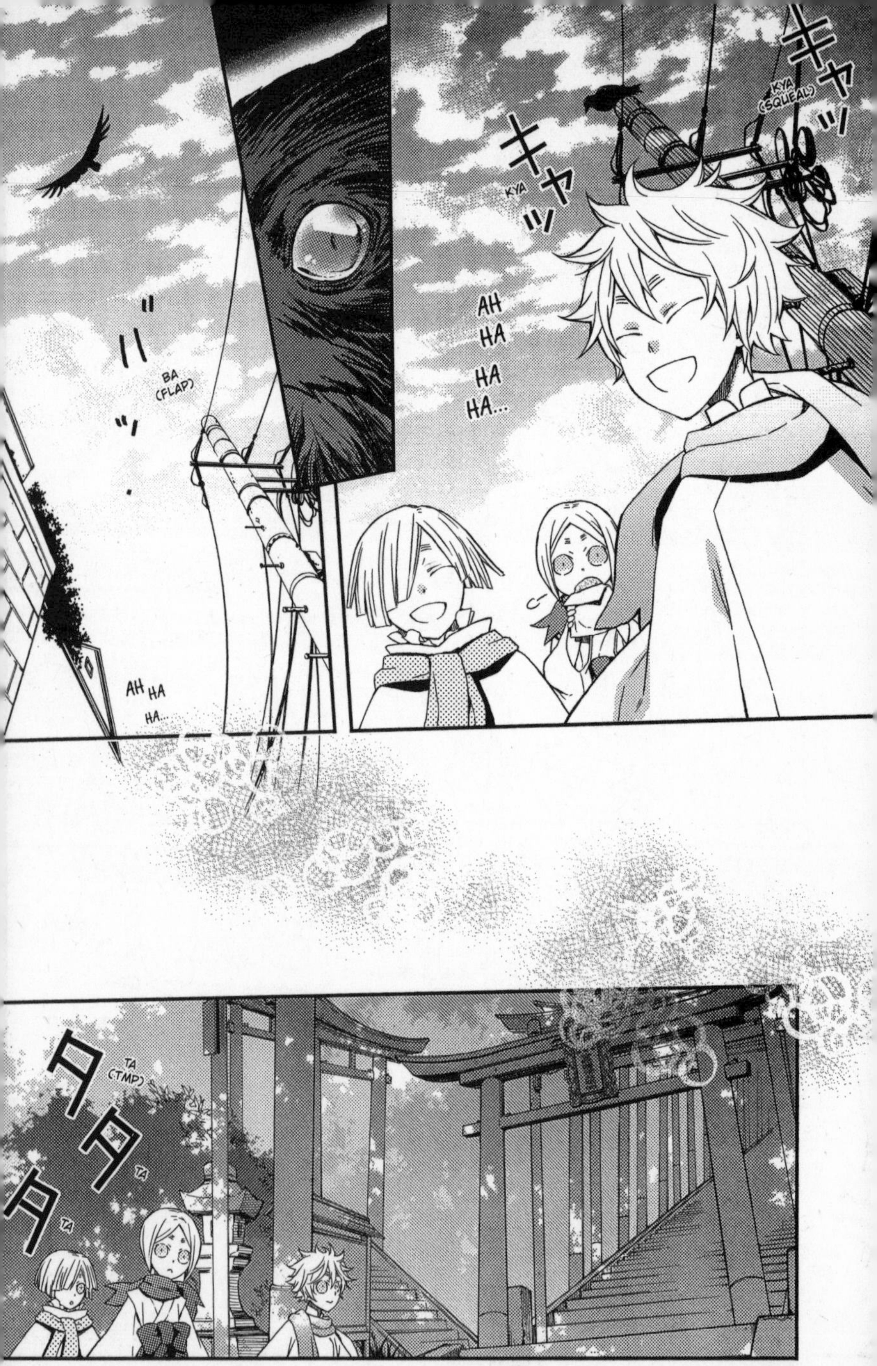
キャーッ
KYA (SQUEAL)
キャッ
KYA
AH HA HA HA...
バッ
BA (FLAP)
AH HA HA...
タタタ
TA (TMP)
TA
TA

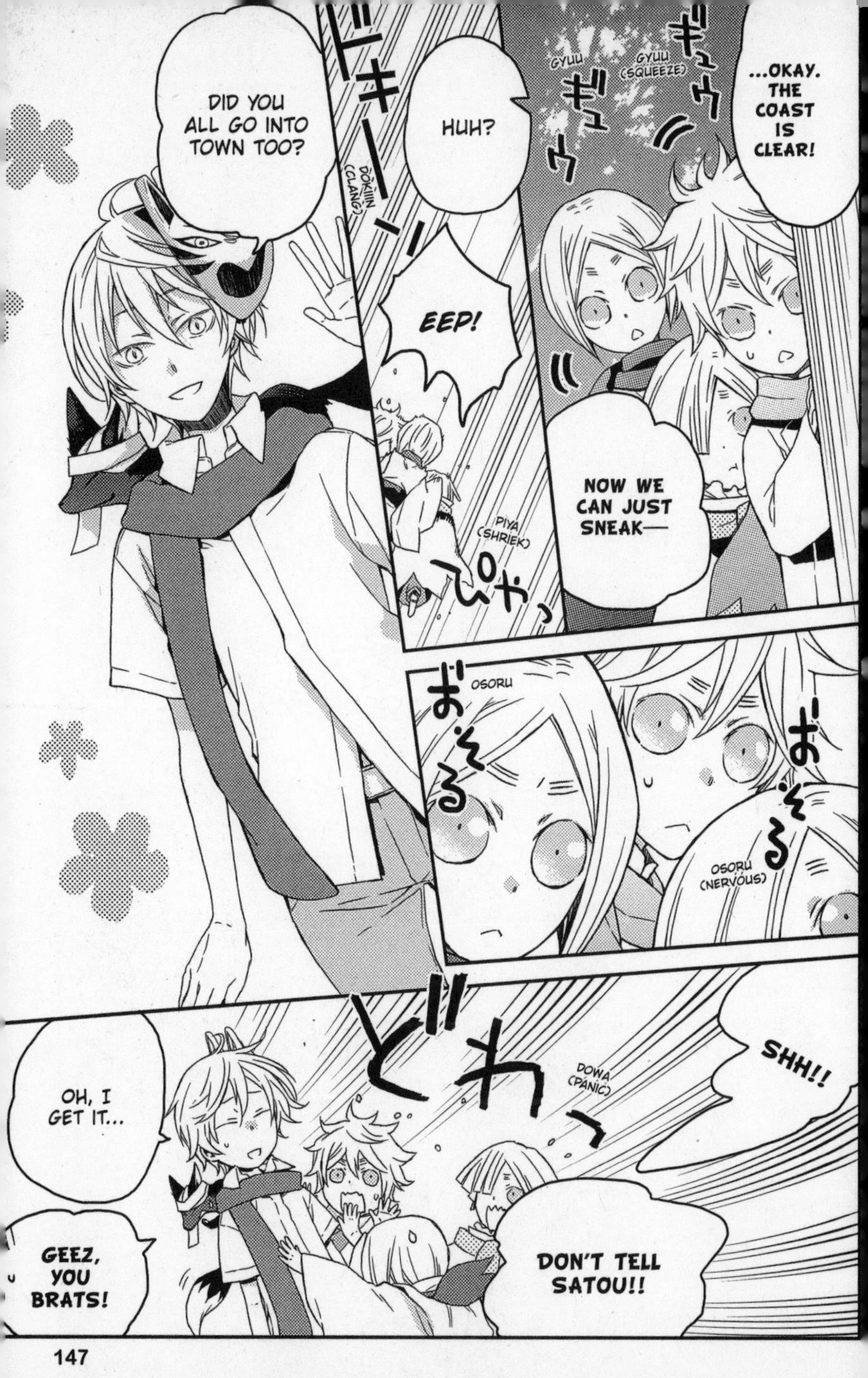
...OKAY. THE COAST IS CLEAR!
ギュウ
GYUU
ギュウ
GYUU (SQUEEZE)
NOW WE CAN JUST SNEAK—
HUH?
ドキーーン
DOKIIN (CLANG)
EEP!
ぴやっ
PIYA (SHRIEK)
おそる
OSORU
おそる
OSORU (NERVOUS)
DID YOU ALL GO INTO TOWN TOO?
SHH!!
DON'T TELL SATOU!!
どわっ
DOWA (PANIC)
OH, I GET IT...
GEEZ, YOU BRATS!

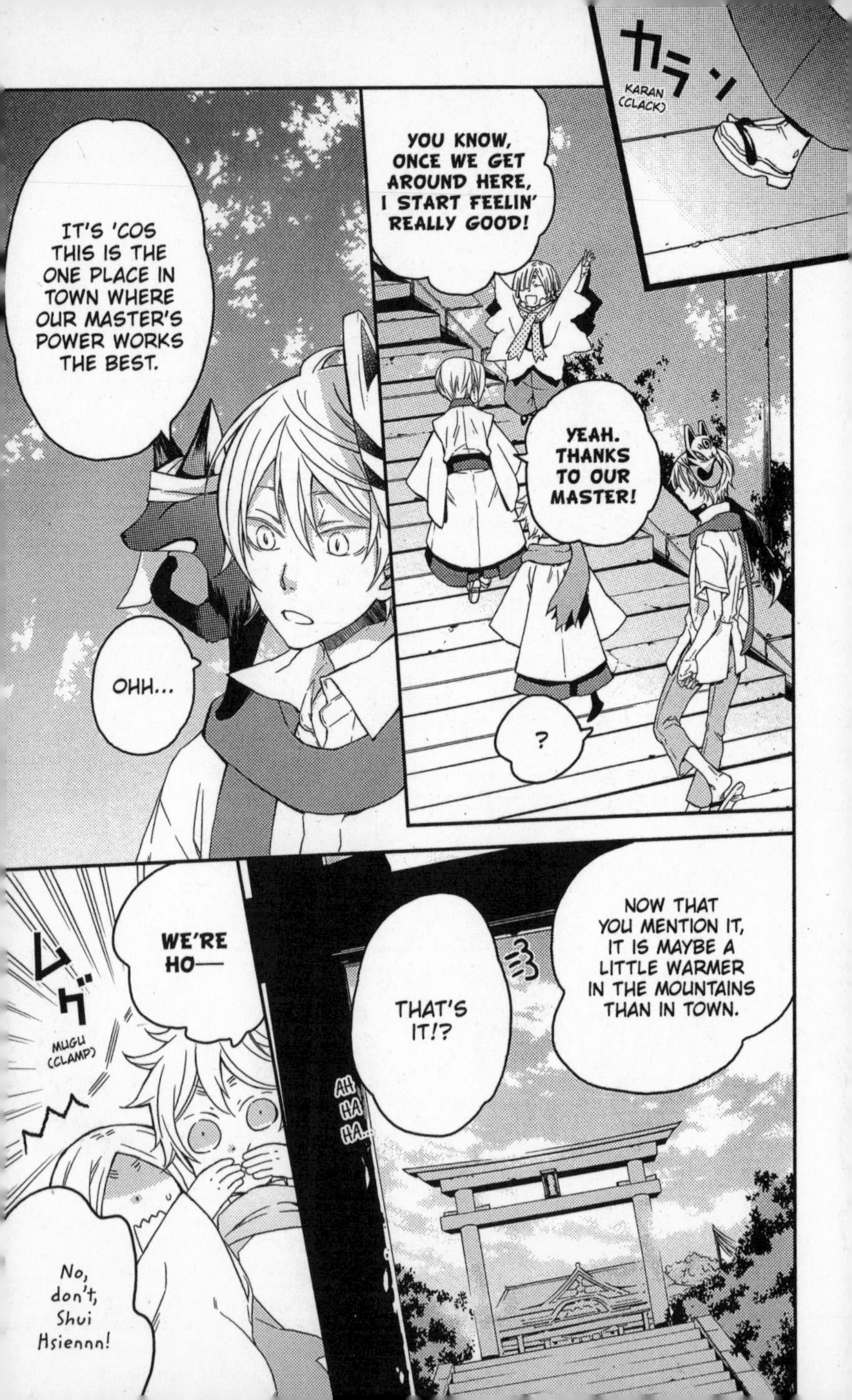
カラン
KARAN (CLACK)
YOU KNOW, ONCE WE GET AROUND HERE, I START FEELIN' REALLY GOOD!
YEAH. THANKS TO OUR MASTER!
?
IT'S 'COS THIS IS THE ONE PLACE IN TOWN WHERE OUR MASTER'S POWER WORKS THE BEST.
OHH...
NOW THAT YOU MENTION IT, IT IS MAYBE A LITTLE WARMER IN THE MOUNTAINS THAN IN TOWN.
THAT'S IT!?
AH HA HA...
WE'RE HO—
ムグ
MUGU (CLAMP)
No, don't, Shui Hsiennn!

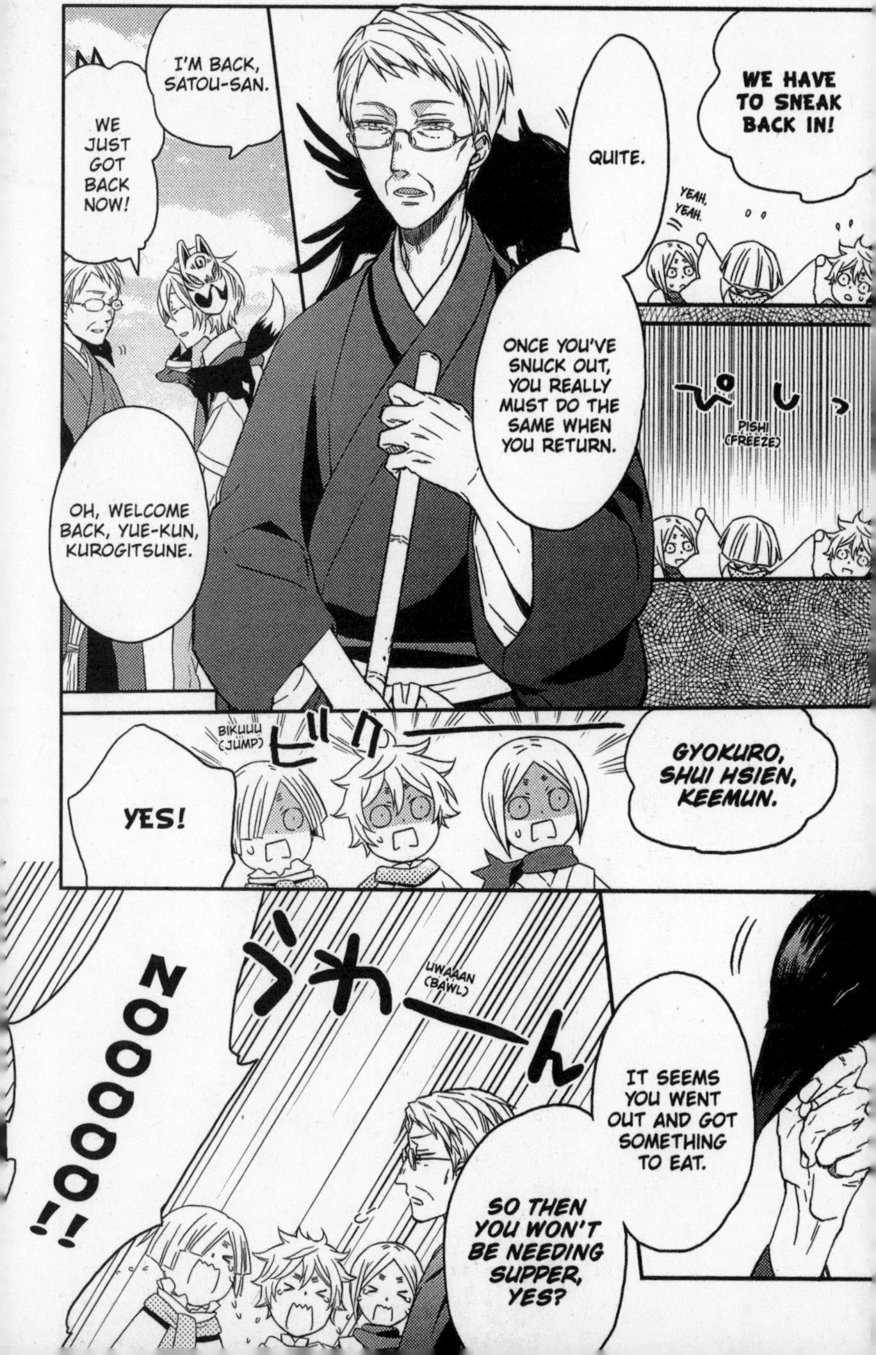
WE HAVE TO SNEAK BACK IN!
YEAH, YEAH.
PISHI (FREEZE)
QUITE.
ONCE YOU'VE SNUCK OUT, YOU REALLY MUST DO THE SAME WHEN YOU RETURN.
I'M BACK, SATOU-SAN.
WE JUST GOT BACK NOW!
OH, WELCOME BACK, YUE-KUN, KUROGITSUNE.
GYOKURO, SHUI HSIEN, KEEMUN.
BIKUUU (JUMP)
YES!
IT SEEMS YOU WENT OUT AND GOT SOMETHING TO EAT.
SO THEN YOU WON'T BE NEEDING SUPPER, YES?
UWAAAN (BAWL)
NOOOOOOO!!

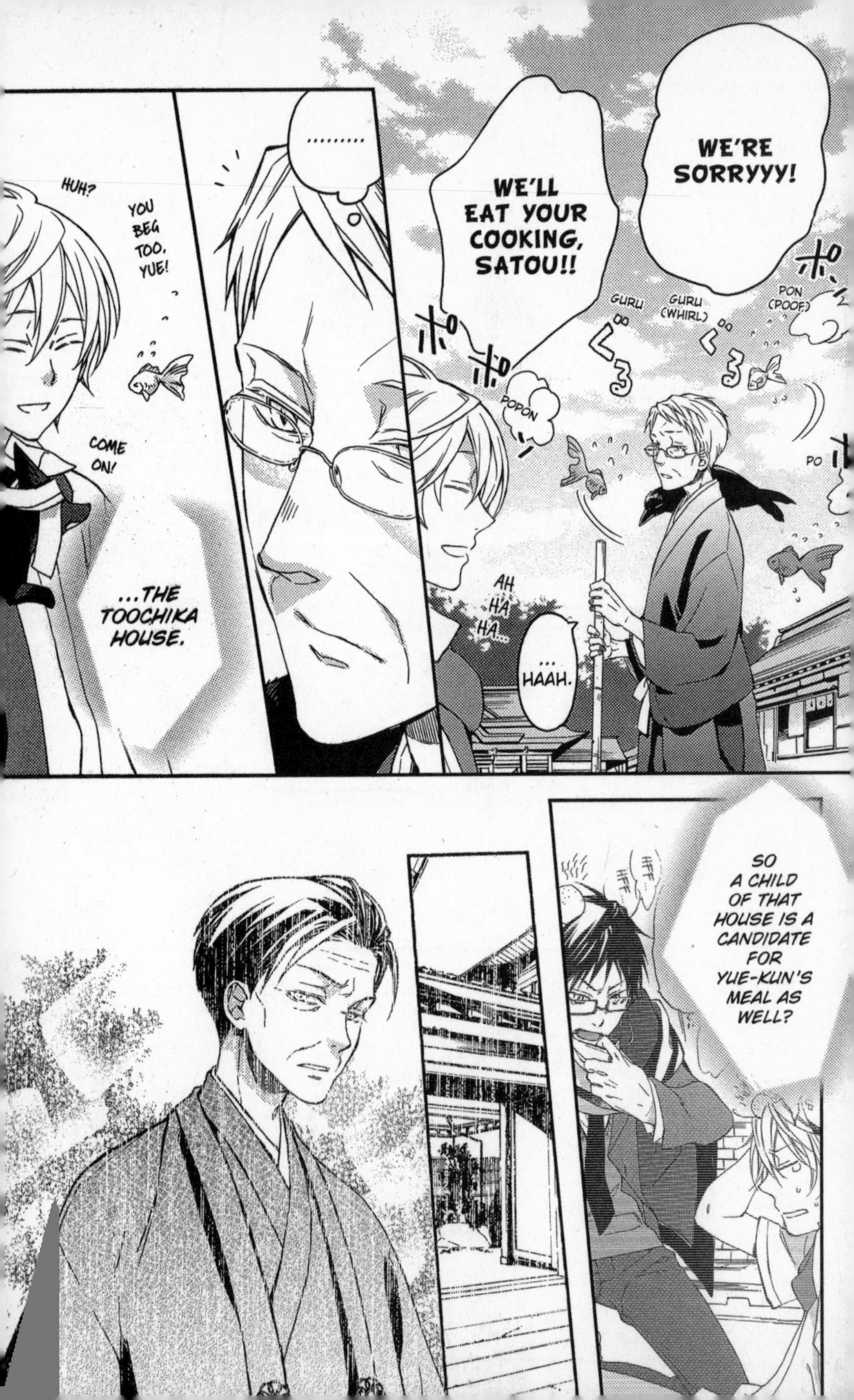
WE'RE SORRYYY!
WE'LL EAT YOUR COOKING, SATOU!!
PON (POOF)
GURU GURU (WHIRL)
POPON
PO
AH HA HA...
...HAAH.
....
HUH?
YOU BEG TOO, YUE!
COME ON!
...THE TOOCHIKA HOUSE.
SO A CHILD OF THAT HOUSE IS A CANDIDATE FOR YUE-KUN'S MEAL AS WELL?
HFF... HFF...

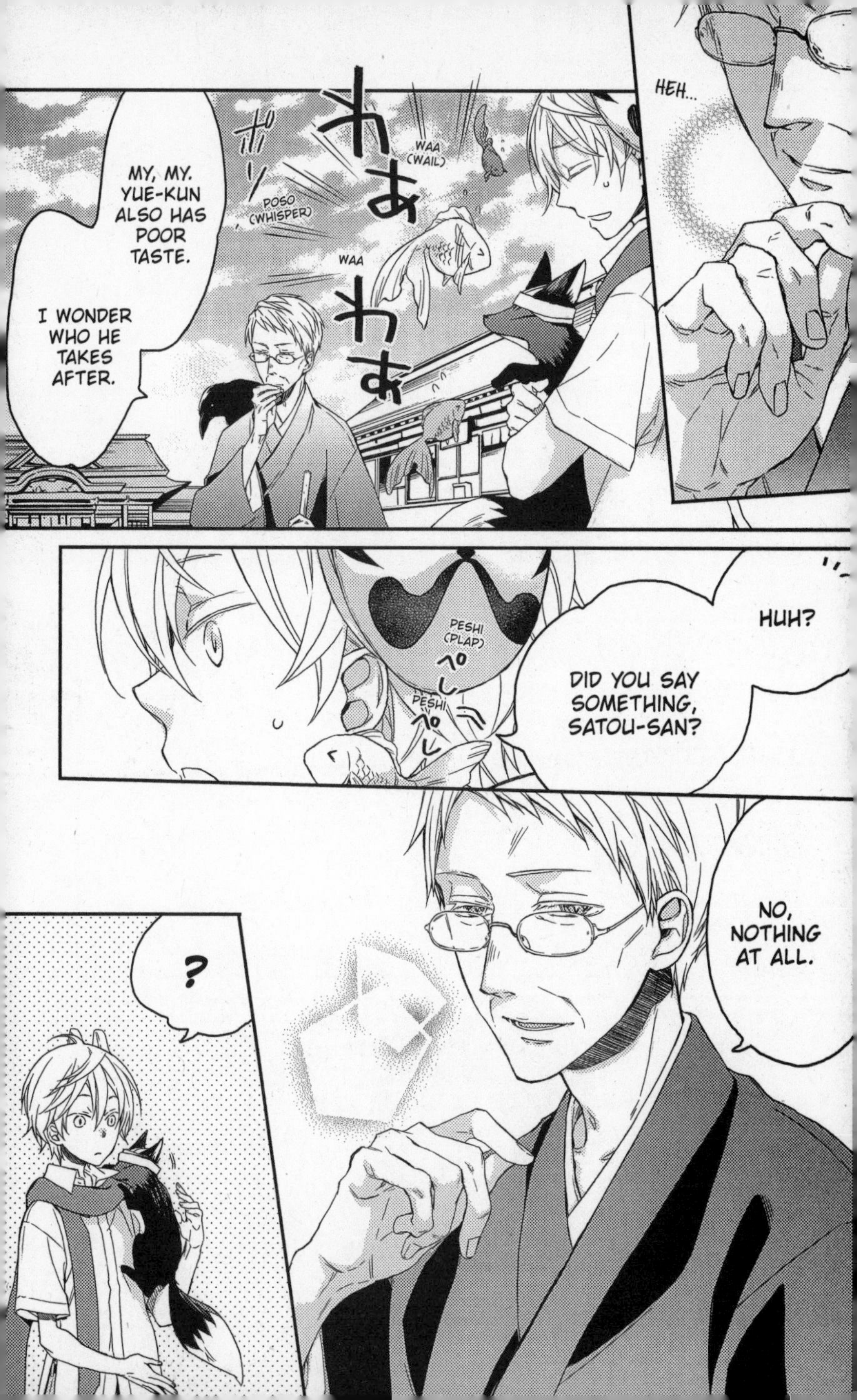
HEH...
わぁ
WAA (WAIL)
POSO (WHISPER)
WAA
わぁ
MY, MY. YUE-KUN ALSO HAS POOR TASTE.
I WONDER WHO HE TAKES AFTER.
HUH?
DID YOU SAY SOMETHING, SATOU-SAN?
PESHI (PLAP)
へし
PESHI
へし
NO, NOTHING AT ALL.
?

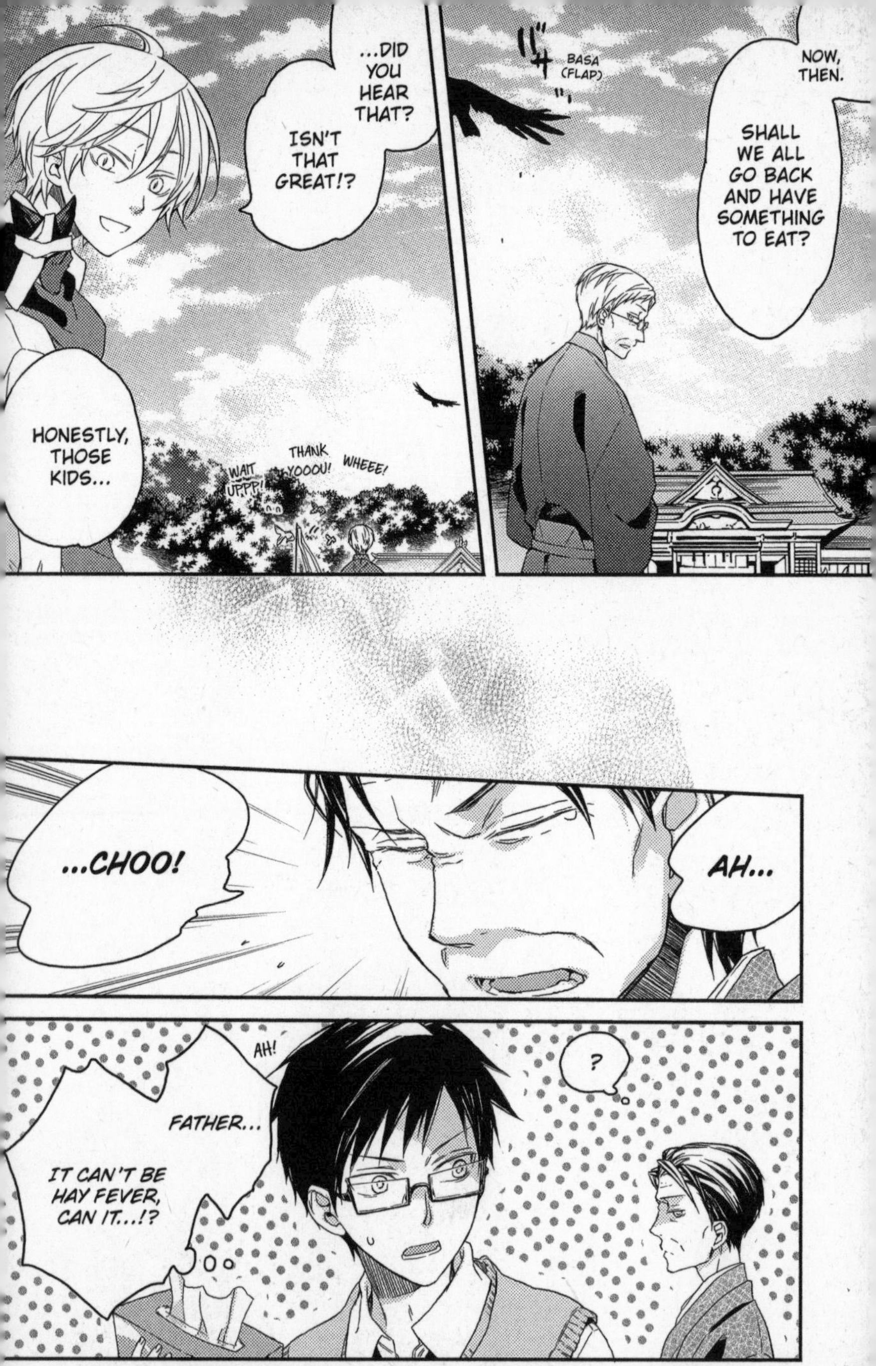
NOW, THEN.
SHALL WE ALL GO BACK AND HAVE SOMETHING TO EAT?
BASA (FLAP)
...DID YOU HEAR THAT?
ISN'T THAT GREAT!?
HONESTLY, THOSE KIDS...
WHEEE!
THANK YOOOU!
WAIT UPPP!
AH...
...CHOO!
?
AH!
FATHER...
IT CAN'T BE HAY FEVER, CAN IT...!?

TISSUES

*Of the Red,
the Light,
and the
Ayakashi*

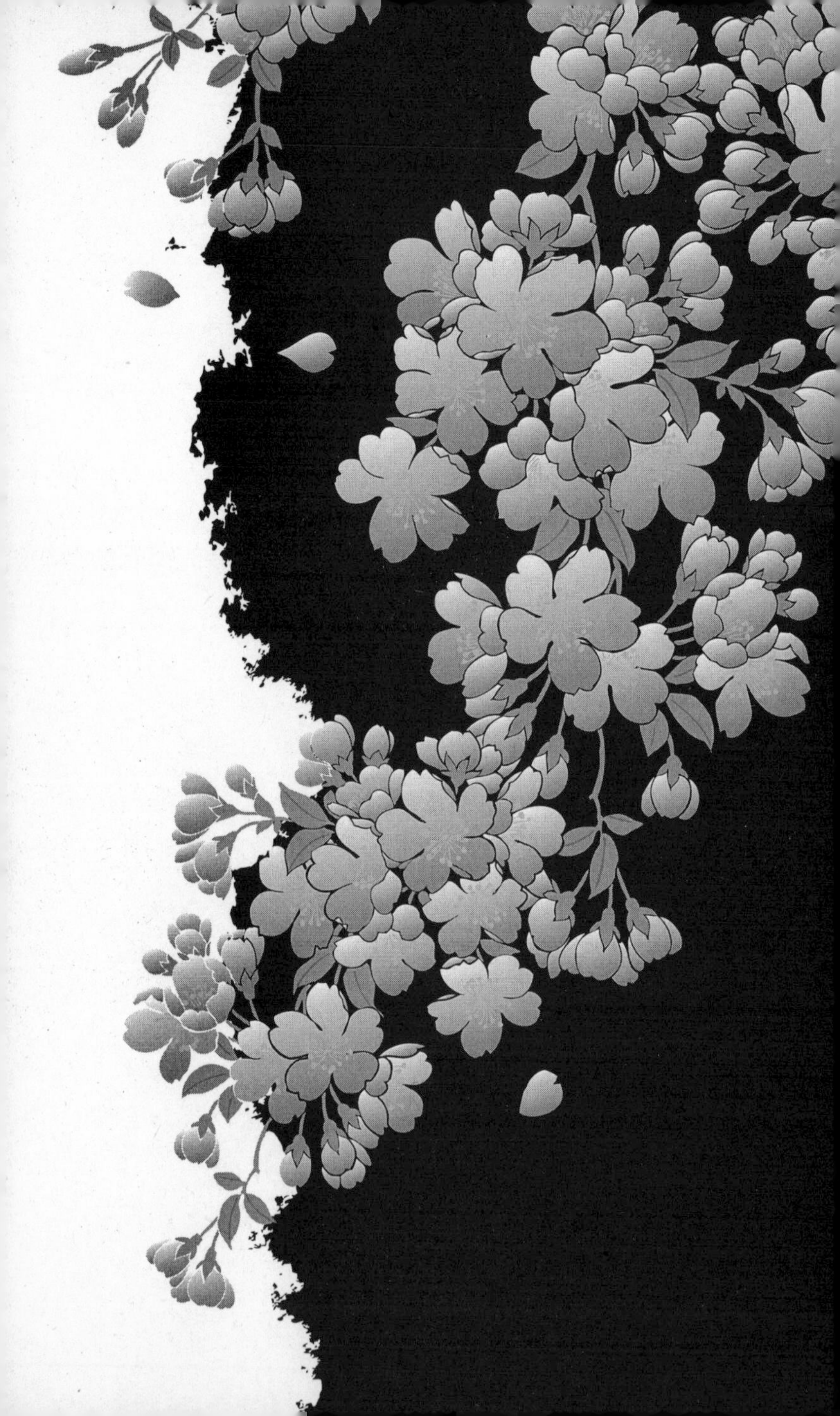

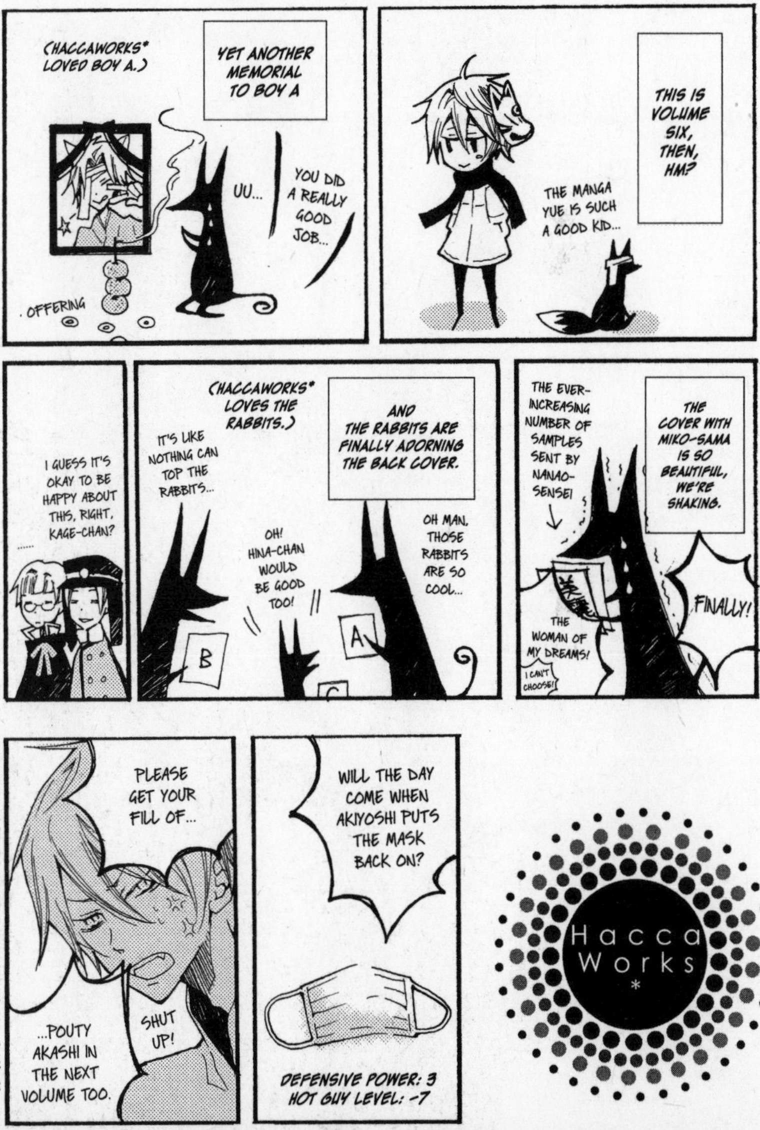
THIS IS VOLUME SIX, THEN, HM?
THE MANGA YUE IS SUCH A GOOD KID...
(HACCAWORKS* LOVED BOY A.)
YET ANOTHER MEMORIAL TO BOY A
YOU DID A REALLY GOOD JOB...
UU...
OFFERING
THE COVER WITH MIKO-SAMA IS SO BEAUTIFUL, WE'RE SHAKING.
THE EVER-INCREASING NUMBER OF SAMPLES SENT BY NANAO-SENSEI
FINALLY!
THE WOMAN OF MY DREAMS!
I CAN'T CHOOSE!
(HACCAWORKS* LOVES THE RABBITS.)
AND THE RABBITS ARE FINALLY ADORNING THE BACK COVER.
IT'S LIKE NOTHING CAN TOP THE RABBITS...
OH MAN, THOSE RABBITS ARE SO COOL...
OH! HINA-CHAN WOULD BE GOOD TOO!
A
B
I GUESS IT'S OKAY TO BE HAPPY ABOUT THIS, RIGHT, KAGE-CHAN?
......
WILL THE DAY COME WHEN AKIYOSHI PUTS THE MASK BACK ON?
DEFENSIVE POWER: 3
HOT GUY LEVEL: -7
PLEASE GET YOUR FILL OF...
SHUT UP!
...POUTY AKASHI IN THE NEXT VOLUME TOO.

Hacca Works *

*HE'S EVEN CUTER HERE THAN IN THE ORIGINAL IF YOU ASK US.

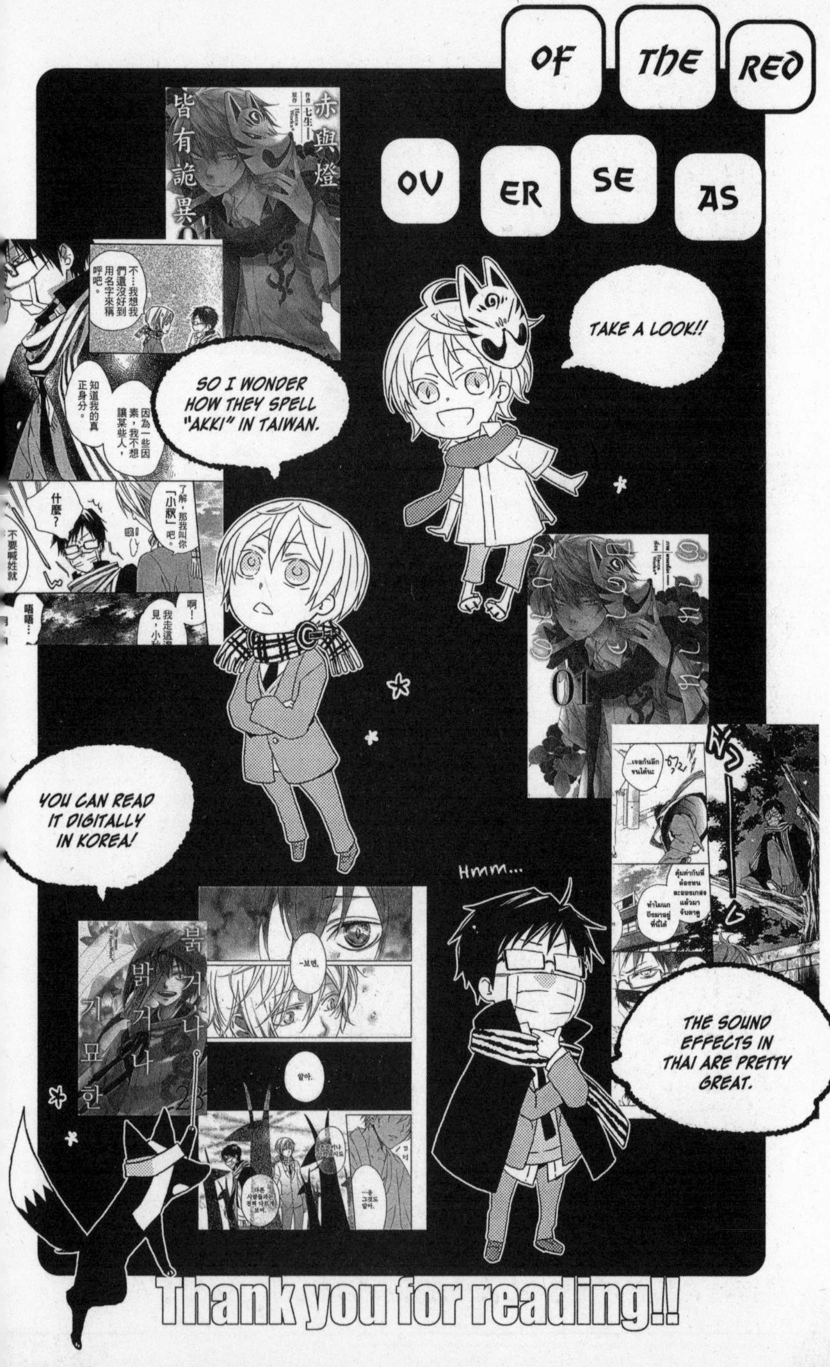
OF THE RED
OV ER SE AS
TAKE A LOOK!!
SO I WONDER HOW THEY SPELL "AKKI" IN TAIWAN.
赤與燈
皆有詭異
不…我想我們還沒好到用名字來稱呼吧。
因為一些因素，我不想讓某些人知道我的真正身分。
了解，那我叫你「小秋」吧。
什麼？
Hmm...
THE SOUND EFFECTS IN THAI ARE PRETTY GREAT.
YOU CAN READ IT DIGITALLY IN KOREA!
Thank you for reading!!

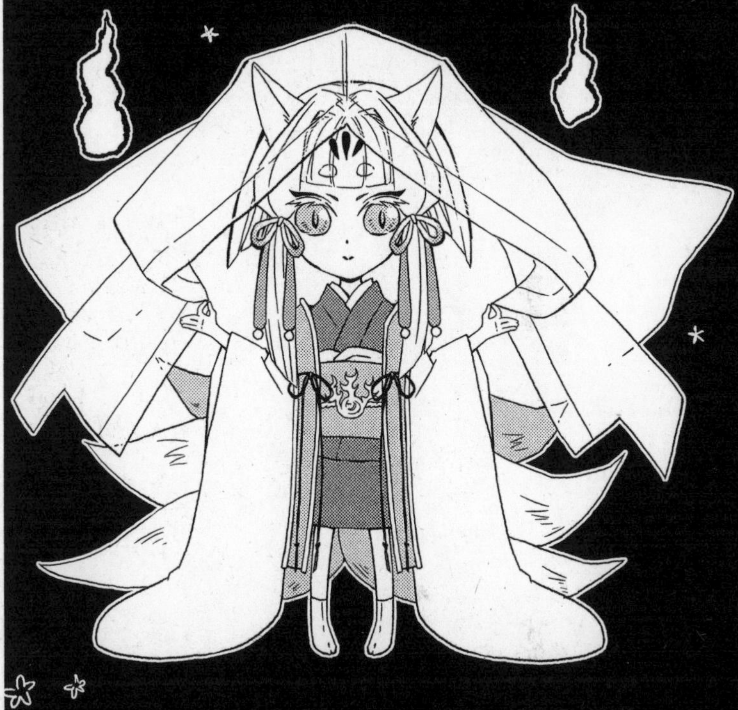

SPECIAL THANKS

HaccaWorks*-sama — YOU'RE SO KIND AND STRONG IN YOUR SUPPORT. THANK YOU SO MUCH!!

The designer — I LOOK FORWARD TO EACH OF THE GORGEOUS COVERS YOU DO FOR ME!

My editor Y-san — SORRY FOR STILL MAKING SO MANY CARELESS MISTAKES...

S-san — THANK YOU FOR SUPPORTING ME WITH BEAUTIFUL BACKGROUNDS EVERY TIME!

Everyone reading!! Thank you so much! DEEP BOWS

NANAO

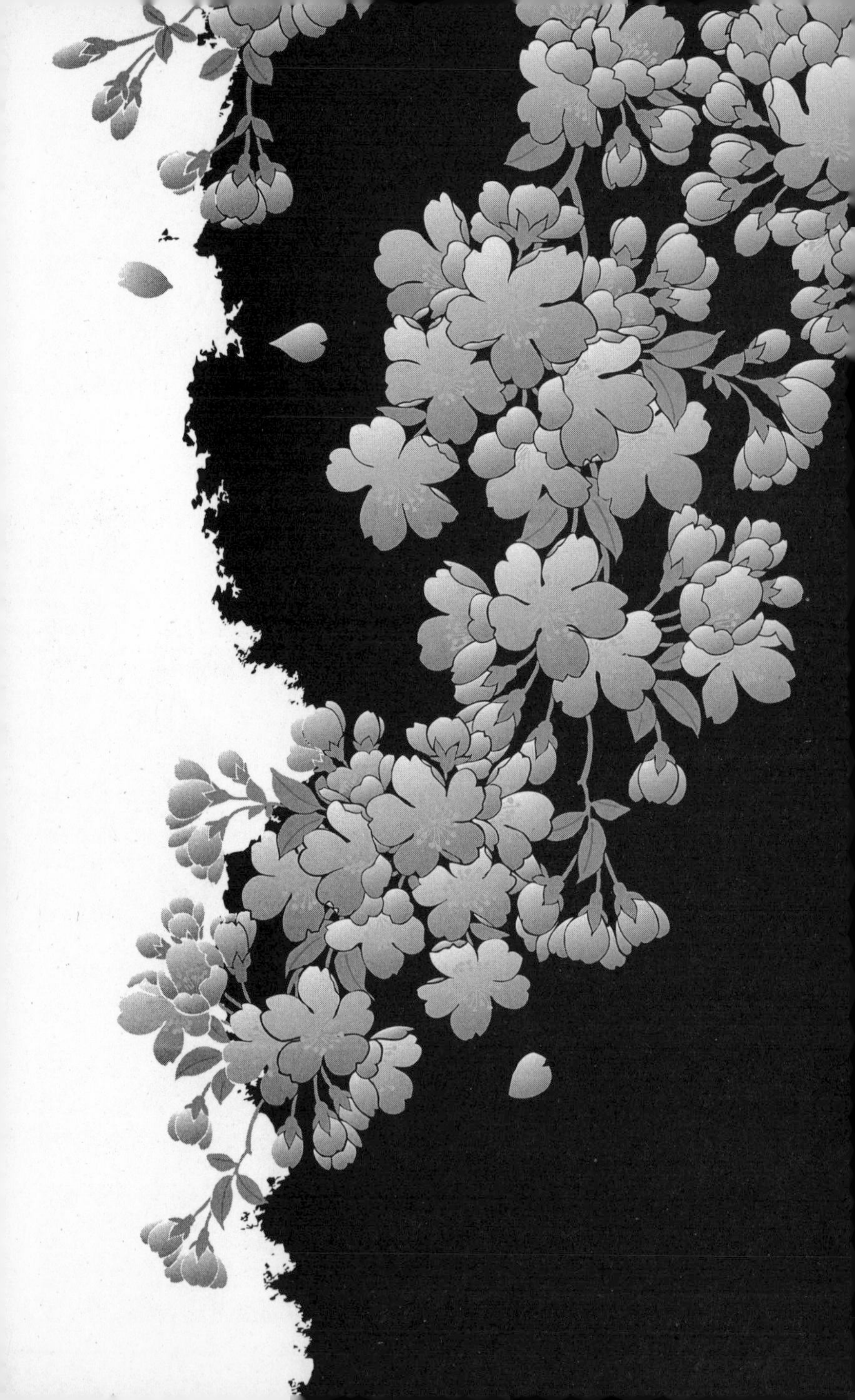

TRANSLATION NOTES

COMMON HONORIFICS

no honorific: Indicates familiarity or closeness; if used without permission or reason, addressing someone in this manner would be an insult.

-san: The Japanese equivalent of Mr./Mrs./Miss. If a situation calls for politeness, this is the fail-safe honorific.

-sama: Conveys great respect; may also indicate that the social status of the speaker is lower than that of the addressee.

-kun: Used most often when referring to boys, this indicates affection or familiarity. Occasionally used by older men among their peers, but it may also be used by anyone referring to a person of lower standing.

-chan, -tan: An affectionate honorific indicating familiarity used mostly in reference to girls; also used in reference to cute persons or animals.

Ayakashi is a general term for ghosts, monsters, haunted objects, mythical animals, and all sorts of uncanny things from Japanese folklore.

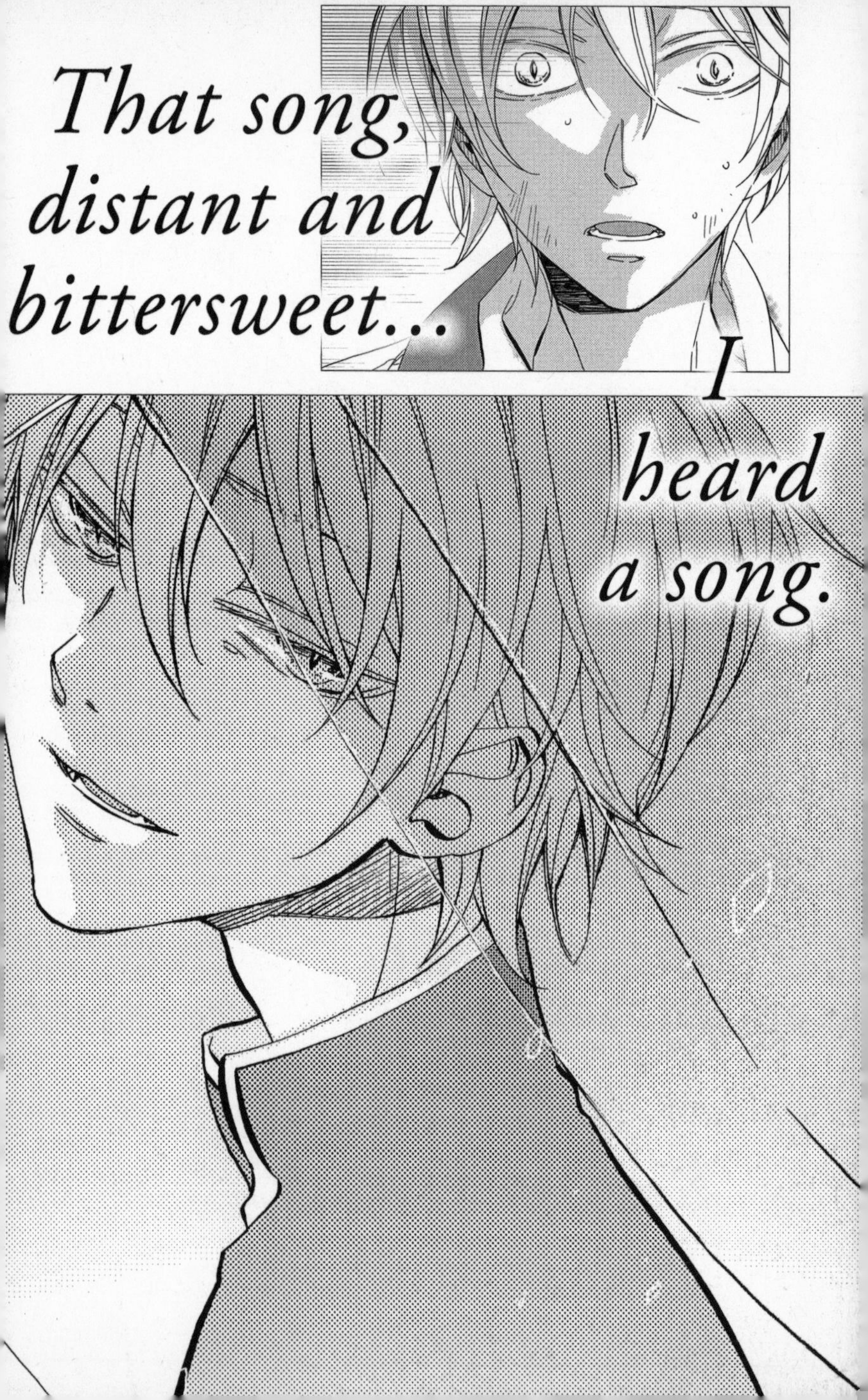
That song, distant and bittersweet...
I heard a song.

"That spirit has already been lost—" Creating the town of Utsuwa, Shin gained the body of Akashi. Thus began the tale of humankind and the ayakashi— with a sin.

...called to me.

THÖUGH I...

...DID TRULY SAVOR IT.

Of the Red, the Light, and the Ayakashi ⑦

COMING IN JUNE 2017

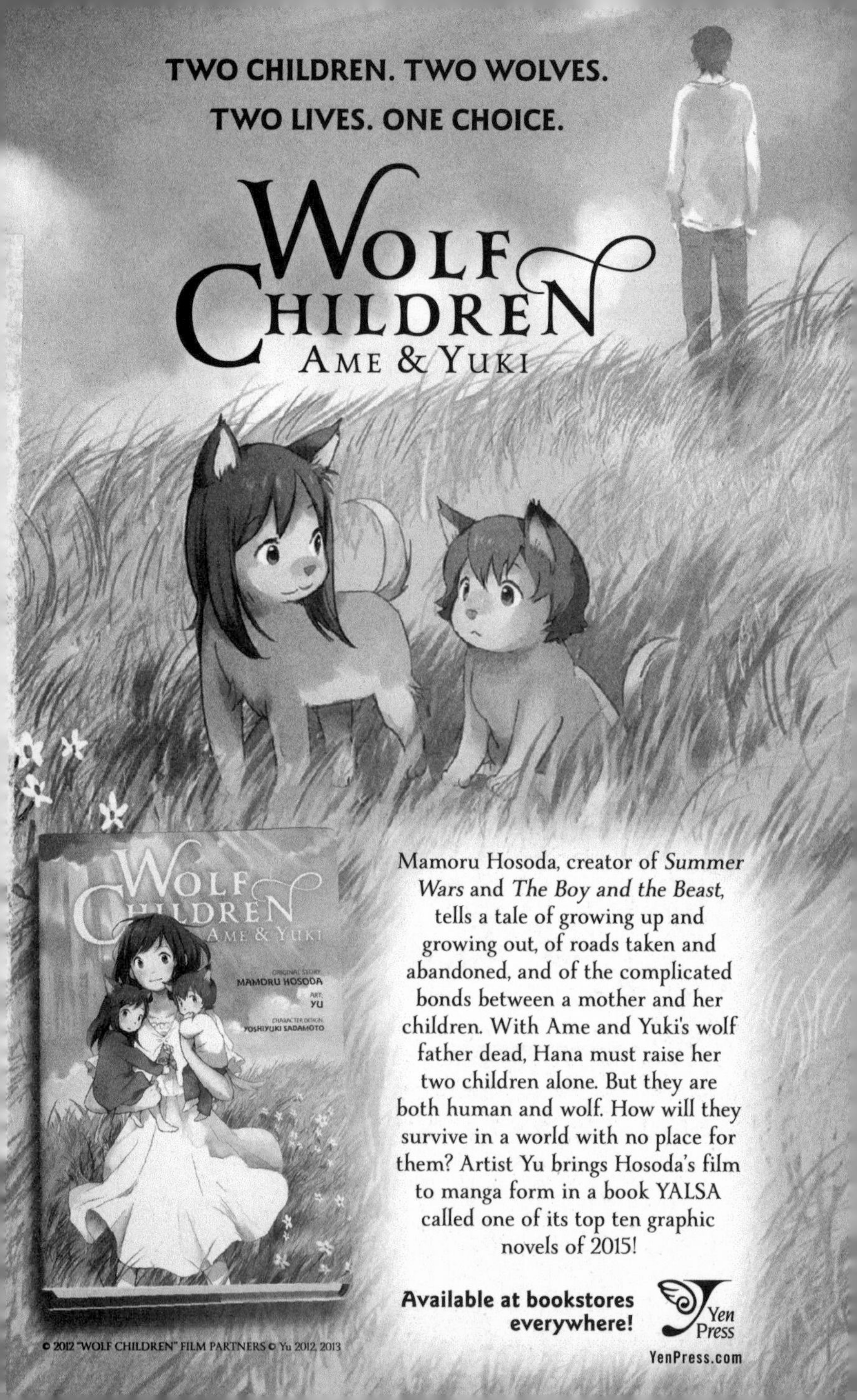
TWO CHILDREN. TWO WOLVES.
TWO LIVES. ONE CHOICE.
WOLF CHILDREN
AME & YUKI
WOLF CHILDREN
AME & YUKI
ORIGINAL STORY: MAMORU HOSODA
ART: YU
CHARACTER DESIGN: YOSHIYUKI SADAMOTO
Mamoru Hosoda, creator of Summer Wars and The Boy and the Beast, tells a tale of growing up and growing out, of roads taken and abandoned, and of the complicated bonds between a mother and her children. With Ame and Yuki's wolf father dead, Hana must raise her two children alone. But they are both human and wolf. How will they survive in a world with no place for them? Artist Yu brings Hosoda's film to manga form in a book YALSA called one of its top ten graphic novels of 2015!
Available at bookstores everywhere!
Yen Press
YenPress.com
© 2012 "WOLF CHILDREN" FILM PARTNERS © Yu 2012, 2013

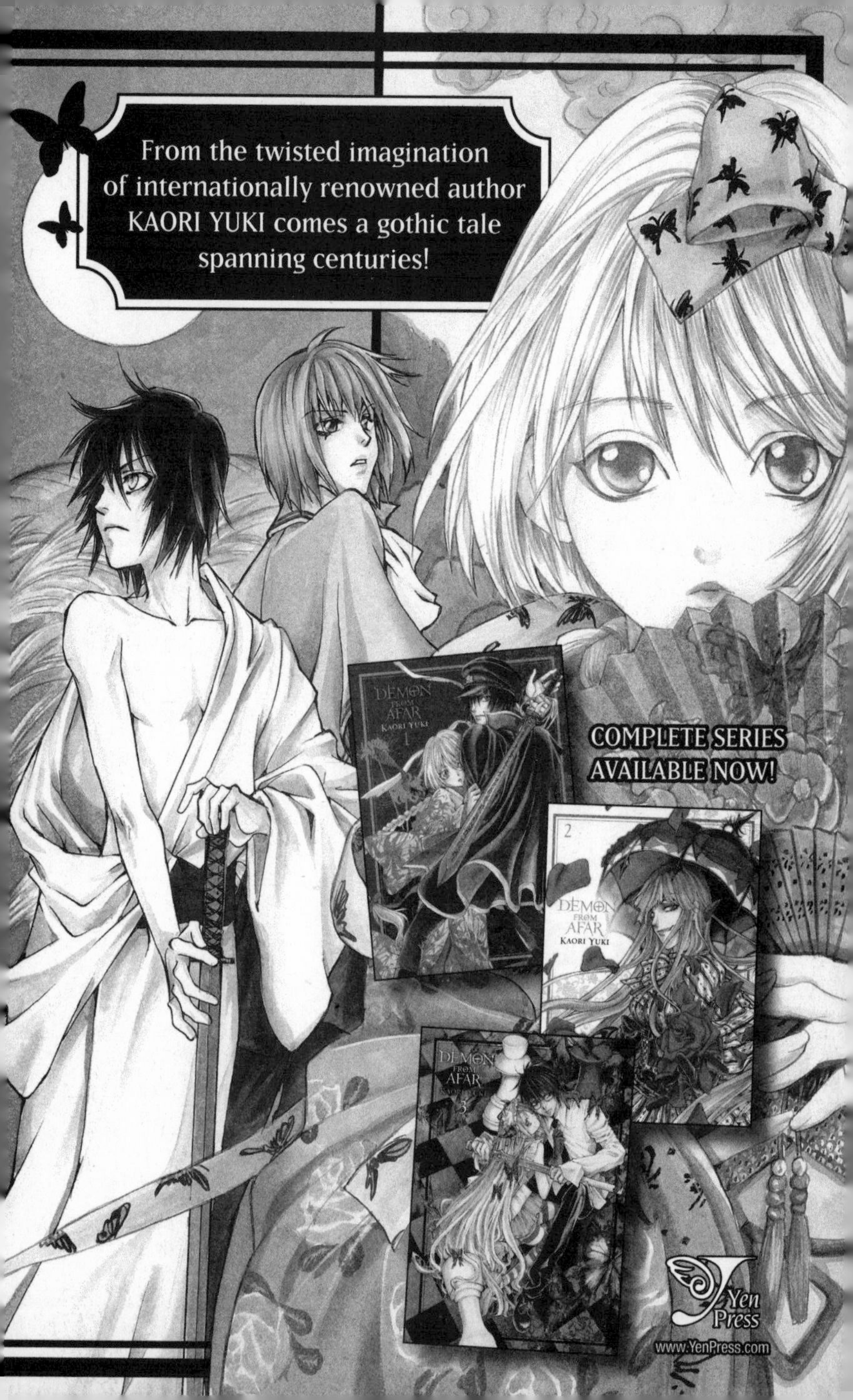
From the twisted imagination of internationally renowned author KAORI YUKI comes a gothic tale spanning centuries!
DEMON FROM AFAR KAORI YUKI 1
COMPLETE SERIES AVAILABLE NOW!
2 DEMON FROM AFAR KAORI YUKI
DEMON FROM AFAR 3
Yen Press
www.YenPress.com

DEMON FROM AFAR

Kaori Yuki

Orphaned in an earthquake, Sorath is taken in by Baron Kamichika, the lord of "Blood Blossom Manor." There, he pledges eternal friendship with Garan, the Baron's heir, and Kiyora, Garan's fiancée. But their friendship turns grisly by events none of them could foresee. The tender feelings each secretly harbors, the machinations of Baron Kamichika, and his strange and seductive female companion, and a fateful encounter with a young girl with bizarre powers...all draw them to the Walpurgis Night and the nightmare's climax!

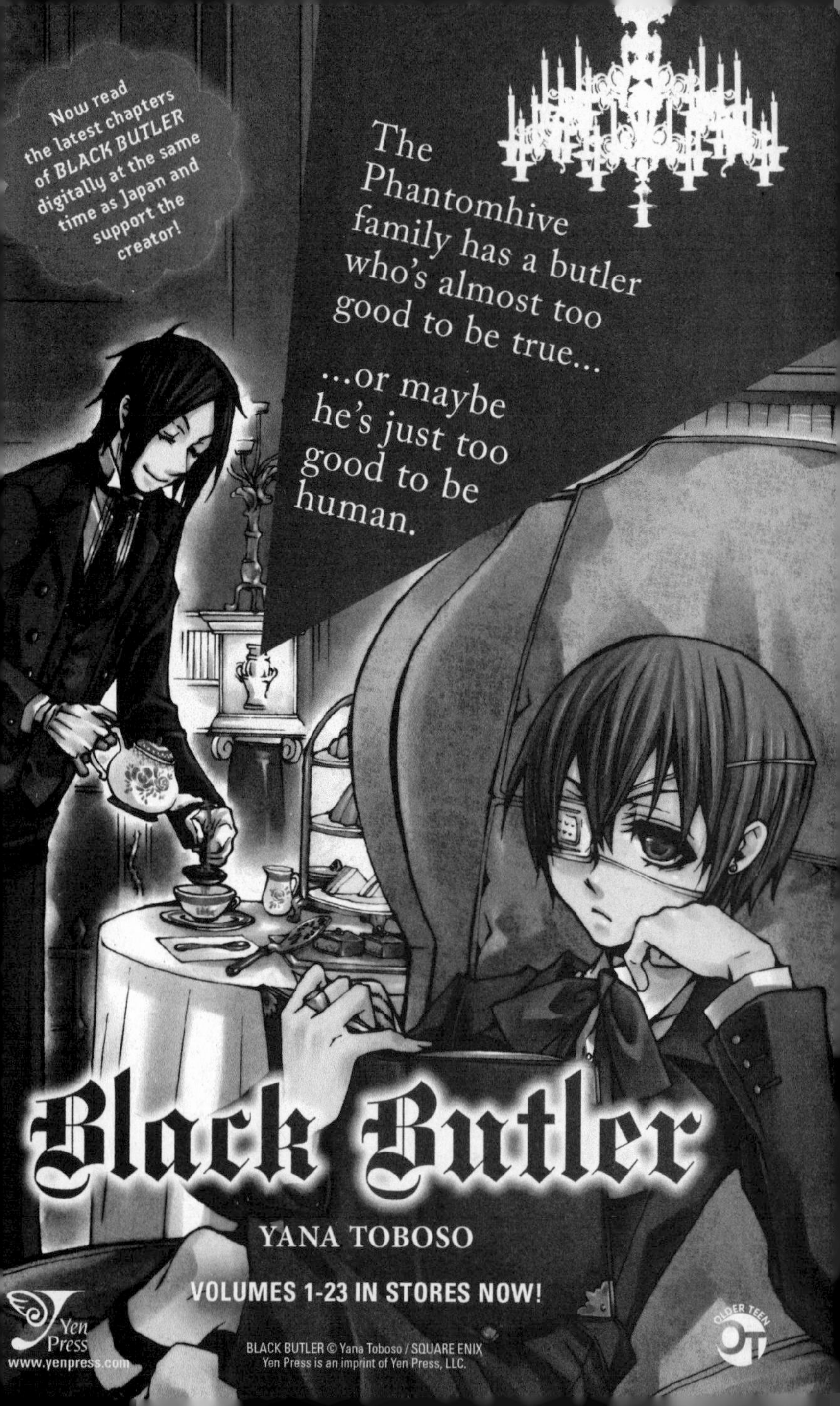

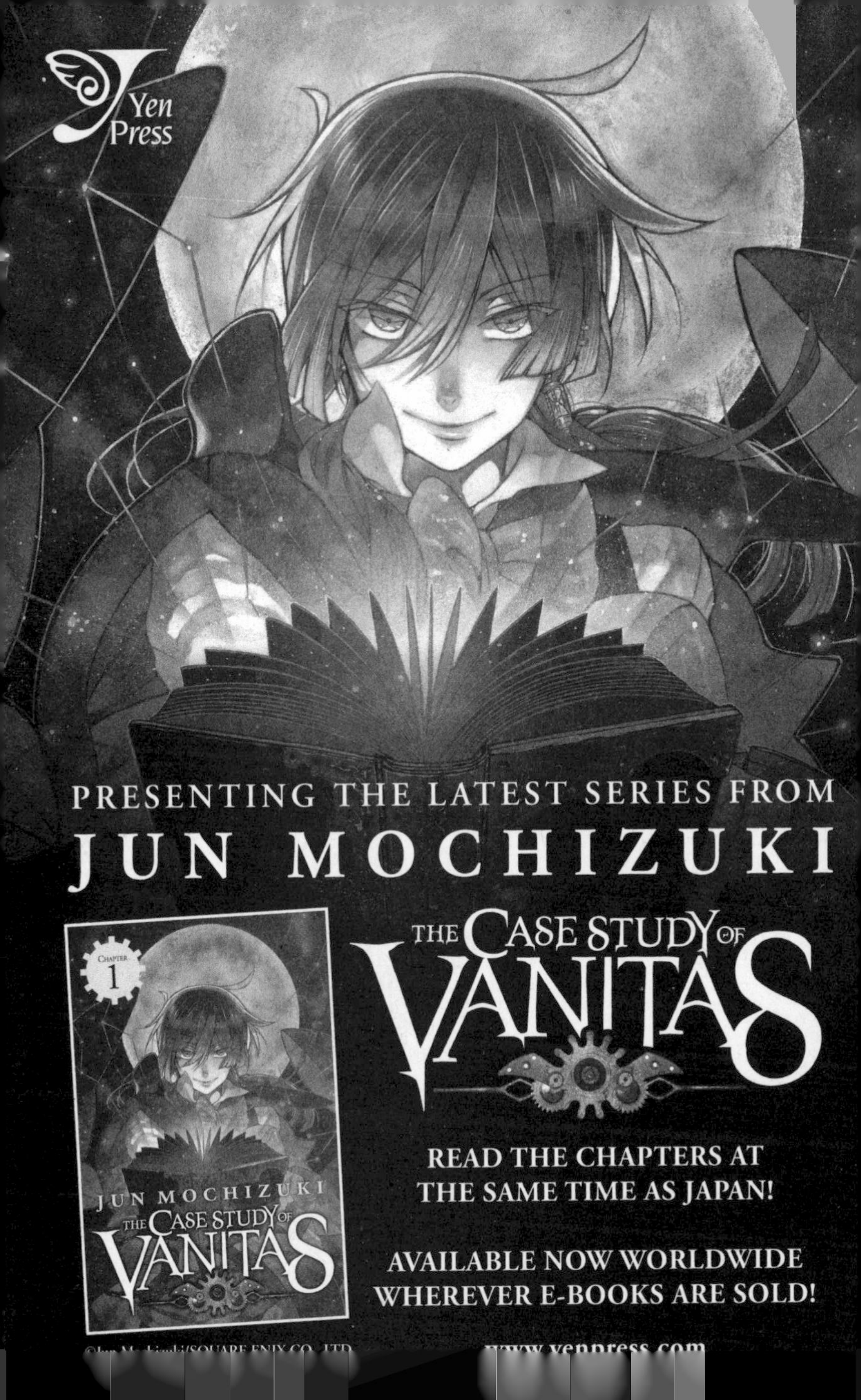
Yen Press
PRESENTING THE LATEST SERIES FROM
JUN MOCHIZUKI
CHAPTER 1
JUN MOCHIZUKI
THE CASE STUDY OF VANITAS
THE CASE STUDY OF VANITAS
READ THE CHAPTERS AT
THE SAME TIME AS JAPAN!
AVAILABLE NOW WORLDWIDE
WHEREVER E-BOOKS ARE SOLD!
©Jun Mochizuki/SQUARE ENIX CO., LTD.
www.yenpress.com

Of the Red, the Light, and the Ayakashi

ART BY Nanao
STORY BY HaccaWorks*

Translation: Jocelyne Allen ✦ Lettering: Alexis Eckerman

AKAYA AKASHIYA AYAKASHINO
© Nanao 2015
© Hacca Works* 2015
First published in Japan in 2015 by KADOKAWA
CORPORATION. English translation rights reserved by
YEN PRESS, LLC under the license from
KADOKAWA COPORATION, Tokyo through
TUTTLE-MORI AGENCY, Inc., Tokyo.

English translation © 2017 by Yen Press, LLC

Yen Press
1290 Avenue of the Americas
New York, NY 10104

Visit us!
yenpress.com
facebook.com/yenpress
twitter.com/yenpress
yenpress.tumblr.com
instagram.com/yenpress

First Yen Press Edition: March 2017

Yen Press is an imprint of Yen Press, LLC.
The Yen Press name and logo are trademarks of Yen Press, LLC.

Library of Congress Control Number: 2016932691

ISBN: 978-0-316-31024-6

10 9 8 7 6 5 4 3 2 1

BVG

Printed in the United States of America